SALTWOOD

SALTWOOD

LEON UNRUH

Meadowlark Press, LLC
meadowlarkbookstore.com
PO Box 333, Emporia, KS 66801

Saltwood

Editor: Cheryl Unruh
Cover design & Illustration: Leon Unruh
Back cover photo: Dave Leiker
Interior design: Leon Unruh

This novel, Saltwood, is fiction. Though the setting and locations are real and seemingly accurate, some liberties were taken for the sake of story, and the characters and events are products of the author's imagination. Any resemblance to actual events or persons—living or dead—is entirely unintentional and coincidental. Businesses and organizations mentioned in the story have no connection to this work of fiction.

Resale and Bulk Orders: Discounts are available on bulk purchases by corporations, associations, and others. For details, contact the publisher at info@meadowlark-books.com.
https://www.meadowlarkbookstore.com/resale-and-bulk-orders

FICTION / Thrillers / Suspense
FICTION / Thrillers / Domestic
FICTION / Thrillers / Espionage

Library of Congress Control Number: 2025938543

ISBN: 978-1-956578-74-4 (paperback)
ISBN: 978-1-956578-75-1 (ebook)

For Julie

*But as we read in golden letters this decalogue of our
inner consciousness and indictment, must we not confess
that as a nation we have been drifting to the selfish, the
grasping, the sinister? As individuals, whether gaining
or not, intoxicated by the conspicuous examples of the
success of a few of those absorbed in the selfish passion
for gain, or recklessly gambling upon the necessities of
others, have we not been ignoring the rights and needs
of a common humanity; or under the pressure of a false,
but criminally legalized system, been mortgaging the
sacred heritage and birthright of children and children's
children, even to alien oppressors? Under this trend, if
continued, what must soon the end be?*

     —G.H. Fish of Wellington, Kansas, 1891

From his pamphlet: *"Hew to the Line.
Master or Slave. Awake You Must, or Lose
Your Place! The Long Roll Beats; the Tide Is
Coming, and Every American Must Take a
Stand"*

Also by Leon Unruh

Dog of the Afterworld
Birchbark Press, 2013

Final Destinations: A Travel Guide for Remarkable Cemeteries in Texas, New Mexico, Oklahoma, Arkansas, and Louisiana [Co-author]
University of North Texas Press (2000)

SALTWOOD

1

The FBI pushed Nick Deveraux out of the nest at nine o'clock on a Tuesday morning in late May.

He had been in custody for more than two years, ever since he fell wounded into the bureau's hands after killing the man sent to kill Nick himself.

Now he, born thirty years earlier as Nikolai Fyodorov in Russia, was being driven from a small installation in Virginia by two agents of the Federal Bureau of Investigation. Their heavy SUV swooshed along drizzly Connecticut Avenue, heading northwest from downtown Washington, DC.

Nick squirmed against his seatbelt while the Explorer with darkened windows swerved from one lane to another, progressing a few yards, then fifty, then sitting at a traffic light.

The agents hunched into their shoulder belts. The one riding shotgun, short red hair and a few years older than his partner, checked his watch.

"Four minutes to time," he said.

The windshield wipers slapped out the seconds, a metronome under leafy trees.

Nick cared about the time much less than his escorts did. The ride through the District of Columbia was gravy.

A clerk that morning had stood him against a blank wall and photographed him "for your driver's license," she said. He was wearing his usual wardrobe—a plaid shirt, khaki pants, dark sneakers.

He could've been a dentist or an assistant produce manager at the grocery store were it not for his expertise in killing people.

On the way out, an agent wearing gloves handed him a billfold stiff with a Virginia driver's license (Nick Deveraux, 6-foot-2, 186 pounds, blue eyes, no eyeglasses required, no organ harvesting), a credit card and two thousand bucks in fifties; a phone and charger; and a blue carry-on canvas rollerbag with sundries and a change of unremarkable clothing. He was surprised the FBI perpetuated the alias he had used in Kansas.

He wasn't asked to sign a receipt. No one wanted a record. Nor would anyone say on whose orders he was being released, deployed, dumped. He wasn't instructed to sign a single nondisclosure form.

His two escorts didn't identify themselves. He asked their names but didn't expect an answer.

"We don't have a chance." The driver slapped the wheel when the light at the oblique K Street intersection turned red. He edged the SUV up to the rear bumper of a sedan.

"Two minutes. It's a half mile. Go easy." The shotgun agent nodded back at Nick. "He'll get there."

The driver glanced into the mirror. "You're a big deal, right?"

Nick had been in the care of the FBI since his near death, although he had never been arrested, indicted, or publicly identified. He did whatever the FBI and a parade of investigators had demanded, up to revealing everything he wanted them to know.

He was angry at the Russians for betraying him both as a soldier who thought he was doing his government's will, and as an assassin who was abandoned by one of the Russian crime organizations. He wanted very much to become an American asset, but he was also wary of again becoming a tool used without moral guidelines.

As the SUV was three-quarters of the way around the expansive Dupont Circle and signaling right to pull off onto P Street Northwest, two dark blue sedans pulled out of nose-to-tail parking spaces. The SUV slid into the vacancies, taking half of each.

Nick had been here along Embassy Row of Massachusetts Avenue, another component of Dupont Circle, six years earlier during his training, taking in a Paradiso pizza and wandering across to the fountain in the circle, sometimes cutting across P Street to practice dead drops outside a bookstore with shelves set up on the sidewalk.

Today, everything felt heavy under the close sky.

People walked warily, glancing with caution at other pedestrians, as if they wondered who among them could be trusted in the present political atmosphere. A few wore masks against the latest covid or the flu or measles or security cameras, looking like a sparse parade of nurses, iconoclasts, and drywall hangers.

The shotgun agent pulled a small notebook out of an inside pocket of his jacket, flipping through until he found a specific page.

"Listen up. This is what you're agreeing to, or we'll shoot you right here."

"Shoot."

"Funny. Screw you." He read his list: "Do not go near the Russian Embassy. Do not approach the White House. Do not tell people who you are or where you've been. If you need help from the Bureau, use the contact number already in your phone."

"Yeah, sure."

"Never mention the president or a former president or any federal official in voice or text communications. Part of this furlough is finding out whether you can keep from being found out by the National Security Agency. You know what it does?"

"Listens to everything. Scans every word."

"Do you agree to each of the items I've read to you?"

"Yes, Agent."

"That's Special Agent, jerk."

Nick sighed. These guys were wound tight.

"Yes, I understand the instructions."

The special agent got out and opened Nick's door. He was a big guy, Nick realized, six-five and two hundred thirty pounds. When Nick stepped down, the agent laid into him just above the belt buckle.

After the fist came a benediction: "Go to the fountain and give the motherland a wet kiss for me, traitor."

Nick stumbled across the sidewalk to lean against a storefront. The agent slammed the back door and hefted himself into the front seat, and the SUV melted into traffic.

"Thanks for the ride, guys," Nick said when he caught his breath. "Have a long happy life."

· · ·

She was a shadow, darker than night, a hole in the world.

Nick glimpsed her out of the corner of his eye, and when he turned his head she wasn't there. Then there she was again, matching his stride as he reached the fountain in the middle of Dupont Circle, bumping him with an elbow to prove she was genuine.

"Are you lost?" she asked.

Nick stared at her. She was the first woman he had met in more than two years who didn't have government clearance clipped to her clothing.

She had fierce eyebrows over brown eyes and straight bangs of dark chocolate. She stood a slender five-foot-five. She wore a black jacket with the hood up, a black blouse, and black slacks. Everything about her said "beware," except for a silver Orthodox cross hung from a fine chain below her collarbones.

And she appraised him. He stood a head taller than she was, a little older. He had dark blue eyes, light brown hair longer than a crew cut, an interesting mouth, and the cheekbones of a Slav.

"Nikolai Fyodorov," she said.

"Not anymore," he said.

"Mother Russia is in your blood."

"I don't have a password," he said.

"You are who you are."

The fountain—the focal point of the tree-heavy park inside the traffic circle overlaying a Metro subway stop and Connecticut Avenue where it went underground—gurgled in its rain dance. Under the elevated stone bowl, three idealized carved figures, a man and two women, posed symbolically.

The woman in black matched him step for step around the yellowed marble until she stopped before the figure that was a naked woman. She pulled back her hood and shook out her shoulder-length hair: toss toss.

In the near distance but hidden by office buildings, police and fire sirens screamed. Nick glanced around; no one else seemed to be distracted by them.

The Russian waved at the artwork. "The fountain to honor an admiral has been here for a century. This figure represents the stars.

The woman with her foot on a dolphin is the sea, and the man wrapped up in the sail is the wind. It is all about navigation. Do you need a map to the city?"

"I've been here," he said.

"You might need it to find where you are going."

"How about if you just say what you want me to do."

"You will kill Harriet Gayfeather, senator from Kansas."

Nick's guts curdled. He had been sent to do that two summers earlier but had broken orders. In the ensuing battle with an assassin sent to make sure both he and Gayfeather died, Nick had won. That's when the FBI had taken custody of his broken body.

He turned back to the statue. "Who sent you?"

"I speak for Orlov."

"Orlov's messenger girl?" Nick spat on the sidewalk.

"Zdorovo," she said with a certain tone. "Vy, dolzhno byt', iz Sankt-Peterburga." Nice, she was saying. You must be from St. Petersburg.

"Make one thing clear for me," Nick said. "Is Orlov working for the Kremlin or the mafia?"

"Kremlin, mafia, oligarchs; what is the difference? You agree or you die."

"Do you even care about the senator's life? You could've taken care of this yourself a long time ago."

"You are right, Nikolai. The game amuses Orlov, but we will win either way. The only way you also win is to do what we require. Among his friends, Orlov has bet against you."

Letting an old gentleman walk past with his French bulldog, Nick and his contact looked into each other's faces. She bent forward and shook the drizzle off her nose.

"Orlov says his people could kill the senator tonight and leave clues that lead directly to you, for now an escaped assassin. So either you kill her, or it will look as if you have killed her. You walk away right now from your pretend friends at FBI, or we will feed you to the FBI dogs. You owe us her life, Nikolai. Either way, we win. If you kill the senator, you also walk away from us alive for as long as you can stay that way."

The Russian touched his forearm.

"Orlov says to think of this assignment as a quest," she said. "Your podvig, your search for glory."

Nick rolled his eyes. That made her smile. They started walking again, another circumnavigation of the fountain.

"Orlov reminds you that he has men in Kansas who can drive a short distance and poison your beloved girlfriend, Cimarron, and be back home for lunch. Or throw her out a window. He said he knows where she sleeps, where she studies, where she buys her groceries. If you don't do your job, the girl dies in pain."

The woman in black stopped and turned to him.

"You still miss her, Orlov says. Does that help you focus, Nikolai?"

Nick thought of Cimi Hernandez, of her eyes after their last kiss, as he had every night for months.

"How did you know I'd be here? I didn't know until I got out of the car."

"The FBI remains not completely our enemy, especially in this new world."

She touched his wrist.

"Nikolai, Orlov said to stress this: The FBI is going to track you. So are we. You mess up, you let the senator go, you're not going to be dead. You're going to be taken apart piece by piece and sent to your mother."

She held her right hand close to her jacket, flipping it palm up so he could see the folded map she cradled. They shook hands, and the transfer was done. He slid his fingers into his jacket pocket, bumping into a folding knife he didn't have two minutes earlier.

"A gift from you." He wasn't asking.

"It's strong, Benchmade brand, American. American way is good. Very sharp and common enough that it is not out of place," she said. "Use it in good health, and never let it be seen again."

"Is that all?"

"You have money and ID from FBI?"

He nodded.

She said, "Use it to make your escape. Then you will be free from us, if you want to be. Try not to get caught by FBI. Or, die trying not to get caught." She smiled.

He frowned in response.

"My name is Anastasia," she said with a sly grin. Ah-na-stah-*see*-a. "If you survive, come back and see me. In the meantime, remember: Heels on ground, Russian found. Heels high, American spy."

He took a couple of steps toward a park bench, hoping to sit and gather his thoughts. When he turned back to ask where Orlov was living, the woman in black was gone.

2

Senator Harriet Gayfeather lived not far from Dupont Circle. The Russian map, unfolded to four by four inches gently under a café awning, showed the location of her house off Cleveland Avenue Northwest. She would be home late in the afternoon for dinner, a tightly printed note said in Cyrillic characters. Look for a two-story house of brown brick.

The drizzle increased into light rain, which, no matter how careful Nick was, fell onto the map and blurred the ink. He memorized the location then spread the map out on the sidewalk. The details of the job blended and streamed into the gutter, and Nick ground the paper into shreds under his shoe.

Paranoia was trained into him. Always look around. Russians were everywhere. FBI agents were everywhere. Every pedestrian was an operative. Every car had a passenger who would remember him. Every woman with a baby carriage was packing an assault rifle. At the very least, teams would be following his steps, agents moving ahead and behind him, sometimes across the street with a parallel team a block away on each side. A satellite, he imagined, was tracking him from a hundred miles above.

If the FBI had handed him off to Russian mobsters, he was a high-value target for one organization or the other.

The Metro had surveillance cameras at every subway station, and in this part of the city every block on every street would be watched, listened to, and assessed on banks of monitors run by embassies, the police, the FBI, and possibly the National Security Agency.

He'd just have to do the best he could with what he had. He had always worked with the idea that he could blend into a city best by absorbing the notion that he lived there. He could most easily try the well-pressed look or devise a homeless look. He doubted, however, that he'd get into the senator's house while wearing charity castoffs.

From the clothing he had been given that morning, he had chosen white sneakers, stiff blue jeans, a red-and-black plaid long-sleeve shirt that still had its packaging folds, and a dark-green nylon jacket. The second set of clothes was more formal: penny loafers, khaki slacks, a light-blue shirt, and a navy blazer with big buttons at the cuffs.

None of the present wardrobe, including his government-issue unisex Weekender watch, was going to cut it in this status-conscious part of Washington. He assumed that everything the FBI had given him was trackable through microchips, RFID antennas woven into the clothing, or transmitters buried in his luggage and shoes.

Using the FBI's money, he overpaid for new clothes at a shop off the circle, leaving with brown and blue blazers, a pair of blue-pattern shirts, navy slacks, adequate briefs and socks, good Cole Hahn shoes, a satisfactory shock- and water-resistant Timex, and a black folding umbrella. He abandoned his FBI clothing, phone, and suitcase in the dressing room.

Down the street, Nick bought a black carry-on rollerbag, a lightweight blue wind-resistant jacket, a replacement billfold, two prepaid phones, and a Faraday bag for his phones and credit card to guard them from being scanned or tracked. He'd use a phone only if he had to. While the location app might say it was off, it would certainly be on and it'd ping cell towers every step of his way.

Skirting morose street musicians, he waved down a taxi and took it from Dupont Circle northwest through the Kalorama district, where the Obamas lived, across Rock Creek to a guest house along Woodley Road. He jaywalked across Woodley and strode through the Marriott hotel, looping back to a Mediterranean cafe along Connecticut Avenue near the Metro subway stop. Keeping an eye open for looky-loos in the pedestrian traffic, he ordered the seafood platter.

At a CVS drugstore across the street, he sorted through baseball caps until he found one with a stylized W from the Washington Nationals, fitting it so the red bill was a shelf just over his eyes. He changed jackets from brown to blue; there was no sense in being too easy to follow. At a hardware store, he picked up a box of nitrile gloves, four six-inch nails, and a short roll of wire for hanging pictures. He pulled out four gloves, all he'd need for cleanup, and stuffed the box into a streetside trash can.

Nick drifted northwest on Connecticut toward his appointment, past the plastic cups men held out in hopes of "just a dollar, sir," and a scowling woman sitting cross-armed under an orange umbrella at a cafe's outdoor table. She was nursing a capped coffee and holding her phone lefthanded against her right ear. He watched her eyes. She watched his feet.

He scouted as he walked, a functionary walking from the Metro stop to a conference at a hotel. He watched for observers lounging in vans under the trees as afternoon slipped toward rush hour, but saw no one. It scared him a little that the watchers were so good.

He felt like an embarrassment to the trade. He always thought he'd be okay at crunch time, but more than two years had gone by since he'd killed anyone, not that he hadn't rehearsed the motions thousands of times in custody. This blindside transfer back to the Russians, however, was a scenario he hadn't thought of.

The logical thing to expect after Gayfeather's death was that the FBI would announce that an assassin who had once defected from Russia had escaped and carried out a mission that he had failed at earlier. The bureau would send his mugshot to CNN and Fox, to TikTok and Facebook, and to every police agency within a thousand miles. Airports and Amtrak stations would be heavy with agents and electronic eyes, a dramatic piece of security theater, and by tomorrow morning everyone from the feds to small-town gunslingers would have learned his face. Facial recognition programs would sort every face on the street and every face that could be stolen from security systems installed in businesses and at the front doors of homes.

The White House would call him by turns a traitor, a Ukrainian terrorist, and probably a French gang member, none of which was correct, and no one would know quite what to make of his Russian ancestry. If the Russians found him first, they might kill him in a grand gesture of goodwill toward the US administration.

He knew he was being set up. Released practically (and deniably) into the hands of the Russians, accepting a map and a weapon—all these pieces of evidence would justify his being shot dead in the street, executed after a show trial, or black-holed into a supermax prison.

Who knew what evidence the FBI or the Russians would plant. Maybe the knife slipped to him by the mystery woman carried spy dust that would show up in Gayfeather's corpse and be a direct link to him.

The 2021 insurrection in DC had raised tensions among the agents and operatives he had dealt with. The loyalty purge instigated by the president four years later had raised the stakes for everyone.

The FBI, Nick thought, would certainly benefit from catching and killing a man it portrayed as a Russian assassin. Some of the allegations in a federal case against him would likely be provable. He had broken US laws along the way, and he was probably going to break more.

He considered his immediate moves.

If he remembered right, the senator was about forty-five years old. He'd have the advantages of strength and youth, but she'd have the advantage of wisdom and maybe a handgun or panic button.

Speed and surprise would be important. The FBI could call at any moment to warn her.

He walked until he found an empty bus stop with a bench. Sitting there, he fashioned a backup weapon, a garrote, from the wire, wrapping each end around two nails that would become handles when he looped the wire around her neck and pulled it tight. The wire resisted his softened fingers, making him wish he'd bought pliers.

He would do the assignment. He didn't care whether Gayfeather lived or died. He didn't have any loyalty to her, and not killing her earlier hadn't been a moral issue. If the Russian threats relayed by the woman in black had any value, walking away a reborn killer was his faint hope of surviving for the day, another week, the next year.

Nick thus needed to escape, and for that he had no plan. His instructors at the academy in St. Petersburg would learn that he died in shame.

•   •   •

The senator's home stood a block off Cleveland Avenue NW, not far from the vice president's residence at the Naval Academy and the Russian Embassy. The two-story home had a rain-shiny brick driveway with small covered porches facing the front and driveway. Ranks of rose bushes stretched under the windows. An SUV with darkened windows sat in the driveway.

Watchers could be hidden along the street. Security cameras were discrete but in plain sight under the eaves and at the doorbells.

Nick carried the garrote rolled up in his left hand, which also pulled the suitcase. He tapped his jacket pocket to confirm the location of the Russian knife, and his slacks' back pocket for his billfold. His gloves were rolled up, a pair in each jacket pocket.

No dogs barked. No strangers appeared at windows as he strode up the driveway to address the less-visible side door. It was made of steel and painted off-white, a nice color with the brick. Under a high thin window was a peephole drilled for an occupant of about five-foot-six.

Noise came from inside—the clatter of silverware and laughter. Friends? Staff?

Maybe he should abort the mission. Come back later, or high-tail it to Canada. Nothing was ideal. He'd adapt.

He set his suitcase down, breathed deeply, and rang the doorbell. Ding ding ding dong, the four first tones of Beethoven's *Symphony No. 5*.

The door opened inward, and there she was.

The senator's blond hair was softly grayer and shorter than he remembered, her eyes a little more tense. She wore a blue silk blouse and a gold necklace. After the shock of recognition, she seemed relieved to see him.

"The FBI warned me you might show up someday," Harriet Gayfeather said. "They said you've been tamed, but I'm not sure I believe them."

She squared away and pulled back her shoulders.

"Do you wish to kill me out here or inside?"

•   •   •

Harriet Gayfeather's mini goldendoodle poked its head between the jamb and her knees. It wagged its tail and sniffed the newcomer, then looked up at Gayfeather for approval.

Gayfeather and Nick stood awkwardly.

"I need your help," Nick said. He wanted to act inside the doorway, away from curious eyes of neighbors and before whoever else was in the house came looking.

Gayfeather pulled her collar open.

"Like this?"

Out on the sidewalk, a young woman with a stroller glanced up the driveway, waving shyly when she recognized Gayfeather. Gayfeather called out, "Isn't it a beautiful day?"

To Nick, she said, "Now you can't do it, can you? She's seen you."

"I'm not here to kill you," he improvised. "I'm here to save myself."

"Do you wish me to call the FBI?"

"Please don't. That wouldn't help."

"Why on earth did you come to me?"

"The FBI dumped me at Dupont Circle this morning. The Russians showed up and threatened to kill me unless I kill you."

"Goodbye, Mr. Deveraux."

"Wait. Please," he begged, his hands open to her. "I don't want to hurt you. Maybe you have connections who can protect me. I just want to get out of this mess and go free."

"Yours is quite a story. I'm sure the Russians would enjoy killing you, but what you're saying is preposterous. The FBI gave you to the Russians? For what? I regret that I can't help you. I just won't. Please leave."

Nick took the handle of his suitcase and retreated into the driveway. Plan A had failed. He still could rush her, fight off that twenty pounds of loyal dog, and do what he was sent to do. In his previous life he would have. But now he had no mafia to call for help, no safehouses in which to hide. He'd be on his own against the world.

Gayfeather knew he was on the loose, which wasn't a good thing. If she were smart, she'd call the cops before he reached the street.

"Mr. Deveraux," she whispered. "Wait."

He turned, a refugee, a beggar in a nice sports coat. A robin trilled three times before Gayfeather pensively approached him. The goldendoodle sniffed Nick's shoes again. Nick didn't like dogs. He stepped back, and Gayfeather leaned down to take its collar.

The senator looked deep into Nick's eyes, then plunged ahead.

"Can you stay for dinner?"

3

B e back at 6 o'clock, Harriet Gayfeather told Nick. She had work to do, but she'd order dinner in. So Nick walked away into the sharp springtime light glancing under the pancake of clouds.

His stomach was empty but his brain was full.

He should expect Gayfeather to set a trap for him, maybe asking the FBI to pull up a third chair at the dinner table. Had Gayfeather already bugged her dining room to compromise lobbyists and other politicians, and now him?

On the other hand, if he really was free from the FBI, he could fight it out against the Russians. He might hope that neither the FBI nor the Russians were sore losers, but experience told him otherwise.

Shortly after 6:00, Nick knocked on Gayfeather's side door before stepping back so he'd have a chance to dodge or fight. Gayfeather appeared in khaki slacks and a maroon cashmere sweater pulled far enough up her forearms to show corded muscles.

Her eyes were piercing, her smile cautious. Nick's eyes darted, waiting for the trap to spring. They shook hands, and she guided him to a walnut table in the dining room. Each stood awkwardly, ready to jump away.

The table could seat eight, but only the places at the head and the seat at its right were dressed with china, silverware, and glasses. A white linen napkin was folded into a tent on each gold-rimmed plate. The dark wood chairs had curved backs and cushioned seats. Below everything was a carpet of deep-sea blue.

She pulled back her chair at the head of the table, and he took the seat to her right. She was gracious and beautiful, her neck elegant with a beaded chain. Tiny wrinkles in her face suggested stress rather than age, and he now guessed she was in her late forties.

On the far wall, facing Nick above a sideboard, hung a painting of a pheasant hunter walking with a retriever in the morning mist somewhere in flatland Kansas. Beyond the foot of the table was the entrance to the kitchen. A glass-doored china cabinet hugged the wall behind Nick.

"So, Nick Deveraux, how've you been?"

"Life's an adventure, Senator. And you?"

"Being alive is good." She put her hand over her heart. "Thank you."

She still didn't understand that he hadn't chosen to save her life. Someone had stolen his attention when he was lining up the kill shot.

She brought up the idea of drinks. Nick asked for a beer.

"IPA? Stout? Amber? Got 'em all," she called from the kitchen. Stout, he replied. "Try this," she suggested. "It's one I enjoy. Wake Up in the Future, brewed across town."

She brought him one, a black bottle with space-alien-green ink, from the cooler, with a chilled glass, and poured herself a glass of California pinot noir from an open bottle she took off the sideboard.

"To the visionary gleam of good government," she said.

"To surviving," he said.

They tasted, and then drank. The stout was rich. Nick wondered whether his drink was stronger than hers.

"This is a nice neighborhood," he said.

"I lived just around the corner when I first moved to town, and I thought I'd stay on the block when this place went on the market. It's a happy place." She sipped. "I feel safe here."

Nick raised his eyebrows.

"Senators aren't safe?"

She shrugged. "*You* found me. I'm not as secure as I hoped."

He nudged his silverware, getting a feel for its heft. She turned her tented napkin on its side. The pause was on the verge of being uncomfortable before she spoke.

"The pup's upstairs," she said. "She's the perfect dog for a politician: cute, smart, doesn't shed, doesn't mark things. Plus, she's a good girl."

"The best kind," Nick said. "Does she travel well?"

"When I'm out of town, she stays with a staffer."

Gayfeather said she had ordered a roasted lamb shank for herself and a strip steak, medium, for him.

"Senators can get delivery from nice places," she said with a self-aware grin.

"Better than the FBI cafeteria," he said.

"There's something you should know," Gayfeather said. "An agent-in-charge at the FBI called me a few minutes before you arrived this afternoon. She said you had gotten loose and I should call her if you showed up. You remember Barbara Pellen?"

Nick did: sharp intellect, athletic, dark hair, dark skin.

"She said she was with the FBI squad in Great Bend and Sandstone," he said. "She knew the shot that missed you didn't come from me. She was fair with me when I was in custody. She came to see me in the hospital, to meet me and not so much to interrogate me."

Gayfeather said, "She told me that you were of no use to the Russians anymore, but that I might notice you somewhere on the fringe. She said you showed no intent to harm me now."

They drank, she more deeply than he.

Pellen had last met Nick in a training-center sunroom secluded by a large monstera plant. Her final advice had been to remember Chapter 18, US Code 351, section 1111: Kill a member of Congress and face execution or life in prison.

Gayfeather added, "I got another call, too, from an Agent Fred Snike. You ever meet him?"

Nick thought about all the agents, from all the services, who had pressed him for answers.

"He was on my interrogation team," Nick recalled. "He said he was originally from Topeka and was there in Sandstone with Pellen during the storm."

"He wondered whether I'd seen you after your release. It felt like he and Pellen weren't sharing notes."

"I didn't know I was that valuable."

Gayfeather poured herself another. "This was a hard day for the FBI," she said. "Did you hear about the two agents today?"

Nick shook his head.

"It happened this morning," she said. "Two agents heading downtown were crushed by a garbage truck that pushed their SUV into an office building on Connecticut. Then the garbage man threw a Molotov cocktail under the SUV. He walked away while they burned."

"That's awful," he said. And he thought: Just the way I learned in St. Petersburg, with napalm. "If it's the pair that drove me this morning, I'm sorry the driver died."

His careful phrasing puzzled her. "I just wondered whether you knew any agents well," she said.

"A few."

Custody had been a parade of agents and officers, some with badges and some without. At the beginning, when he was locked in his sparse bedroom or in interrogation rooms, he measured the passage of time by changes in the agents: who worked five days and was off for two, who hadn't shaved, whose cold sore finally healed, who wore the same shirt and tie two days in a row, or maybe it was just one day under torture.

"I saw you twice while you were in custody," Gayfeather said. "The first time, you were sedated and didn't know I was there. The FBI wanted to know whether I recognized you or your name. Your friend and my constituent Cimarron Hernandez told me why you didn't pull the trigger on me, but that might've been just a story. The second time, you may remember that visit. I think you were surprised to see me. We talked a bit."

Nick remembered. She asked a lot of questions. An agent told him later that she had visited a third time to ask more questions, but by then Nick was under tighter security during official sessions.

"Did you know," Gayfeather said, "that this part of town once had another resident you might have heard of? Alger Hiss."

"Senator, I don't recall."

She laughed. "You're one of us, all right."

"After World War II," she said, "when the Cold War was getting started, the District was full of fearful people. This was before the blacklists were a big thing, but being a Communist and gay was still dangerous. Whittaker Chambers, who was a spy for the Soviets, renounced the Communist Party and gave up some film that had been hidden in a pumpkin at his farm in Maryland. He was setting up a case against Hiss."

Nick nodded. Hiss had come up in a half-remembered lesson at the academy in St. Petersburg. He had been accused of being a Soviet spy in the State Department but was convicted only of lying about being a communist.

"Hiss lived just a couple of miles south of here. I thought you'd like the connection, even if Russia's not exactly communist anymore."

Nick laughed. He raised his glass: "To history."

"Someday," she said, "I want to hear your full story. The good people of central Kansas have never forgiven you."

"I thought you were popular. They re-elected you."

"It wasn't by much. I was the only surviving Republican in the race in a state that hasn't elected a Democrat to the Senate since 1932. But that was before the real craziness took hold."

"What's going on?"

"You know about the president and his policies, right? A lot of Kansas Republicans have been reactionary that way for years," she said. "It's a Civil War border state that sometimes forgets which side of the border it was on. For example, *Brown vs. Board of Education,* the desegregation case in the 1950s? That started in Kansas because of an official segregation policy.

"Now, for a lot of the party, it's worse. No one can be conservative enough, evangelical yet Old Testament Christian enough, vicious enough. If you didn't kill Muslims for breakfast and vote against blacks and gays by lunch, then deport Mexicans and make a tribute to the president in time for the evening news, you were a liberal making up hoaxes."

Gayfeather took a deep breath, settling back in her chair.

"Politicians used to win by being beige, the most inoffensive people in the room. Now voters want garish colors, and I'm not garish," she said. "There's no more visionary gleam, I'm afraid. It's all divisionary now."

She looked off across the room.

"My opponent, Fontaine, the one who was killed, was that kind of person. He was as corrupt as could be, but he had wrapped the Stars and Stripes around his actions and the public saw little of what he was up to. And his people have never forgiven me for not taking the bullet instead of him. God, now he'd fit right in."

Gayfeather poured herself a third glass and set the bottle down within easy reach.

"It wasn't just him." She pointed a crooked-back index finger at Nick. "Look at any of the Republicans elevated out of Kansas during the president's previous administration. That should tell you something about the quality of our party's leadership pool."

She halfway smiled. "I'm sure you remember Vernon Lister. He'll never forget you."

"Ragweed" Lister, hired by one of Fontaine's backers, had been aiming at Gayfeather but missed and shot Fontaine by accident. Instead of doing the smart thing and driving to Mexico, he had gone home and gotten tied up watching another family's homemade porn.

"There are bumper stickers on pickups all over Kansas that say 'Lister missed her. Try again.' Forgive me if I don't have fond thoughts for the hard-right sect of the Kansas Republican Party."

"When I was being questioned by the FBI," Nick said, "all I could tell them about Lister was that he was in a separate world. I knew he was a jerk and he tried to kill me, but his willingness to do something so stupid, without training, surprised me."

"A professional's approach, I'm sure," she said after a moment.

"I had a better plan and a way out," Nick said. "The only problem with my plan was me."

"As I said, I'm grateful. I've been looking over my shoulder every day since then, now that the rules against shooting politicians are gone. Not necessarily watching for you, but for someone who thinks he's better than you."

"Look, I apologize for how bad you must have felt when you learned about me. If it weren't for that kidnapping business and last battle in Sandstone, I could've just disappeared and no one would have known." He raised his glass. "To stupid morals."

Gayfeather and Nick were leaning in. Their eyes met and then their knees did.

"Tonight, Nick, you can call me Harriet. In front of others, I'm Senator. OK?"

Nick sensed a night of romance in his future. "Harriet."

Gayfeather removed the lamb and beef from the warming oven and brought the plates to the table. She lifted the lid of a stereo and started an album of cello music, then dimmed the track lighting until the room was restaurant-moody.

"I saw you looking at the pheasant painting," Gayfeather said. "That's a scene outside Beeler, a little place off the highway up in Ness County. You know of George Washington Carver, the scientist who made all kinds of things from peanuts? He lived there awhile in the late 1800s. Anyway, the story I'm going to tell you doesn't have anything to do with Carver.

"This is how I understand it. A Beeler farmer came home from World War II with a German wife, and they lived up in the limestone hills. They didn't get along, and after a while the farmer told his friends that his wife had gone back to Germany. At his death, he revealed that he had killed her and that she was buried in a corner of the pasture. He asked for someone to bury her in a cemetery.

"I guess the moral is that people do horrible things and, when it's too late, they try to atone for it," she said. "The story's usually about the farmer and the hell he went through knowing what he had done. To me, this is a tragic story about the German wife."

They didn't talk much while they ate. Finally, as Gayfeather pushed the last of her julienned carrots onto the fork, she asked Nick whether he went to church.

"It contradicts my lifestyle," he said.

"At least you're honest about it. I'm sorry to go on about the ultra-conservatives, but maybe you'll understand, since you're an outsider."

He raised his eyebrows. "Understand?"

"I'm not married now. I don't have kids, and I don't stand in the way of abortion. So these people, all wearing their crosses on their sleeves, whisper in their churches, from one church to another, that I'm a lesbian yet somehow hate all women. It's as if there's a jealousy incubated by women who choose a life of Bibles, babies, and Bubba instead of having careers or going into public service.

"To be fair," she said, "some women find real joy in raising families. And, in some cases, a genetic disposition or bad parents kept them from succeeding in school or demanding their rights. And their men are just as bad about women."

"That has to be hard," he said, nodding.

"H.L. Mencken, who used to write a newspaper column over in Baltimore, called those people Puritans. He said they were people who suffered from 'the haunting fear that someone, somewhere may be happy.' It's my favorite quotation, but not one I can ever use in a speech."

"You said, 'Not married now.'"

"I was once. He—Steven—was an officer in the Army. He was killed in 2003 in the second Iraq war about a year after we married. He was thirty-eight, leading an engineering battalion, and I was twenty-seven years old, a bright-eyed world-beater economist. He was West Point, and I was University of Kansas and Yale. When the war was over, we were going to be a power couple."

They raised their glasses in his memory.

"Now I'm a perfect pre-MAGA Republican," she said. "Pro-military, a gun owner, in favor of lower government aid to people and higher subsidies to farmers and industry."

She laughed at herself.

"Kansas is a big stage where emotions should've been played out all along. A lot of folks have repressed their feelings all their lives, though, and now they're starting to let everything loose. It's not pretty. I tell you, another stupid culture war and I'll be ready to junk it all."

Gayfeather poured more wine and brought in another beer, and the two of them sat companionably for a long moment. She asked Nick to slide his chair closer to hers.

"You mind?" she asked. She smiled warmly.

"This is nice."

Did she want to hook up? He hadn't had even a kiss for two years.

The FBI had brought Cimi Hernandez to Army and Bureau posts a couple of times to use as a wrench against him, but she'd finally had enough and said she wouldn't be back. Maybe a year ago, he convinced himself that he gotten over her.

Gayfeather was talking.

"What are your plans?" she said. "Are you going back to Russia, or to the FBI, or to Canada, or what?"

"First, I like the United States. I want to stay. Second, I need to find a job doing the kind of work I understand."

"Are you really not going to kill me?"

He looked her in the eye and didn't answer.

"OK, then," she said. Again, her gaze wandered and returned. "If you're not doing anything special for a couple of weeks, can you come work for me?"

Nick sat back. "Would the FBI approve?"

"Let's not tell the FBI."

He smiled. "Okay."

"I have a staff member, a deputy in Kansas, who might be involved in activities that are way beyond her years and pay grade, and it's causing concerns that she's working for a foreign government interested in weakening America."

"Why not call the FBI? Or fire her?"

"I don't want the FBI involved in keeping my office clean, and I don't want her running off to CNN, Fox News, or the *Washington Post*. This needs to be done quietly. You know what the government's like now. The worst Americans hold so much power, and this is my effort to help clean up the mess while we still have a chance. Maybe we can save our country."

"What can I do?"

"I want you to get close to her. Laura Eisenhauer. You're a bright guy with an exceptional history, and I don't think you'd have any trouble striking up a conversation or even a relationship. She's smart, perceptive, and connected, and she's no pushover. She's so organized that she lives fifteen minutes in the future."

"What do you want?"

"I want to know what she's up to. If she can harm me, I want you to persuade her to stop talking."

She started to say more, but paused.

He played with his glass. She laid her fork and knife across her plate.

"There is maybe a point," she said, "where I don't want to know what's going to happen. It'll be up to you."

"This is a risky conversation," he said.

He searched her face for further meaning. Maybe the offer was the bait in her trap. He wondered where the bugs and cameras were hidden.

Gayfeather said, "Go to Kansas. You'll be safe there. The FBI never did release information about you or confirm anything that was brought up, so you may be more forgotten than you think."

She placed her hand over her heart.

"Nobody would suspect someone working for me," she said. "And who'd think of looking for you in a place where half the population, if they remember anything about you at all, thinks you're a ghost in a false-flag conspiracy launched by the deep-state FBI?"

She warmed to her idea. "Go get connected with Laura and don't tell anyone else who you are, other than I just hired you to be my new constituent liaison. Laura will know your true identity and abilities. She's seen parts of the classified report and the FBI showed her your photo, and she was there in Great Bend. Earn her trust."

Gayfeather watched Nick's eyes. He hoped it didn't show that he was thinking he could handle this Laura, finish off Gayfeather, and escape by melting into the breezy distance of the plains.

"Laura's just starting her vacation," Gayfeather said. "I'll tell her you're coming. I have to take care of some business here and then I'll fly into Wichita on Thursday or Friday. I have a Memorial Day speech out there on Monday."

"What didn't you want to tell me?"

"Be careful of traps, Nick," she said. "Laura's had emotional trouble over the years, and she has a fragile grip on her promiscuity. I want you to be her next mental breakdown."

She put her hand on his forearm, and he bent in so she could whisper in his ear. Her grip tightened.

"Hiring you is probably one of the stupidest things I could do," she said. "If word got out, if your identity and history were exposed, it would open a door to questioning everything about the assassination attempt and every vote I've ever made."

"I understand," he said.

"This is high-level security work, and there's more to be had later," she said. "I want to trust you, Nick. But if it turns out that I can't, I will punish you hard."

4

Nick moved to the front room and peeked around the drapes. The sky had gone to dusk, and streetlights turned the neighborhood into a scene of harsh light and deep darkness. He didn't spot any troublesome silhouettes under trees, no shadowy operatives lit by cellphone screens in bland sedans.

He stepped aside when the senator walked back in.

"I don't want you to think I took your participation for granted," she said.

Nick shrugged. He smiled, which seemed to seal the contract.

"But I arranged for a ride to Dulles tonight for you."

She checked her watch. She texted someone.

"It'll be here in five minutes," she said. "You have time to relieve yourself. First door on the left. After that, everything you need will be provided. Until you're set up, just go with the flow."

Gayfeather picked her glass off the table.

"To your success and long life, Nick Deveraux," she said. "We'll solve this problem in Kansas, if it's the last thing we do."

He rationalized: If he's going to kill Gayfeather, he might as well do it in Kansas, the home of her natural enemies.

•   •   •

Into Gayfeather's driveway hot-rolled a Ford Excursion, a dark beast simmering down as the driver lowered the grayed-out passenger window in the contrasty porch light.

"Get in front with me," he called to Nick. "Keep your bag with you. Keep your face forward."

Nick sensed another passenger, seated directly behind him. He buckled himself in and positioned his rollerbag between his knees. The driver, wearing thin leather gloves, handed him an envelope.

"Open it, see for yourself. Five thousand dollars from her office to cover your expenses."

Getting to work for Gayfeather while plotting to kill her and escape was a complex bit of good fortune. Would Laura, the assistant, be part of the work? Maybe he'd end up killing them both. Everybody wins.

Heaven help him, though, if someone came in later tonight and killed Gayfeather. He'd get the blame. His fingerprints were on the dinnerware; his DNA could be pulled from his fork and glass.

Gayfeather had created a position on the spur of the moment, Nick realized. He was just the bumbling godsend to make filling it possible. Considering his fumbled approach to killing Gayfeather, he hoped he was better prepared for the expanded assignment, even if it was just to stall for time.

He didn't speak to the driver, nor did the man in the back seat, as the SUV headed out Massachusetts Avenue to Nebraska Avenue, then south across the Potomac River into Virginia. From there, the driver followed state highway 123 to 267 to Dulles International Airport. He took an early turnoff and pulled up at a fixed-base operator at the north end of the easternmost runway. By Nick's watch, the drive took fifty-one minutes door to door.

The man in the back seat opened his door first.

"Follow me," he said, an executive directing a distant underling.

The man's posture was straight, his pick-stitched suit pressed, his dark hair trimmed neatly above his pale blue shirt collar. He didn't wear glasses. There was no bulge suggesting either a firearm or love handles. His shoes bore a hard shine, and he walked with grace.

Only once did he glance over his shoulder, apparently checking that Nick was tagging briskly along through in the terminal's passenger lounge. Under the LED fixtures, he was tanned and appeared to be well tended, although perhaps unpleasantly thin lipped.

The man had a briefcase but not a suitcase, which Nick found curious. Did he have two homes and flew between them? Would he be flying back to Dulles tomorrow? Whose business jet with the open hatch were they headed toward? It wore no company livery, just the N-number on the white tail above the twin engines and *Learjet 75* painted discreetly on the lower fuselage.

At the base of the steps, a ramp attendant tucked Nick's bag into the hold. Nick followed his host through the hatch behind the cockpit, hunching over to fit under a ceiling less than five feet above the deck.

Each side of the cabin had four plush leather seats along the windows, the first facing the second, the third facing the fourth. The man took a forward-facing seat in the front half of the cabin, joining two other men sitting one on each side with their backs to the cockpit. An attendant aft gave Nick her warmest smile and gestured to the fourth seat on the starboard side as he sidestepped down the narrow aisle. He felt like he was tripping over the base of every seat.

The plane's auxiliary power unit kicked the twin turbofan engines into service. White noise filled the cabin. He settled into the stitched leather seat and peeked out past the winglet into the light-studded darkness, the long necklace of approaching jets. He overheard a questioning voice from the front of the cabin and the muttered response: "Gayfeather's new aide."

The attendant placed before Nick a tray holding orange juice and a pair of headphones. Nick smiled at her and drank the juice but didn't put on the headset.

"It's policy for guests to wear these, sir," she said. "Delicate matters are often discussed, and our men prefer to speak freely."

Nick plugged the phones into a wall panel, and his ears filled with classical music. Brahms, according to the digital readout. The attendant put Nick's glass in a trash bag, checked with the men in front and the flight deck, then pulled the cockpit and cabin doors shut and belted herself into the other rear seat.

A moment later the engines kicked up their whine and the Learjet began its roll to the north end of the runway. The three men in the front looked at him again and turned away without expression.

• • •

Nick awakened to the attendant pressing his shoulder. The plane was quiet and empty but for the two of them.

"Sir, we've landed."

He handed her his headphones, then pressed his hand against the inside pocket of his jacket to be certain Gayfeather's money was still there.

"Where are the others?" he asked.

"They've caught their rides and asked that you be allowed to finish your nap."

Nick looked out the window into the darkness. "Where are we?"

"Colonel James Jabara Airport. It's a small airport on the east side of Wichita, Kansas. Have you been here before?"

"I didn't really want to come back."

Nick stood up, felt queasy, and slowly sat down again.

"Give me a minute," he said.

The attendant turned away and fussed with her gear.

A moment passed. "I'm heading to the terminal," she said, "and I'd love it if you'd keep me company."

"The time?"

"About 11:30 Central."

She handed Nick his suitcase and walked him inside to the terminal counter of the fixed-base operator. She left without another word, although she did squeeze his arm and smile as she passed him off to the desk agent. The agent, a forty-something clean-shaven man in horn-rims, stood up and handed him a folded phone message.

The note was terse and in the clerk's printing: "Wait in the lobby. I'll get there about midnight. Laura."

"You do this for everybody who flies in?" Nick asked.

"I do when they come on that plane."

At midnight, the woman who stomped through the automated sliding glass doors was ready to bite. The attendant nodded toward Nick.

She was five-foot-eight and lean, her brunette hair fixed under a ball cap. She wore purple sneakers, old blue jeans, and a purple sweatshirt with an image of a snarling cat.

She aimed a finger at Nick. Under the harsh fixture, it looked like the skeletal hand of the Ghost of Christmas Yet to Come, and it beckoned him.

She led him to a burgundy Ford Flex parked under the tall lights. The roof and hood were dimpled with hail damage, dark rims of rust showing where the paint had cracked. The license plate bore a design like a round campaign button from the 1950s: I LIKE IKE.

"Laura?" He smiled at her. "Thanks for picking me up."

She acknowledged it with a nod. Slightly, one time.

"The senator ordered me to put you up for a few days," she said. "Although I can't imagine why a hotel's not good enough, or even what I'm supposed to pretend you're doing here. I don't like you or anything you represent, or what you tried to do to the senator only two years ago, so let's not talk."

I wouldn't be happy either, Nick thought. It's midnight on your vacation. But maybe you won't have long to suffer.

Laura pushed south on Webb Road to Kellogg Avenue, and then west on the six-lane freeway through the state's largest city. The ride was a little rough. The dashboard had a rattle and small cracks, and Nick's seat was worn at the seams.

Signs directed traffic south to McConnell Air Force Base. To the north, a stream of lights traced the path of Interstate 135. Laura and Nick crossed the southbound Arkansas River west of downtown and turned north on Eisenhower Airport Parkway.

"Eisenhower. Related?"

He thought she grimaced, but the streetlights made it hard to tell.

"Eisenhauer." She spelled it for him. "Sounds the same."

The parkway devolved into Ridge Road. She steered into an apartment complex, her Flex becoming one of fifty cars under metal canopies.

Laura led the way up the outside stairs to her second-floor apartment, entering and not holding the door for him.

"The couch is yours," she said tonelessly. "The bathroom is the first door down the hall. If you make a mess, clean it up. If you open my bedroom door, I'll shoot you."

5

An unfamiliar alarm bleated Nick awake.

Eyes wide open, he lay still until he figured out that he was not in an FBI unit's barracks, surrounded by low-bidder furniture and a five-foot dowel rod masquerading as a closet. He was under a fleece blanket on the brown leather couch in Laura Eisenhauer's living room in Wichita. A knife's edge of sunlight pushed through a crack in the curtains.

There was no dog, a good thing. The apartment smelled of sauteed onions and roasted meat. He must've been too tired last night to notice.

What had he gotten himself into?

Nick put his feet on a reddish rag rug and looked around for the alarm. He found it in the kitchen: the microwave timer.

A cursive note was taped to the microwave's door:

Use the towel on the counter for your shower.

I went to the office. Take all your stuff to the Log Cabin Diner 5 blocks south of here and eat breakfast. I'll pick you up at 8:30. —L

PS. Heads up, a drug dealer was stabbed to death this winter in a parking lot this side of the diner. Don't buy any drugs.

The clock said 6:01. Nick pulled out the stem on his watch and adjusted it back an hour to Central time.

The apartment was small but had sturdy, overweight secondhand furniture and clean cookware. A countertop wine rack held seven bottles, and there were two bottles of Prosecco in the fridge. Black-and-white landscape photos were framed on the walls. Two pairs of women's running shoes rested under a row of coat hooks near the door. Nick held apart the curtains until he saw his naked reflection in the balcony window of the facing apartment. He stood to the side of Laura's door and quietly tested the knob; it was locked.

He shaved and showered in the hallway bath, luxuriating in the feel of the terrycloth towel drawn across his back. He picked a blue shirt and slacks out of his suitcase, then repacked it with his travel clothes. By 6:55, when the sun was burning full over low buildings to the southeast, he was in his jacket and out the door.

•   •   •

Muehling's Log Cabin Diner was a design transplant from the North Woods to a city where spruces suitable for cabins were not native. Nick ran his hand over a shaved log; it was real. The highway neighborhood, however, was built to accommodate chain restaurants, chain hotels, and chain stores.

He claimed a two-top table under the big window in the front wall, snuggling his suitcase next to his chair. A fly lay dead on the sill behind a tied-back red curtain at the far end of the table, beyond a gentleman's reach if he wanted to brush it to the floor.

Tables lined the window wall, and a counter with stools ran across the other side of the room. The kitchen had a pass-through hole, with unfilled orders hanging on the kitchen side. The floor was linoleum tile with a bland striped pattern where foot traffic hadn't worn it down to the gray backing.

Nick's stomach, unsettled last night from the drugs and long day, was back to normal, but he didn't trust it in a cafe that smelled so thickly of bacon grease. From a laminated menu, he ordered whole-wheat toast, two pancakes, a slice of ham, and a couple of eggs over easy with unsweetened iced tea. With a thin paper napkin, he wiped the menu ickiness off his fingers. Clerks on their way to the office paraded in and out, buying coffee and a burrito to go. A few singles, the odds and ends of Wichita, took their breakfast at the counter. Older men in big-box-store shirts and women in oversize glasses were holding down chairs around two tables at the far end of the room, the men talking national politics and the women chatting emphatically about the need to kick members off their grandkids' school boards.

The view to the south was of a grassy embankment supporting Kellogg, doing double duty as US 54 and US 400, where it passed over the parkway heading into the airport. A bank time-and-temp sign on the way over had flashed 57 degrees; he was glad he'd worn his jacket even though the day would warm up soon. Bright leaves in the young trees on the embankment swayed, hinting at the day's breeze to come.

He drummed his index fingers on the edge of the table. This mission was the first time he had ever gone freelance, postponing a certain opportunity then flying halfway across the continent to, he assumed, delete another target first. He was alive, for the first time in his life enjoying self-agency, and he was grinning when the waitress brought his plate.

"Well, ain't you the happiest boy in town," she said. "Pay at the register when you're done, hon."

Nick winked, and she walked away sharing his smile. He spread marmalade on a triangle of toast and looked around casually while he chewed through the eggs.

At the counter, behind a thick man in a taut mechanic's shirt and a skinny blond woman, stood a skittery twenty-something with slicked-back hair, a ducktail obscuring some of his neck tattoo. He wore a black T-shirt with an oversize neck hole and saggy black denim jeans with keys on a belt chain, and he was holding court for two cooks he had called out of the kitchen.

Laughing, he slid a knife out of its sheath. "I was looking at blades at the Walmart, and the guy showed me this one." He held up a bandaged finger. "I sliced my trigger finger open. Almost to the bone."

So you still bought it? a cook asked.

"I said, 'I'll take this one since it already has my blood on it.'"

The cooks exchanged glances, but the man seemed content to admire his knife and they went back to work. Nick considered a man waving a blade around to be a threat, unless it was that guy. He felt in his pocket to be sure of the Russian knife.

Nick spread grape jelly on his second triangle of toast and took a bite. He sipped his tea before using the toast to guide remnants of the eggs onto his fork.

That's when the blond woman set her plate and iced tea on Nick's table and slid into the facing chair. Two-thirds of a pancake lay on her plate with the fork, and a half-eaten sausage link rolled around.

"May I join you?" she asked.

She was pretty. Bemused, Nick said, "Sure."

"The knife guy gives me the creeps. He's so Wichita." She pronounced it Which-tah.

"I don't scare you?"

"Don't flatter yourself." Her brown eyes twinkled. "The waitress likes you."

They meandered through the small talk: the weather, the food, the chatterboxes at the far end of the diner. She listened to him attentively.

Her skin was translucent. She was slightly built, gangly to the point of looking like a handful of straws held together by elastic thread. Her collarbones were prominent under the open collar of her plum polo shirt, and her smile revealed a slender gap between her front teeth. Her eyes were kind. The blond hair came from a salon, he thought. It was slightly wavy and perfectly trimmed above her shoulders.

Nick figured she was in her late twenties, maybe thirty. Her manners would make any grandmother proud.

"Your accent, from the east," she said. "Where's your family from? Is the wind blowing you in or out"?

Nick laughed. "In. My family's from eastern Europe, but I've been on the East Coast."

"Ha. I was going to say Kansas City."

"Are you from here?"

"I'm from northwestern Kansas, near Hays. You know it?"

Nick had been through that area in the summer. A couple of years earlier, Hays was his hot, dry, windy introduction to Kansas.

"It's big country out there," he said. He got the last of his eggs. "You work here in town?"

"I'm taking a few weeks to drive around, see all of Midway USA, get to know people." She frowned, adding, "I gave up on my job. I random-tested urinary catheters at a factory, for strength and cleanliness. It just wasn't fulfilling."

He wrestled with his thoughts about that work. "Are you here long?" he said. "I'm waiting for someone to pick me up."

"Is this that kind of place? Who're you hoping for? An escort, your girlfriend, or your mother?"

He laughed. "More of a taxi driver. Maybe she's secretly a nun."

"My bio dad's brother was a minister. That's as close as I come."

"You have a big family?"

"My birth mom and dad died when I was a baby, and I don't have any kids. My mom's sister lives in western Oklahoma with her two kids, my nieces."

"That's sad about your parents."

"Now, my foster mom was a math whiz. She multiplied until she had twelve kids. It was as if she and her husband threw a bunch of spaghetti babies against the wall to see which ones would stick. Eight turned out okay, two are in halfway houses, and two moved to Wyoming to make meth. I was fourth oldest but always the thirteenth kid, kept to be a babysitter."

She drank until the ice clicked against her teeth and a bit of tea splashed out onto her shirt. She set her glass down and patted the spill with her napkin.

For half a minute, she rolled the bottom of the glass back and forth in its arena of condensation. Her nail polish, a light pink, had grown away from her cuticles.

She asked, "You have a big family?"

"No brothers, no sisters, no wife, no kids, no attachment," he said. "My dad died in a plane crash, and my mom has been busy with her work."

"Two drifters on the prairie."

They were clinking their glasses when the building yelped, a sideways kick followed by rolling waves. A cup vibrated off the lunch counter and shattered on the floor.

"Fracking quake," she said. She hadn't even lifted her elbows off the tabletop. "A gift from the oil companies."

"We don't need to get under the table?"

She shook her head.

Nick didn't seem convinced. He'd been in quakes in Alaska, but that was to be expected in wild country.

"So Kansas has both earthquakes and tornadoes? Where do you go to be safe?"

"Colorado."

Nick raised his eyebrows. "To Colorado."

They sat companionably, alternating their views between the waitress sweeping up the broken cup and the rush-hour traffic. Background conversation in the room shifted from the quake back to politics.

The woman gazed forlornly at her plate. Nick leaned forward, asking, "Is your drifting going all right?"

"Mostly," she said. "I'm just tired." She raised her eyes. "I get to think a lot. Lately it's been about the purpose of life."

"Do you find that in Kansas?"

She frowned. "You know life is bigger than where you are at the moment."

It sounded woo-woo, but Nick conceded with a nod.

"You have to find an idea to hold onto and keep it in your heart," she said. "You have to love someone, to believe in something, to know that you're doing the right thing. You've got to be willing to give up everything. Like an artist, because you're creating your life."

Nick played with his fork, chasing an imaginary scrap of egg white with a bit of syrupy pancake, and she watched his face.

"You know what I mean?" she asked.

"Sometimes I get a glimpse," he said, "but it fades away."

"When it comes back, hold on tight."

She scooted her chair out and rolled her shoulders. She dug a ten out of her jeans, smoothed it with the side of her hand and placed it with the ticket under her plate.

"It's sad," she said, "to meet people you might never see again."

Nick stood up with her. "What's your name?"

"Kelli, with an *i*."

"Nick, also with an *i*."

"See ya, Nick." As she backed out the door, Kelli blew him a kiss.

She held the door for a woman coming in. The woman—Laura Eisenhauer—turned to watch Kelli, whose hair danced in the wind as she glided across the parking lot.

"Pay up," Laura told Nick. "Let's go."

Outside, Nick said to Laura: "Three things, and then I'll not talk. First, thanks for putting me up last night. Second, thanks for letting the senator force you into babysitting me on your vacation. Third, before we go wherever we're going, can we pick up a few things at Walmart?"

She got in the car, so he did too, although he wasn't the one who slammed the door. They pulled across a side street into the store's parking lot.

Her voice defrosted, but she kept both hands on the wheel and looked straight ahead.

"You're welcome," she said, "but don't press it. I'll help you shop, because you're going to work at my ranch and you don't know what you need. I will not put up with any whining later."

In the store, she told him to get a cart.

"Just so you know," she said, "I'm not pushy and I'm not picky."

"We'll get along fine," he said.

"But sometimes people think I am. On my own time, my way is the only way, so it's the right way."

With her begrudging guidance, Nick filled his rattle-wheeled cart with work shirts, work gloves, underwear, a pair of sunglasses, and blue jeans.

"Really," she said, "you won't look like a grandpa in those. Just get the damned jeans."

She had him add shoes, shorts, and shirts for running.

He modeled several straw hats for her, clowning a bit. Finally she pointed to a blue Kansas City Royals baseball cap and said, "That."

Nick walked past Laura to the electronics section, where he pulled a quartet of pay-as-you-go phones from a rack.

Nick grinned at Laura and brandished a phone.

"They're always handy," he said. "Tell the world your problems."

She made a point of texting the office while Nick discussed details with a clerk he called Karl (who corrected Nick: "Karlton, not Karl"). Karlton, a bit stocky with brown hair halfway over his ears, was bland but handsome in a way, having a sincere disposition with a mustache-beard trimmed into an attention-focusing tight circle around his mouth. He knew his merchandise, and he knew how to draw.

Nick nodded at a pencil sketch on a pad lying on the counter. "That your dog?"

"Nah, that's Garmr. He's a Norse monster guarding the gates of h-e-double-hockey sticks. That's my hobby."

"Interesting," Nick said. It was a term he'd learned from the FBI.

Karlton rang up the clothes and phones and took Nick's cash. He was bouncy.

"Today's my eighth anniversary here!"

"Congratulations," Nick and Laura said at the same time. They looked at each other and added, "Good luck."

•   •   •

Laura kept her thoughts shut up tight as she sped northwest on Kansas Highway 96 out of Wichita. They were in the Arkansas River bottomland he was familiar with from his previous mission upstream in Sandstone and Great Bend, which lay two hours northwest of Wichita.

The day was humid, threatening to rain, but patches of blue peeked through the low clouds. It was the kind of day that wanted to be all things and wasn't good at any of them.

Uneasy at the thought of being near Sandstone again, he finally asked, "Where're we going, exactly?"

"West."

"How far?"

There was silence, and Nick surrendered.

Going far enough west on K-96 would put them in Great Bend, and he'd be happy not to go there either. But, man, he'd never get any secrets out of Laura if she didn't talk.

He had to keep in mind, however, that she was his secondary target. If he handled Gayfeather first, it didn't matter what happened with Laura Eisenhauer . . . unless he could sell her trove of supposed secrets to the FBI or the Russians. In any case, if he had to run he still had $4,257 of Gayfeather's cash left.

Laura would warm up to him or she wouldn't. Laura would live or she wouldn't. Nick didn't care.

She was in a hurry, running a little over seventy miles an hour on the four-lane. Her jaw muscles were taut, and she kept glancing at Nick. Finally, she blurted:

"You fucking Russians think you own this country!"

"Where does that come from?"

"You know as well as anyone," she said. "Election interference.

Giving us this president and his gang. Putin. Traitors in Congress. Money laundering. And this is really good: The fact that you can walk around killing Americans."

Nick had to admit it, the last part was right.

"Harriet Gayfeather is the only American politician I've met," he said. "I don't have anything to do with money."

Laura flipped him the bird. "You're part of the machine."

"Besides," he said, "wasn't a lot of this region settled by immigrants from old Russia?"

"Ukraine. Crimea."

"You think I'm here to mess up aid to Ukraine?"

Fields of wheat rolled in vast but shallow green waves, ripening to gold slowly as the kernels matured. Whole young cottonwoods swayed as the southwest wind pressed through them. The Ford Flex, substantial though it was, was pushed a little to the right each time a semi-trailer hurried past, then lurched leftward into the vacuum following the trailer.

The sun wasn't hot but it was bright, and Nick put on sunglasses. Laura, already opaque to Nick, wore wire-frame glasses that turned dark in direct light. A freckle decorated the tanned cheekbone under her right eye. Her shirt, of periwinkle and white checks and fastened by pearl snaps, was open two buttons at the top, and she wore jeans and running shoes. She looked fit, in a runner's way. Her thick hair was brought into a ponytail with an elastic tie. She wore a watch on her left wrist and no jewelry. He guessed her to be in her mid-thirties.

She had cracked the rear windows for circulation. The flop-flop turbulence forestalled conversation with the city slicker assassin still in his East Coast clothes.

Road signs carried the conversation.

"Abortion kills a gift from God."

"Make America Great Again."

"Contrails = Poison!!"

"Visit Dodge City's Boot Hill! Left on US 50."

On paper peeling from a billboard: "The sun will shine again in Kansas."

Little towns: canopied by old elms, grain elevators rising above the trees, barren subdivisions leaking into farmland.

At a dirt-road intersection with the highway, a man driving a black Amish carriage, covered but open in front, waited behind a gray mare. Cattle grazed in pastures where prairie dogs stood as sentinels. Bags of trash spilled their treasures in broad ditches. Expansion joints thumped beneath the tires. Seed grain was advertised on small signs along fields.

A mile to the north, the dark tree line of the Arkansas River tagged along, a distant frame to fields of wheat, soybeans, and irrigated corn.

Past Hutchinson, the country opened up, more of it in pasture. Side roads were sandier. A hundred yards to the north, a dust devil spun across a plowed field. In front of the car ahead of them, a redtail hawk flapped hard to get off the road, and within seconds the Flex straddled a roadkill rabbit ripped part by beak and talons.

Nickerson, ten miles. Bull Creek, twenty-one.

"That's where we're going," Laura said. "West of Bull Creek."

"What's out there?"

"My ranch. No cattle, no livestock, no crops. Natural grassland. I go there when I can, and since this is my vacation and I have to babysit you, you're going too."

"Roll up your window. I need to tell you something."

She frowned, but pulled the toggle that raised the window.

"Here's the deal, and it's probably a state secret. Do you want to hear it?"

"Sure," she said. "Tell me your lies."

"I was released yesterday in DC by two agents from the FBI. An operative for the Russian mob was waiting for me and ordered me to go back to work for my old boss."

"Are you writing a movie script?"

"She gave me the senator's home address, and I went there hoping Gayfeather would protect me because I hadn't shot her. She gave me dinner and offered me a job, this job, to get me out of Washington. She said you're the only person out here who would know me."

"This is complete bullshit, but I applaud your imagination."

"The agents who dropped me off were attacked and killed a few minutes after giving me to the Russians."

"Uh-huh."

"Ask your office about the agents. Google it. It's the kind of thing that'd make the news."

Five miles later, she spoke again.

"What's your cover story for being here?"

"I'm a new constituent services aide in Washington," he said. "You're helping me learn how the office runs. You're cautious around me because you suspect that I'm after your job."

"I don't have any idea what you're after. The whole thing is squirrelly."

"Absolutely. I'd like to just be invisible."

"I'd be happy if you were out of my sight."

"Look," Nick said. "That mess was two years ago. I thought I was going to perform an honorable duty for my country, and you know it could've turned out much worse for the senator. I apologize for the situation, but I'm not sorry I didn't shoot her."

"Right."

"I'm not even the one who shot at her," he said.

"What if you had?"

"Everything would be different."

6

Now Laura was talking up a storm. "The land came to me from my grandparents. They owned it for more than forty years," she said.

"It's almost a whole square mile along the Arkansas, about six hundred acres of scrub brush, walnuts, cottonwoods, and bluestem. Grass," she added when Nick raised his eyebrows. "I have a creek, a pond, a house with three outbuildings, and lots of barbed wire. There are deer, pheasant, quail, sometimes an armadillo, prairie dogs, coyotes, and the usual opossums and coons. The pond has ducks, catfish, bass, and bluegill."

"Are you close to anything?"

"Other than the river and Quivira National Wildlife Refuge, no. My place is nestled in the big bend of the Arkansas, just south of the middle of the state. I'm far enough away from town that I can see the stars and hear the coyotes."

"You drive from Wichita every week?"

"I come mostly on weekends when the senator isn't in the state. It's a little over eighty miles from my apartment to the ranch. Once I kayaked from my ranch almost to my apartment in Wichita. The river is a national trail, according to the Park Service."

The countryside was changing from flat irrigated fields into dryland sand dunes with dark-leaved shrubs and tall wiry grasses. Windmills—four-legged steel towers topped by fan blades and a vane to keep the blades at the correct angle to the wind—used gears, a cam, and a sucker rod to bring water out of the ground and pour it into open steel tanks for cattle. Some trees, their limbs wrapped toward the north, were permanently bent by the wind.

"The ranch is like this?" he asked. "It reminds me of Ukraine."

"It's not exactly a farmer's paradise. The soil's kind of crappy," she said. "But the drainage is good and groundwater is close to the surface. Fortunately, so's the oil."

"You have oil? Are you rich?"

"There's an old well on a corner of the ranch," she said. "I get enough in royalties to keep the lights on."

When they turned off the highway south of the town of Bull Creek—"There's a couple of little towns across the river from me, but Bull Creek's where we get gas and groceries"—it was onto a washboard sand road. Nick braced his hands against the dashboard and Laura laughed as the Flex regained traction and she slowed to twenty miles an hour. The snare-drum beat of pebbles pinging the car's underbelly relaxed.

"After all the pavement, that's my little celebration," she said.

Nick smiled at her, and she smiled back. He thought: This is where she's at home.

"Sorry about the ride," she said. "When traffic or the grader goes too fast, it leaves ripples, and then I hit them the next time."

"Anyway," she went on, "I like oil. I'm not a tree hugger and I don't think solar and wind are going to save the world. But there are problems with drilling. We didn't have earthquakes before the drillers started fracking. There are other problems too, like the chemicals they frack with."

Laura slowed to swerve around an ornate box turtle trundling in its black-and-yellow shell from one weedy ditch to the other. In the ditch outside Nick's window, insects zipped around the waxy cream-colored blossoms hanging off a yucca spire.

"You know fracking, right?" she said. "The drillers force sand and chemicals down the well to break open the rock and let more oil and gas out. They also push drilling wastewater into some wells that go below the water table."

Nick nodded. "I know it can get messy, like fracked gas getting into houses' well water. It's been in the news."

"Oil companies are willing to cut corners for a buck," Laura said, "and they play with big bucks." A hundred yards down the road, she added, "I had a friend who was looking into that."

Nick rolled down his window and hung his right elbow out, hoping they'd get to the ranch soon. The open country made him want to run. The FBI had let him use fitness tracks, always with a chaperone, and usually an agent doing his own workout would circle the track with him fast enough to keep them both sharp. He needed to run now, just run until he couldn't lift another foot, run until he was away from all the people he knew.

"Have you ever watched a crew drill a well?" Laura asked. "One of my neighbors has a well going in. Oil prices are so low that nobody can figure out why Saltwood started drilling, but maybe we can get up close so you can see the magic happen."

She turned south and then west and south again, passing black and brown cattle clustered in pastures behind barbed-wire fences. Pea gravel popped against the car as they approached a turnoff near a shuttered rural school, its untrimmed bulbous eastern cedars shading a pickup.

"This isn't the most expensive place to drill. The oil's close to the surface, usually a little more than three thousand feet. The drillers just have to find the right place to punch the hole down."

"How much does that cost?"

"Half a million bucks or more, plus the cost of leasing acreage from the property owner."

About half-past 11:00, they drove over a ditch culvert and through a wide gap in a five-strand barbed-wire fence. The fence post on the right was adorned with a small sign identifying the project as Saltwood 7. A short oiled road led them into the pasture.

"It's Saltwood's seventh exploration of just this one old oilfield named Saltwood," she said. "The company maintains hundreds of wells in the US alone. This site is just outside the refuge."

Rust-blemished bottom-line sedans and a mismatched squadron of oversize pickups were backed in against the property line's fence, and Laura backed in as well near the entrance. Off to the side beyond the cars squatted a well-traveled white thirty-two-foot office trailer with basic amenities: four wooden steps with a handrail leading to a landing at the door, and a blue plastic drum of the sort that forty-two gallons of liquids are shipped in. A portable fiberglass-walled toilet waited just beyond the trailer.

Standing a hundred yards across the field was a derrick, a four-sided truncated pyramid of steel crossbeams based on a platform surrounded by trucks and tanks. It reached a hundred fifty feet higher than the windmill they passed earlier. Pipes were stacked on end under a block that traveled up and down inside the derrick.

Laura pointed at the derrick, saying, "Those pipes are threaded so they fit together, and there's a drill bit at the end of it. A mixture called mud is pumped down the hole with the pipe, and the rock that the bit grinds up is washed back to the top with the mud. Every time the drill pipe goes up and down, it has to be taken apart and reassembled. On top of the hole is a blowout preventer, which holds back a gusher in case the drill hits a high-pressure pool of oil or natural gas."

Even at a distance the thrum of machinery offended their ears, and the late-morning air carried an overtone of diesel exhaust and mud that overwhelmed Nick's sense of smell.

Fifty yards away beyond the derrick was a weathered wooden barn, the remains of a farmstead. The saplings that would have been cared for by the rancher's family had grown into trees that were now at the end of their lifespans, bare branches a perch for predatory birds, and hollow trunks that would be home to raccoons and bees.

The next shift, fourteen or fifteen men in orange safety vests and hardhats, clustered at the trailer's steps, listening to a man on the landing read from a clipboard. As Nick and Laura walked toward the trailer, one of the men noticed them. He lifted a couple of white high-density polyethylene hardhats off a rack and hustled over.

"Insurance rules," he explained.

"We're neighbors," Laura said. "Can we stand here and watch? How far down are you?"

"Almost three thousand feet," he said. "We're going for oil, but there's nothing yet."

The meeting at the trailer erupted with cheers.

"Got to go," the guy said. "You can probably stay, but you should stand back here." He waved away a bee and laughed. "Insurance rules."

The sun was getting through the clouds and growing warm on Nick's back, and the temperature must've risen into the seventies. He and Laura wore jackets against the breeze; hers was a light fleece and his was the sports coat he'd traveled in from DC. He adjusted the hard hat to cut the glare as he watched the roughnecks jostle one another and laugh, guys being guys.

The roughneck hadn't left. He was staring at Laura and blushing.

"Haven't I danced with you at the Hitch?" he asked her. "Chris. Remember?"

"Maybe . . . tell me more."

Rather than intrude on an oil-patch seduction, Nick kept his eyes elsewhere. A worker picked a scrap of two-by-four lumber off the ground and tossed it underhand into the blue drum, which must've been used as a trash barrel. Nick, swatting at a buzz past his ear, sensed that the block must've been heavier than it looked.

In a flash, the drum exploded.

•   •   •

In the incomprehensible first moment of the explosion, the pressure wave—the full-body shove, a head-slamming percussive thud—threw Nick against Laura.

They tumbled backward, heels up, arms flinging, bodies scuffing hard along the ground.

The shrapnel followed. Metal bits flying faster than sound left whispered trails, if anyone could hear them.

And then the shrapnel that had been blown high in the air began to rain down, a torrent of nails, nuts, bolts, wire, and circular power-saw blades whirling and fluttering at the mercy of aerodynamics, all of it more of a sensation than a known thing.

Nick awoke slowly, already in shock and numbed, and deaf. His body felt bent and awkward, and his eyes hurt too much to open. He felt around and discovered that he was lying across Laura's head and torso.

He forced his eyes into a squint and lifted himself off her. Was she alive?

He touched her face and then her belly. She was breathing rapidly, almost panting.

He yelled her name and held her face. She opened her eyes, and her pupils were wide. She moved her lips, but he heard nothing. His ears hurt.

Nick sat up and looked around. A column of yellowish smoke was drifting away from him, away from the place where something had been. The trailer, the men.

The driller, Chris, who had stood beside them, was sitting with his hands braced against the ground, his eyes fixed on five inches of jagged saw blade peeking out of his lower thigh. Gouts of arterial blood rose against the blade and flooded the sand between his thighs. Nick got up on his hands and knees, coughed and vomited, and in a minute he made it to his feet, a prairie dog in a murky world.

Laura was holding her hands over her ears and crying. Speckles and splashes of blood dotted her clothing.

Chris died as he sat, bled dry. The men who had been standing at the trailer were gone. Nick edged toward the crater. The wiry grass was flattened outward, slick and repulsive with blood and flesh.

There were legs and scorched body pieces. Two heads, one cut in half, the other smashed flat. He found four men who had all their limbs but were unresponsive to his touch.

The acrid odor of explosives and ruptured entrails was the scent of the world. Even as the unheard drilling rig made the air throb, Nick knew he should be hearing wounded men howl and kneeling men retch. He blinked but couldn't clear his vision, obscured by dust and smoke and tears from the smoke and the sureness that he wasn't really seeing the empty hardhats lying on the swept ground.

An instant of memory: a yellow-white burst, a single frame from a video, but nothing before or immediately after.

It was a new world, and he was alive, and he would act.

Nick staggered back to Laura and draped his jacket over her shoulders.

With his Russian knife, he cut the hem of his blue shirt and tore the fabric into wide strips. He wrapped one around a gash on an unconscious worker's arm, the cotton flooding with blood as he tightened it. The second man he came to had surrendered his jaw and his eyes; he lost his pulse as Nick held his wrist. He knelt beside another twisted man, rolled him over flat, swiped at the cloud of flies and pressed his hand against a sucking chest wound.

Nick's hearing was coming back, and he realized that the drilling rig had been brought to a stop. The vibration in the air was gone. All he could hear over the klaxon in his brain was pleading and crying. Some of it might have been his own.

Men in red coveralls were running from the drilling platform. The first man was yelling into his phone. The second carried a large first-aid kit and directed traffic like a battlefield veteran. Nick waved for him.

The medic opened his box, and the two of them wound plastic wrap around the victim's chest.

"What happened?" the medic shouted.

"A barrel blew up."

"Fuel barrel? Propane tank?"

"Trash barrel. Blue."

"How close were you?"

"Fifty yards."

The medic ran to the next guy, and the next, before finding someone he could help. Nick stayed for a minute, making sure the plastic held, and moved to another victim and another. His shirt was used up now—a tourniquet on the last man's leg; on the next man, a bandage to hold a sundered scalp tight against his skull.

In ten minutes, the medic was back at his side.

"Show me where you're hurt."

Nick stared at him.

The medic pointed a blue-gloved finger. "Let's tape your neck and wrap up your arm before you bleed out."

Nick looked in amazement at a long scrape in his forearm.

Using gauze, the medic wiped most of the blood off and poured disinfectant on.

"You're not on the crew," the medic said.

"A bystander. A tourist."

The medic leaned back and looked him over. The sun, behind him, lit up his crew cut.

"Talk to whoever's in charge and make sure they have your name."

Nick weaved as his knees weakened, his vision fading out of focus.

"You're going into shock," the medic said. "Get someone to help you stay awake, and wash all the blood and guts off right away. Get a tetanus shot. Can you do that?"

"Sure," Nick said on his way to the ground.

"You have small cuts compared to the rest of these guys, but see a doctor today about stitches and internal damage," he said.

Nick repeated the gist of the instructions and turned his head to the side as far as the wound let him. The grass wasn't as green anymore, the sky not as blue. All the dust was blown away, and he felt surprised.

The medic patted Nick's chest and said, "And don't go anywhere for a while. As many scars as you have, you know the drill."

"How many? Hurt?"

"Nine dead and three or four in bad shape. Others, not hurt bad-bad. You saved two yourself. Medevacs and ambulances are coming from all over."

Shivering on his back, Nick propped himself up on his elbows and looked beyond the bodies.

The explosion had torn apart the trailer, shredding pink fiberglass batts and papers and lifting the material into the wind. The trailer's metal chassis was torn and bent, and the toilet was blown over and collapsed. The nearest vehicles had broken windows and shrapnel punctures, sheet metal peeled back, dents from debris. Several had flats.

The south wind was picking up. Much of whatever was here now would soon be gone, brought to rest in fences, brush, and trees. The air stank, and gray powder dusted everything north of the crater.

Why was there a bomb out here?

Nick clambered to his feet, his body protesting, and staggered around the perimeter of the shallow crater and then made a circle that encompassed most of the pieces. There were furrows torn by scraps nine or ten inches long, and by shreds, all with tortured edges.

Laura was yelling into her phone, sweeping her free hand across the scene. She took a long sloppy stride to avoid stepping on a steel-toed boot with a foot in it.

"That's all I know, Senator," she shouted in exasperation. "Eight or nine dead so far, I'm basically okay and your new man is wounded. It's in my pictures. Nothing happened to the rig. No ambulances yet."

She finished with an angry "You're welcome, Harriet" that sounded like she hung up second. She took more photos and shoved the phone into her pocket.

When he walked up, Laura clung to Nick's bare arm.

"These men were attacked. Set up. They're just pawns," she said. "This guy, that one, that dead guy—oh my God, that's Chris, all that blood—they didn't know what's going on."

"Do you?"

"This is wrong. This is not the way to stop it."

"What are you talking about?"

"Where's your shirt? Your coat? Get it back. Don't leave anything."

Sirens were coming from the east and west. A white pickup with a steel-mesh headache rack was newly parked near Laura's Flex. Her car wasn't blocked in, but it would be once the responders and rubberneckers showed up.

"Do you know who did this?" Nick asked.

"Don't say another word. Don't ask me any questions. It's under control here. We have to leave. Now."

An oversize white pickup raced up the section road and turned in, parking in front of the first pickup. Flashing lights appeared over a rise a half-mile away and quickly sank out of sight. Within a minute, cops would be asking questions.

The big pickup, a Ram like the other white one, bore "Saltwood Exploration" in no-nonsense black logo type on the door. The driver stepped down and was joined by the passenger, a man in a suit, no tie, who had gotten out the other side and come around the front. The driver of the first pickup hurried to them, pulling hearing protectors from his ears and letting them hang on their cord against his khaki work shirt.

Nick felt sure that the man in the suit had flown him to Wichita last night. When Laura caught Nick staring, she took his arm and led him toward her car.

The man from the plane looked down his nose at the shirtless, bloody mess Nick had become. If he recognized the wretch, he didn't show that he cared. The two other men followed his gaze. No one asked Nick and Laura who they were, or how they were, or why they were there.

The first ambulance slowed at the gate and roared onto the field, followed by a car from the Rice County sheriff's department. A wide-eyed deputy in a bulletproof vest parked hastily and with waving arms instructed the men and Laura to stay put, but Laura pointed to Nick and said she was taking him to the clinic. The deputy, talking into his shoulder-mounted handset, signaled them on and hurried to claim the blast site.

Laura's car now had a cracked windshield. She tossed a blanket from the trunk to Nick, instructing him to spread it over the passenger seat before he sat down. Ignoring the seat-belt warning, she cursed loudly and gunned the car onto the section road. Nick wiped his bloody hands on the blanket and braced himself for the ride.

It was less than twenty minutes after the explosion, and the well site was more than an hour's drive from Wichita. How, and why, did the man from the jet get there before the ambulance from Bull Creek?

Nick chewed on that for the entire bone-shaking six-mile run to the ranch, while Laura shouted to herself and connected dots only she saw.

7

Karlton Cooper, excited about his Walmart work anniversary, twirled his pocket pen between his fingers. He had spent a quarter of his life wearing a blue vest, and much of that time toting a handheld computer.

He cornered the other clerk in Electronics.

"I'm going to walk into Jim's office and tell him I need a fifty-cent raise," he said. "Don't you think I've earned it? I deserve fifty cents."

"Shhh. I like working here. I'm not going to talk about pay with you," she said, refusing to look at him. Sometimes he stared too hard. "You know they have ears."

"I do a lot of work."

"Whatever you're making, sure, you deserve a raise," she said. As soon as a shopper in Cameras raised his head and looked around, she scuttled off to help.

Karlton leaned sideways against the counter and surveyed his kingdom. He was everything that was good about this gigantic company. He had bought his phone, tires, TV, handgun, groceries, and computer here, even his mustache clippers. He stroked his facial hair, grown to compensate for his hidden chin, wishing his dad could see him now.

The old man, who lost a finger in a training exercise during the US invasion of Honduras in 1988, owned his late cousin's jacket embroidered with a map of southeast Asia and the words: "Even though I've walked through the valley of the shadow of death, I shall fear no evil, for I am the meanest son of a bitch in the valley." His dad used to call the boy "Karly, the chinless wonder" and beat him once a month to toughen the boy up.

"You got my cousin's name, you better earn it," his dad said. Dad's favorite cousin Karlton was killed in action during the American incursion of Cambodia twenty-three years to the day before Karlton was born. Dad was gone now, too, dead from lung cancer. He had been a jig builder at the city's airplane assembly plants, Boeing Military Aircraft, Cessna, Learjet, and Beech, when that's what those companies were called.

And here Karlton was, himself a key part of a worldwide corporation. He was dedicated to this store, like he had been to the one in south Wichita close to where he grew up. This was the best job he ever had, much better than standing behind the counter at two convenience stores and McDonald's, his first three jobs.

Over the years, he had spent his thirty-four hours a week stocking shelves and helping customers in Groceries, Bakery, Auto, and now Electronics, plus Sporting Goods, working the cash registers nights and days and weekends and holidays, and if anyone thought selling beer or hunting licenses on a Friday evening just before duck or deer season was a piece of cake, they were wrong.

Most of the money he made went to gas, food, and his southside rental duplex with the rent-to-own washer and dryer in the garage instead of his Toyota Corolla. He was proud of having moved out of his mother's house two years earlier. Living with her, Mama Filene, was stressful, because she never did anything quietly. She plopped down bags and boxes, and she scooted her feet on every floor. She began to talk even when people were already talking about something else, and she lingered at the end of her sentences out of fear that someone would try to grab control of the conversation. She laughed "huhn huhn hee hee hee . . . snort."

For years until the old man's death, she had shrunk from Karlton's stern father, finding her pleasure in the bosom of hellfire religion. Now a single woman in her early fifties, she was free to express herself, which she did by forcing hugs on everyone she encountered. She loved Karlton and his help with her rent, but not as much as she loved Father God as revealed on TV.

Karlton lived a clean life and tithed to the River Jordan Cathedral, giving an extra 2 percent because Pastor Luke had promised again and again that the Lord rewards those who put their financial trust in Him. Karlton's investment in life everlasting far exceeded his earthly savings.

He worked and went to church and enjoyed his hobby: Norse mythology. He first read about it in a book from the library, and then he checked out a second book too. His personalized license plate—he almost slugged a coworker who questioned his sincerity by calling it a vanity tag—said ODIN.

The tag became Karlton's joke to himself after one of the Corolla's headlights burned out. The original Odin himself had just a single eye, having given up the other one in order to drink from the spring of wisdom. Odin was cool. He died to gain wisdom from the dead, and then he was reborn to use that wisdom in the living world.

Karlton sometimes wondered whether he should've gone with his first choice, Tyr. He thought Tyr was pronounced "tire," which also would've been perfect for his Corolla, but he backed off when he learned it was pronounced "tier." Or "tear," and Karlton was not a crybaby.

Tyr was a warrior of great wisdom who sacrificed an arm so the dangerous wolf Fenrir could be tied up. Karlton sometimes saw himself as the Tyr of Walmart: a god of law, justice, the sky, war, and heroic glory. He had even scratched a "T" into the walnut grips of his Smith & Wesson .44-caliber Magnum revolver.

The other clerk returned to the counter.

"Jim wants to talk to you," she said.

Jim had been an assistant manager at this store since the previous November, having come from Tulsa, Oklahoma. He was a little younger than Karlton, Karlton thought, but it was impossible to get to know him. Jim wore a plain gold wedding ring and kept a picture of two small blond children on his desk. His short-sleeve shirts, worn over a white T-shirt, were snug even though he could've bought the right size at a discount. His shiny neckties had strings of tiny stains, and his glasses always had reflections that masked his eyes.

Jim's office was in the back, and standing guard at the door was Warren Snarr, a bulky, bearded tattooed guy, six-three or six-four, who usually worked in Auto. All of Warren's facial features struck Karlton as exaggerated except for his forehead. He was a couple of years older than Karlton, and respected. Without saying a word to him, Warren nodded, knocked twice on the metal door, and twisted the latch open.

Jim motioned to a hard plastic chair situated away from the desk, and Karlton pulled the chair close. Jim edged his own chair backward a bit and complimented Karlton for his eight years of service and helpful attitude.

"But you know how tough times are," Jim said. "Our store's labor costs have skyrocketed, and we've had to look for ways to keep our doors open."

This was an odd way to open the conversation. Karlton felt himself floating, anxious.

"What can I do to help?" That was the right thing to say.

"We're letting you go, Karlton."

Karlton was sure he had misunderstood. "Say that again?"

"We have to let you go. You're laid off."

"Eight years and I've never let the store down. You've never even had to give me a coaching."

"You've been a superb employee. That's not why this is happening. It's not personal."

"Not personal . . ."

"I understand that you may have trouble accepting this. I have no say in this, and it's final," Jim said, reading from a typed page on his desk. "You can continue to shop here, without a discount, and we will welcome you as long as you show the common courtesy we expect of all our guests. Leave your vest and all other company property with me."

Karlton shrugged himself out of his blue vest and folded it.

"Can I keep my name tag?"

"Sorry, no."

Karlton laid the vest and his handheld on the desk.

Jim took a long envelope from a drawer and extended it toward Karlton. The sound of the drawer being pushed shut echoed in the little office.

"Here's your final check." Jim glanced at his watch. "You're paid through noon, right now. We'll mail your tax form, the W-2, to the address we have on file. Thank you, and good luck."

Jim walked around the desk as Karlton sat stunned, looking at Jim as if he expected to be told it was a prank. Jim pushed the envelope at Karlton, who finally accepted it. Jim kept his hand forward, not to shake but to guide Karlton out the door. He pushed it shut on Karlton's right heel.

Karlton couldn't understand how his good service and moderate pay had put this superstore in such a dangerous position. The place was always busy, even moreso now when customers couldn't afford to shop at Target. When he got around the corner, he slumped against the wall.

Warren from Auto came up beside him.

"Sorry, man. I'm supposed to make sure you leave the store. You got everything that's yours?"

"My jacket."

The two of them got his jacket off its hook—Karlton didn't need it, because he could handle the chill at the beginning of the shift, but sometimes it was raining when he got off—and walked where few could see them, across the back of the store and out through a steel door near where the semis unloaded. Karlton knew for sure that everyone in the store was watching him, stripped of his vest, and laughing at his shame. He carried his envelope between his fist and his thumb. None of this would be official if he refused to stuff it into his pocket.

Warren held the door open and let Karlton pause a moment then edge into the sunlight. The big guy wedged a scrap of pallet lumber under a hinge to keep the door open, and looked around. He pulled a cigarette out of a half-empty pack of American Spirits and offered one to Karlton, who shook it off.

After a puff, Warren leaned against the wall and said, "You didn't hear this from me, okay? You're being replaced by a Mexican chick because she speaks Spanish."

"You're kidding."

"I heard it from Juan in Sporting Goods. She was a teacher at his high school, but the schools laid a bunch of teachers off. She's going to make fifty cents less than you and work in Electronics."

"Fuck!"

"Sucks, don't it?" Warren said. He ground his smoke onto the asphalt. "See you around."

•   •   •

Karlton Cooper wore away the afternoon on the streets of Wichita.

Gentle rises and falls in elevation trained some city dwellers to think they knew what hills were, but those folks were wrong. Wichita was flat. That suited Karlton just fine.

He didn't enjoy the high-speed, high-traffic freeways, which would have demanded too much from his sun-blistered teal 2000 Corolla with its sporty aftermarket spoiler on the trunk. The 1.8-liter inline-four engine had just 327,664 miles a month ago, the last time he poured two quarts of 10w-40 oil down ODIN's throat. Instead of racing the speed demons, he took the long mile roads. On the north side of town, his route was 29th, 21st, 13th, Central near the homeless camp, and Douglas. The south side, beyond Kellogg, had Lincoln, Harry, Mount Vernon, and Pawnee. He savored the sight of the new arena downtown, because it reminded him of how much fun it had been to see flames erupt out of the exhaust pipes at a monster-truck show.

His windshield cracked, his radio inoperative, he drove back and forth, east and west, and a mile north or south at the end of each run. He liked the stop-and-go traffic, which was busywork but also a chance to scope out women: mothers in mommy cars picking up kids, high school girls in pickups less dented than his car (and with less Bondo filler in the dents), black women, Mexican women (until now), Korean and Filipina women, tattooed white women in tank tops on the concrete sidewalks squinting in the sun and turning away from the wind when they could.

At 3:27, he decided he'd had enough.

He turned ODIN down the street behind the dumpster of an auto parts store and pulled into his half of the shared driveway of his duplex. It was a point of pride to park each time directly over ODIN's sludgy puddle of leaked oil so it didn't grow. But this time, he was too depressed to get out. Even now, with the windows closed and the car hot in the sunshine, he shivered with desperation.

ODIN's heater and air conditioning had given up two summers ago. Twice last August he had bummed a ride to work from Braylynn Huckstep, who lived on the other side of the duplex, just for the AC. The third time he asked, she said no, her boyfriend didn't like it.

When Karlton moved into the duplex, he never should have let her see his blue vest, because she badgered him almost every week to do her shopping. She'd hand him a wad of bills and a list, compiled and signed BRAYLYNN in her grade-school printing, but her estimate of the cost was always five or ten dollars short. He had to make up the difference. In addition, he had to use his employee discount and give her the receipt so she could get refunds, because otherwise she could have invented some offense by the "rude clerk" and gotten him some coaching, a sure black mark against his career.

Karlton heard her voice—*that voice*—every day, every night through the walls at home. Often enough he heard it at Walmart, her complaints flying across the racks like a thrown knife. She would shriek her nickname for him, even though he pleaded with her not to. She thought "Karly Coopie" was cute, and he sensed that using the nickname made her feel as if she owned him.

Braylynn was in her compact Chevy at this moment, filling the driver's seat, too plump to bring her arm up and shade her eyes as she half turned to bitch at her boyfriend, a balding forty-something wearing a striped muscle shirt over his beaten-down shoulders and bowling-ball belly, shorts with stripes running a different direction, and sky-blue plastic clogs.

"I would've went to see my motherfucking mother three motherfucking years ago," she shouted. "And I didn't because you wanted to go see your own motherfucking mom, and now mine's dead." She laid on her horn for emphasis.

Karlton once asked Braylynn's boyfriend, a hospital orderly, why he put up with her yelling. "She's the best I ever had, man," the boyfriend said. "You know." Then he shrugged and went inside.

She noticed Karlton now and honked again. She yelled something at him too.

Karlton leaned his forehead against the steering wheel and covered his ears. "Jesus, please help me," he prayed.

There are some people you just can't polish up, his mother liked to tell him. His mother was polished. She was never without her tiny spray bottle of White Shoulders perfume.

Karlton unlocked his duplex's deadbolt and turned on the TV. He dropped onto the heavy dark chair his living room shared with his dining room, and let game-show noise envelop him. Aside from the broadcast-only TV, he had bought himself one indulgence: a ten-gallon aquarium stocked with discount goldfish swimming around a little castle. The air pump burbled away, the three fish unaware of his difficulties. He liked talking to them and the responsibility of feeding them.

The only decorations on the walls, both here and in his bedroom, were his thumb-tacked pencil sketches of a famous woman named Kelli who had autographed his arm and said he was cute, like she had a real crush, when they met three weeks earlier. He looked her up on the internet at the library, but she didn't seem very Christian and hadn't come back to his store.

He grieved for himself. Not only had he gotten laid off for a reason he didn't understand, but he'd also said "fuck" at the store. It was a word he sometimes thought but never spoke, because he was a man with integrity and a desire to know the Lord.

Sometimes he felt frustrated by the world, as if he were dressed in raingear walking through a forest, seeing the trees but not getting wet and not experiencing the whole event. Right now he felt worse. He was a marble rolling loudly around in the bottom of a soup can. Everything he depended on yesterday had been shaken loose.

Money. He needed money and a job right away. He had never not had a job, never not been able to keep up with rent. This would be the first time he'd have to beg the landlord for time, just the way his coworkers talked about every month.

He didn't even feel like dinner tonight, not knowing how long he'd have to stretch his peanut butter and jelly.

When he went to deposit his half-paycheck, he'd look for a new job. He should go to the library and look online, since he ran out of money two months ago for internet. Anything, he thought. Anything but a convenience store again. Maybe a grocery store this time. Maybe another Walmart.

And, ding-darn it. He had left his drawing of Garmr on top of the Electronics counter. He wished the dark dog could slip its chain and avenge this injustice, but the drawing was probably already in the trash after being laughed at.

Focus. Find a job.

Pastor Luke might be able to help with a job. He had said his door was always open. But then, so had Karlton's boss, right up to when the door hit him in the foot.

Karlton drank two glasses of tepid water from the kitchen faucet and turned his glass upside down in the red wire rack next to the sink. He'd go see Pastor Luke.

If he hurried, he could get to the church before Pastor went home to dinner with his loving wife and daughter.

As he showered, Karlton thought about the wife and daughter. Those two always sat in the second row at church, two brunettes right in front of the pulpit.

Noelle was a cheerleader at the city's biggest Christian high school. He had gone to a basketball game once to watch her, and she jerked her head with surprise when he yelled her name and she discovered him in with the students. She sometimes wore yoga pants to church, and he paid respectful attention as she walked up the aisle after the service. Once in a while, when she walked out to the family car and her mom stopped to talk to a friend, Noelle would strike the pose Karlton remembered from the game: shoulders back, chest out, arms akimbo, right leg forward, foot on tiptoes, tossing her hair.

If he were being honest, and a good Christian tries to be, he'd admit that he had a crush on Noelle, even if she was seventeen years younger. But he also really liked the TikTok star, Kelli, who signed his arm. She held his wrist as she wrote with a Sharpie, and he felt the connection deeply. It was hard to get her out of his mind. Sometimes his coworkers would let him watch her videos with them.

Pastor's wife, Christmas, was as pretty as Noelle but with hair that stopped above her shoulders, and like her daughter she looked past Karlton's head when he spoke to her. She didn't smile much either. Even in warm weather, she wore a blazer.

Karlton pulled his Corolla into a space on the empty west side of the mustard-yellow metal and brick building housing the River Jordan Cathedral, much closer to the front door than he parked on Sundays, and made sure of the bungee cord holding the trunk shut. He walked along the knee-high, oxblood-red brick fence protecting the evergreen hedge to reach the smoked-glass entrance with chrome door handles. By his watch, it was ten minutes until 5:00 P.M.

The air in the foyer, even in May, was so still he could smell the whole church—the carpet, the trash can of the coffee stand down the hall, the flowers left over from Sunday's service in the big sanctuary.

Pastor Luke Meriwether was in his inner office, his door open. Karlton saw him from the hallway and pushed open the glass door to the outer office, where the receptionist would be sitting except for this late in the day. He called out "Hello" as he stepped onto the carpet, so thick it was like walking on God's top floor.

Without looking up from his laptop, Pastor waved him toward a chair. He wore a royal purple polo shirt, and a sports coat hung on a rack behind his desk.

"Sit for a bit," he said.

Pastor was typing. As the minutes passed Karlton looked at framed photos on the paneled walls. It was awkward to try to see them from a distance, so he walked over to examine them. Pastor with President George W. Bush, Pastor with President Trump, Pastor with a man Karlton thought was once the governor, Pastor with a Miss Kansas, and again with another Miss Kansas.

Karlton had seen it before, through the glass door, but this was the first time he'd gotten a close look at an oil painting of Christmas Meriwether. Her painted hair was a little brighter than in real life, but her smile was just as cheerless.

There was the younger Pastor in a framed newspaper clipping from an anti-abortion protest, waving a Bible and leaning over a woman. Pastor shaking hands with this person and that person. A framed screenshot of Pastor being interviewed on TV. There was also a framed picture of Our Lord Jesus.

A dozen or so copies of Pastor's autobiography rested on a credenza. It was *My Wealth Comes from Jesus,* and Karlton knew that Pastor handed copies to his new friends.

Behind Pastor's desk, above his head, hung his diploma and certificates. Above them was the king of his credentials, an AR-15 rifle housed behind glass in a horizontal shadowbox.

Pastor hit an emphatic keystroke, skimmed his writing, and closed the laptop. He stretched his arms and laced his fingers behind his head, a man whose workday was over. His face, as handsome as any fifty-two-year-old television preacher's, when resting nevertheless gave Karlton the impression of a mostly inflated balloon. His hair was dark brown and wavy, his eyes a lighter brown. His nose was straight and his teeth were perfect.

"What's up, young man?"

"I need a prayer, Pastor. I was laid off today from Walmart after eight years, and I need Jesus's help. I need a new job."

"Are you a thief or a pervert? A terrorist?"

"No, sir."

Pastor often preached against perverts, which bothered Karlton because he knew and liked several. Pastor didn't care what man's law said, just what the Bible delivered from God Himself and not always what Jesus Christ said and sometimes only tiny bits of the first chapters of the Bible. He'd look down into the congregation and say "homosexual" as if he were experimenting with each syllable, daring anyone to disagree with God.

"Why were you laid off?" he asked Karlton.

"They hired a woman who speaks Spanish."

"I see. Walmart's a good company. I have a thousand shares of their stock." Pastor thought about this, as if he'd left the room.

By leaning forward, Karlton could read the gold plaque under the black rifle: "Our Prince of Peace, Pastor Luke Meriwether."

Pastor's attention returned to Karlton. "Remind me of your name," he said.

"Karlton. Cooper."

"Yes, that's it. You told me once you worship Norwegian gods."

"Norse gods, sir. Just to read about."

"Do you remember my sermons about how Jesus rewards those who give freely to the church and believe upon Him?"

"I give 12 percent of my take-home to Jesus. It's all I have after gas, rent, and food. And now I don't have any take-home."

"The Bible tells us to give until it hurts and then give a little more."

Karlton nodded. Pastor often said this.

"Jesus rewards those who love Him fully, Karlton. I'm sure He appreciates your generous tithing but you can have no other gods. Exodus 20, verse 3."

"Do I need to buy my car a new license tag? It says 'ODIN.'"

"If you love Jesus, you do."

"I will, Pastor. Will you pray for me to get a job?" Karlton wanted to nail this down even as Pastor guided him out of the office and into the lobby.

"I'm sure Jesus will find you something. I'll pray at dinner tonight. Right now, I'm going to offer you the right foot of fellowship," Pastor Luke promised, fishing in his pocket for keys with one hand while pushing the outer door open for Karlton. Pastor glared around the parking lot and scowled.

As Karlton turned to shake Pastor's hand, a tall woman in a snug green dress appeared in a sanctuary doorway, starting toward them but hesitating. Karlton had seen her in Sunday services.

She called out: "Before you leave, Pastor, may I have a word?"

Pastor asked her to wait. He said to Karlton: "Do me a favor. You see the gardener out there, tell him I said not to park that turquoise piece of crap close to the church again."

Karlton found himself standing alone outside the doors, facing his car, the only one in the parking lot.

"Teal," he said.

Maybe his new job would let him buy a car that didn't embarrass Pastor Luke. He turned on his heel and went back to thank Pastor yet again for the inspiration. He pulled on the handle, but the door was locked. He leaned in against the smoked glass and put his hands around his face.

Pastor Luke wasn't alone. In the home of Our Lord Jesus Christ and Father God, Pastor was walking back to his office with his arm around the waist of the woman in the green dress, and they were smiling at each other.

8

Laura Eisenhauer talked herself down by the time they reached the beginning of her driveway. It was a double track that crossed a cattle guard, made of horizontal pipes aligned with the ditch, before entering a pasture fenced by barbed wire. Clusters of shrubs grew along the quarter-mile-long driveway as they drove north, with an occasional cottonwood rising where the land collected water. Partway up the driveway a dense shelter belt of eastern cedars and honey locusts began on the left.

Swales of soft sand pulled the car from side to side.

"Sorry," she said. "I'm kind of stressed."

"We'll be okay."

She looked at him as if for the first time.

"You don't seem too torn up about all the blood," she said.

"They weren't my first corpses."

The driveway made a long curve west into the yard, and Laura parked in a large sandy oval between the house and three outbuildings. She instructed Nick to stand near the back porch.

She hugged him, carefully because of his bloody torso and because of their injuries, and then squeezed him for a moment with more certainty. She stepped back and considered him.

"I'd hose you down out here," she said, "but then you'd have to be naked and you'd make a mess all the way to the shower."

She went inside and came back with a handful of old newspapers. She laid pages on the concrete steps before disappearing into the kitchen. "You wait," she said.

His body was regaining its poise, although every muscle was aggrieved and his head pounded. His ears rang, but even so the south wind brought him echoes of the blast site's commotion: the sirens, the circling helicopters, the occasional bullhorn.

The afternoon breeze sifting through the windbreak was strong enough to move the leaves and flowering racemes of the locusts and the cedars' stiff branches, but not enough to discourage flies from settling on his shoulders.

Lazy heat waves shimmered over the sandy soil, half desert and half prairie. The ground was warm and he sank to it, his back to the sun. As he adapted to the stench of dried blood, a smell so strong that it tasted like a mouthful of copper, he began to pick out the aroma of the warm grass. His arms and legs relaxed, and he wanted to melt into the earth.

He inventoried his injuries.

His chest ached from the explosion's wallop. His arms ached from being flung backward as he became human shrapnel. His right thigh must've landed hard on Laura's knees or hips, because it was sore to the core and was developing a large bruise. His eyes didn't focus well, and his throat still felt full of pasture dust. His hair hurt.

The stress of performing battlefield triage exhausted him.

He gazed blankly up into the clouds, wondering just for a moment whether he was dying. Maybe it was a lot of moments.

At some point, the world wormed its way back into his awareness. He moved onto his side, pulled his knees toward his chest, and rolled up onto them so he could push himself onto his feet. He felt like a poor traveler through all he surveyed.

The spread right in front of him was part driveway, part parking lot. It was sandy loam, worn by years of tires rolling into a shallow sandbox. Grass—yard grass and not the rough tall stems of the pasture—reached out with thin runners.

The house looked about thirty feet by forty feet, with the broad sides parallel to the driveway. The back door and a curtained window faced west, overlooking the parking area and three outbuildings. The front door opened to the east. A large bay window, flanked by rose trellises and a lilac, dominated the south wall.

Near the back porch and within easy reach of the driveway stood a gray-green fiberglass tank, maybe eight feet high and eight feet wide.

The house was a simple one-story place on a concrete foundation, lap boards painted white with dark-red wooden doors. The back door, the one that rural people used for almost everything, was fronted by an aluminum screen door above three roomy steps sagging slightly to the left. A pair of tubular aluminum lawn chairs with woven green and white plastic webbing leaned against the back of the house.

The roof was covered by dark asphalt shingles. A satellite dish, mounted near the ridgeline, pointed over the southwestern horizon. Electricity came in on a single line along the driveway from a string of power poles following the county road. A transformer dropped leads to the house and to a pole with a yard light out by a two-door barn. A propane tank squatted in the front yard, away from the house.

The barn wasn't elegant. It had red-faded-to-pink corrugated metal siding and roof, a small door on the left and a large sliding door open to a bay housing a square-sided, white-over-dark-red Ford pick-up. Thirty feet to the right of the barn, a long one-story frame building with wire screen over the windows might have been a chicken house. The outbuilding arc was completed by a shed listing toward the chicken house. The shed and chicken house were weathered brown.

One shelter belt hindered the south wind, and another would help deflect winter's north wind. The Arkansas River—or at least the tall trees bordering the riverbed—was a half-mile away to the north and east.

Laura was back within ten minutes. She had changed into a loose green T-shirt and shorts but hadn't washed the dirt off her face.

"Rub the dry stuff off out there, and then you can come in," she said, holding the door open. "Try not to flake off. Or flake out."

Leaving his shoes in the yard and holding one hand against his wounded neck, Nick padded along the path of newsprint from the door through the living room to the bathroom and onto the yellow linoleum in front of the shower.

The blood from other victims had dried, leaving his arms, chest, and hands crusty, mottled, and dark. Scars on his chest and back glared dully: the pale medals of his life.

"Your dirties go in this bag." She pointed to a trash bag by the tub. "Get wet, turn off the water, scrub, rinse. We don't have much left in the tank."

Nick pushed aside the shower curtain and sat on the edge of the tub. He cautiously took off his socks, slacks, and underwear, shaking loose bits of shrapnel from the fabric. The slacks had caught a lot of the bloody mess at the beltline and on the thighs, where he had wiped his hands again and again. He washed his hands in the sink and fished his billfold out of the slacks.

In the mirror, his wounds didn't look too bad, and they didn't hurt much. Another inch and it'd be a different story, he thought, like anything else in life. The neck wound would become just another scar. The scraped arm would be scabbed over soon enough.

The latest insult before this day was the result of a US Army corporal who took Nick's Russian background the wrong way and slashed his belly with a combat knife before Nick broke his arm and flattened the arch of his left foot. The abdominal scar joined a round scar, which was from a bullet to his back, and a through-and-through pair on his upper thigh. His face bore the tiny marks of shrapnel from a rifle shot that blew apart a metal railing atop a grain elevator near the conclusion of his previous Kansas adventure. He was lucky he hadn't been blinded.

The FBI and Army had taken care of his medical needs: dental, eye, cardio, bones, internal, psychological. Nevertheless, he wondered whether he had been injected with tiny antennas that would trigger radio-frequency ID scanners. Someday he'd look for an amenable X-ray tech with free time.

The shower sloughed the drillers' blood away, clotted red strings running off his fingertips and down the drain toward a septic tank out under the yard. He borrowed Laura's soap and wash rag, scrubbing himself until all the dried blood disappeared. He washed the Russian knife, too, making sure the blade wasn't carrying spy dust or that Russian specialty, a Novichok nerve agent. With the tip of the blade, he scraped the dark curves of blood from under his fingernails. He wasn't so much afraid of disease as he was just plain unwilling to eat dinner with someone else's blood on his hands. Always, the victims' blood washed off. The shampoo smelled of flowers.

The bathroom door opened. His Walmart bags crinkled as they plopped to the floor.

"Short shower," Laura shouted.

Nick rinsed quickly and stepped out. He dressed in his new grandpa Wranglers and long-sleeve shirt, brushed his teeth, combed his hair and wandered into the living room. Laura, still in her torn clothes, was on her cell, facing out the wide window. She addressed her answers to "Sheriff" and enunciated what she had seen at the rig.

The newspaper pages on which Nick had walked had been stuffed into a trash bag at the kitchen's screen door. He went back to the bathroom, gathered the bag with his fouled clothes, and shoved it into the kitchen bag as well.

The living room's attitude was country. The floor was dark wooden planks with an oval green rag rug between a plaid-upholstered couch on one wall and a pair of rockers that framed the window, which from the far right side looked out past the roses and lilac toward the county road. The walls were papered with roses on a field of cream from the wainscoting to the painted ceiling, which was just higher than Nick could reach standing flat footed. The room wasn't large but felt airy.

Shelves held twenty or so hardbacks and paperbacks and a vase of dried sunflowers, and next to the vase sat a solved Rubik's cube. A silk painting of a Chinese floral scene, the only picture in the room, hung out of the direct sunlight.

The air was warm and soft and dry, and Nick stood for a moment and watched the elms sway before he picked up the cube, twisting the pieces around into a mess as he wandered into the kitchen.

An old Tappan stove of white enamel had propane burners, and the linoleum in front of it was worn to the planks. The countertops were covered in square-cut orange Formica, with a chipped section over a drawer by the gold-colored fridge glowering in the corner.

The kitchen window overlooked the outbuildings and parking area. Under the window, a double steel sink held one plate, one fork, one spoon, one knife, and one wine glass with a dried ruby eye.

Two wooden chairs were pushed under a square table covered by a red-and-white oilcloth with salt and pepper shakers in the middle. Over the table was a battery-powered clock in the shape of a black cat, its tail swinging back and forth.

•   •   •

A red Jeep Rubicon pulled up next to Laura's car. A fit-looking man, a redhead perhaps in his early fifties, lifted a leather satchel out of the front seat. He looked askance at Nick's bloody wallow in the sand before he climbed the steps and rapped on the kitchen door.

"Hello, newsmakers!" he called out.

"Orion, come in," Laura shouted from the living room.

He looked Nick over.

"Pleased to meet you," he said, putting the bag on the kitchen counter and offering his hand. "Sam Orion. Laura tells me you're from the home office."

Laura swept into the kitchen and hugged Orion.

"Thank you, thank you," she said.

"Hey," Orion said. "It's okay. You're okay now."

She held on to him but talked to Nick.

"He's a physician's assistant," she said. "He lives a couple of miles over. He's going to check us out."

"Appreciate it, Sam."

"Call me Orion. O-r-i-o-n. People think I'm Irish, but I'm just the son of hippies and a gift from the heavens."

Laura asked, "What've you heard?"

"The radio and TV are repeating that there was an explosion and that ambulances and medevacs took several people to hospitals in Hutch and Wichita. There's no official death toll, no real info. No one's taken the blame, and I guess there aren't any suspects. The site's blocked off for a mile around. Cops are everywhere. TV trucks are everywhere."

Laura worked the faucets for him as he washed his hands and gloved up.

"You two sit," Orion said. "No fainting while I'm here."

Nick, with his obvious injury, went first. Orion found Nick's blood pressure unremarkable, listened to his heart and lungs, and shone a small flashlight into his eyes.

"Your wrist tattoo," Nick said. "Afghanistan?"

"You were there?"

"My parents were."

"Thanks for making me feel old," Orion said.

"A different time, a different war."

"Ohhh. CIA."

Nick let it sit there.

"Rib pain? Bruises?"

"My whole gut is sore, and my thigh."

"So far, so good," Orion said. "You've probably noticed that your eyes are bloodshot from the percussion and that you're bruised. Take acetaminophen. Your neck needs a few stitches. I'll do that now and give you some antibiotics for that and the little punctures. Put Bacitracin cream on your arm, and wrap it loosely in gauze. Laura, you have that here?"

He pulled new latex gloves from a box and a needle and surgical thread from the kit.

Nick knew the drill for stitches. He didn't ask for an anesthetic, but didn't complain when Orion applied a topical wipe followed by an injection of lidocaine before pushing the curved needle in three times and pulling it through.

With a bit of flair, Orion tied and trimmed the knots.

"OK, Nick. Keep it dry and take your pills," Orion said. "You, especially, are going to hurt like hell in the morning. Ms. Eisenhauer, you're up."

Laura shooed Nick away. "Go sit outside."

•   •   •

"You know, I could've stitched you up," Laura said as they slouched outside in the lawn chairs after Orion left. They each had a glass of red wine on a table between them. "I learned to sew in 4-H and how to stitch in a nursing class. Farm girls do this all the time."

"Orion seems plugged in," Nick said.

"I called him when you were in the shower. I trust him completely. He's semi-retired from a practice in Hutchinson and lives out here."

Nick moved to touch his stitches, but she held his hand down.

"What you did after the explosion was impressive," she said. "If you weren't who you are, you'd be a hero."

"Let's keep that our little secret," he said. "I'd rather be invisible."

"How are you? Really."

"Sore. I'm going to be a black-and-blue mess where I landed on you, and I'm already getting stiff."

"You're such a flirt," she said.

They both stretched their arms up and groaned.

"We won't take you to a clinic unless you're about dead. Bull Creek is probably crawling with the FBI and Alcohol, Tobacco, and Firearms, and every injured stranger in every clinic from here to Oklahoma will get a lot of questions. Plus, you don't want to be dragging the senator's name through all this."

· · ·

"Look, I hate to bring this up, especially today, especially for me," she said, looking in the fridge. "But my grandmother's favorite cousin died a couple of days ago, and now you and the bomb have almost been too much."

"Did you know her well?"

"She was a lovely person. A good cook, patient with me but cranky when the neighbor's cattle got in her yard," she said. "And here I can't even offer you anything to eat. My plan to stop at the grocery store got derailed."

"Let's go now."

"I'm not sure I could handle the excitement. Also, I don't want to cook tonight."

She slid into the second chair, taking the Rubik's cube from Nick and absentmindedly twisting the layers until it was perfect again. Still holding the cube, she rested her hands in her lap. Her eyes closed, and her face tightened then slackened.

Nick looked at her closely. Pasture grass remained woven into her hair, and dust outlined the creases of her face.

"Are you okay?" he asked. "You sure you're not hurt bad? Physically? Mentally?"

"Mentally? Really? How do you not get hurt mentally by what happened? Every muscle is sore and my ears ring, but mostly I'm just tired. Adrenaline's wearing off, I guess."

"What did the sheriff say?"

"He asked what I saw," Laura said. "I said we were talking and then a bunch of us were dead. I told him you had flown into Wichita that morning for a familiarization tour of the state. *This* morning. I said we were at the rig on a whim because it was close to my place."

She paused, as if she were counting to ten. "I didn't give him your full name, said I don't know it. He knows what I do, who I work for."

"I'm grateful."

"I called Harriet first," she said. "She said to stay away from this."

"Did she ask whether you were hurt?"

"She has a lot on her mind, I guess." Laura kneaded her forehead with her fingertips. "She said there was another bombing, at a small tank farm up in North Dakota. Williston, I think. There was only property damage, because the people there were far enough away. The bomb went off on a timer, apparently just a few minutes after the one here."

"Do they know who did it? At either place?"

"Not a clue. She said the networks don't have anything, and the FBI and ATF people haven't told the Senate anything. People are floating a lot of ideas about eco-terrorists and Muslims."

"The usual suspects."

"Yep," she said.

The wall clock's tail ticked back and forth.

"God, I need a shower. A quick shower," she said.

"My apologies about the water. Don't you have a well?"

"The groundwater isn't very good, and I don't trust it on my skin and I won't drink it. I had that 3,200-gallon tank set up next to the house a month ago, and a truck fills it up with city water when I call. That's another call I made when you were showering. We'll have more water tomorrow, so don't get dirty in the meantime."

Nick checked his watch. It was somehow only midafternoon.

Laura walked out of the kitchen, then turned around.

"Put your suitcase in the bedroom next to the bathroom, then unpack your cloak of invisibility. The senator says I'm supposed to keep you close and quiet, but tonight we're going to dinner at the finest joint in Bull Creek."

9

Three tired sedans, two all-terrain vehicles, and a half-dozen jacked-up pickups lounged haphazardly on the unpaved lot in front of Bull Creek's finest joint.

The Trailer Hitch was a decommissioned wooden church with a half-shingled, half-open steeple. It claimed space on a broad gravel pad along old Kansas Highway 14 in the floodplain north of the Arkansas River bridge and south of the town of Bull Creek, population noted on a sign as 2,248.

"There used to be a bell up there," Laura said. She got out of her old Ford pickup and smoothed down her gray-plaid shirt and fluffed her brushed-out hair. "Drunks would come out outside and shoot at it with their deer rifles, and one year a ricochet winged somebody so they took the bell down."

Nick pointed to MAGA bumper stickers. "Your crowd?"

She shrugged. "The food's good."

Rusted screws fastened a metal sign to the door: "Patriots welcome."

"Ignore it," she said.

Taped below it was a second sign, this one written in Sharpie on paper: "If we don't know you, you're not welcome today."

Behind the door, a sturdy bouncer in a black Harley T-shirt blocked the entry hall.

"Laura," he said. He took in Nick's wounds but also his polo shirt and clean but weirdly faded jeans. "Your friend from out of town?"

"He's with my office, Jake," Laura said. "He's not a reporter, not a cop."

The interior motif, bathed in warm light, was beer signs and brown wood textured by spilled beer. Whatever was once sacred must've been exorcised years earlier, although the two unremarkable stained-glass windows that remained were protected by wire screens. Six other windows were fitted with yellow glass on the upper sash and painted plywood on the bottom. The ambiance spoke of cheap drink and fried meat, with an overtone of petroleum.

"I'm way overdressed," Nick whispered to Laura.

Most of the other guys wore work clothes with ground-in dirt and oil, and a couple of them had bandaged arms with blood showing through the gauze. A few were clearly ranch or elevator hands, jeans running down over their dusty shitkickers.

They clustered together, now and then looking up at a Wichita TV station's helicopter coverage of the explosion site. Another TV played Fox News, and the video was of talking heads every time Nick looked up.

Laura waved to the thick-chested bartender—"our friend Stan"—and led Nick to a wood-plank booth under a stained-glass window along the far wall. They slid onto benches wide enough for three butts, leaning against the wall on opposite sides. The server, a tatted girl in a college T-shirt, eventually took their order for burgers and Shiner Bocks.

"A church-college town," Laura said, "with I think eight churches and maybe that many places where you can get a drink. It's a nice place to live near."

"This looks like a place that would've been lively before today."

"This place plays real country music. Some classic rock, but also Willie Nelson, Marty Robbins, Loretta Lynn, George Strait," Laura said. "None of that stuff with whiny emotions and cheap patriotism. There's enough of that on Fox."

"I don't like jingoistic music," he said. "It reminds me of Russian propaganda. Different flag, same kind of songs."

"At the Hitch, the conversation's not so much political as it is up-and-up about lost love, bad bosses, and getting laid."

Nick swept his head around. "Not tonight, it isn't."

"Come back in a week, it'll be an orgy with dancing. Zippers will be dropping like flies."

He looked around again, trying to imagine it.

Someone pushed the jukebox buttons for "Dust in the Wind," by the classic rock band Kansas, and a hush settled on the bar. "Oh, man, that's us," said a guy, and he sank into a chair and cried into his palms.

"Why are we the only ones not crying?" Nick said.

"We had the hell beaten out of us, but these guys lost friends and maybe brothers," she said. "You were right there with them. You know what they went through. They're angry at an unidentified killer. So am I. I'm also pissed at Harriet Gayfeather for not giving a shit about whether we were hurt."

She drank half her beer, belched a little, and thumped the bottle onto the table.

"Here, look at this." She tapped the urethane-covered table, into which an abstract cat's head was stenciled with purple paint. "Kansas State Wildcats. My alma mater. Political science."

"Good school?"

"Good old Silo Tech," she said. "The pride of Manhattan."

Nick nodded toward bumper stickers and T-shirts stapled to the wall by the bar: "Ditch the Bitch at the Hitch" and "Ditch the Witch at the Hitch." A sign below the shirts advised: "Wear one to the Hitch. Wear the other home to Mama. $20 per."

"Women must feel special here," he said. "It looks like a place where you never know who'll show up."

"Just the opposite." Laura raised her eyebrows and kind of laughed. "When you walk in, you know exactly who'll be here. Your man, your last man, your next man. A woman with a pregnancy test stick and a knife."

Nick blew out a laugh that ended in a pained grimace. Laura tapped his forearm like a conspirator.

"Someone's always on the make here," she said. "This place is notorious for affairs, flings, cheating lovers, and cheating spouses. You'll never find a woman with a boyfriend for a chastity belt. You can get hitched and unhitched in the same week. People get in fights then find someone new. They come back to flaunt their new sweethearts and check up on their exes, and half the time that leads to another fight. It's not a love triangle; it's a love pentagram. Sometimes people get married on the deck. Half the fun of coming here is guessing who's in and who's out."

"You ever pick up guys here?"

Laura pretended to be offended. "Ha! These dudes have better taste than that."

He smiled at her, always gauging her responses.

The waitress arrived with more beer.

"You think of yourself from Bull Creek?" he said. "You get around a lot."

This time she shot him a deadly glare.

"I didn't say that right," he said. "I mean, around the state."

"I live here, but I'm not from here. My grandparents were accepted pretty well, because they were honest and treated the land kindly for four decades and had my dad, and of course they had a name that sounded like the best Kansan ever. Dad met Mom at K-State, and they settled in Salina and had me and my sister. I don't think I'll ever be accepted here unless I marry a guy who played high school football here, was in 4-H here, and gets me pregnant here. And even then, I'd be on probation."

They ate their burgers, onions and mayo on hers but only ketchup on his, and watched the sea of plaid shirts swirl. Oil crew and field hands, still, and a few office workers who arrived after five o'clock.

It was a somber evening. Fox News, every ten minutes, right after commercials extolling a drug that will "improve the appearance of your intestinal lining," ran a replay of the explosion investigation with a drumbeat graphic: "Terror at Saltwood 7." Talking heads denounced a slew of usual suspects and the previous presidential administration's green-power policies. The explosion in North Dakota, where no one was hurt, got hardly a mention.

The crowd quieted each time copter footage showed the trailer, crater, and line of body bags. The video showed nothing new, and the rotating panels of pundits said nothing that hadn't said earlier.

It was as if not acknowledging the bags each time would be disrespectful. The men in the bar barely spoke beyond cursing, and the women draped their arms around the men.

Nick and Laura were about finished when a large-shouldered man, five-foot-ten with a goatee, carrying in one hand three Budweiser bottles by the neck, loomed at the end of the table. Laura nudged Nick with her knee and shook her head slightly.

"Hey, folks," the guy said. "I'd like to thank you for helping us out at the rig. I hope you're doing all right," nodding at Nick.

"It was a terrible thing," Laura said. "Are the guys who lived going to be okay?"

Nick recognized him. He was the man from the Saltwood truck parked next to Laura's Flex at the well site, the one in the khaki who talked to the man in the suit, the one who arrived immediately after the blast. Nick nudged Laura's leg and raised his eyebrows.

"I'm Lance Sterrett," the man said, shaking Nick's hand but looking at Laura. "I'm a troubleshooter with Saltwood Exploration. I saw you at the explosion. We can help you cover expenses if you need medical care or have questions."

He set the uncapped bottles on the table and pulled a chair up to the open end of the booth.

"Mind if I join you?"

Laura shrugged.

To Laura, he said: "I didn't catch his name."

"Roy," she said.

Sterrett's voice was pitched higher and was more nasal than Nick expected for a guy with a trimmed four-day beard and a high-and-tight haircut.

Sterrett pulled out a cigarette.

"Please don't," Laura said.

"I really don't. It's just a habit to play with them."

His front teeth said otherwise, Nick thought. Maybe he should go ahead and smoke. His face said he'd had a long day.

Sterrett looked closely at Nick and shook his head at the wonder of it all.

"Wells are complicated beasts," he said. "Lots of geology and hydrology to take into consideration. Sometimes we have accidents."

"I imagine so," Nick said. "Trash cans must be complicated too."

Sterrett flicked him a look but continued: "Head pressure and spectrographic analysis. Fracking solutions. You ever get to deal with those?"

For all his pleasantness, Sterrett had dense eyes. He was a hard man.

Something about him bothered Nick, but he couldn't figure out what it was.

"I do office work," Nick said. "In the District."

"The District?"

"Washington, District of Columbia," Nick said. "Just visiting."

"You okay?" Sterrett said. "You look uncomfortable."

"Nobody who was there is comfortable today, I imagine."

Near the bar, two men, one in plaid and one in a black T-shirt, crowded each other. Nick glanced at them and returned to Sterrett.

"It's been a rough day," Nick said. "I was passing through, and Laura here took me out to see how a well gets drilled. We just happened to be there."

Sterrett broke his unsmoked cigarette at the filter and dumped the tobacco into his hand and then onto the floor. With his thumb, he separated the filter from its paper and spread apart the fibers, making them less likely to be noticed. When he noticed Nick watching, he smiled in a sad way.

"Habit. My dad taught me to do that, and two tours didn't help."

Laura said, "All the news aside, it's odd that Saltwood is drilling there in the first place, and I think something big's going on. I heard that the feds are talking about leasing to a company out of Dallas to drill test holes around Quivira and the river to check water quality, but maybe that's just a coverup for an exploration well."

Sterrett focused on her. One, two, three, four, five seconds.

"I haven't heard anything about that," he said.

She shrugged and lifted her Shiner.

To Nick, he demanded: "Are you an investigator? A journalist?"

The tussle by the bar became a skirmish. The man in plaid pushed his rival into a bar stool. Two other guys pushed the pile across the room and into Sterrett's back. His flailing arm knocked over his bottle, and Bud spilled onto Laura's shirt and pants. As soon as the men saw who it was, they backed off.

Nick started to get up, but Laura grabbed his wrist.

The man in plaid cursed at Nick.

"Not your fight, asshole," the fighter said.

A third guy stepped in and spread his arms to keep the others back. "He was there," the guy announced. "He did first aid."

He put a heavy hand on Nick's shoulder, ignoring the flinch. "Stan! These two get whatever they want."

The oilfield men and women pulled up chairs. Nick and Laura asked about the dead and hurt guys, their girlfriends, their kids. There was swearing and laughing, and a lot of beer and onion rings. There were toasts to field supervisors, a directional drilling specialist, a rig chief, and men who mud-wrestled the pipes into and out of the ground. One worker said they'd been told the rig was being shut down for the investigation, but they'd be paid for at least the coming month.

Under it all were the questions of why it had happened, and why it had happened to them.

Without a word and without being missed, Lance Sterrett had disappeared. Neither Nick or Laura drank the beers he had put on their table, and they asked the server to take the bottles away before anyone took a sip.

• • •

It was nine o'clock, with brightness lingering over the western horizon, when Laura drove them back to the ranch. Neither was drunk, and Nick was so exhausted that he imagined flashes of light in the ditches. Fireflies, reflections off insect wings; who knows, she said. Look at all the toads, she said. Those fat gray splotchy blobs hopping in the headlights? They come out for the bugs. Her clothes smelled of beer.

At home, she handed him bottled water from the fridge. "You know," she said, then paused as she tucked Nick's bottle of antibiotics into his shirt pocket and poured two Tylenol caplets into his hand.

"You know, the Hitch has always been a friendly place for me. Most of the guys around here are nothing but pud-strutters, bumping chests and yelling in each other's faces and making outlandish threats about 'the next time you try something like that, I'll . . .'"

"Tough guys," Nick said.

"But this oil guy, Sterrett, there's something behind his eyes that says he could kill us."

"Yeah, I think he'd do that."

She slid a chair under the kitchen fluorescents and gestured for him to sit down so she could inspect his wounds. She pulled back the tape, rubbed in more ointment, and replaced the bandages. His stitches had survived, seepage be damned. His arm would be okay soon enough.

He yawned. "Where do I sleep?"

"Spare bedroom," she said. "Same rule as in Wichita. If you come in my room, I'll shoot you."

He had a dresser, along with a plain wooden chair and a high-standing double bed with a squeaky brass and iron frame. The quilt's pattern was a series of stars: a dark square canted inside a light square, all surrounded by four triangular bow ties. She had put his suitcase and shopping bags under the window next to the dresser.

"Don't be in a rush to get up in the morning."

Nick sat on the bed and bounced.

She said, "It was my room when I was a kid, when I stayed with my grandparents. Don't you dare mess it up."

"Hey, quick questions," he said. "At the well, who was the main man who got there after the explosion and talked to Sterrett? The guy in the suit, he was the big shot who flew me to Kansas. Whose plane was that? And who is Sterrett, really? Were you bullshitting him about the other wells?"

"Later," Laura said. She walked into the bedroom across the hall and pushed her door shut.

A moment later she opened the door.

"This is what I went to the Wichita office for this morning. The senator set this up for you." Like tossing a Frisbee, she spun a letter-size manila envelope across the quilt. "Goodnight."

He was wedging the Russian knife's blade under the taped and sealed flap when she knocked again.

"Here's an old towel to put under your neck in case it leaks," she said. "No blood on the quilt, please. Goodnight again."

The envelope held another $5,000 in twenties and fifties, maybe meant as blood money. He thought, already blood money.

He put the cash back in the envelope and tapped the edge against his palm to straighten out the bills. Poor Laura.

With a slug of bottled water, he swallowed his pills. He left his door cracked open until the light under her door went out.

In the dark, Nick stripped to his underwear and stood at a window overlooking the farmyard. He raised the double-hung glass and listened to the cool night.

The Milky Way was out; a jet blinked past the stars. Another minute of watching, and gray details developed out of the darkness: the falling-down shed, the barn, the outline of the shelter belt. A red spot bloomed in the darkness, gone after Nick blinked. Just enough breeze floated across the farm to whisper soothing music in the trees. One coyote called and another answered.

"From Washington to nowhere," he told himself, "and still I'm lost."

Nick pulled the sheet and quilt back and arranged the towel on his pillow. He stretched out and pulled the sheet to his shoulders. Letting out a deep breath, he slid into sleep.

THURSDAY

10

Nick woke out of a restless sleep to sunshine and a blaring TV. He sat up, stiff and deeply sore as he twisted and edged his legs over the side of the mattress. The tautness of his neck stitches reminded him of the bombing, but his fingers came away dry when he checked for seepage.

"Nick!"

Laura was in her room, standing barefoot in a long purple sleep shirt. He shuffled in, patting down his hair. She pointed with her phone.

"Look at this," she said. "I can't believe it."

A Wichita TV station was working its way through a breaking-news report from Washington, the replay showing a grim Gayfeather backed by a half-dozen senators Laura said were from other oil states.

Gayfeather said, "Nine oilfield workers in my home state of Kansas lost their lives yesterday to an act of terrorism. There was a second attack, timed with the first, at a crude-oil tank farm in North Dakota. We must not let that happen again. We will not allow eco-terrorists or vicious groups from other countries to endanger the security of our nation's energy industry."

The camera angle changed, and she shifted to look the second camera in the eye.

"I with my fellow senators, along with industry members and intelligence officials, spent yesterday and most of the night creating legislation that will prevent terrorists from endangering our energy dominance. We assure our fellow Americans that we will do all that can be done to ensure safe drilling practices and keep cheap energy available."

She took a deep breath.

"To that end, I and the senators here with me will today introduce the Petroleum Extraction, Transportation, and Refining Oversight Act. The PETRO Act. We hope that every member of the Senate and House will do right by Americans and vote for this bill, and we call on the president to immediately sign it into law."

Laura sat down on the bed.

"That goddamned Gayfeather," she said. "I was almost killed and she didn't even have the courtesy to tell me about this. Wichita called to let me know."

She pressed a button on her phone. She mouthed "office" to Nick.

"Thanks, Darla. Yeah, that was a surprise. Any word from DC about when she's coming out?"

Laura nodded, said, "Okay," and hung up.

"Busy day at the office?" Nick said.

"For them, and it's going to get worse. This is still my first vacation in three years, and I'm keeping it even if not being at work kills me. They're emailing me Harriet's bill."

After her phone dinged, she scrolled through the bill.

"Most of it's boilerplate, jargon, and flag-waving. This is the office's assessment:

"It indemnifies petroleum companies from spills and leakages of oil, brine, fracking materials, and all other fluids, gases, and fuels stored, transported, or used aboveground, underground, or intended to be injected or reinjected or used in generators and vehicles, and even from sabotage and from the disinfectant used in portable toilets.

"It covers all surface and subsurface ground and mineral rights, and all surface water and subsurface water. It indemnifies energy companies from lawsuits concerning all damage caused by geological changes created by hydraulic fracturing of the bedrock; all air pollution; all transportation by rail, pipeline, highway, and water; all workplace injuries; and all surface landscape issues in exploration. Injured employees cannot sue for damages."

She looked up from her phone. "Exploration is just a pretty word for drilling."

"And it covers production—refineries and storage—and financial interests, including trading in derivatives. And listen to this: It grants energy companies the right to use deadly force to protect all their installations. Anyone protesting any part of this can be charged with inciting terrorism."

She read it again, to herself.

"Remember how Donald Trump said he could shoot somebody on Fifth Avenue and get away with it? That's what the oil companies are asking for here. And they'll get it, because Congress has just enough cowards."

Nick sat on the couch. "And the senator is their way in?"

"Yep. Who would've thought?" Laura tossed her phone on the bed.

"Is she really that worked up about oil production?"

"It's Saltwood, Nick. Saltwood owns her. That's whose plane flew you here. The Saltwood suit you were asking about is her lover and personal lobbyist. He's the vice president for governmental relations."

"They drugged me on the plane."

"They're shits. They did that to me, too. And you know what else? Gayfeather's pretty bright, but several of the senators with her are dumber than fence posts. There's no way they came up with that bill overnight. Either the oilies handed it to them, or she wrote it in advance because she knew something like this was going to happen."

"And the guy last night at the bar?"

"Lance Sterrett is a class-A creep. Even from a mile away, it feels like he's invading my personal space. He works for Gayfeather's lover, maybe as an enforcer, but I don't know exactly what he does."

Laura crossed her arms and stalked into the living room. Nick followed and stood beside her at the big window.

The wind hadn't come up yet.

She spoke without looking at Nick.

"Go get your running shoes," she said.

•   •   •

Both of them hobbling on bruised legs, Laura led Nick along a six-foot-wide path recently mowed through the grass and weeds west of the barn. At a graveled circle, they sat on a discount-store park bench to tighten their laces under a tall pole bearing the yard light. In the distance, a high-tension power line stretched off to the northwest.

"You have cattle?" he asked.

"My grandparents sold off their last cattle when they got too old to throw feed. The fences discourage trespassers and keep other peoples' cattle out. Grandma kept chickens until the coyotes got the last of them."

The morning was pleasant, the sun having been up for a couple of hours in a sky with few clouds. Nick inhaled the grassiness of the air, as well as the pungent scent of a distant cattle feedlot. Birds chirped and darted, and one came to rest on a fence post.

He pointed: "Meadowlark?"

"Dickcissel, maybe. Different kind of chest marking. Meadowlarks have a beautiful trill and brighter colors, and dickcissels have a snappy little song. We get so many species here because of the refuge that I'm sometimes not completely sure which bird I'm hearing. Sandhill cranes, whooping cranes, eagles: those I know. This time of year, the big flocks are grebes, falcons, orioles, and turkey vultures, like that one circling above us."

Nick looked. The vulture was an enormous black bird, six feet from wingtip to wingtip, spiraling on a thermal updraft.

Nick and Laura stretched their legs and backs, Nick feeling awkward because he hadn't run for days. His shoes were stiff, and he didn't care for the smell of the spray Laura put on them to keep ticks away. Laura, wearing a purple shirt of tech fabric, smiled at him and loped away down the sandy trail.

For the first two hundred yards of being paced by Laura in the dunes, Nick was sure his body had forgotten how to run. His core muscles cried in pain. Cut stems from last year's dried grass scratched his ankles. His new shoes, worn for the first time, didn't fit right.

Laughing at him, Laura slowed to a backward jog.

"I created this track last summer," she said. "It makes a half-mile loop inside the property. There's also a trail that follows Salt Creek down through the new acreage to the Arkansas, the land my family added on about fifteen years ago. I used to run the dirt roads, but now there are too many jerks in pickups. I even get Harriet to run with me once in a while. When I'm in Wichita, I run along the Riverwalk."

"Any wildlife besides birds and bad drivers?"

She answered in rhythm with her steps. "Deer, mink, raccoons, armadillos. Skunks. Coyotes. Turkeys. Rattlesnakes and blue racers."

"Wait." He stopped running. "Rattlesnakes?"

"Massasaugas. The good news is that they're death on mice. They're only about two feet long and are fat all the way down to their rattle, which is skinny. The bad news is that their venom destroys your flesh and keeps your blood from clotting, so a bite really hurts before you swell up and bleed to death internally. Or so the rumors say. Stick to the path, and don't reach down without looking."

Nick made sure his feet hit the center of the path.

"We also have prairie rattlers," she said. "They're bad, too."

"You ever been bitten?"

"Not me," she said.

A couple of minutes later, he asked, "You hunt?"

"I don't anymore, and I don't let anyone hunt here. It's my piece of peace and quiet. There are lots of hunters, though, and a few poachers, even though it's all posted against trespassing." She waved at the trees beyond the fence. "Guys on off-road vehicles go up and down the river and shoot at anything they want. Some of them have hunting stands back in the cottonwoods. If I see anyone on my land, I toss a .22 in their direction. Not to hit them, but to remind them."

"Ever kill anyone?"

Step step step step. She looked him hard in the eye.

"Hey," he said. "It's just professional interest."

At the north end of the track, they thumped across a wooden bridge over a shallow stream that was in no hurry. "Salt Creek," she said.

Nick bumped into her. "Oops. Watching for snakes."

Laura pointed west across the fence. "Quivira is over there, a couple of miles. It's federal land, about thirty-five square miles of sand prairie and salt marsh on the Central Flyway. This is the edge of Rice County. Over there west, Stafford County. North a little, Barton County. Closer to Saltwood's rig, Reno County."

The southbound stretch of the loop crossed the creek again. She waved at trees lining the bed. "See the ones blooming? Catalpas mixed with walnuts. You can go there, but watch out for poison ivy."

"Around again, race you to the end," Laura shouted.

Nick thought it was his imagination, the music in the air during the second lap. As he stumbled toward the gravel circle, it became obvious that the *1812 Overture* was playing from a speaker mounted under the yard light.

Laura raised her arms as she reached the bench. He mimicked her finish, and she clapped.

"I saw a picture of Jim Ryun winning a mile run that way when he was in school in Wichita," she said. "I copied it every race I ran in high school, even when I finished seventh."

Nick, hands on his knees, raised his eyes as the music climaxed.

"I was a terrible athlete," she said, "even for a kid. No motivation. But then when I was a sophomore, I discovered politics. It didn't take me long to realize that successful politicians were good-looking, highly motivated people. So I put my heart into running as hard as I worked in class, and I turned into the gorgeous athlete you see before you."

She pirouetted, and Nick saw her beauty. He rewarded her with a ha-ha that grew into a belly laugh. She joined him, because they had beaten death.

If he had thought through the situation further, he would've traced his joy to his freedom. He was on his own for a day, loose in the wind, even if it was in Kansas. He had just run without a keeper, and he could simply disappear if he wanted to. There were no badges in sight, no feds, no Russians.

There was only the woman he was there to spy on, and she was making him laugh. He'd kill her or not, but just not right now.

"Thanks to you, I have a library of Russian music," she said. "Tchaikovsky, of course. *1812,* and I sometimes play *Hymn of the Cherubim* at dawn and dusk. Prokofiev's 'March' from *The Love for Three Oranges.* The myth of you appeared in our lives in Great Bend, and then you were in and out of FBI custody. You're the forbidden fruit, the snake, the pale rider."

"You're making me more than I am."

"I'm fascinated by you and frightened of you. It's an adrenaline rush," she said. "People who know you, they die."

11

Sweating in the humidity after their ramble around the pasture, Nick and Laura drank iced tea at her kitchen table.

"You liked the music?"

"How'd you get it to start playing?"

"Electronic remote. I spend so much time outside that I figured it'd be worthwhile to put up a big speaker."

He raised his glass to her. "It made me feel like a champion."

"I play mostly symphonies and operas. Mozart, Beethoven, Verdi, the great composers All the great tragedies, with the baritone and tenor fighting to the death. The baritone wins and gets the girl. It's how I counteract the cooties I bring home from the Hitch. There's romance on the prairie wind."

"What else do you do for fun out here?"

"Mostly go to funerals. In fact, you and I are going to one in two hours. It starts at 10."

"Seriously? For the explosion already?"

"It's for one of Grandma's cousins, Alice. I told you about her, a nice woman who lived south of the refuge. She and Grandma grew up together."

Nick said, "It sounds like she meant a lot to your family."

"I'd drop in on her every month or so. Her granddaughter's about my age, and she's cool."

"She live here?"

"Out in Denver."

"We're sweaty."

"The water truck came while we were on the track. The tank's full now."

Nick poured himself more tea, asking, "When did your grandma die?"

"A couple of years ago, a year after Grandpa went. Grandma was a hypochondriac about other people's health. 'He looks sick, does he feel well, I bet he has a heart attack soon'—and then she had a heart attack while driving in town and ran into two cars and a light pole but was probably dead before she hit the pole."

"That's awful," Nick said.

"I think maybe she said all those things about other people's health because she suspected her own problem and wanted to believe she was no worse off than they were. So everybody was somehow sick and she wasn't alone."

"No one wants to be alone," Nick said. "No one wants to die alone."

•   •   •

Laura drove them to the funeral, arriving from the east on a patched-asphalt county road that transected the southern part of the wildlife refuge. The church was a white frame building behind a pair of thick cottonwoods. The church's cemetery was on the west side in a large rectangle protected by a cedar shelter belt.

A dozen cars and pickups were lined up side by side on sand and mowed grass in front of the church.

"Everyone parks where they've parked for decades," Laura said. "I'm parking in Grandma's old spot. So many of her generation have died that there aren't enough new people to fill the spaces."

A pianist played "Rock of Ages" as Laura led Nick to a cushioned pew halfway up to the wooden pulpit. She waved subtly to people already seated. Alice's walnut coffin rested on a wheeled catafalque in front of the pulpit.

Nick looked around. Stained-glass windows glowed on the sunlit side of the airy sanctuary. The choir loft must've been useful when more people came here.

"When I was a kid," Laura said, "this was my idea of a real church. I imagined that I'd get married here and buried here. Now I generally don't go to any church unless it's with Harriet for work."

Laura stood up and hugged two women in their seventies who were seating themselves one row back. Laura introduced Nick as an aide from Washington. The women looked him up and down before returning to tiny talk with Laura.

"They found Alice in her pea patch, next to her garden gnomes," one said, waving her funeral-home-issued pasteboard fan. "She had fallen, and it looked as if she just gave up."

"It might've been a stroke," Laura suggested. "That's what the doctor said. Or a heart attack."

"Or maybe she just got tired of it all."

Laura said, "She gave everything she had to that garden. When her dogs and parakeets died, she'd bury 'em in there as fertilizer."

The pianist segued into "This Is My Father's World."

"You know about Alice's granddaughter, right?" one said. "She moved to Colorado and had a baby with a poet, and that's just something she'll have to live with."

The other said, "He must've been . . . poetic in bed."

"I wouldn't know. I'm not a gossip." She fiddled with her purse, pulling out a tissue. "Was he a Longfellow?"

"She's probably had verse."

The second woman snorted. Everyone else turned and frowned, then waved when they recognized the source.

"She married the guy."

"At least one part of this is traditional."

"But they got married on a Thursday."

As the granddaughter found her seat in a pew at the front, the preacher rose and the pianist wrapped things up. Laura whispered to Nick: "I once fell in love with a half-assed poet, and that's a shame I'll just have to live with."

The minister began by asking for a moment of silence for the victims of the bombing. Then he spoke of Alice's various good works with the township's 4-H club and in the church charity.

"Maybe her best-known anecdote was about people," he said. "About all of us." He cleared his throat, and looked at the thirty or so mourners one by one. He paused for a beat when he noticed Nick's bandaged neck.

"She'd say, 'You will find, Reverend Scott, that as we age, we become more distilled versions of ourselves.' And that's what she did. She became kinder, more insightful and more deeply in touch with the earth. Let's now join in celebrating Alice's life and glorious homecoming by singing 'In the Garden.'"

The congregation didn't need a hymnal for the chorus:

> And He walks with me, and He talks with me,
> And He tells me I am His own,
> And the joy we share as we tarry there,
> None other has ever known.

As the hymn's refrain softened into an echo, one of the seventy-somethings whispered to the other: "She'll really be in touch with the earth now."

Nick's face flickered with a grin but that faltered as his thoughts drifted off to the Gayfeather challenge passed along in Washington from his mobster nemesis, Gregori Orlov.

"Make it your podvig, your glory," his Russian contact, Anastasia, had told him at Dupont Circle.

Alice had found her glory with a kind heart. How would he ever accomplish anything of the sort, especially with the mess he was in?

•   •   •

Alice's granddaughter asked Laura and four of Alice's least-mobile friends to sit with her in the row of folding chairs under the funeral home's graveside canopy. Nick stood behind Laura. On the other side of the hole, a large piece of fake turf hid the mound of soil that would be shoveled back in after the service.

The sun, less than a month short of the summer solstice, was high but not directly overhead. The wind had come up at midmorning and had strengthened enough to make ancient cedars sway and the canopy rustle against its supporting pipes and guy wires. Beyond the cemetery fence, wheat moved in waves. Behind the minister's voice, a meadowlark on a post trilled an angelic chorus from deep in its bright yellow vest.

The minister intoned a few Bible verses and wished Alice well as her spirit walked with Jesus on Heaven's streets of gold even as her body returned to dust inside the coffin and vault.

"You know," Laura said later, as she and Nick climbed into the car, "that whole thing about Heaven's streets of gold, that's such a religious hangup."

"Churches and other royalty love gold," he said. "Having lots of it seems like a weak person's idea of true happiness."

"The whole Quivira area is best known for being the promised home of a city of gold. Coronado, one of the Spanish explorers, the conquistadors, came up here from the southwest in 1541 following the rumor of gold and found the Wichita people living as farmers and bison hunters in grass huts."

"Was there any gold at all?" Nick asked.

"Not a bit. Coronado had his Native guide killed for leading them to Quivira. It wasn't the last time Indians suffered because of expectations the Europeans had of them. Now 'Quivira' is a symbol for an unrealistic goal. For example, the state of Kansas used to publish textbooks for subjects like grammar, math, and history. Grandpa gave me a little history book from a hundred years ago that sums up how the government wanted students to think. That book was published in 1919, which is when the country was going through labor riots, white riots against blacks, and scares about communists and labor activists. The Ku Klux Klan was in full swing.

"Anyway," she said, "in that history book there's a poem about Quivira, and I learned it for a presentation in high school, back when I was a full-throated believer in the American Way.

"The poem starts by telling about how the conquistadors came looking for streets of gold 'in the kingdom of Quivera,' with an *e*. The last stanza goes like this."

She took a deep breath and recited:

> *Thus Quivera was forsaken;*
> *And the world forgot the place*
> *Through the lapse of time and space.*
> *Then the blue-eyed Saxon race*
> *Came and bade the desert waken.*

"So you have the conquistadors looking for gold and you have the buffalo, and finally you have the northern Europeans turning the place into a moneymaker. Nowhere in there are Native Americans except for the mention that it's their 'kingdom.'"

"Are there still Indians here?"

"Not really. The census says the whole gerrymandered First Congressional District of Kansas, which includes us, is less than one percent Native Americans. Rice County, where my place is, has even less than that."

"Sorry to be snarky," Nick said, "but isn't that how it usually works in a state named for Indians?"

"One of Coronado's priests came back to establish a mission," she said, "but he was killed. The Catholics called him a martyr. There's a giant cross honoring him up by Lyons, north of here."

Nick looked around, finding it easy to imagine settlements along the river when it had more water.

"The Indians survived on the lower plains until the mid-1860s, just after Kansas became a state. That was when an Army unit massacred a village of Cheyennes at Sand Creek, not far across the state line in Colorado Territory. The good people of Colorado named a town after the regiment's colonel, and what's worse is that the town still has his name."

"Was that part of American exceptionalism? Manifest Destiny? Weren't the Indians also attackers?"

"They were protecting their homeland. Their methods of warfare weren't any more heinous than the Army's, I suppose," she said. "It could be simply a willingness of men with guns to become bullies, and pushing out heathens was the American way of life. Plus, God is on our side, so it still is. The Indians are gone, so people can say what they want about them."

"You sound a little harsh about American history."

She shrugged. "It is . . ."

". . . What it is," he said.

· · ·

As Laura drove slowly east through the marsh, Nick kept an eye on the grassy ditch for rabbits that might try their luck crossing the road.

"You probably never heard about Quivira Jesus," she said.

"He was here too?"

She frowned, a look of exasperation for a second, before pulling the car over to stop with the right two tires off the asphalt. Her hands rested on the steering wheel, her eyes on the distance.

"A few years ago, another morning early in another May, a man was driving through here, just up the road. He pulled over when his little pink Mercury Mystique ran out of gas. He was taking his six-year-old to Hutchinson to live with her grandparents."

The breeze stirred the pasture grass and wildflowers. Cloud shadows swept across the landscape.

"There's a saying that when the weather's bad, nature's asking for a victim," Laura said. "A tornado came up and ran right over the two of them. The kid wasn't hurt, beyond some scratches, because tornadoes are fluky, but the father was caught by loose barbed wire. A power-line crew found him whipped up against a pole, his head hanging down and his arms out like Christ on the cross. That by itself sounds like something from a bad movie, but he also had two strands spun like a wreath around his head."

"Dead?"

She nodded, her eyes following the fence line.

"He bled quite a bit from being wrapped up," she said, "so the cops knew he stayed alive for a while."

"His poor kid."

"It was a completely random situation. That the dad and kid were there, that the storm came up, that the fence was torn apart." She drew the back of her hand across her eyes.

"The dad, for as much as God apparently hated him, got a big funeral so people could talk about everything he did wrong. The guy was poor. His daughter was sick. The car was a piece of crap. He should've known better than to drive during a tornado warning. It also was an act of God, everyone said. Mysterious ways, and all that. Some true believers went to the funeral sure he'd be resurrected."

Laura put the Flex back in drive and let the engine draw the car through a stretch of potholes and patches. She pointed to a squad of broken, leafless trees in a shelter belt running parallel to the south side of the road.

"There's where the tornado came across," she said.

"That's a lot of power in a small place."

"The scary thing was that a mile to the east there was a half-full school bus, and a mile to the west was the church where we buried

Alice. This man died, and his kid was left sitting in the ditch chanting 'Daddy, Daddy,' all because the storm followed a path laid out by God, on God's timing."

She turned to Nick.

"And that's life," she said. "Sometimes you deserve death, and sometimes you don't. People make up stories about how you deserved to die so they can say it's God's will."

12

Laura parked downtown close to Bull Creek's traffic light, off the street and within easy walking distance from the town's café. The place, with the name Farmtown painted in silver and black on the plate-glass window, was fashionably dressed outside with slats of worm-tunneled eight-inch-wide barnwood and inside with rusted farm tools. Conversation hushed and folks stared as Nick and Laura sat themselves at a table for four.

The crowd was a third hometowners, a third cops and agents, and a third reporters hitting up everyone else for quotes. Once, in an election-year conversation with the senator, Laura described situations like this as "a captive audience waiting for its food, and predators hustling to feed the machine."

Nick sensed every face turning toward them, and after a nod to Laura he headed down a cheaply paneled hall to the men's room, up in front by the coat rack.

The waitress headed over with a couple of laminated menus and a Diet Coke. She got as far as asking, "The usual, dear?" but was nudged away by A.B. Abbey, a metro columnist for the *Wichita Eagle,* the newspaper with the largest circulation in south-central Kansas. Abbey had what was once described as a voice meant for opinion journalism: nasal with a down-bending whine at the end of phrases, like a rusty knife spreading soured frosting across a cake.

"Give us a moment, dear," Laura said to the waitress. Glaring at Abbey, she added: "This won't take long, will it."

"Laura," Abbey said as she pulled out a chair and sat down uninvited. She laid her phone on the table and tapped "record" on the voice memo app. "I'm so sorry you got caught up in this. How're you doing?"

"I'm hurt, but I'm alive. Nine guys aren't."

"What kind of injuries do you have?"

"Not your business."

Abbey ran her hand back along her glasses to arrange her auburn hair. As always, she felt self-conscious next to Laura, who a year earlier she had described in print as the "glow-in-the-dark Eisenhauer."

"You're of course Senator Gayfeather's top deputy in Kansas," Abbey said. "Has she had any personal messages for you or her new aide? By the way, what's his name?"

"She's deeply saddened by this terrible attack. As you know, she was up all night preparing a defense for our essential oil industry against such misguided attacks."

"Any ideas on why terrorists struck that well?"

"Seriously? Why would I have an idea about that?"

Laura lowered her voice.

"And, really, after the hard-hitting exposé you wrote about the senator's buying her next-door house, maybe you ought to cut her some slack for responding so quickly in a time of national need."

Abbey fiddled with her hair again. "You know how it all works."

Laura put the menu down and caught the waitress' eye.

Abbey pressed on: "The aide was on the spot with first aid. Former military? What can you tell us about him?"

"Nothing. I hardly know him. When he came to town, I wanted to show off a drilling rig, so we went to that one because it's close. It's terrible that he was involved, but he saved lives through his quick response even though he was injured."

"What can you tell us about his injuries?"

"A.B.," Laura said, "this was traumatic for us but the story isn't about us. It's about those nine dead men and their families and coworkers."

She gave the waitress the order and drank from her glass before speaking again.

"Senator Gayfeather's aide did what anybody who knows first aid would've done," Laura said. "Like everyone else, we're still shaken up by all this. Tell you what. I'll ask him about his reactions and text them to you alone. I have your number."

Abbey wasn't happy at being dismissed, and even less so about being escorted to the cash register by the hostess at the bidding of the hometown celebrity. In her visit to the cafe, however, she had acquired quotes from an eyewitness victim, a state law enforcement officer, a pair of federal agents in suits, and two farmers whose land was near the well.

•   •   •

While Laura was thumbing through the news on her phone, the waitress delivered a pair of Farmers and Merchants platters—chicken-fried steak with cream gravy, home fries, a dinner roll, and a bowl of corn. A man in a worn-shiny suit left his table of sheriff's deputies and highway patrol officers and strode past her table, slowing as if he might stop, but he walked on to the restroom. He tried to twist the lever on the hollow-wood door of the men's room, found it locked, and leaned back next to the coat rack to wait.

After a few minutes, he returned to his table, said a few things to the crew, laid a five and ten on the check, and left.

A couple of minutes later, Nick came out of the men's room. Laura raised her plastic glass in his direction.

"Let me guess," she said. "You're a private person with intestinal issues."

"Yeah, something like that."

"That's handy if you're here to kill someone, but what about when you're saving lives? People want to meet you. You're not even identified, but they know which one you are."

"It's a way of life," Nick said.

She looked over his shoulder, and her face lit up.

"Speaking of life," Laura said, putting her napkin on the table and rising, "here's the life of the party."

She whispered to Nick, then hugged Sam Orion. Orion glanced at Nick, back at her, nodded, and pulled out a chair.

"I'm Sam Orion," he said. "People think I'm Irish, but I'm just a gift from the heavens." He laughed. "Laura tells me you're from the home office."

Nick grinned. Clearly they were supposed to have never met. They awkwardly bumped fists and sat down next to each other.

Laura said, "Orion's my best friend out here. He runs a nudist . . ."

"Naturist!"

". . . Naturist colony a couple of miles southeast of town, out in the sand where only the jackrabbits, coyotes, and people who crave an even suntan gather."

"Membership is only a dollar," Orion said. "We're all buck naked."

Nick raised an eyebrow at Laura.

"Once," she said.

"But you're smiling when you say that," Orion said.

He turned to Nick.

"It's safe and nonjudgmental," he said. "You can wear clothes if you want, and we all carry towels to sit on because none of us is as clean as we think we are."

Laura interrupted. "Orion, stop!"

"Hey, listen, are you and Harriet coming to the memorial service Saturday?"

"I probably will, but our office is advising the senator to stay home so it doesn't look like a political event piled on top of her oil-industry protection bill."

"Really? Because that would be just perfect for Fox to whip America's heartland into frothy fear."

"Exactly," she said.

"Are you getting medical care?"

"Nah. My ears still hurt and I got a bunch of bruises, but it would've been a lot worse if 'Roy' hadn't been in front of me and taken the blast hard."

Nick mouthed, "You're welcome."

"Not that I don't think about it every hour."

"Well, then," Orion said, "have you entered a pool for Who Will Kelli Kill?"

"God, no. What if it's Harriet? I've lived through that a million times since she was shot at."

Nick blushed, but no one noticed.

"She's 10-to-1 at the Hitch."

"Remember Kelli's video in Topeka?"

Laura pulled up YouTube on her phone and handed it to Nick. "'Roy,' you met her, but do you know about her?"

The video started. Kelli Ochs, blond and thin, was making a selfie in front of the bear cage at a zoo.

"I'm going to kill someone who really deserves it," Ochs said on the recording. "I'm an expert shot with a rifle and pistol, fluent with knives, know my way around electricity. I'm a walking danger zone."

Nick asked Laura, "You knew about this?"

She answered with a bit of exasperation. "I didn't say anything about her yesterday because she's our problem. Whether she's serious or a fool, she's a Kansan, and you're not. You didn't mention her so I didn't. And besides, Jesus! I've met more famous people than I can count. She's just one more. Famous, right now, for nothing except being on Facebook and saying she's going to kill somebody. That's not exactly a small club."

Laura put her forehead in her hands.

"Nevertheless, Gayfeather should be afraid," she said. "She thinks she's invincible. Ever since Great Bend."

Nick said in a soft voice, "Kelli's determined, but I think she's also scared. Both of them are."

Orion and Laura sighed together. Then Orion stood up, hugged Laura again and whispered to her. She nodded.

To Nick, he said, "You, sir, are invited for a swim in our heated pool if you want to try out our camp."

Nick laughed. "Your guests don't want to see my body."

* * *

The man in the shiny suit was leaning against the front panel of Laura's Flex. He showed his badge and identified himself to Nick as Captain Loren Hornish of the Kansas Highway Patrol.

"I'm part of a task force set up by the governor last year to keep an eye on radical individuals and groups, left wing and right wing, to prevent terrorism," he said. "Our members are in the Kansas Bureau of Investigation, the Patrol, and several sheriffs' and police departments. With the FBI in town, my role in the bomb investigation is peripheral, but Kansas has its interests to protect."

The trooper was a couple of inches shorter than Nick and built solidly, about the age of Nick's father. Nick remembered Hornish from his earlier time in Kansas, but didn't mention it.

"Ms. Eisenhauer, there've been a couple of developments," Hornish said. "Topeka's going to announce them this afternoon. I figure telling you is almost as good as passing it along directly to your boss, in case she hasn't already heard."

"She's flying into Wichita tomorrow afternoon," Laura said.

"Plus, if I tell you, maybe you can add something to it."

Laura nodded. Hornish had turned toward her, leaving Nick out of the conversation.

"The FBI determined that the explosive was made of Tannerite, a two-part off-the-shelf powder that explodes when struck by a high-velocity mass. A bullet from a hunting rifle, for example."

Laura nodded. "That doesn't narrow it down in Kansas. You know guys with guns: If it moves, shoot it. If it doesn't move, shoot it."

"It fits with what we found, a segment of a blue trash barrel with what could be a bullet hole. But a hole like that could've been made by anybody in the past month, which is how long the rig's been there."

"How much explosive was there?"

"The barrel held actual trash like paper cups and pieces of lumber, and buried in there was a five-gallon steel bucket filled with Tannerite, metal scraps, and nails. Maybe fifteen pounds of powder, like about four sticks of dynamite. The bullet hit that, and it blew. It's a wonder every one of you wasn't shredded."

"Who set it off?"

"That's also part of the news. Late yesterday we found a bolt-action, scoped Remington Model 700 back in the cottonwoods not far from the old farm, maybe three hundred yards line of sight from the blue barrel."

Hornish paused to watch a pickup roll into the parking lot.

"It was at the base of a deer blind, one of those rickety ones with a pipe frame and a camo-painted plywood shelter on top. Our working assumption is that a sniper fired and then was traumatized or overly excited, so he dropped the rifle with the bolt open and skedaddled down the ladder and ran away. The FBI took the rifle, saying they'd lift fingerprints from the stock and the one casing we found on the ground."

Laura was surprised. "He left his rifle? Surely at that point nobody was looking his direction."

"That's also part of the news. This morning Stafford County deputies found what might be the shooter's Chevy Silverado pickup and camper behind the house at an old farm a couple of miles south of the well. It has current North Dakota tags."

"Jesus. Whose was it?"

"We don't know yet for sure. The insurance card and truck's registration were missing, but if the tag's accurate we may have a lead. The owner ground off all the vehicle identification numbers some time ago. The FBI is hinting that the owner is an anti-government radical, and that the ID matches fingerprints found on the rifle."

"So he left his rifle and his truck?" Laura asked.

"Maybe someone drove him away," Hornish said. "Everything's open to conjecture."

Hornish raised his index finger to pause the conversation. Laura thought his expression was a smirk as he closed his hand and then raised his right ring finger.

He waited, though, as a woman they'd seen in the cafe strode past. She waved to Laura: "Say hello to the senator, dear."

"Thank you, Mrs. Brightwell. Always good to see you."

As Mrs. Brightwell reached her Subaru, Laura explained: "My dad's English teacher."

Hornish continued: "One more thing. We found an extra digit."

"What? Whose?"

"We don't know yet. Our highly educated and suspicious minds think a crow picked it up somewhere and was flying over when the barrel blew up. The crow dropped the finger, coincidentally on the outer circle of the site."

"How do you know it wasn't from one of the rig guys?"

"Theirs are all accounted for, or at least enough of their fingers exist that we know it's someone else's. Plus, even though the flesh was cut, it was by something clean, not shrapnel."

Laura looked dazed.

"Fingerprint?" she asked. "Could it be the gunman's?"

"Probably not. It looks like it's been in water for quite a while, and things nibbled on it. Maybe a turtle, maybe a catfish. Crawdads. Maybe birds. It's a finger that's seen some tough times."

"So there's no way of knowing, . . ." Laura prompted.

Hornish cast a quick, sharp look at Nick, up and down.

"Until we run the DNA," Hornish said.

. . .

"You don't look good," Nick said after he and Laura were in the car.

"I ate too much."

"I thought it might have something to do with what the cop said. About the finger."

She put the Flex in gear and drove out of the lot, pounding the brake to avoid T-boning a pickup.

"I have a friend who's gone missing. I wondered if maybe it's his finger."

"Why didn't you say anything about him?"

"To protect his privacy."

"This sounds interesting."

"It's not what you think, and it's more than you can imagine. Let's leave it at that."

Despite her upset stomach, Laura drove them to the grocery store.

"I need food at home," she said. She had him wait in the car.

13

All Pastor Luke Meriwether wanted was time alone in the River Jordan Cathedral, so he directed the office manager to take the staff of five women to the Applebee's a few miles away for lunch, his treat. He locked the front doors after they left.

He was a nervous wreck. He had phoned Christmas an hour ago and left a message: "I can't believe this. Nobody from the *Eagle* or TV, not even a podcast, has called me. I called three reporters, and all of them let it go to voicemail. I called Saltwood to offer the Cathedral for a memorial service, and they transferred me to a secretary who put me on hold for five minutes and then said that everyone was busy."

He also phoned the governor's office, the two senators' offices, and the office of Wichita's member of Congress. Not one person had returned his call.

The only two times his phone had rung all morning were when that Norse wannabe Cooper left two voicemails before 10 o'clock, pleading for news that Jesus had gotten him a job. Pastor suspected he shouldn't blow the guy off, but Jesus doesn't work miracles, buddy.

Pastor walked into the sanctuary and plopped down in the last pew, the twenty-sixth row back from the stage. This seat in a protected corner offered the grandest view of the sanctuary. During his sermons, he sometimes imagined his heroic profile as he stood before the eight-foot wooden cross bolted to the wall, raising his arms in exaltation and being the very picture of a successful pastor as he called down from Heaven the mighty power of Jesus Christ through an ear-mounted Bluetooth microphone.

He loved the sanctuary. The pews were oaken and cushioned, and the carpeting behind the pews and on the stage was a resilient rich green. The stained-glass windows didn't open to the outdoors; they were closed in and illuminated from behind because the TV and streaming crew complained that the uneven sunlight messed with their pan-tilt-zoom cameras mounted on the walls. Two aisles divided the sanctuary into pie-shaped thirds pointed at the stage.

The stage was big enough for the glass-and-metal pulpit, chairs with plum-colored upholstery for Pastor and visiting pastors when they weren't wandering with the microphone, risers for the choir, and a small band. Because—Pastor pursed his lips—you can't celebrate Jesus without a saxophone.

Twenty-two men and women made up the choir, which sang one or two light hymns every Sunday and guided the congregation through the praise music. Most were plump, but a half-dozen members, runners and gym rats, had dramatic faces and were often singled out by the livestream cameras. Pastor thought they easily could be wooden statues trimmed by an adze. The choristers' forced smiles weren't much different from scowls, and there was always a brunette with blocky hips wearing a skirt with a geometric pattern that reminded Pastor of an internet eye test.

The best part of the choir was that young singers from the state university became members so they could earn performance practicum credits. Praise Jesus, their pretty faces drew TV viewers. Once in a while there was a singer of such ethereal beauty and talent that people actually came to the church and paid good offering money to hear her for a semester or two.

Pastor sighed when he dwelled on music. Like so many other churches, the Cathedral early on installed a pair of gigantic video screens for people who got lost in the repetitive words to Christian karaoke: "All Things Are Possible," all fifteen verses of it, and intimate love songs to Jesus.

"People like it," good wife Christmas said. "But my Lord in Heaven, the hymns you and I grew up with are in a forgotten language. Nobody knows how to sing 'How Great Thou Art' anymore. The most complicated melody they know is 'Onward, Christian Soldiers.'"

Pastor had read in a ministry-industry magazine that churches were replacing paper versions of Sunday bulletins with boxy QR codes tucked into racks on the back of the pews. Click on a code, go to the Cathedral's website (where the phone's info was recorded and user identified), and see the weekly notices.

"People are going to be on their phones anyway," he said. "I look across the sanctuary and see all those bent heads, and I know they're not praying. They're probably not even using the QRs, just some stupid games."

Christmas Meriweather, more than Pastor Luke, bemoaned the loss of tradition.

"We're already selling out real worship," she said a couple of weeks ago. "We preach politics, sell our congregation coffee loaded with sugar, draw money automatically out of their bank accounts, and have them sing along to drivel. Your speaking in tongues is completely fake. I don't mean to criticize what we're doing, but don't you ever miss the way church used to be?"

"I don't really care as long as the offertory buckets fill up and my name stays in the news," he said. "I hate that I sound so mercenary, but look at the worship center I've built."

Sometimes, after one of those conversations, he sensed that he was drifting away from his moorings. But not all that far.

Luke's old man, Josephus Meriwether, had been a pastor as well, southeast of Wichita in a midsize town in northeastern Oklahoma. His message was delivered in the poetry and hellfire of the King James Version, both in person and on Sunday morning radio.

The son's day of enlightenment came from Josephus, who in the fall of Luke's senior year of high school came home from recording his radio show and sat the boy down at the table in the church's parsonage. He put a beer before each of them. The skinny old man went on about his day and swerved into the joys of preaching.

"There's only one way to Heaven," Josephus said, "and that's through Jesus Christ. Remember, my boy, that you hold the key to Jesus. You are the key. And all you're asking in return for guidance to eternal life is respect and a beautiful gift of love in the offering plate."

Luke, who was still using his birth name, Gerald, nodded like he was taking notes.

"And," the old man said with a smirk before he drained his beer, "the occasional dissolute daughter of a rich man."

A Pentecostal threatening souls with Deuteronomy and damnation, the old man made a good living on the hilly outskirts of Osage oil country. About the time of the kitchen-table talk, Josephus was taking up with a young Baptist woman down in Tulsa, and word got around to his wife. After lunch one spring day, she snuck up on the philanderer as he snoozed in his recliner and slid a bread knife between his ribs. She topped off the day by plowing the family station wagon through a crossing gate and broadsiding a Union Pacific locomotive.

Gerald Meriwether collected the scant insurance money paid on his father's death and the car and went to the Charles Parham Bible College in northwestern Arkansas, forty-five miles from home as the scissor-tailed flycatcher goes but ninety miles by road.

In his sophomore year, the handsome, charismatic young man was called to a small church of hard-cores, a post he expanded into a fifteen-minute radio TV show recorded ahead of time and played at 6:00 A.M. seven days a week for an audience of Ozarks retirees and blue-collar workers. His on-air name was Luke Meriwether, a name more virile, more Biblical than Gerald. Thirty years ago last April, he walked into the courthouse in Bentonville, Arkansas, and changed his name officially to Luke so it would appear on his diploma that way.

On the Memorial Day weekend after his graduation, Luke married Christmas, the prim, attractive, and discreetly pregnant daughter of the gospel-singing radio stars Oremus and Nellie; Christmas, who swore on their wedding night that if he ever raised his hand against her she would kill him and who, while three months pregnant and on a trip to see a college friend in Wichita, called Luke in tears.

"The baby's gone," she said. "The pain was terrible, and then it happened on the bathroom floor." She caught her breath. "I miscarried. It's all my fault, Luke. I'm so sorry, so sorry."

Luke convinced himself that she had gotten an abortion, but she denied it. He became more strongly against the procedure for any reason, and soon founded the River Jordan Cathedral in Wichita during the 1990s Operation Rescue aftermath as a show of dominance. She resented it but didn't dwell on the situation. Christmas, who still wouldn't say *shit* if her mouth were full of it, grew into her beauty and her role as a minister's wife. She felt she had no choice, and she enjoyed churchwork.

Now here he sat, lord of all he surveyed, the king of holiness nestled between bars where local girls pursued officers and randy enlisted men stationed at McConnell Air Force Base. He was on the fast ladder to success—no more services held in bankrupted farm implement dealerships with congregations so small that the offering plate often held little more than sofa change.

He didn't care that people called River Jordan the Tiny Camel Cathedral because of Pastor's apparent belief that some camels are small enough to fit through the eye of a needle. Nor did he care that the Cathedral, erected with corrugated metal walls, bore an architectural resemblance to shops that sold tractors and road graders.

The camels weren't the only reminder of the Holy Land. On a row of poles along the edge of the parking lot, four Israeli flags flapped in the same breeze as six US flags, plus a thirty-by-fifty-foot American flag out front that sometimes misled drivers trying to find a car dealer's lot.

To be sure, stalwart members of Pastor's congregation wouldn't invite a Jewish family to dinner. The blue-and-white banners symbolized admiration of Israel's government, as well as the contradictory justification to kill Muslims and to punch their own Jesus tickets for the Rapture once Israel was taken by the Muslims.

One Sunday morning, in a Teens Ask Questions session, a smart-mouthed girl asked Pastor in front of the congregation why, if God wanted the Muslims dead, "doesn't He just kill them Himself with a plague or something? Is He making us take a loyalty test?"

"Because the Bible says specifically to kill Muslims. You can look it up," Pastor said. "We follow God's orders."

"No, it doesn't," the girl said. "Pastor, you also talk about a war on Christianity. But you say God is all-powerful. Isn't it enough if we believe in His love? Can't we turn the other cheek?"

"Young lady, they're taking our rights."

"Our right to believe?"

"Who's next with a question?"

The girl was prepared to ask more. Instead, she picked up her coat and purse, walked out right then, and never came back. Pastor still bristled at that memory. But at least he was still wrapped in the American flag.

If the Red, White, and Blue works for car dealers, Pastor's reasoning went, it ought to work for the Cathedral. Plus, his services competed with Sunday auto racing and football for the same audience, so he might as well use their tactics.

His sanctuary—he was thinking of rebranding the room as "The Celebration Center at River Jordan Cathedral"—was usually filled, sometimes with city leaders who ventured out of their Presbyterian and Methodist neighborhoods, but more often by people attuned to a remark he made once about a black civic leader he nicknamed "Dudley Do-Rag." He felt at the top of his game, except for today, when God's voice needed to be heard above the reverberations of oilfield terrorism.

Pastor Luke did his best to keep everybody happy on their way home to heaven, but he'd be the first to admit that running a cathedral was difficult. It was a godsend that wiser men had shepherded him toward the light.

A preaching instructor in his Fundamentals of Fundamentalism college class pointed out that folks can go anywhere to join a club. The trick, he said, is to create a need.

"Listen," the instructor said, "you can't run a thriving church without money. You have to understand that sometimes religion isn't just a matter of people prostrating themselves before Our Lord. For a lot of people, it's a club where they pay dues, wear club symbols, sing club songs, and beat up people from other clubs."

He pointed at each student in turn. "When the parsonage's electric bill comes, those people's money is just as good as a widow's last dollar."

Prosperity is the ticket, the instructor said. Praising the acquisition of wealth brings in the riches, but you have to be smooth. The safest way to build your congregation and new sanctuary is to focus on God's revealed will: praise the rich, ignore the adulterers, and go hammer and tongs after liberals and high taxes on capital gains.

Pastor drank beer with the deacons and bourbon with the governor. He attended every Republican fundraiser, saying his donations had come out of his own pocket. He was known to be available for graduation services and public celebrations.

"I'm a passionate evangelizer," he liked to say. Although those words didn't mean much about the quality of his efforts, they projected a halo over his career.

Still, almost nothing was more effective at spreading the River Jordan Cathedral's goodwill than its private gun club. The church had bought eighty acres of wooded bottomland along the Arkansas River southeast of Wichita and turned it into a shooting range, a fishing pond, and a family party zone that could be rented for high school proms, and, if the post-prom romances and pregnancies held together, for wedding receptions.

A couple of years ago, he dropped a few hints during Sunday services, and before long a cadre of two dozen like-minded men with four-day beards coalesced into a paramilitary group that wanted to be known as the Christian Crusaders. Although that name was put forward in good faith by several members who had fought Muslims in Iraq and Afghanistan, several influential church members, and a substantial number of posters on Facebook, laughed at the abrasive cliché. In a heated meeting, the Crusaders voted to limit their roster to fifteen and rename themselves the Almighty Rifles.

The Almighty Rifles quickly received sponsorship from a firearms manufacturer covering half the cost of their weapons, uniforms, body armor, and accessories such as matching watches. After a story about the squad, in a national religious magazine intent on destroying the secular government, labeled them the AR-15, donations poured in and several other churches formed similar squads.

The men served as honor guards at local military funerals; they protected stores (those bearing the fish symbol) against deportables, libs, and people who spoke against unlimited gun rights; and they watched over picket lines outside clinics where family planning was provided.

Inside the church, the Security Ministry was created for men who had not been invited to join the Almighty Rifles. They dressed in gray slacks and blue blazers, like department store security guards, and carried concealed Glock pistols. Officially, the group was a shield against hostage takers and madmen, but the presence of the security ministers also encouraged church members to behave themselves in disagreements over religious dogma and seating in the pews.

Every May, the River Jordan Cathedral celebrated both Mothers Day and First Responders Sunday, inviting law enforcement officers, firefighters, and ambulance crews to a service. The visitors were asked to stand and be recognized, and the congregation gave them a standing ovation. A few first responders and their young families became members. Most Sundays a couple of patrol officers in civilian clothes attended services with the wives and kids.

"I," Pastor Luke told Christmas, "have checked all the boxes: mothers, children, military, and the flag. The Lutherans and Baptists have nothing on us."

14

Pastor felt protected. In fact, life in the church was all good. Except for the busybodies. He called them the biddybodies.

"Pastor Luke," they'd say after the service, "why do you and Ms. Christmas have only one child? We'll pray for you to have God's own married sex and bring forth a blessed second soldier of the Lord."

The truth was that he had gotten a vasectomy thirteen years ago to prevent any misconceptions. He felt no need to mention the operation to his wife, who was now in her late forties. To be honest, Pastor and Christmas, or Mrs. Pastor as she was often called in church, weren't the best of friends and confidants.

Mrs. Pastor once bought a handgun with the intention of killing a woman who criticized her husband. That's what Pastor told the court when he was explaining why he had called the critic and warned her that Christmas was dangerous. The police, however, said Pastor himself had bought the gun and threatened to kill his critic. The critic subsequently received a gift from the church, delivered by the captain of the Security Ministry, in return for moving to another church and asking the police to drop the case.

Pastor described the whole event as a bonding experience. Mrs. Pastor, who had never held a handgun in her life and certainly had never bought one, refused to speak of the episode.

Despite what he took as forgiveness after she swallowed her fury, Pastor found that Christmas often exasperated him. For example: He has a recurring dream, and he wakes her each time to describe how a glowing dog carrying a silver tray accosts him.

"I boast of no heroics," he recites, as if his speech is part of his dream. "I did not flip the tray up or cleave the beast in two. Nor did I cower under the blanket. I instantly tried to clap, but I couldn't move my arms. But right away, the bright messenger disappeared into the gloom. And then I fell back asleep. In my dream."

In the dark bedroom, he couldn't see Christmas' eyes, but he felt the derision in her voice.

"Do not tell me again about that made-up dog," she said. "See a therapist. Make an appointment."

Pastor and Christmas, of a bumper-sticker church, had settled into a bumper-sticker marriage: Coexist.

And now their first intentional attempt to have a child, the lovely Noelle, induced almost fifteen and a half years ago to be born on December 25, had popped up as a problem.

The kid was unhappy, which was not unexpected from a teenager, but not in the way of pot-smoking high schoolers, who were useless scruffians. Her complaint, festering from December, was that she had never had a birthday party of her own. Right there in Sunday school, she proclaimed pity for herself and a classmate named Nevaeh.

"Look how holy her parents think they are," she explained that night at the dinner table. "But who would name a kid after *Heaven* backwards?" she said, staring right into her parents' eyes. "That seems Satanic. Or timing your daughter's birth to Jesus' birth, just because you're a preacher, and then naming her Noelle for all the people who didn't get the joke. Right, Mom?"

Twice in the past month, Noelle had stayed out after her 10 P.M. curfew. Last week the girl, going into her junior year at an expensive Christian school, announced her plan to get a tattoo. When Pastor tried to talk her out of it, she snarked him: "Put a penny in the Facebook prayer box."

Pastor's wife had this very morning, not three hours before Pastor took his seat in the sanctuary, waved a pee stick in his face.

"I just found this in Noelle's bathroom trash," she said. "Your daughter is pregnant."

•　•　•

Pastor Luke heard the church's big glass door being unlocked and felt the air pressure inside the sanctuary change.

Joyleen Sterrett, the church's bookkeeper, appeared in the sanctuary entrance. She stage-whispered "Hi" and waved, either not noticing or ignoring his grimace at the intrusion. She sidestepped between the pews toward him.

She smiled. "I wasn't as hungry as the others, but thanks for lunch. Can we talk?"

In Pastor's experience, this would be very good or very bad.

She sat down an arm's length away. When she raised her eyebrows, Pastor looked around and nodded, and she slid over.

"I wanted to thank you for Sunday's sermon," she said. "It's as if you were speaking directly to me. As if your voice was the very voice of our Lord Jesus."

"Thank you, Joyleen. I did have you in mind when I spoke of the love of a good woman."

"It was so deep. Your voice was so, so mellifluous. I just wanted to close my eyes and float on your words."

Joyleen sagged her hard body against him, her eyes wide as she drank up the sound of his voice, the scent of his cologne. It was impossible now to slide a sheet of paper between them.

Pastor didn't think Joyleen was as bright as he was, but that wasn't a shortcoming. She certainly was a relief from his previous lover, the luscious, tattooed, but cloying Mona Leesa. Mona Leesa got married a few weeks ago and went away, following her business-school grad husband to an oil-company position in South America. Pastor was relieved it ended without recriminations because he didn't want anyone in the congregation to think of him in terms of adultery.

Joyleen brought him back to the moment. She whispered: "Yesterday, when you put your arms around me after work, I was the happiest woman in Wichita."

He glanced again around the sanctuary, then pecked her on the cheek. Not a stupid man, he put his hands on her shoulders to protect himself from imminent rapture. This was their game.

"God's love will make you whole," he intoned. "And maybe I can help."

She smiled demurely. "We have to stay careful."

As they walked to his office, Pastor's mind flashed to his wife, as it always did, but his manliness didn't sag. Joyleen gave no indication that she had seen worry flash across his face. She had come to terms with what she and Pastor had been doing, and his wife and her Lance be damned.

• • •

Joyleen Sterrett's parents, and she told them this some time ago, were trapped in a bubble of fear, afraid that someone was taking advantage of them, that the blacks and Mexicans and gays and liberals and other religions were getting special treatment, that the whole system was rigged against them, them personally more than any of their patriot friends.

Joyleen wanted more than life in that bubble. She dropped some of her parents' teachings and stepped into a wider world, going so far as to marry a lapsed Catholic. Her soldier-man, Lance Sterrett, had by then given up the pope in favor of all-American Protestantism and relentless baby-free sex with his yoga-practicing, aerobically fit, eight-years-younger wife.

But even now that Lance was back from the wars, he felt as if he were still gone. He was always out doing the bidding of Saltwood—her parents may have been right about it being an oil war—and when he was home he sometimes just didn't connect with her.

"I've seen and done things overseas that I can't forget," he said on their first date.

During their engagement and years of marriage, he often apologized, and when he was actually with her he tried to be an active part of her life.

He wouldn't go anymore to her parents' place for dinner. Joyleen's mother spit in his mashed potatoes after she found out he was raised a Catholic.

"You're not my people. You have a heart of darkness," she said.

"Fuck you," he replied.

But he shopped for groceries with Joyleen, cuddled her after making love, and sat beside her in the fourth pew in the right third of the sanctuary.

Pastor knew exactly where to look for her.

Joyleen had gotten here by deciding quite consciously that she would take all the life she could grab. Her muscular if enigmatic husband brought home good money, and she bought a few nice things for herself with what she made in the church office. That wasn't enough. She had designs on a man who despite being a sly heartless adulterous bastard also was rich, powerful, and mentioned among the political leadership of Wichita, the state of Kansas, and, to hear him say it, the national Republican Party. Good God, the guy had his own half-assed militia and thought he would someday be a senator.

She liked the promise of spiritual gains Pastor Luke promised in return for office sex in the nearly soundproof room in which he counseled couples about fidelity. Conversely, she was sure he wouldn't let godliness get in the way of his passions.

This lustful man, she thought, should be grateful that he was ugly only on the inside. Well trained in the basics of his religion, he was not self-aware enough to realize that there were things he didn't know. One Sunday he showed her a copy of Sinclair Lewis' tragic novel *Elmer Gantry* that a wise member of the congregation had urged him to take to heart—and a week later from the pulpit he thanked the man for sharing "the fictitional uplifting tale of the preacher Elvis Gentry." The next week, it was "arch-itecture" and "athalete" and "Realator," Joyleen noticed, but maybe adding a syllable was just a way preachers kept their rhythm during a sermon.

She suspected there was hidden money behind the hubris. With that in mind, everything else was easy. A bookkeeper, especially one working for a man who didn't read books or see beyond himself, can find things.

After the first time they had done it in his office, they lay side by side on the floor next to his shirt and pants and her green dress, his favorite of everything in her closet. He had been a gentleman and fallen off the couch first.

She put her hand on his sweaty chest.

"When's the last time you got laid by a woman without a tattoo?" she said.

15

By midafternoon Thursday, Laura had fended off newspaper reporters calling from Wichita, Hutchinson, Topeka, Kansas City, Dallas, New York, and Washington, and all the television networks from heavyweights such as CBS down the spectrum to Newsmax and One America News.

She and Nick had been interviewed at the ranch by sheriff's deputies from Rice and Stafford counties; by agents from the Kansas Bureau of Investigation; and by an investigator from the Bureau of Alcohol, Tobacco, Firearms, and Explosives. After all that, a pair of good-cop bad-cop agents from the Wichita office of the FBI arrived at the ranch.

Laura spoke first with the FBI duo. When it was Nick's turn, he showed his driver's license and insisted on talking only with Special Agent-in-Charge Barb Pellen in the DC office.

Speaking to the agent playing the bad cop, Nick said, "Call Pellen and let me hear her voice."

"Who are you?" the agent asked.

"A family friend."

The agents conferred, and one of them sent a text.

A few attempts were made at conversation in the living room—"Is it a good year for wheat? Is that what you grow here?" "How's the hunting?"—but they went nowhere, and silence reigned.

Four minutes later, the agent's phone buzzed. He handed Nick the phone.

"Hang on, please," Nick said into the phone and took it into the front yard, settling in under a redbud tree's cranky branches.

"I'm glad you're not dead," Pellen said.

"Twice in Kansas, almost dust to dust twice."

Office chatter erupted on Pellen's end.

"Hang on," she told him. To someone else, she said, "The Quivira bomb."

And then the chatter was gone.

"Senator Gayfeather told me you came by her DC house on Tuesday," Pellen said.

Nick gave Pellen a quick rundown on his hiring.

Pellen was annoyed. "She didn't tell me she had you over for dinner, and she sure didn't tell me she was going to offer you a job."

"I think it was spur of the moment," Nick said.

"Well, that was certainly nice of her."

"I asked her for help getting away from the Russians."

The call went silent for a moment.

"The Russians?"

"Your agents dropped me off a block from Dupont Circle, sucker punched me, and then sucker punched me again by pointing me toward the fountain. A Russian operative was waiting for me. Russian mob, more than a security service."

"You have a history with the mob."

"Not a happy one," he said. "You do remember that the mob tried to kill me and would've killed Gayfeather."

He heard Pellen typing. She had been there in Sandstone for his final gunfight, she told him when he was in the hospital.

"Had you seen the operator before?" she said. "Describe him."

"Her. Five-foot-five, brown/brown. Used the name Anastasia. Slender, subtle, good English and native Russian, Moscow accent. She recited facts about the park's fountain. She made fun of St. Petersburg. I assume she had Gregori Orlov on speed dial."

"Did you talk with Orlov?"

"Not directly. According to Anastasia, Orlov hinted that he had sources inside the FBI who told him I'd be put on the street. He didn't say who made that happen. Your guys didn't seem to know what was going on, more like errand boys, but were stressed about getting me to the dropoff at a certain time."

"Agents Cardiff and Johnson were firebombed Tuesday on the way back to their office. They died in the street."

Confirmation in hand, Nick thought about that. Pellen spoke first.

"The Russians are up to something," she said. "It looks like you might be part of it. At the very least, a distraction."

"You know I'm not with them," Nick said.

"You're sure? Because this is already sounding messed up. And because this could be life or death for you," she said. "If you're lying, I'll pull the trigger on you myself."

Nick said nothing.

"You gave your clothes away," she said. "You disabled the phone we gave you."

"Wouldn't you?" he said. "Who was tracing it, the FBI, the Russians, or a Putin groupie in the FBI?"

"Point taken," she said.

"If you had given me a new name on the driver's license, I might've pitched that, too. The Russians knew I left with my present name."

"Do you want new ID?"

"Now that you know where I am and why I'm here, yes. Please."

She seemed to think about that.

"I'll try to get you something in the next few days," she said at last. "Now, exactly what did Gayfeather hire you to do?"

"To be an independent observer in the Kansas office."

"Bodyguard?"

"I don't think so."

"Because if she needs security, the Senate itself can arrange that. And we can help."

"I don't think she's afraid in DC. She talked about how much she's hated in Kansas."

"And she hired you because . . ."

"Because I refused to shoot her and took care of the guy who tried to."

Pellen typed, a pause in the keyboard coming every fifteen seconds or so.

"I'm going to look into the situation here," she said. "Don't speak to anyone but me, and don't call any number but this one." She recited the number.

"Hey," Nick said. "One more thing. A guy I talked to here said they found a rifle back in the woods."

"Hold one," she said.

Nick shuffled his feet while he waited.

"Here's the deal," she said when she came back on the line. "I'm telling you this despite the obvious legal hazard that you're involved, but you seem to find out things that our personnel don't. Anyway, keep this to yourself, because while we're sure of these facts we don't know everything."

Welcome to the club, Nick thought.

"The owner of the fingerprints is a forty-three-year-old part-time farmer, part-time mechanic from West Bonetrail, North Dakota, named Ray Brehm." She spelled his name. "There were some tree-hugger fliers in his camper, and his fingerprints are on them. The FBI and ATF out in Bismarck are checking out his place."

Nick asked, "Did he do the Dakota bomb too?"

"Could be. The explosion was less than a dozen miles from his home, northwest of Williston. Maybe he set the timer and hurried down to Kansas. The employees there say they look over the tanks by noon every day, so we know that a bomb placed where it was couldn't have been there before Monday noon. Still, it'd be quite a feat to place the Dakota bomb after dark, if that's when it was done, on Monday evening or Tuesday and then drive sixteen hours on two-lane roads to rural Kansas and place a device at the well without being seen. He might have been so wired on meth or caffeine that he'd be lucky to hit the trailer instead of the trash barrel. Crime Scene guys confirmed Tannerite at both sites, plus plastic explosive in North Dakota."

"He wouldn't have known about the deer blind in Kansas, right? Unless he'd been here before or had a friend here."

"I imagine he might've stumbled on it. He could've just as easily set up behind a fallen tree, from what I understand from our tactical guys."

Nick pictured a guy, having driven all night, walking into unknown territory, placing a bomb, and scouting out a location from which to shoot.

"The cops out there say he has one ticket for a broken tail light and a single charge of carrying a firearm in a bar, which is why he was fingerprinted. He has a local reputation of being a full-blown enthusiast of the Second Amendment, which isn't what we expect of a radical environmentalist, but he also loaded up Facebook with pictures of himself brandishing guns."

"Why'd he pick an obscure well outside Quivira?" Nick wondered. "How'd he get the explosive into the trash can?"

"Good questions," she said. "I don't have answers, but we're looking into this hard."

She wished him well, and they hung up. Nick went inside to write down Pellen's number. He erased the call info and handed the phone back to the smug bad-cop FBI agent.

•   •   •

Laura had ordered Nick to get out of the house while she fixed dinner. Maybe go to the pond, she said.

On the verge of the pond, Nick untied the ropes holding a brown tattered tarp to Laura's red polyethylene canoe and righted the sixteen-footer off its wooden sawhorses. A bleached-out paddle, its epoxy coat flaking away, slid out and landed softly on the grass.

He carried the seventy-pound canoe awkwardly to the pond and plopped the bow into the glassy water, creating ripples that made abstract art out of reflected reeds and young cattails. He stretched his left leg out into the hull and drew the canoe close before dropping the paddle in, leaning out to grab the gunwales and move his center of gravity over the hull. He pushed the paddle against the mud in the shallows just hard enough to move outward.

Satisfied, he laid the paddle across the gunwales and leaned forward, hands on his knees. The pain of the wellsite explosion was leaving his arms, but his torso and legs had a long-muscle ache that experience told him would take days to fade.

The rectangular one-acre pond had been bulldozed out years ago to provide year-round water for the Eisenhauers' long-ago herd of Black Angus cattle, Laura had said. The excavated soil, now grown over by grasses and chest-high shrubs, was piled into low dunes to the west. Nick guessed that the impoundment was a hundred feet wide by four hundred feet.

At 7:30, the day was within an hour of sunset. Redwing blackbirds sang their evening songs, and barn swallows skimmed the water. Bats swiveled low, feeding on a cloud of insects above the reeds.

Every few minutes, Nick touched the clear water with the paddle just enough so that he wouldn't drift onto the mud of the shallows.

"The main fun is just being on the water," Laura had said. "You can't go far, so you sit there and relax. It's zen boating."

Along the shore, bluegills sucked insects off the mirrored surface. He didn't need a license if he wanted to fish, Laura had said. The rods and tackle were stored under the canoe, but he was happy to leave the bluegills where they were.

Be careful, whatever you do, she said, because the water gets deep quickly about twenty feet from shore, and it's not warm enough yet to enjoy swimming in.

Laura said she wanted him out of the house. She was cooking a late dinner of steak and sliced potatoes in cheese sauce, but she also needed to rest and think about not being dead. As in, her world had come undone. Her boss didn't care that she was nearly killed. Nick's presence, she said, was disruptive.

Cimarron Hernandez, his Cimi, the girl from Sandstone, had told him the same thing at the end of their relationship.

A freshet spun Nick's drifting canoe, and he decided he'd had enough fun. Cumulus clouds were rising against the sunset and the air cooled quickly. The darkening sky and the breeze filled his peripheral imagination with flickers of lightning, and with an occasional stroke he guided the canoe toward its sawhorses.

There had been lightning when he was in Kansas before, lightning that illuminated their first kiss and lightning that almost killed them both. During his recovery, late-summer thunderstorms over the military hospital in San Antonio had left him screaming in his dreams.

Cimi was the only woman he had loved in the four and a half years after the death of his adored Anya in Russia. Now, after two years in custody with little to do but confess, exercise, and think, he had given up loving and hating Cimi. Instead, he hated himself for becoming so vulnerable, for giving her all of himself and asking nothing in return—asking nothing but nevertheless expecting much.

He knew he'd ache over Cimi until his dying day, and yet he no longer loved her. Sometimes he imagined her as a specter.

To great fanfare, Cimi had been flown to New York as a guest of network morning news shows. On the *Today* show, for example, she described her intrepid role in breaking up a statewide kidnapping operation and in helping the still-anonymous Nick kill a Ukrainian hitman, and she had gone back quietly a couple of times to New York to talk to FBI investigators. After the first FBI meeting, her cooperation was rewarded with a full scholarship to the University of Kansas for the last two years of her undergrad education.

After she received her degree, she said, she was expected to go to law school and pursue a career in the FBI. From that perspective, Nick understood, a lingering affair with a known Russian assassin could be more of a roadblock than a career gift, but it would give her connections that few others had.

Nick and Cimi had been granted time together on her visits. Neither experience was satisfactory. Almost immediately he felt her pulling away, attracted by the world that had opened up to her. Their second visit brought the end of their relationship. He had been confrontational and afraid, and he pushed so hard that he buried the last remaining thing he liked about the world under six feet of self-hatred and remorse.

Her story about the kidnappings, vetted by the FBI, had been optioned by a movie studio for a quarter-million dollars. But still, she told Nick, he was a jerk for endangering her. Many of Sandstone's residents had come to resent the pressure put on the town by police agencies, the media, and souvenir hunters. Her mom's café, for example, had become a nest of conspiracy nuts who sat for hours and ordered nothing but coffee and faster wifi.

"In Sandstone," Cimi said, "almost everything you did was mechanical, although I think you rescued me out of real affection. You had that one moment when you gave yourself up for me or for your old lover and pulled the hitman over the ledge. And that was your redemption."

She put her finger on his chest.

"But you put me in that position because you were calculating. You used me. You have a forceful personality. You can be kind and loving, but you're still all about yourself."

Nick asked whether she loved the guy she had moved in with at college.

"I never said I wouldn't sleep with other men," she said.

She looked at Nick, weighing her thoughts about the other guy against Nick, whose last impassioned kiss had been preceded by "I've loved you for a long time, and you know it," and who two days later told her to go to hell.

"It's complicated," she said.

Their final conversation came a day later.

"Think about this," she said. "Are you nothing more than a killer? Is that the only reason you have left for living?"

•   •   •

The stranger arrived out of the sunset, rising piece by piece over the grassy horizon of a dune at the western end of the pond: a nearly flat view of his head, under a long-billed baseball cap and behind dark glasses, his chest dark with camouflage. He was maybe fifty feet away.

At his waist, the stranger held a rifle. It was an AR-15, Nick knew without thinking.

Nick edged the canoe backward. As he paddled unevenly, the bow yawed to his left.

The stranger raised his right hand, maybe saluting. He kept his eyes on Nick, who squinted against the brightness.

The man raised the rifle to his shoulder. The barrel was fitted with a thick suppressor.

Nick felt the crosshairs on his forehead.

If the man was any good, Nick knew he wouldn't have any better chance on the mud and grass than he had sitting like a duck on the water.

Nick slipped into what he called "combat mind." React first, assess second.

Trusting that the gunman was watching the target with tunnel vision, Nick let his paddle slip away from his right hand. He glided both hands to the gunwale at his left side. Taking a quick breath, he rolled overboard and capsized the canoe behind him.

As his head hit the water, a bullet smashed through the stern of the canoe, making it jump.

Nick held the canoe midship with one hand and kept his body as low in the water as he could. It was hard to stay vertical and bouyant without lifting the hull, but it would be deadly to let his back and feet rise to the surface.

He couldn't hide behind the polyethylene hull, but maybe he could confuse the scene. If he kept the boat between the gunman and himself, he'd present a smaller target with more of his body under the surface. Not that that would stop a military round tunneling through the water until friction bled off the speed, or a bullet aimed at the low point of the canoe itself.

The canoe vibrated in Nick's hands as the bow disintegrated. Then another shot hit the stern. Blown open at both ends, the craft settled deeper into the pond.

Nick hated that the gunman was toying with him. He decided he'd ride the canoe down if he had to and swim underwater to the farthest bank. Maybe the sunset glare would mask his movements. If he were to have a chance, he'd have to pull himself out of the muck and run across the grass.

He'd probably still get shot, but he'd die trying.

He peeked through a hole in the hull. The gunman was gone, or had hidden behind the brush on the dune.

Nick breathed deeply for half a minute. He exhaled completely and inhaled as much as possible.

Abandoning his cover, he dived deep, twisting toward shore. The daylight was nearly gone, and Nick was looking through dark water as he pulled hard with his arms.

When he caught the first shore grasses in his fingers, he pulled his knees forward until they rested in the muck. He moved his hands down to the roots, looking for a secure grip.

In a burst, he scrambled out of the muck and staggered onto the shore.

Gasping, he ran. He swerved to the left and to the right. He didn't care where. Just away. Every ten yards made a gunshot slightly less accurate. It was the rhythm of life, one foot in front of the other, always moving forward.

He tripped, falling hard into a bed of bindweed.

He didn't think he'd been shot. There were no sounds of someone creeping through grass. No voices. No firearm actions being cycled.

Keeping himself low, he rolled onto his back and raised his head just enough to see over the plants. Nothing.

Without thinking more, he stood up and juked to his left then spun to his right. A quick step, and he was off at a run, picking his feet high and watching his footing as he thundered around the pond and up the grassy, slippery forty-five-degree angle of the dune.

Little sunlight was left, and what there was skimmed across the ground. His own shadow seemed to be a hundred feet long.

Movement in the distance caught his eye. A man, a long object in his hand, was quick-walking to a dark-colored pickup pulled over at the side of the road beyond the field. The man went to the passenger door and got in. As the truck's aspect changed, a window flashed a sunset reflection and a dust cloud rose behind the truck. Three seconds later, the gruff noise of the engine reached Nick, and at that moment the sun surrendered the scene to dull gray twilight.

Nick walked the length of the dune but found no shell casings. Perhaps the shooter picked each one up.

The pond reflected the bright evening star Venus as Nick skidded down the dune. Ahead of him, in the still water, the shattered red canoe floated upside down like a bad memory.

He caught the driveway and followed it to Laura's house. The yard light created a scene of high contrast, and the gentle light inside the house welcomed him.

He strained to hear more footsteps behind him, quiet words of warning, an eruption of pasture birds. He refused to turn backward and look.

• • •

"Oh my God." Laura laughed when Nick rapped on her back door.

"I fell in," he said. "Your canoe broke."

"That old thing will never wear out," she said. "You, though . . ."

She shook her head and waved him in. "Take a shower. And don't track up my floor."

"Seriously, your canoe . . ."

"Just admit you fell in the mud," she said.

16

The casserole of potatoes au gratin and a plate of asparagus were already resting on trivets when Laura pulled a brace of salted ribeyes out of the broiler after four minutes on each side.

They ate like starving sailors.

"I don't think I'd ever get tired of this cooking," he said.

She blew him a kiss.

Nick had the whole time to tell her about the gunman at the pond, but he didn't.

Later, Nick and Laura sat in her bedroom watching the late Wichita news when the anchor presented an update on national reporting of an oddball celebrity in Kansas, a "how others see us" feature. The image switched to a photo of Kelli Ochs, whose smile was disconcerting against the words next to her: "Who will Kelli kill?"

"There she is, your breakfast date," Laura said, not kindly.

"What do people think of her?"

Laura waved the remote at the screen.

"This sums up the state. Kelli Ochs has driven around Kansas for a month, not really doing anything but posting on Facebook and TikTok that she's going to murder someone."

Nick thought Kelli was kind but carried anger and grief, like a soul who has felt the cold breath.

The story said she attended Fort Hays State University while in the National Guard. She was beloved by first-year students for coaching them in math, and she graduated at twenty-three with degrees in psychology and history. Then she worked six years at a catheter factory, climbing to a supervisory level before giving two weeks' notice at the end of January.

Nick asked, "Why's she doing this?"

"Why kill someone," Laura said, "or why post about it? Cops in three or four counties have threatened to arrest her, according to her posts, but she called their bluff because apparently there's no law against vague threats. She could be locked up in a mental hospital as a threat to herself or others, but there haven't been any pictures of her with guns or possible targets. The cops have searched her car, and there was never a weapon. And in the post–January 6 world, threats by public people are rarely prosecuted."

"Speaking professionally, though, her strategy seems counter-productive. Who's she after?"

"Who knows? Anyone from a foul teacher to a banker to a politician to someone who gave her a disease. She hasn't given anyone a clue. And now she's got people in other states trying to start the same game, and it's getting dangerous. People see it as Me Too mixed with the Hunger Games, and the whole thing is perfect for CNN and Fox." Laura spread her arms in exasperation. "And then we've got state officials patronizing her—'The little lady has some issues, and we're concerned about her.' That just riles up more people."

"In Russia," Nick said, "the government calls people it arrests crazy, because only crazy people would dare challenge the laws of the mighty will of the people. Everybody sees through that, because they were born knowing the government lies."

"I'm surprised she hasn't been shot dead by some dude who wants her pelt on his wall."

They paused to imagine that.

"The funny thing," Laura said, "is that Kelli's escapade has made everyone with even the smallest guilty conscience think about whether they're on the list. Or the next killer's list."

"What does the senator think?"

"She wants security when she's in the state. Maybe that's why Harriet hired you. Anyway, I haven't told the senator that you and Kelli are friends."

"Accidental sharers of a table is more like it." Nick explained how they had come to eat together so she wouldn't have to have breakfast next to a man playing with a knife. "She seemed nice."

"Most everyone seems to think she's just trying to become a TikTok star," Laura said, "maybe get a movie or reality show made about her and her cult of justice seekers. It doesn't hurt that she's cute and blond."

Nick was glad he wasn't bent toward conspiracies, because otherwise he'd wonder whether this was a long play by the FBI or Russians to take out the senator and him. Or maybe Gayfeather had sent a backup who was guarding her in secret against Nick.

It was something to think about, that Kelli Ochs was waiting at the diner Laura had recommended.

And now Nick was being trailed by his own mysterious gunman. Who will the stranger kill?

•   •   •

A Punisher decal—a comic-book symbol originally promising trouble to criminals, and lately co-opted by the criminals themselves, or those thinking of themselves as badasses—was the only political statement on Kelli Ochs' twelve-year-old Chevy Malibu.

Over five weeks starting in late April, the twenty-nine-year-old from western Kansas had been crisscrossing the Sunflower State in her pale-gray sedan. She had bought it in Hays from the family of a widow, paying seven thousand dollars cash. The woman's son had maintained it, and the four-cylinder engine had fifty-six thousand miles. It was the nicest car Kelli ever expected to own. She washed it weekly and had added six thousand miles to the odometer.

A saleswoman without a tangible product, Kelli chatted up folks in diners, college students in hangouts, other drivers as they pumped gas together, and the occasional sheriff's deputy.

The diners were all different but the same. There'd be a bottle-blond waitress in her sixties. A half-dozen hefty men and six skinny men wearing ball caps, each cap advertising an agribusiness brand or a vulgar political message. An old man would spill his coffee on the table and floor, and always a churchy lady in sneakers would spring forward to mop it up with her napkin. "You're so nice to me," he'd say, and she'd reply, "It wouldn't do us any good not to be."

The next customer would come in, ringing a bell over the door and letting in a blast of midday wind, and everybody would look up hoping to see someone they either knew or could gossip about. Tables were set with heavy white cups, Tuxton brand, made in China. The fork, knife, and spoon were rolled in a paper napkin sealed with a paper band, if it was a fancy place and the waitresses had extra time in the afternoon to fuss with silverware. Ice water was served in translucent, easy-to-grip cherry-red plastic glasses with slightly chipped lips. Guests ate from plates laid on white Formica, brown Formica, orange Formica, all of those colors worn out by elbows and bellies and coffee cups.

And no matter where Kelli Ochs was, her presentation was as familiar as the diners. Each conversation ended the same way. "Demand justice and accountability from those in power," she said. "I plan to kill someone because of injustice. It's not you."

In rural Kansas, common ground was hard to find when she was among older citizens. Younger listeners took her message to heart, not so much at first but more and more. City folks listened attentively and asked questions.

Many of Kelli's conversations were online. She had two Facebook accounts, one for her frequent posts and a secret account for "the responsible opposing viewpoint," on which she'd play devil's advocate. The second account supposedly was a troll, but a useful troll who would ask sharp questions that somehow helped Kelli make her point. She never ran short of useless trolls, mostly self-righteous women and men denouncing her for having opinions. Their messages could be simmered down to "Stay in your lane, get back in the kitchen, get laid, shut up, die."

Her TikTok viewers, who didn't overlap much with the Facebook audiences, were much more supportive. Short videos were also more fun to produce and publish than screeds. Her viral episodes of yoga and weightlifting casually revealed her five-foot-six physique, her two-sentence messages showed wisdom, and her jokes and spirited expressions enticed everyone who wanted or needed a friend.

She never showed herself with a weapon—no firearms, no knives, no ropes. As for her target, she never mentioned a name, a gender, a career field, a specific reason.

What she did best was raise the question of who should feel like her target. It quickly became a truism that people who spoke the most loudly against her had something to hide.

When she started, she amassed almost four hundred followers by the end of the first week. By the end of the second week, fifteen thousand. And now, after five weeks, more than three million people around the world were interested enough to commiserate with the downtrodden, laugh at the trolls, or just be abusive and coarse. And for every hundred trolls, there were ten souls who offered her their cooking, their shower, and a couch for the night.

· · ·

Despite all of Kelli's new friends, she had no one she was very close to.

She'd had a couple of boyfriends as she developed the dynamic persona she would use online, but she ended the first relationship to focus on her plan and dropped the second boyfriend when he tried to set rules about her behavior.

The biggest problem on the road became overeager guys. Touch them once on the shoulder, she discovered, and they think you're theirs to stalk.

And cops. Four times already she had fended off being arrested on false charges by giving sheriff's deputies a hand job. It seemed like the smart thing to do. She had no doubt that a spurned, embarrassed deputy could always find official cover to kill her. The rule of law didn't offer much protection to poor rabble-rousers traveling alone.

She followed all the rules: no videos or photos taken while driving, and no images of children. She posted regularly in the morning and afternoon. One day last week she overslept, waking to a panicked audience speculating that she had been arrested or killed. They demanded answers.

Five weeks of feeding the digital beast day in and day out, in city after city, town after town, used up her savings. She thought of herself as a rogue broadcaster, like old-time legends Wolfman Jack and Goat Glands Brinkley, their radio stations broadcasting from Mexico, but she posted her broadcasts from cellphones bought in bulk two months earlier in Nebraska, Missouri, and Iowa and used for only one day each.

On her more paranoid days, she felt like Saddam Hussein, always on the run after being deposed when the US military invaded Iraq in 2003. The difference between her and Saddam was that she operated openly in the thin layer of society between the criminals and the self-righteous.

She had no real friends, but she had a plan.

17

Laura started off Friday by showing Nick the wild parts of the ranch. There were the songbirds and the thermal-riding hawks, the squawking crows and the buzzing damselflies. Laura named a dozen flowering plants, what he had mistakenly called weeds. He was taken aback when a five-foot bull snake hissed at them.

"Unless you're a rat, you don't have anything to fear," she said.

"I've been called worse," he said.

Dressed in jeans and sneakers, and she with a backpack, they made their way to the eastern side of the property. Laura had him hush and stand motionless. Within a couple of minutes, a dozen black-tailed prairie dogs climbed out of gentle mounds, watching the sky and the people before scampering away to chew on grass. A hawk approached out of the sun, and immediately the air was full of squeals and the acre almost simultaneously was empty of dogs.

"They have tunnels and chambers and spend a lot of time down there, day or night," Laura said. "It's a whole society under the surface. They mate, sleep, nurse. They can make it night anytime they want."

"It sounds like a good life."

"Can you believe that guys beg me for access onto the property just to shoot these dogs?" Laura said. "What would they get out of that, killing a bunch of three-pound dudes?"

Finally Nick and Laura made it to Salt Creek, a languid stream. They backed down the bank and paused in the current, letting it press against their calves.

"This is beautiful," he said.

"People always ask why anyone would live here," she said. "Well, it's because of this. There's still a mystery about what's beyond the next dune, around the other side of the cottonwoods, what colors the sunset will be, the power of the storm. You've been in the Arkansas before, so you know how pretty the rocks are that get washed down from Colorado. When we live on the plains, seeking out these mysteries is what makes us better people."

"You're lucky to have this," Nick said. "It's certainly not Wichita."

Laura nodded. She began talking with her hands, drawing the path of Salt Creek in the air.

"Rattlesnake Creek feeds into it from the south, but a lot of water comes from the refuge itself," she said. "It's like any old flat-land stream. It wiggles back and forth, and when there's a river flood and the creek backs up, sometimes it'll cut through a bend and make a new channel. What's left is an oxbow pond, and those are little wildlife refuges in themselves. And sometimes I find bones washing out of the banks. Horse skulls, that kind of thing."

At the second oxbow, sleek leopard frogs startled by human footsteps and shadows splashed to safety in deeper water and thicker brush. One frog, however, didn't sense the great blue heron standing quietly, and so played its role in the circle of life.

"You know this place pretty well?"

"When I was a kid, I camped here, right by those trees. There was more water then, before the water table got pumped down by irrigators and feedlots."

They followed the creek east until they came to a point that Laura said was a quarter-mile up from the Arkansas River. From a bank three feet high, she pointed into the clear water.

"There in the shallows," she said. "The perc spring. No algae, no minnows, no tadpoles. No beavers or muskrats. It's like that for a hundred yards downstream. It's been like that for at least a month."

Nick shaded his eyes against the glare. He sniffed something sweet with an edge, and in a moment he realized it was what his clothes smelled like after he picked them up at the dry-cleaner.

"Do you smell it? The dead zone," she said. "Perchloroethylene. It's a solvent."

"I thought it would be bubbling," he said. "Boiling up."

"Four weeks ago, it was, pushing up against the surface. It's apparently under less pressure now."

"So it's safer?"

She shook her head.

"Don't drink it. Don't even wade in it if you want to walk in my house again."

"I won't."

She wagged her finger at Nick.

"You didn't ask, but here's what really pisses me off."

"What really pisses you off?"

"This is Salt Creek, okay. It flows out of the Quivira salt marsh."

"Sure," he said.

"Does any part of that name sound familiar? One guess which multinational oil and chemical giant got its start almost a hundred years ago by drilling within a mile of here."

"Saltwood?"

"They appropriated the idea of what's now my creek, and now they're killing the creek. The perc is nothing, relatively. It'll evaporate and go harmless in the wind, unless you sniff it hard. Then you'll probably have a headache, or get confused or want to throw up. You might ruin your liver or kidneys. But the chemicals that escaped with the perc are poisoning my creek and the river."

Nick swatted at a gnat, a flock of gnats, around his ears.

"This is my home," Laura said. "My pump draws water from the big belly of sand below the creek. That's where the chemical plume is spreading."

"Can't the state do anything about it?"

"Maybe, by feeding microbes into the plume to eat the chemicals, or sparging it with holes to let air neutralize them. But this stuff can stick around for years. We have a conservative legislature, a talent show of has-been talent, so it probably won't do anything. If PETRO passes, nobody will ever do anything about it."

"What worries you the most?"

"The most?" she said. "Which cancers will the chemicals cause in Bull Creek and in Hutchinson, in Wichita, on farms along the way? In me? What's going to be pumped up and drunk by families and sprayed on irrigated corn? What will fishermen carry home to their tables? It's bad enough that the surface water is already tainted by herbicides and pesticides and feedlot runoff. What will happen to little kids wading in the water on Saturday afternoons?"

Laura found an old muskrat slide in the grass and half-stepped, half-slid sideways down to the creek. She opened a small jar and dipped it into the creek at the spring, then screwed the lid on tightly and sealed it inside a zip-lock plastic bag.

"Have you called the EPA or the state water people?"

"No. The EPA banned most uses of perc when Biden was leaving the White House, but companies got years to stop using it. And the EPA now, who knows? Still, something's being done."

"But what about this spill? If you're so afraid of it, why the hell not tell the people downstream?

"Because a river scientist got me to avoid the Environmental Protection Agency and the state agencies. He was studying how much the water table was dropping, and diverting to study a single leak would take too much of his time."

"Wow."

"Yep. I was a wuss."

"I heard that the river used to be much higher."

"Kansas tries to be something it isn't. It has never really been the Great American Desert, but by sucking so much irrigation water out of the riverbeds and the Ogallala Aquifer, it's going to be. The state is farmed within an inch of its life."

"There's irrigation everywhere I look."

"This hydrologist, Dr. Cletus Purkeypyle . . ."

"Not his real name."

"'Fraid so. He was testing out here on the river as part of his post-doctoral work at Kansas State University. Current flow, tributaries, turbidity, nutrient load, erosive forces, loss of groundwater to trees, that kind of stuff. Prairie fires used to keep water-sucking trees out."

"Smart guy?"

She nodded.

"Clete, in his ivory tower wisdom, wanted to suggest ways to intervene with voluntary actions by farmers, ranchers, and towns. The problem is that Kansas has always been steadfast in avoiding doing what's in its own best interest."

"Surely not the only place to do that."

"A big part of the Dust Bowl in the '20s and '30s was caused by farmers overplanting to scrape every penny out of the postwar wheat market. Now it's all about irrigation to grow corn and alfalfa for the cattle feedlots, plus soybeans for foreign markets, such as they are. The farmers will get their bucks and their government subsidies, and then they'll complain about the size of the subsidies and demand more support when the aquifers dry up. For the record, Gayfeather supports the farmers. Off the record, she doesn't support them very loudly."

She double-bagged the water sample and put it in her pack, then got out bottled water for each of them.

"Clete wanted to nail down the source of the pollution before everything got tangled up in red tape and yellow tape and tapeworms for all I know. He needed Saltwood's cooperation to see whether it was their well, before he pissed them off."

"This sounds messy."

"Life is messy. God knows, my life is messy. Oilfield history is grade-A messy. And good ol' Clete pissed off Saltwood."

"And now he's hiding?" Nick paused. "Seems like a good time to call the water people."

"Here's the deal. My water well is shallow and can pull five hundred gallons a minute. That's way more than I need. But I had to buy a water tank and have it refilled until I'm sure the groundwater is clean. So I'm testing this water every two weeks to see whether it's worth undercutting my property value to make any of this public."

"That seems . . . selfish."

"Maybe so, but it's how any of us out here would do it. If Saltwood's going to pay, I'm golly damn going to be first in line."

They began to walk back to the house. Nick finished his water and squeezed the bottle flat and wedged it into his pocket. It squeaked with every stop.

"You have an oil well," he said. "Aren't you part of the problem?"

"It's an old stripper well that's been there for a couple of decades, and I watch for leaks in the pipeline from the pump jack to the storage tanks over there. There've been two little leaks ever that I know of. It's shallow, it doesn't use fracking, and it's not a disposal well. A vacuum truck picks up the oil, and every month a royalty deposit appears in my bank account. Those kinds of wells are necessary, but they have to be done right. Demanding that does not make me a hypocrite. It pisses me off that Saltwood holds the lease."

They were heading back into the house when Nick said, "Golly damn?"

"It's a politeness thing."

Laura opened a snack bag. "You know what?" she said, working her words around a chickpea puff. "We could use a break. Let's take a drive around the refuge, look for deer."

•　　•　　•

Laura lay flat, bracing her hands against the low concrete curb of a short bridge spanning a small stream in the Quivira refuge. It was the third time they'd stopped her rattling pickup along the yellow-sand road, the third culvert along the eastern rim of this segment of the marsh. She tugged her seed-company cap on tighter, snugged down her old demin shirt and scooched forward far enough to bend down to see into the bridge's shade.

Nick sat in the truck, swatting at flies, and switching the radio from one canned station to the next. He rolled down the window, flinching at the screech, and called out, "Anything new under this one?"

"Two carp," she said. "Minnows and water striders and mosquito larvae. No deer. Same as everywhere else."

They pulled into an observation point along the northern rim of the large pool. The breeze enveloped them in the scent of mud and decay, but Nick breathed deeply.

Laura shoved him a bit. "Don't step in that." He was two inches from landing on a pile of scat. "Coyote poop."

They sat on the ground, back a couple of feet from the water's edge on a spot with the fewest anthills, and there was no shelter from the sun or wind. Their jeans, long-sleeve shirts, and ball caps were comfortable enough, but still the two sat shoulder to shoulder while she looked around with field glasses.

"Quivira has a couple of big marshes and some smaller wetlands. This area gets twenty-eight inches of rain a year, so it's more lush than places not far to the west." She laughed. "Do you like my geography lesson? I don't get many assassins here, and it's fun to show off."

"I do. But if it's okay, I'll recommend that no one send more assassins this way for a while. It's a killer assignment."

Laura squeezed her lips together, then laughed.

"Anyway, Quivira is federal and it's more of a natural site than Cheyenne Bottoms, an enhanced swamp north of here, outside Great Bend. They had to divert water from the river through a canal to a creek to another canal to fill it. It has lots of Central Flyway birds too.

"Over there," Laura said, pointing east with her field glasses, "is where Rattlesnake Creek passes north through the refuge. It comes up from southwest Kansas and gives fresh water to the south marsh. Up here, the Rattlesnake joins Salt Creek, which drains the north marsh and crosses my land going to the river. I used to fish for bullheads in there."

"Is this all salty?"

"The marsh water contains salt and gypsum. It's too brackish to drink. The water where my pump reaches is below this. It's groundwater that's more associated with the river, flowing through the sand. But there's a lot of salt, because Kansas is the bottom of what used to be an inland sea. There's a salt mine up in Lyons and another under Hutchinson. I think there used to be one in Sandstone, where you were. Oil companies pipe away a lot of saltwater when they drill through a layer of salt, and they usually stuff it into a deep wastewater well."

"Kansas is a land of surprises."

"Okay, here's another bit of trivia. Almost all the streams south of the Arkansas around here were called salty by whites or the tribes. The Rattlesnake, especially after it joined with the Salt, was known as Salt Creek the last few miles to the Arkansas. The feds changed its official name of that part to Rattlesnake in the 1970s. Here, it's all about salt, and this creek is very salty.

"So, in my world, on my land, the stream remains Salt Creek."

•   •   •

"What about live animals? I don't see much wildlife here."

"Watch those reeds in the water. Use these binoculars, and you'll see redwing blackbirds hanging on to rushes. Over there, wading along the shore, are black-neck stilts. It's the middle of the day, so most of the mammals are asleep or hiding out. The refuge lets some cattle graze here, to imitate the bison that were here before. They trim the grass, fertilize the soil, stir it up with their hooves. In the summer, there'll be thousands of white pelicans out there. "

She pointed to a stand of cattails where turtles were sunning themselves on a half-submerged log. "And there's a water snake. See how it floats?"

"People would kill for a place out here," he said.

"Tell me more," she said dismissively.

Laura took back the glasses, eyeing the length of the road and each stand of cattails.

"Maybe they wouldn't kill for it," she said, "but there's a lot of money involved."

He raised his eyebrows. "Does the refuge sell its water?"

"Remember how Purkeypyle was looking for evidence that the river water was being used up by the biologically recent arrival of trees and brush along the bed? His project was following up on a decision by federal Fish and Wildlife to not complain that farmers out west were pumping groundwater and lowering the water table, which meant that the Rattlesnake was bringing less water to the refuge. Kansas' other senator, not Harriet, supported giving irrigators, a.k.a. campaign donors, the first right to the water. The aquifer out west went down more than a foot a year ago."

Laura waved at the open water.

"Oil companies have drilled around Quivira for decades without a problem. But if they spill anything now, it's going to be obvious and there'll be a big cleanup cost and public-relations problem."

"I'm guessing that's already happened."

Laura tucked her cap under her arm and swept her hair back.

"After Clete found the dead zone in Salt Creek," she said, "he tested it there, downstream, and upstream." She mimed scooping up liquid and tightening the lid of a jar.

"The first question was, 'What chemicals are here?' And then it's 'Where did they come from at a rate of eight gallons a minute?'"

"And . . ."

"And the third question, 'Where is it going?'"

Purkeypyle needed samples from sites in the refuge and from ditches and wells outside it.

"That was anyplace where fluids could be dumped or pumped," she said. "That included the Saltwood well. There are a number of working wells on leases in the refuge, but Saltwood's is the only new one."

"Doesn't pumping take out oil and water?"

"Water and chemicals are also pumped in as lubrication and to wash out the rock that's ground up in the drilling. And if the drillers are fracking, they're using an unholy mixture of chemicals. Although," she said, "it could be that the drillers are just drilling a deep hole so they can inject a million gallons of dirty water from other wells so it's safe, way below the aquifer."

"Just before the explosion, your pal who was killed said they were drilling for oil, not for injection. Would any of that use perc?"

"Nope. What makes it a real puzzle is that Kansas was slow to regulate the dumping of perc, because the dry-cleaning lobbyists owned enough of the legislature. So it's possible that the perc came from some other source—dumped in a ditch, poured into one of the conservation pools here, piped in through some forgotten pipeline from a storage tank miles away. Clete needed to test all the possible sources to rule them out. If they didn't have perc, he wasn't interested."

"What was the problem?"

"He thought that if the chemicals found with the perc matched the composition of what was in the Saltwood well's mud, it would prove that the leak resulted from the well. It could be shameless dumping, he thought, or even a burst well casing in a soft spot in the soil."

"He'd have a direct link to the source of pollution. What then?"

"Perc isn't the only problem. It's a carcinogen, but it loses potency. The other serious concern is the other chemicals and maybe the petroleum itself that show up with the perc. The perc is just the canary in the mine."

"Why would Saltwood set itself up that way?"

"They didn't get where they are through self-sabotage. But if Clete tracked that chemical trail to the well, every downstream farm and city would have a deep-pockets corporation to sue for damages and remediation. And then you're talking real money—enough to annoy even Saltwood."

"Does the water you have delivered come from a place that's safe from the leak?"

"Maybe not, since it's from Bull Creek," she said. "But the volume of water in the riverbed might push the plume down past town, so I have more time."

"Gayfeather's timing with the PETRO bill is pretty lucky, if no one finds out about the leak until the president signs it," Nick said.

"Yeah, that dang PETRO Act. If it's enacted, it could be the death of life along the river. If it doesn't pass, it might be the death of her career, because her lobbyist donations would dry up."

"There's one guy who could settle this," he said. "Where's the hero? Where's Purkeypyle?"

•　　•　　•

"You have a driver's license?"

"State of Virginia," he said, and caught the keys. Laura said she'd rather watch for whitetails while he drove.

The steering wheel was tight in his grip. He tested the suicide knob, its scratched orange acrylic fastened tight with a hose clamp at 2 o'clock on the wheel. On the way over, Laura had steered with the knob, which let her turn the wheel completely with just one hand. Everything felt solid but used hard. She said her grandpa had bought the truck new in 1989.

It might be too much for Nick to say he was delighted by driving, but he was grinning. Seeing for miles was optimal. They passed an area where bright green shoots rose through the black ashes of last year's grass.

"We're close to the explosion site, right?" he asked. "Did the blast cause this fire?"

"Probably not," she said. "The managers burn off grass in the spring to kill saplings and keep the overall fire hazard down. Fire's a part of nature out here. It's all healthy. Look at the road, and you'll see fresh deer prints."

Laura cleared her throat. "So, back to the leak," she said. "At first, Clete wanted to tell everyone about the pollution. Call the newspapers, the TV stations, put it on the web."

"But then . . ."

"But then he started hedging his desire for glory. He said he should nail everything down first. Get his results. Build his spreadsheets. Map everything."

"That's logical."

"But I think he realized that as soon as he went public, he'd be targeted by the oil, chemical, and cleaning industries. Ranchers who depend on their oil royalties and center-pivot irrigation would want to kill him. Inspectors would be everywhere with their drones and high-resolution photos and chemical sniffers and utility records, so all the ranchers growing pot also would be at risk."

Nick laughed. She didn't.

"His contract at K-State would protect him, but how long could that last? If he made any mistakes or got on the wrong side of politicians, million-dollar grants could be held up for years. It would end his career and maybe his life. What agency under the Republicans would hire someone known to be against oil?"

"He's a grownup with choices," Nick said. "You have an oil well and work for Gayfeather, but you suspect that you have dirty water. Didn't he take people like you into consideration?"

"That's where it gets really ugly," she said. "Morally."

•   •   •

A year ago, while still a doctoral student, Purkeypyle published a book about riverine ecology, Laura said, and he had been interviewed by the *Wichita Eagle*. The Saltwood people bandwagoned on that and asked to sponsor two years of his research at K-State.

"He couldn't turn down a quarter of a million dollars and access to a lab," she said.

"But there's more to the story, I bet," Nick said.

Laura tucked her leg under and turned to face Nick, which distracted him so quickly that he nearly T-boned a whitetail buck that popped out from behind a sandhill plum. Not missing a beat, Laura braced herself against the braking and swerving.

"Clete's wife. A second-year law-school student in Topeka. He said she was too immature and demanding, so he accepted the Saltwood grant to get her off his back. She got most of the money, and he got to be on the river. Everybody wins."

Nick was fiddling with the suicide knob, spinning it under his palm as if he were twisting on and off a jar lid.

"But then the chemical leak showed up in his river samples," Laura said, "and he traced it up Salt Creek. He was ecstatic. He wouldn't talk about anything else. Saltwood figured out that something was up when he asked to take samples from the well. The company told him outright that he wasn't being paid to observe that one. Put another way, he was being paid not to.

"At that point," she said, "Saltwood might not have even known about the leak but just didn't want to take the chance that something had gone wrong at Quivira. A lot of their second-tier executives probably hunt ducks and geese there, and they didn't want to spoil their welcome."

"Is it possible that Purkeypyle bombed the well site?"

"I don't think he would've hurt the workers. He might've done it if he could've gotten the big shots."

"So, where is this guy?"

"Gone. I don't know where. Nobody talks about him."

"Just up and left?" Nick was driving now with only his right hand on the suicide knob.

"He was going radical. Like the Earth Firsters. Or even like the Tea Party, ragging on oil companies even though the big oil companies created the Tea Party. Maybe he went out west and joined a militia."

Nick stopped the truck at the intersection with the county road.

"Were you two close?"

"What?"

Nick held up two fingers together.

"No. Different worlds. And Jesus, Nick, can you imagine me hanging around with someone named Cletus Purkeypyle?"

18

Nick wondered whether he had pissed off Laura, who had gone silent after he pressed her about Purkeypyle. At last, as they turned onto the county road that'd take them to the ranch's driveway, she found her voice.

"Don't you dare tell the senator I said this," she said, "but it's suspicious that her boyfriend from Saltwood flew back to Wichita the night before the explosion, just in time to drive up to the well right after the explosion."

Nick agreed. "If you and I hadn't been there, no one would've known."

"Given the way the world is now, I kind of think Saltwood is making a play with or against the Russians, or the Chinese. If the company can get Congress to play along with American drillers and to deregulate the industry, they could undercut the world market and still make enormous profits."

"And Gayfeather's part of that?"

"Willingly or not," she said. "She's not stupid."

"But money . . ."

"It's the second biggest oil and chemical company based in Kansas, and it too is privately held," she said. "It owns dozens of subsidiaries and runs seven refineries around the world. Saltwood used to have a decent reputation. They'll remodel museums and give a million dollars to universities for an arena or to influence business-school professors. They sponsor soccer leagues for kids.

"But," she continued, "that's chump change for a multi-billion-dollar private corporation and its band of half-percenters. They've bought off hundreds of legislators and judges around the country, some for as little as two hundred dollars and the cachet of being recognized by a big oil company. And now, with this president and Congress, Saltwood has a chance to make a killing."

Laura was jabbing her finger at Nick.

"See, we have our own oligarchs. Just like you Russians."

"Russian by heritage," he said. "Not Russian anymore."

"I hope that's true," she said. "If I'm going to be killed in my sleep, I don't want it to be by a Russian."

Nick smiled until he saw how earnest Laura was.

"Maybe the next war will not be between nations but between oligarchs and their corporations," he said.

"Saltwood's political action committees have corrupted the political system in Kansas and the rest of the oil states. Look at Congress. Gayfeather gets half a million a year from Saltwood. PACs make politicians do crazy things."

"The world over," he said.

She snorted.

"Were you in Alaska," Laura said, "when old Frank Murkowski gave up his Senate seat in exchange for being governor? He appointed his daughter, Lisa, to the Senate as his legacy, but really, who thinks about leaving the Senate in his fourth term to run a regressive state that was basically a colony of Seattle and British Petroleum? Maybe he thought that if he didn't appoint Lisa, who became a decent senator, the seat would be filled by some fool. And even though Murkowski politicked hard to open the Arctic National Wildlife Refuge to oil drilling, he lasted a single term as governor. He was beaten in the primary by Sarah Palin, who quit halfway through her term and was succeeded by a guy who actually worked for an oil company."

"That happened before I was there," he said. "But the bigger thing is that I think you don't like oil companies and corporate welfare. Why are you a Republican?"

"I used to believe our party was good people," she said. "But you've seen what it's become. Our legislation is so obviously self-serving that it has to be greased for the public's sake. So we create fear. Like some vague but immediate threat to our energy independence."

"Isn't that tactic obvious? It's so clear that you can spell it out standing in a field with coyote poop."

"We're not the folks who count, bucko. Most of the people around here are level headed, but you'll still find regular evangelicals lining up with the hardline Christian nationalists to be used by the Project 2025 overseers. And the libertarians. All those people without empathy."

Laura said under her breath, a whisper: "Screw it. Just screw it." She rolled down her window and screamed into the wind.

19

Karlton Cooper left his fifth message with the church receptionist and clicked his phone off. Pastor Luke hadn't called him back, and the receptionist said she'd heard nothing about any jobs. And here it was Friday afternoon.

Where was Jesus, the man of miracles, when you needed him?

The end of the month was coming fast. With the short paycheck Karlton was handed on his way out of the store, he'd have to kneel before the landlord.

The day had started with hope. After calling Pastor's office to see whether any job leads had fallen from Heaven—"I'm sorry," the receptionist lied, "but Pastor Luke has gone to the lake to work on his sermon. I'll be glad to take your message."—he had driven to two grocery stores and a Target, filling out applications.

"We'll let you know," each assistant manager had said.

His fourth application was filed at yet another Walmart. He had come here only twice before, because he was almost perfectly loyal to the store where he worked.

It was dispiriting to find so little was different from one store to the other. He wondered whether he'd ever see Walmart as a happy place again.

He wandered through the grocery aisles, thinking that maybe he could try shoplifting. He got trapped behind a guy about his age who had too much neck hair above the stretched collar of his T-shirt, pushing a shopping cart containing a little blond girl who listened intently to her dad's phone conversation.

". . . Like your sister," the guy said, "working with kids that are crazy. She don't have any right to be around kids that are crazy. She's batshit crazy herself."

Karlton thought: Another day at Walmart, another real-world shopper.

He found the right assistant manager and filled in another application. The assistant manager had known Karlton from the other store before getting promoted to this one, and after he checked his computer he gestured for Karlton to have a seat.

"I'm sorry, my friend," he said. "I didn't know you'd been let go. But we can't hire you."

Karlton looked down at his hands.

"Your file says you were fired because a customer filed complaints against you. The same customer each time. A Ms. Huckstep. She said you were rude once and insulting, gosh, a half-dozen times. All of the complaints were made in the two days before you were let go."

Karlton opened his mouth, but then figured, What's the use? Without a word, he nodded, stood up, and turned away. Like a zombie on the edge of tears, he walked out through the sliding doors.

In the sun's glare, he stopped to collect his thoughts.

A woman churned toward him, shouting, "Wait. Wait!" Her black pants were adorned with yellow blossoms. Under her mud-colored shirt, her breasts heaved like an angry sea. Her plastic clogs grunted: "clomp grate, clomp grate."

It was Braylynn Huckstep.

She seized his arm as she leaned over to catch her breath.

"Thank God I caught you," she said. "Go back inside and get me some chicken."

Karlton shook her hand off and headed toward ODIN, but then he spun around and got something off his chest: "Your name is stupid. It should have an *e* at the end."

Braylynn screamed, "I'm telling the manager you were rude to me."

He flipped her the bird and went on to his car.

•   •   •

Karlton put ten dollars' worth in ODIN's gas tank and drove for a while to calm his nerves. On the south side of town, on a street with heavy trucks, he bounced his car hard over the curb and into Kan-Do Pawn's gravel parking lot.

The pawnshop, squatting at the end of a row of airplane-industry shops, started out as a pizza restaurant, then became a Chinese restaurant before settling into its present occupation. The brick exterior had big windows around the front and two sides, with a glass door on one side between the window and former kitchen. Steel bars protected the windows, and a collapsible metal gate was drawn back from the door.

Karlton parked and thought about this. Pay the rent, hang on for another month, Jesus will send a job. Jesus wasn't sending it fast enough. Jesus wasn't the one who'd have to move back in with Mother.

Karlton reached under his seat and pulled out a white plastic shopping bag containing his revolver. He always left it in the car, because the car had never been ransacked.

It was a Smith & Wesson Model 629, a .44 Magnum. Forty-one and a half ounces. Six-and-a-half-inch barrel. It was the biggest handgun Walmart sold back then. Heavy hollow-point bullets that could kill a moose and make a mess doing it.

Karlton had bought it shortly after he started working there because the big guy, Warren Snarr, said shooting it would make him a man. Warren, who had worked at a couple of pawnshops, also told him how the shops work in case he needed to sell the gun.

He settled the checkered wooden grip in his right palm and ran his left index finger over the stainless steel barrel. It was big in his hand. With his thumb, he released the cylinder and spun it. Five bullets left, plus an empty shell.

With a flip of his wrist, he snapped the cylinder back into place. He smiled at the solid sound of metal on metal. It was the best-made thing he'd ever owned.

Karlton pulled back the hammer and sighted down the barrel at a trash can behind the pawnshop. He remembered the first time, the only time, he had fired the .44. The day after he bought it, he drove out into the empty part of the next county and found a stop sign to shoot at. He flinched with muscle memory. His ears had screamed with pain, and the recoil from the gun felt like it had nearly torn his hand off.

He would be prepared this time.

Karlton had never robbed a store before. He did remember talking with Warren Snarr one day at work about how Warren would do it, not that he ever would.

"What has to be done has to be done," Karlton told himself. "Even when it sucks."

He opened the car door and slid the revolver under his belt at the back of his jeans. Out of the corner of his eye, he noticed that another chunk of Bondo had cracked off his fender.

Maybe Pastor Luke was right about the car. Karlton would worry about it later.

He pulled the shop's door open under a tinkling bell. The pawnshop's clerk, a barrel-trunked man draped in a black leather vest, already had his right hand on his cocked but holstered 9-millimeter semiautomatic when Karlton sidled into the air conditioning.

Karlton first examined power tools, then ran his hands over fiberglass fishing rods poking out of a trash can. No matter where he went, he stood so he faced the clerk. He was the only customer.

"First thing," the clerk said, almost shouting, "I want you to use two fingers to lift that revolver out of your pants and lay it here on this pad." He tapped a rubber mat on the top of a glass cabinet where fancy watches were displayed.

"What're you talking about?"

"We got cameras. I seen you stick it in your belt." He pointed a thumb at two screens behind him;

Karlton saw himself and stood up straighter.

"I got a right to carry," he said, puffing up his chest but careful to not let the heavy revolver twist out of its nest.

"I got a right to shoot you," the clerk said.

"Hey, man. I just want to sell it to you."

"We'll talk when it's out in the open. Don't bullshit me."

Karlton wanted this to go faster. Customers could arrive anytime, and then there'd be witnesses. He bent his head over and raised his shoulder to rub his ear.

"Can you pay cash for it?" He walked slowly to the counter.

"Gun out, dude."

Karlton raised his left hand, and with his right reached with care for the checkered grip of his .44.

The clerk wrapped his fingers around the butt of his weapon. He braced his left hand on the counter.

Sweat slid down Karlton face. His guts were jelly. He was close enough now to see the clerk's nametag: Wayne.

"It's okay," he said. "I'm not going to do anything."

Karlton pressed two fingers onto the grip and lifted. When he shifted his hand to carry the weight better, the clerk squinted and seemed to get edgy.

"I'm taking it out now," Karlton said.

"Turn and let me see."

Karlton swiveled his hips a few degrees to the left.

Wayne chuckled. "Don't shoot your own ass off."

Karlton's spontaneous decision to just shoot the guy was interrupted when the .44's front sight tickled his lower back. He grimaced and instinctively bent backward.

Wayne reacted like a quick-draw gunslinger, thumbing down the safety but bringing the pistol smack up into the back of the glass cabinet. He jerked the trigger unintentionally, and the gun leaped out of his hand as it fired into the shelf of watches.

When he raised his eyes, the only thing Wayne saw was the big barrel pointing from Karlton's waist. The last thing Wayne saw was the hammer of the .44 start to move. He blinked.

Karlton staggered, dropping the .44. He had sprained his wrist again. He stuck his fingers in his screaming ears and was surprised they weren't bleeding.

Wayne wasn't bleeding much either. Karlton's bullet had gone right through the center of his chest, and he collapsed, a pile of flesh and clothes behind the cash register.

•   •   •

A year ago, Karlton and Warren Snarr were BS-ing as they ate at Walmart's employee picnic table. Warren described the methods used by a friend of his who robbed stores.

Don't worry about the body, the list began. It's fine behind the counter. Secure your .44. Find the keys. Pull the door's metal gate shut and lock it. Lock the glass door. Turn off the "open" sign. Find the digital video recorder. Remove the memory cards and put them in your pocket. Ignore the safe if it's not open. Take the bills from the cash register. Search the guy's pockets. Look for a cash box. Don't take anything else, because it's listed in the ledger. Turn off the lights. Make sure you have your gun. Wipe down everything. Ease out the back door and lock it. Walk casually to the car. Don't look around. Drop the video cards into a trash can on the way home. Get rid of the gun.

•   •   •

It wasn't until Karlton was in a discount barber's chair having his hair trimmed above the ears that he realized that he could've blown out his own spine if he had touched the trigger when he lifted the .44 out of his belt.

He broke out in a sweat, beads gathering on his forehead.

The barber stopped cutting.

"Everything OK, Karlton? You don't look so good."

"Sure. Life's good."

But he thought: It could've been all over. Go to God, Garmr, whoever. I should just kill myself. Or kill Pastor. He promised to help me get work, and now I'm going to Hell. Or prison.

"Tell you what," he told the barber. "Cut it all off. The mustache and beard, too. I want to be bald."

"You got it."

As the barber wiped the last of the shaving cream off, Karlton was thinking: Pastor and his thoughts and prayers and lake cabin. I bet he's out there with Green Dress, cheating on ol' Christmas Pastor.

"Yes, sir. You got a fine-looking head, Karlton. Needs a little sun, though."

Karlton stared at his shiny white dome in the mirror. If he looked at just his eyes and mouth, he'd recognize himself. He doubted anyone else would. Now he was just another tough son of a bitch.

He paid for the haircut and shave with the pawnshop's money, and had $822 left over to help with the rent.

Life would go on.

•   •   •

Karlton stood at his front door, a bag of NuWay crumbled-meat sandwiches at his feet, and looked around at his neighborhood as he fiddled with his keys. His life was different now. He was a felon, no doubt about it. He'd need to survive on his wits.

His neighbor unlatched open her screen door.

"He ain't here," Braylynn Huckstep said. "Who're you?"

He took his time to turn and show her his deadest expression. There wasn't any recognition in her eyes, nothing on her face but nosiness.

He turned away. Time had slowed down.

A man drove past, left to right, in his rust-patched pickup with a brown steel fuel tank nestled against the cab. His windows were open and he was blowing a duck call.

The house across the street was losing its light-green paint in big flakes. Three years ago Karlton had sold the owner the paint, tried to sell primer to go with it, but the owner didn't have the money for primer.

Chain-link fences up and down the street, yards containing antsy chihuahuas and pit bulls treading paths inside the fences. Tired pickups in gravel driveways, oil spots in paved driveways, and oil-patched cracks in the street. In the yard at the corner, big lilacs shuffled in the wind, dark green in a yard of gone-to-seed crab grass.

A hollow-wheeled plastic tricycle sat where one of the kids had left it on the sidewalk. No one would steal it. No one cared.

Karlton picked up his sandwiches and got back to his neighbor. She was prattling on, louder now, about how Karlie owed her money for Walmart chicken as soon as he got home. She grabbed for his bag of sandwiches, and he slammed her arm against the wall.

She was stunned. He caught her eyes, holding them for a beat.

"Fuck off," he growled.

He unlocked the door. He went inside. He shut the door. Before he had turned the deadbolt she was already there: knocking, pounding, cursing.

He pulled his chair close the aquarium and ate in front of his three goldfish. One of them hovered just inside the glass and stared at him, its mouth opening and closing, and he wondered whether the fish knew who Karlton was: God. He made the manna fall, he drained the red sea (green, really). He took the dead away and brought new life.

The notion came to Karlton that he lived in God's fish tank. Some faceless God that the people thought looked out for them but really kept them around for amusement and was troubled only when he had to get out the net.

Dead fish went down the toilet. Where did dead people go?

•   •   •

Karlton's phone buzzed just once that evening, shortly after he had turned on his box fan and gotten under the sheet of his double bed. It was a text from Warren Snarr, who two days earlier had walked him out the back door at Walmart:

> Bummer u lost job to mex. Ur our bro. Want to join us? 9 Sat nite
> @ Emils. Beers on me.

20

Senator Harriet Gayfeather stared mindlessly at farmland and small towns Friday afternoon until Wichita slid into view outside the window of the American Eagle CRJ7 twinjet. It had been three weeks since she had been in her native state and adopted hometown.

She was bored with Wichita, with its endless squabbling over tax giveaways to billionaire oilmen and airplane-factory executives. She hated being asked to campaign for insurance sharps, county attorneys, and scions of wealthy families who wanted a state legislator in the family.

Gayfeather had been first elected to the Senate at age forty-one, then re-elected a couple of years ago. Serving as one of America's least popular senators, judging from Facebook postings, had nudged her emotionally and physically a little past her actual years. She got her blond hair brightened every six weeks, battling subtle streaks that were trending gray, but she was fit and electric and maintained the look of a woman who would never appear old.

Gayfeather was comfortable with her political opinions—pro-women's health, not anti-immigrant, and dismissive of the National Rifle Association's fear-inciting campaigns—and usually voted with the party majority on the budget and military bills. She had never asked a president to endorse her campaigns.

She didn't need the job anymore, exactly. A secret contract with a Chinese business group to steer sales of agricultural commodities brought $50 million a year in tax-free income into her secret offshore bank accounts. The administration's trade policies with China would either screw that up or make it even more profitable.

But the whole deal could be spoiled by her snotty assistant, Laura Eisenhauer, who let people think she was a great-granddaughter or distant cousin of Dwight Eisenhower, the Kansas-grown World War II heroic general and two-term president. Eisenhauer suspected something, Gayfeather knew, but the kid didn't have the street smarts to put it together. One way or another, Nick Deveraux would have to make her go away.

The senator's situation of living in a brick house in a flat city in a landlocked state that was a three-and-a-half-hour direct flight to Reagan National Airport in Washington, even longer on layover flights to New York and Los Angeles, annoyed her, and she knew it was a sentiment shared by many of her Plains colleagues when it was advisable to take a common carrier instead of a corporate jet. One Kansas senator, now retired, had simply rented out his house and moved to the DC area. He stayed with friends when he came back to the state. Gayfeather accepted the reality that the Senate would be her last employer, and the ability to influence policy and be known by everyone in Kansas still made her tingle.

On this flight, though, she steamed with resentment.

She felt manipulated by Saltwood into accepting a lobbyist-written oilfield anti-terrorism bill. Despite being the recipient of an immediate wave of donations and political support, she felt betrayed. But it was politics, and, to be honest, she *was* working for Saltwood.

Approaching Wichita's Eisenhower Airport from the north, the aircraft landed and nosed into its gate. Gayfeather walked a gauntlet of hand-shakers through the terminal of the self-proclaimed Air Capital of the World.

A young assistant from the field office escorted her to the sidewalk outside the terminal. They stood for a minute, waiting for the senator's Tahoe, a full-size SUV, and squinting in the sunlight and breeze. Yes, Gayfeather assured the aide, she had had a fine flight, and she complimented the aide on her haircut. And yes, the political winds do favor the PETRO Act.

The driver, Kevin Perdue, headed north out of the airport, taking the underpass to cross US 54/400, the main route transiting southern Kansas. He stayed on Ridge Road for a little more than a mile, turning east on Central Avenue, and then north on McLean Boulevard to follow the Arkansas River upstream as far as 13th Street. From there, it was only a mile to the senator's North Riverside neighborhood.

Perdue was free for the rest of the day, he said. Plus, he didn't say, his wife was probably still exhausted after a sleepless night entertaining her lover and getting to her early morning tennis lesson. Perdue knew what was going on.

Perdue knew a lot of things. He was Saltwood Exploration's executive vice president for governmental affairs, having built his grass-roots credentials as an oil-funded astroturfer for the Tea Party. His present duties were planting ideas in Harriet Gayfeather's head, bundling donations for her campaigns, and keeping her happy enough in bed that she wouldn't be seduced by the other giant oil company in town. It was cheaper to maintain and motivate a used senator than to buy and train a new one every six years.

The state's other senator didn't need tending. He would always dance with the one who brought him.

In the spring before she was first elected, Perdue had met candidate Gayfeather at an oil-industry golf tournament at Tallgrass Country Club, a square-mile development with an eighteen-hole golf course in the middle, houses and business parks lining the links, and a mammoth church built into one corner.

Perdue had walked up to her, waited for her to look at him, and said, "Will you marry me?"

"I'm nobody's fool," she said.

"Then will you be mine?"

She dropped her gaze to his hands.

"You're married."

"She's right over there. The one who's not paying any attention while I talk to the most beautiful woman on the course."

"You're brash."

"I represent money."

She snorted. "OK, hotshot, let's play."

He was a head taller than she, younger by three years, strong with a gym-maintained body and reasonably pleasant to look at. His hair was brown, his eyes dark brown, his teeth gleaming white. She considered the notion that he was an acceptable piece of arm candy.

Later, as they approached the sixteenth tee, she told him: "Better not drink too much afterward. This is not the night you want whiskey dick."

Kevin Perdue and Harriet Gayfeather never golfed together again at Tallgrass, but she arranged a weekly tee time for him at the Congressional Country Club outside Bethesda, Maryland, about five miles northwest of Gayfeather's home. He kept a set of clubs at her DC house as well as at her Wichita house. He stashed a third set in the District quarters Saltwood owned for its executives and lobbyists, and a fourth set at his own home in Wichita. The sets were identical and top of the line.

Wife Sarah once accused him of having a fling with someone, she didn't know who. He walked away, saying, "Who cares?"

That's why Sarah, a former college cheerleader who remained blond and taut skinned and decorated with bejeweled crosses and chunky turquoise necklaces, took up with the first liberal arts major she found wearing a necktie: an editor who ran the news desk at the Wichita paper. The fact that her choice of a politically correct lover wasn't a knife in Kevin's heart puzzled her. On the other hand, she told a tennis confidant, her lover "fixes my frittatas like no one else ever has."

After a few weeks of this empty-the-fridge-of-eggs arrangement in their home in Wichita's residential enclave of Eastborough, neither Sarah or Kevin cared what the other was up to as long as everyone remained discreet.

She didn't even bother looking at Kevin's phone when he left it open on the table, as he always did, and walked off to the bathroom. She did wonder whether he was taunting her or was just really stupid for someone in his chosen career.

• • •

Perdue pulled into Gayfeather's two-car, stand-alone garage, next to his Saltwood truck, and pressed the remote button to close the door. He hustled around the back to her side and helped her out, putting his roaming hands to work even before her feet were set.

"Cocktail?" he asked.

"Frankly, I'd just as soon have the whole thing."

He smirked. "Well, aren't we glad to be back in Kansas."

"But here's how it's going to go," she said. "Bathroom. Shower. Dinner. Bed. That order."

"I missed you," he said. "Tuesday was a long time ago."

"Wednesday morning was a long time ago. It's been hell."

"We'll talk," he said.

"That can wait until after bed."

They kissed hungrily, and she hugged him with her head against his shoulder.

"I'm never wrong," she said, "but I need to know I did the right thing."

•   •   •

Sarah Perdue had a hobby. She was the leader of a loose band of white authoritarianistas who hated taxation, blacks, immigrants, Democrats, tree huggers, and the poor in general. They gathered twice each month in back rooms of restaurants and talked of border walls and militias, leaning right until the anger in their brows surpassed the septic vehemence of their bumper stickers.

Although Kevin Perdue once described the club as "a zoo, but not animals you want to see," he threw a few thousand anonymous dollars into the kitty every year so the group could bring in speakers well known for publishing books that were praised on the vicious fringes of the internet. The group's activities didn't hurt Saltwood's cause, and the money helped make the Queen of Diamonds willingly oblivious to Kevin's long weekends away.

Sarah's lover found the group distasteful, but he enjoyed the risks of sleeping with democracy's enemy. He agreed explicitly to keep everyone's secrets, if for no other reason than he liked Sarah's kitchen.

21

Glad to be back in Laura's house after their tour of the wildlife refuge, Nick wandered into the living room, where he flipped through paperback romances, pestered the Rubik's cube again, and snorted in good humor at scrapbooks of snapshots Laura had taken.

"You think my pictures are bad?" she said, prepping for dinner. "Wait till I shoot you."

Picking up a plate from a shelf and seeing its maker's mark on the bottom, he asked, "Did your grandparents go to China?"

"They went twice," Laura said. "They brought back boxes of souvenirs during the Mao days and left some of it to me. I got a Little Red Book and the Chinese china."

"And the ranch?"

"They were old-style conservative tax lawyers in Wichita who loved the land and knew I did too. It would've gone to my folks, but a drunk driver killed them when I was in college."

Laura paused, and Nick said, "It's awful that happened to you."

"I guess Grandpa and Grandma assumed I'd outgrow the present Republican Party but love the ranch forever. My sister's a priss. She hates bugs and living anywhere that's not within five minutes of a Target, so they gave her money instead. Grandpa died during the pandemic, long after they moved out here for good. Grandma died two years ago."

She put her hand on his chin and twisted his head around. The shrapnel wound, marked by a thick line of proud flesh, was healing without leaking pus or other signs of infection.

Playfully, with gentle touches, he checked her for wounds.

"Did you work anything out with the senator?" he asked. "Has she acknowledged your nearly dying?"

"I don't think she ever will."

Nick sensed Laura's resignation.

"There are just some things I don't expect from her," she said. "I'm never going to be like her. I follow her around at meetings, always ready to whisper a name in her ear, remind her of a topic, get her coffee, and all the time I feel like the fourth runner-up to her Miss America. I'm jealous, but I'm not going to become her. She has this sense of control like a ratchet wrench. Always tighter, always to her advantage."

Laura relaxed her hands and let them fall.

"But she's been tense lately, like she senses that something's up," she said. "Maybe it's the PETRO Act or the election, or maybe her jerk boyfriend. I'm afraid she's going to explode."

"You work so closely with her. Do you two ever share boyfriends?"

"God, no," she said. "We are not in the same circle. I'll get passes from wheeler-dealers who think they'll strike it rich if they can get close to her. You're not that guy. Your access is as good as it gets."

The kitchen timer went off, and dinner was served with beet-bloody hands.

"Ta-da! Borsch for my Russian friend. Beef, beets, onions, potatoes, and a lovely dollop of sour cream."

Nick placed his arm around her shoulders. He beamed.

"Spasibo. Ty menya udivlyayesh'."

She furrowed her brow.

"Thank you," he said. "You amaze me."

"Russian nights and Holland days."

This time, Nick cocked his head. She laughed.

"For breakfast, eggs Benedict Arnold."

He didn't get that one either.

Afterward, Nick cleared the table and washed the dishes. Laura supervised from her chair.

"My great-grandma used to wash them in Tide laundry powder," Laura said. "It was cheap, and it was strong enough to take stains out of underwear, so you know it was good enough for our forks."

Nick opened cabinet doors until he found a pair of water glasses. Laura's stash of alcohol wasn't rich, but she had restocked it and the fridge, at his request and expense, on the way home from Quivira. He set vodka and brown ale on the table next to the glasses. He poured each glass two-thirds full of ale, then topped them off with vodka and mixed the drinks with a spoon.

"An interrogator in Mother's unit, a real alkash, a boozer, gave me the recipe."

"Are you going to interrogate me?"

"No. Cheers."

"Do you get your targets drunk before you kill them?"

"I have twice." He put his finger against his chin. "Four times."

"Tell me about your parents."

"Mother, the last I heard, runs an intelligence unit near the Black Sea. Father was a general in the Russian Army. My FBI overseer said he was killed in a plane crash."

"That's rough," she said. "I'm sorry."

She held her glass up against the light, squinting at the translucent swirls. She brought the glass down so she could look over the rim into his eyes.

"Do you intend to get me drunk?"

"Maybe."

"You're not going to kill me."

"Not tonight."

They smiled. They clinked the glasses, their eyes never wavering.

•　　•　　•

When Nick asked about what Gayfeather was like—who were her enemies and friends—Laura joked about how private the senator was. Still, over the years the two women had shared a few insights.

"I've been with her forever," she said. "I was one of her first volunteers and the one who was the most competent."

Nick nodded. "I'm not surprised."

He mixed the second round.

"Okay," Laura said, rising with a little wobble. "I'd better go to the bathroom first. God bless vodka."

Nick waited patiently. He'd probably get answers, which he hadn't ever really demanded before in his career. Get a bit of confirmation and do his job; that was his old mission. Back then, the orders were to do and to die if necessary. During his stay with the FBI, he had decided that he could still do, but he wasn't going to die and he wasn't going to make anyone else die without a reason he agreed with.

Laura flushed the toilet, walked slowly into the kitchen, and gripped the back of her chair. She leaned toward Nick.

"You will find, Nick Deveraux, that as we drink vodka, we become more distilled versions of ourselves."

"And . . ."

"You're so handsome," she said. "You make me feel like a cougar. I'm thirty-five, you know."

She giggled. Nick pretended to be surprised. They laughed.

"Now you answer a question for me," Laura said. "Have you seen people killed?"

"Some."

"Of course you have. Silly me."

"Doing my duty has bothered me sometimes. You kill somebody, Laura, your life might be wrecked. You'd have nightmares, unless you're a sociopath. When I do it, I might feel bad for being glad it wasn't me who got hit, and I then get over it."

He tapped his temple.

"I see them in my dreams sometimes," he said. "But I suppose I'd have to be a bit of a sociopath to have been there in the first place."

"Okay. That sounds right, you being a hitman."

"Please, Laura," he said with feigned exasperation. "Remember when you called Orion's people nudists and he demanded they be called naturists? This is like that. I was an assassin, not a contract killer. I was on a payroll. I completed assignments and cleaned up problems as needed."

Laura sat down and sipped her drink. She patted her thighs and clapped her hands, like she was going to play patty-cake, but then she sighed loudly, brushed her hair back, and rested her jaw in her hands. She worked at focusing on Nick's eyes, but she was all over the place emotionally.

"You think Gayfeather's timing is weird?" she asked. "Let's say Gayfeather gets a ton of Saltwood money and she's been making deals in the Senate, all of it building up to this PETRO bill. And if she had the bill ready to go, just waiting for an event like the explosion, if she's not charged with conspiracy she'll at least be vulnerable in the next election. If anyone catches on."

"I can hear her not being on the ballot as we speak," he said.

Laura set her glass down. Nick let her run with the topic.

"It's funny that she's the Republicans' most expendable senator. There's so much riding on her, but she could also be kicked out of office—or shot—if the whole thing works. Hey, if she's shot, she'd become a martyr. The evangelicals and other right-wingers could do anything and say it's in her honor. Kansans may hate her, but America loves a dead blonde."

Laura raised her glass to dead blondes.

"She'll be vulnerable anyway, because of what she knows," Laura said. "Think of the scandal if she's found out for whatever she's doing. Saltwood will have to either pay her off or kill her."

She burped. "This drink's pretty good."

Nick sipped his.

"But there's something off about her and Saltwood—no matter how much money they give her, she acts like that money is just a tool for staying in office, like she won't need any personal money in the future. Like she has a second stash already. And that's something, when you look at how rich other senators become when their salaries are only $174,000 a year, and then they still become lobbyists."

Laura walked over to the fridge and moved some things around, finally opening a package of pressed ham. She laid slices out with Ritz crackers on a dish in the middle of the table. She folded a piece of meat over twice and nibbled at it, her gestures becoming expansive.

"Her houses, you know? Wichita, the District, a place in Arizona. She thinks I don't know about this, but she also bought a decomissioned Titan II missile silo out by Kingman, west of Wichita. Her contractor asked me questions about it. You're not writing any of this down, are you? All these places, they're worth millions, and it's not inherited money. Her dad drove a truck for a coal mine until he beat her mother to death, and her dead soldier perfect husband didn't leave her diddly.

"Arizona's far from the Russians," she said, "but there's Chinese money there. Plus the university. Military contractors. Space scientists. Mobsters from Chicago."

When she paused to pick her teeth, Nick said, "The Russians are involved here? Or maybe the Chinese?"

"It was a big deal a few years ago when a bunch of senators went to Moscow to talk to Putin over the Fourth of July. The other senator from Kansas went, but Gayfeather didn't. Especially because they sent you to kill her, she hates Russia and its oligarchs and would do anything to undercut them.

"So if I were you, Nick Deveraux, . . ." Laura belched, crossed her eyes and covered her mouth. After a moment: "She'd love to use their own tool against them. I'd be really careful. And her Saltwood boyfriend knows Russian, so be careful around him."

"It's easier to say than do," he said, "especially when Russians are involved."

"If it's not the Russians," she said, "maybe Saudi or China is paying her for something else. She has power, connections, and a degree in economics. Her committee assignments include both Agriculture and Energy and Natural Resources. She'd know how to hide big money in very dark places."

Spreading her arms to show how big the money could be, Laura knocked over her glass.

"A drunk drinking accident," she exclaimed with a giddy laugh. But then, "Oh my god, my parents. How can I say things like that?"

•   •   •

A half hour later, after washing the glasses and holding Laura's hair back while she vomited, Nick crawled under the sheet of his host's childhood bed. He wondered whether the springs creaked when little girl Laura moved her shoulders around to make the linens scratch her back. Did girls do such things? Girls and youth . . .

There was an afternoon, half his lifetime ago, when he was fourteen and swimming in Lake Lisi with the sons and daughters of Russian intelligence officers who were his parents' friends working in the Georgian capital, Tbilisi.

From among a gaggle of kids holding on to a black inner tube, a girl three years older than Nick had climbed aboard. When she straddled the tube, her gracilis muscles lifted her taut yellow bikini off the inside of her thigh, exposing dark curls.

"Stop staring at my crotch," she said when she caught him lingering. She wasn't coy, nor was she angry.

Soon after, Nick's parents rotated north to the uprising in Chechnya, where there were no peaceful lakes and no more bikinis.

From Chechnya, Nick was granted admission to a military academy in St. Petersburg. He couldn't remember the girl's face or her name.

In the coming years, until he met his first true love, Anya, a woman's face and name didn't matter much. But the sense of the girl in the lake stayed with him. He enjoyed women who had an easy sensuality paired with a confident attitude, and who would tell him no.

He considered the odds of the girl's family surviving that war and the next and the next. Had she gone into the service like her parents? Did anything ever break her heart?

But he was done with love. Falling in love, no matter how pure, had bent his life. First it was Anya. He learned to kill out of revenge after her death, and that made him a tool of the state and then the mafia and now probably some oligarch. On his previous mission to Kansas, his infatuation with Cimi became an all-consuming flame that took him to the edge of death but was also his salvation and his torture.

Now here he was again among strong women. This time he would not allow himself to seek the luxury of a warm heart, for failing his assignment would trap him forever in the afterworld.

22

First thing in the morning, Laura's phone pulsed with the senator's ringtone. She answered in a hungover, flat tone suitable for Saturday: "Harriet, hi."

She took notes: "You'll be in Bull Creek at 2:00 for the memorial. Got it. Yes, he's here. OK, I'll tell him. Six o'clock at your place."

She was in the kitchen an hour later when Nick came out of his bedroom. With a flourish she slid a plate in front of him: a pair of toasted English muffin halves topped by round slices of Canadian bacon, poached eggs, and vibrant gold hollandaise sauce.

"Voila!" she said, bringing her own plate. "Eggs Benedict Arnold."

"You have a fixation with traitors," he said. "Are you projecting?"

"Humpf. Eat your breakfast."

Halfway through his plate, he looked up.

"Is it all eggs and butter? This is really good," he said. "Anything new on the bombing?"

"Nothing new on Twitter, nothing in the email, nothing on Facebook that isn't soaked in conspiracy. Aside from that, my body still feels beaten up."

"Mine too. Headaches, sore neck, and abs I can barely use," Nick said.

"Because of your damned drinks last night, I had terrible dreams."

"The bombing?"

"I was walking in the wildflowers, and then there was a gunshot and a white flash and the shrapnel, all together. Suddenly you were on top of me and I couldn't breathe or hear, and there was blood everywhere."

"A gunshot?"

"It came from behind us. Maybe I'm mixed up about when it happened."

"Maybe we should tell the highway patrolman. I believe what you said about the bullet. The thing is, we weren't between the hunting blind and the blue barrel. If your dream is right, the bullet didn't come from the blind. "

"Yes, we should tell Hornish."

She brought up her napkin and wiped her face.

"That mystery finger stumps me," he said. "Who and where did it come from? Are there more bodies out there?"

Laura put her fork down and looked at her hands.

"It could be some farmer lost a finger in an auger," she said, "or a stray that got cut off in a car wreck."

"Doesn't seem likely."

She shook her head.

"You know what?" she said. "I could use a break. Let's do some actual work, like I promised you."

"Sounds like fun."

"Also, Harriet called. She wants you to show up at her place in Wichita this evening. You can take my truck. I don't know what the meeting's for, but take your clothes in case you don't come back."

23

Joyleen Sterrett had gotten started in business as a poorly paid bookkeeper for a small Wichita real estate firm. One day, when she was the only person in the office, she picked up a call from a gentleman who wanted to rent an apartment for his niece, a college student named Mona Leesa who sang at his church.

Joyleen quickly ferreted out the true relationship but said not a word about it. When the lease was signed, the gentleman, who identified himself as Pastor Luke Meriwether, offered her a bookkeeping job at his large church, steady work at better pay.

What put the pep in her step last January, after a few months working for Pastor, were discoveries in the church foundation's books.

The first was deducing that Pastor was spending almost two thousand bucks a month of the foundation's money on items, such as room and board for his mistress, that provided the charity with no obvious return. What had prompted Joyleen's interest was Pastor's request for a 100 percent boost in the outlay, payable to him for "outreach."

"My—our—costs are rising," he said one day in his office, "and the foundation can help."

She bent closer and cocked her head, a good listener.

"We'll talk about this in person only," he said. "No phones or email or texts, okay?"

Joyleen glanced down demurely, then back into his eyes.

"We don't want an un-merry Christmas," she said.

Joyleen winked, and a flash of understanding crossed Pastor's face. He smiled and held a finger to his lips.

It struck her as funny that Pastor was protecting his image in front of the very person who had helped him rent his love shack. Especially considering the first time she visited him in his office, how she had stared at the portrait of Christmas on the wall and remarked on the subject's penetrating gaze.

Pastor didn't bother to look up. "Art imitates wife," he said.

The second discovery came in her second month on the job. A financial advisor called to double-check the church's bank account number for the records of a client. The advisor, softened by Joyleen's attention, mentioned in a braggy way that the church's foundation was a transfer-on-death second beneficiary of an irrevocable $3.7 million trust.

Joyleen worked this over in her head for a week before she approached Pastor. In the middle of an afternoon, wearing the green dress she knew was Pastor's favorite, she popped breathlessly into his office.

"The IRS is looking at church foundations," she said. "I just heard about it on the grapevine."

"What's that mean for us?"

"We'll need to show how we've spent our funds according to our charter. We need to be solvent."

"Sounds easy enough."

"Except for the part where you're spending us into a hole."

"And? Can't we throw a little cash in from other accounts?"

"The auditor will ask where the money's coming from and where it's going."

"Jesus in Heaven."

"Word will get out. The congregation will draw conclusions. You and I could both go to prison."

Pastor rolled back his chair and strode across the room to his coffee machine. He pointed at it and raised his eyebrows to her, but she shook her head. He picked up a mug and the pot, then put them both down.

"God in Heaven," he said.

She said, "I didn't come on board here to get caught between you and the IRS."

She smoothed her skirt down and took a chair. She stared at the wall ahead of her, and after a few seconds she yanked a tissue from the box on the end table and dabbed her eyes.

"I don't know whether I can hide the deficit anymore," she said.

"There's no way around this?" he said.

She looked at the floor and then decided to speak.

"Maybe."

He returned to his desk.

"Maybe?"

She looked straight at him.

"I need to trust you absolutely before we even talk about this."

"I have everything to lose," he said. He thought: Christmas, Noelle, his chance at becoming a senator, his mistress. He added: "The sun shall be turned into darkness, and the moon into blood, . . ."

Joyleen cleared her throat and got his attention back.

"You know Hank Ross, who was a retired engineer at Boeing. He wrote the foundation into his will."

Pastor shrugged. "Ol' Hank has been a long and faithful deacon, but he's deep into Alzheimer's. I heard he's close to the pearly gates."

"Attention, please. A lot of money. Anyway, we're the contingent beneficiary. We're not guaranteed the money. It'll go to his son."

"Who isn't a member," Pastor Luke said. "How generous would he be?"

"I imagine he'd be flexible. Open to discussion. With me."

She wiggled her shoulders and parted her knees slightly.

"I see."

"What I'm thinking is that you and I could work out a deal, just between us. I'd get 10 percent of the donation, and you'd get to screw your niece in peace."

Pastor blanched at the phrasing, but nodded.

"How much?" he asked, leaning forward over the desk.

"Enough to make you a legend."

"God bless."

"The money I get has to be in cash and come out of your personal funds," she said. "The donation has to appear in the foundation exactly as it was given. It's too traceable to mess with."

With that, the deal was done.

"We're not going to write any of this down, and we'll never talk about this arrangement in public," he said. "You have to agree to keep my secret, and I won't tell your husband about your business skills."

They took each other's hand cautiously, then grinned.

Hank Ross died the following week, a comatose passing mourned widely in the city's aerospace industry. He left without knowing that his son, also a mechanical engineer, had been killed in a drug deal.

When Joyleen brought in the breathless news that Hank Ross's trust had delivered the church a surprise bequest of $3.7 million, Pastor swept her off her feet. He laughed, he howled; he was an animal freed from a cage.

"I got the son to donate the whole thing," she said. She made a quarter turn, thrust her breasts forward. "The son was just a man."

"I'm a man, too," Pastor said.

"Well," she said, "the son was a man until he got murdered. The cops said it was over fentanyl."

Pastor backed away. "He was going to be a millionaire and he was messing with drugs?"

"It was on the TV news. He was stabbed," she said. "Anyway, he's dead now, and the foundation will be solvent."

"The son should've stayed away from drugs," Pastor said. Joyleen picked her purse off the floor while he rambled about the annoyance that is the IRS versus a man's right to love donating to the church as much as he himself loved God.

"Remember," she said, "the deal's not done yet."

"Maybe you and I should renegotiate."

"In what, a hundred back-breaking installments? A better idea would be for you to pay what you owe me, and maybe we'll work something out after that."

"How much?"

"You know how much. Three hundred seventy thousand."

"Where will I get that?"

"You have places. You have reasons for getting it."

Pastor sank into the couch.

"It's not so bad," she said. "You still need to pay in cash. I don't want the IRS after me either."

"Two weeks."

She sashayed up front of him, her hips not far from his face.

"You do that, and you might discover that you don't even need that tattooed niece anymore."

Pastor and Joyleen began their casual affair around Valentine's Day, after Joyleen had reluctantly accepted Pastor Luke's plea for a quarterly installment plan—starting with $92,500 immediately—and an eternity of guaranteed mutual secrecy.

It was delicate, as they had to fit the fling in around her husband, Pastor's wife, daughter, current mistress Mona Leesa, and such things as funerals, Rotary meetings, political-action committee sessions, and Bible classes. Coincidentally, Mona Leesa broke things off within a few days when her boyfriend proposed.

"Just because I hold the key to Heaven doesn't mean I have to stop liking sex," Pastor Luke bragged to Joyleen.

He wasn't willing to have his wife killed, although the subject did come up. (Maybe his troublesome daughter, though, but that was just an idle thought. Like Joyleen said, "The thing I like about you is the thing I can't stand about you: You're too nice to your daughter.") Anyway, neither death would have put much money in his pocket.

On this Saturday in his office, he struggled to keep thoughts of sex, money, and political intrigue out of his mind. He was trying to develop a theme for his pre–Memorial Day sermon based on Acts 2, and it needed to encompass the terrorist explosion at the oil rig.

He certainly could paint a fulfilling picture out of five verses, Acts 2:20–24, the ones starting with "The sun shall be turned into darkness, and the moon into blood, before the great and notable day of the Lord comes. And it shall come to pass, that whosoever shall call on the name of the Lord shall be saved."

Even the start of the chapter was like a bomb: "And when the day of Pentecost was fully come, they were all with one accord in one place. And suddenly there came a sound from heaven as of a rushing mighty wind, and it filled all the house where they were sitting. And there appeared unto them cloven tongues like as of fire, and it sat upon each of them."

Pastor felt a strong kinship with Acts 2. For one thing, it described the Pentecost, a gathering of apostles and Jesus' mother, Mary, and others shortly after the ascension of Jesus. And the River Jordan Cathedral was based on Pentecostal beliefs, among them baptism in the Holy Spirit, prophecy, healing, and exorcism. It would be the perfect speaking point for America's Day of the Dead weekend.

For another thing, the traditionally acknowledged writer of the New Testament book was none other than the disciple Luke. Praise the Lord!

24

Lance Sterrett sat in a wobbly old deer stand tucked into the Rice County cottonwoods and walnuts where the Arkansas River formed the northeastern edge of Laura's ranch, absentmindedly nibbling his military surplus Meal Ready to Eat. He ordered two dozen at a time over the internet, so he could keep a stash in his truck.

He watched Laura and Nick through the scope on his sound-suppressed rifle, waiting for Dr. Cletus Purkeypyle to pop into the picture. All Kevin Perdue talked about was the need to get Purkeypyle. No one knew where the hydrologist had gone.

Sterrett was spinning his wheels, sitting for hours, driving around Bull Creek, bushwacking along Salt Creek in hopes of spotting the target and stopping every fifteen minutes to pick ticks off his legs, cursing himself for not using his permethrin spray. He had waited long hours in Afghanistan and Iraq to knock down a target, but at least then there was the excitement of protecting his men. These two pretend ranchers would go down like tin cans on a fence rail.

Lance followed Nick, who was dragging brush away from an old shed as the day edged closer to noon. Then he aimed at a locust tree over by the house and in his mind pulled the trigger, before leaning the weapon against the railing to finish eating. He was looking almost directly south, and the glare would be a problem if he had to shoot this time of day. Even the ringneck pheasants were taking the day easy, hardly a rough cackle coming from the roosters out there in the grass.

The MRE chicken burrito bowl—actually beans, rice, and chicken—was like all the rest he had eaten in his military career. Mildly warm, mostly filling, bland, about 1,250 calories. Food for the warfighter indeed. Or, in this case, the babysitter.

Lance picked his teeth with the corner of the empty meal bag and rinsed with the last of the thin and sugary lime drink. He folded the bag and stuffed it and the heating component back into the mud-colored plastic envelope they came in, and the envelope went back into his pack. The dozen sheets of four-by-four-inch tissues went into his pocket; you never know . . .

It didn't take much to fill him these days. Maybe it was the late-spring chill or his nerves, or maybe he was just failing to see the point anymore. His appetite was down. He'd been out of town much of the week and was exhausted from driving. It was one thing after another, and even though he was, or maybe because he was, a soldier and the son of a sergeant, his instincts told him the whole thing was screwed up.

He set his M24 rifle, the military's standard sniper weapon, back on the sandbag he had brought for a gun rest and sighted in for the fourth time on the pinnate leaves of one gently swaying twig on a low branch of the locust. He checked the rangefinder again: 723 meters, 2,372 feet, less than half a mile and easily within range. If he saw the woman and the senator's new aide leave, he'd fire a round into the tree to double-check the bullet's drop in these conditions.

This M24, based on the Remington Model 700 and its .300 caliber cartridge, was his best rifle. It looked like a simple firearm, much like a regular deer rifle with a bolt action and a 24-inch barrel, but it was extremely accurate in good hands. His second-best rifle—another M24, another $5,000 wonder—was in pieces strewn into the ponds over at the salt marsh.

Out at the oil rig, the plan had been for Lance to blow up the drilling crew at 11:45 when the Saltwood bosses were walking toward the office trailer, the intended assumption being that some terrorist wanted to kill the bosses but got overeager and shot too soon. The crew members were being gathered to be told that they were getting bonuses, so they'd greet the bosses warmly and maybe provide some human shielding between the bomb and the bosses.

The trouble with that plan, it was clear to Lance, is that people would care if a bunch of real people died. No one would mind if some suits almost got blown up. "Almost" was too strong a word. They wouldn't even get close to the shrapnel zone until after the explosion.

Ego. That's all that mattered to the suits. Bragging rights at the club, at the resort, at the stockholders and board meetings when bonuses were brought up.

But then Laura Eisenhauer drove up unexpectedly with a strange man, and she and he were walking toward the bomb. There wasn't any time to alert the bosses before they arrived, so he took executive action in his post at the old school down the road. With his rifle already lined up over the cab of his pickup, he squeezed the trigger a few minutes early so Senator Gayfeather's aide was less likely to be killed. He needed her alive if he were to ever find out where Purkeypyle had gone; those were his overriding orders.

If Eisenhauer had brought the scientist, he could've been blamed for the bomb. It would've been easy enough to rewrite the timeline if he were wounded. Amid the foggy memories created by the blast, he could have been spirited away. If he were dead, that'd be okay too.

What remained was the big picture: Nine men were dead, and Saltwood had its pawns.

That's what Lance was explaining to the bosses when they showed up. It's why they all stared at Nick and Laura. Lance had explained again how the Tannerite wouldn't explode without being hit by a high-velocity bullet, how no one would hear the gunfire because the bullet would arrive half a second before the muzzle blast and after that everyone's memory would be wiped clean by the explosion. There might be survivors who'd testify that the new man hadn't brought a rifle. As it was, shrapnel had nearly killed the guy.

Within two hours of the blast, after Lance had talked to the sheriff about what he had seen after he arrived, he drove into the neighboring wildlife refuge, to the far end. He dismantled the rifle and wiped all the parts with rubbing alcohol, then sanded the pieces so the salt marsh would destroy them more quickly. He flung them piece by small piece into the water. The rifle would never be matched ballistically to the shot that ignited the bomb. His path wouldn't be traced electronically, because long ago he disconnected his truck's GPS tracker.

He had just had the most important week of his professional life, and all he felt today was exhaustion. He was tired of this whole screwed-up Quivira business.

He had completed another job back in late January. That one was refreshingly simple, and Lance hadn't had to answer to anyone.

It was a gift to his wife. Joyleen, crying in his arms, had told him how that afternoon a guy at church had put his hands on her hips, rubbed his cock against her, and suggested that they fly up to his place in Wyoming for a week. Could Lance please, please fix this?

Ten minutes on Facebook told Lance what he needed to know.

At 4:46 the next morning, Lance walked up behind the man—a mechanical engineer whose respected father was at death's door—outside a west Wichita condo as the engineer carried a gym bag to his BMW sedan. He grabbed the engineer and shoved a blade through the target's puffy jacket and into his heart.

To mislead investigators, Lance, wearing a black mask and latex gloves, pressed a zip-lock baggie containing three fentanyl tablets against the engineer's fingertips and pushed the baggie into the engineer's pocket, then shoved into the engineer's mouth a playing card drawn randomly from a deck the night before: the six of clubs, on which he had spray painted a red slash.

He got no thrill out of that death, he acknowledged to himself as he walked the half mile to his personal pickup, stashed in another apartment building's lot. It was necessary for enforcing order and dominance. The sex afterward was great. He couldn't remember Joyleen ever being so enthusiastic, and that was saying a lot.

Why he was still doing this crap puzzled him. He'd had a life before the Army, but now that he was out it seemed like he was being drawn deeper into the muck. The only smart thing he'd done was refusing peer pressure to join the church's Almighty Rifles militia.

Lance made it to sergeant in the Army because he liked the work. And it was honest work. What he did before that may have been honest, but it wasn't work.

Back after Lance broke his arm playing high school football, his uncle, an accountant, taught him how to buy and hold stocks. At age 16, he used his summer earnings to buy a thousand shares of Apple at $7 in 2003, after the iPod came out but before the first iPhone, and sold half three years later just before the shares peaked at $80. Then he invested in young Google, buying at $12 and selling half at $142. And so on.

Eventually he got bored watching the stock market make him a millionaire, so he joined the Army. Now here he was at 38, olive skinned with a trimmed goatee, white sidewalls, and a crew cut. He had become as tough as a fence post sawn from Osage orange.

Lance's father had served as a bulldozer operator in 1991 in Operation Desert Storm, the first Iraq oil war. He had the stickers on his pickup and the bad dreams to prove it.

The old man had been in the First Division, driving a bulldozer behind Abrams tanks and Bradley Fighting Vehicles—a gray-green Caterpillar D-9 with a turret for a cab, bulletproof windows and anti-grenade screens around the turret. A machine gun atop the turret. Headlights atop the columns holding the blade.

His advice to Lance:

"Don't stand there in a trench and shoot small arms at a fifty-ton pile of armor and hydraulics that'll rip you in half. Bravery alone doesn't make you a hero. Get out and find another way to fight."

He and his men scraped away the defilations and collapsed dozens of Iraqi trenches on the coalition's path to the Highway of Death.

"I must have buried a hundred men myself," he said over Sunday dinner a few years after he came home. By then, he had a new job using his veteran's status and only marketable skill, driving a D-9 on highway projects.

"Buried alive," the old man said. "That's how the Iraqis gave their lives for their country. They got covered up by the most basic thing—a diesel dozer that shoves dirt around. I think about them poor boys every time my dozer sags into soft ground. The glory of war."

Young Lance volunteered in 2007. After sniper school he was sent to a small forward operating base near Turkey, right in the middle of the second Iraq war. He killed twenty-one Iraqi men and boys and two women, all from at least eight hundred meters.

When Iraq II was wrapping up, Lance rolled straight into the arms of a private security subsidiary providing covert observation and protection for Saltwood Exploration operations on three continents.

Joyleen came on to him after a softball game in Oklahoma, where he was living for a time, and they were married within six months. He never got around to telling her he was a dividend millionaire, and he sure didn't live like one.

With Saltwood, he had been back in Kansas for three years, three months, one week and four days. He visited his parents' shared grave in the Kansas Veterans Cemetery in Winfield, a scant hour's drive south of Wichita, every month and fought with his wife every other week.

He had come home into the arms of Dysmerica.

Kansas wasn't his happy place.

•   •   •

Hints of white paint clung to the lapboard walls of the Eisenhauer ranch's sagging machine shed.

The shed once had swinging doors tall enough for pickups and small tractors, but the hinges had rusted and the wood had rotted away from the screws holding the doors on. The doors now were lying on edge lengthwise under a window, the shed having become a catchall for material not easily thrown away. Glass jugs and five-gallon metal and plastic buckets lined the wide wooden shelves or sat on the dirt floor. At the back, piles of old furniture rose nearly to the rafters under the pine boards and wooden shingles making up the roof. The nasal whack of greasy dust with an underlying animal stink seemed to be a permanent fixture.

The building was surrounded on three sides by weeds, already a foot and a half tall after the spring rains. Beyond the shed and its neighbor, the dilapidated chicken house, was a long trench, eight or so feet deep, backed by a tall berm of recently dug soil. The tracks of the backhoe that dug it were still evident in the dirt and crushed plants along its path.

Laura led Nick around the shed, bracing herself against the wood as she stepped over rotting lumber and rusted gear sets. She looked at her hand and swept the tiny splinters and paint flecks off against her jeans.

"The farm was built up in 1938," she said, "and that was probably the last time the buildings were painted. We haven't really used the shed for decades. Now it's just a fire hazard. At first, I thought I'd burn it all, but then I realized that an intentional fire was not much better than a fire hazard. So, I'm going to collapse it and bury the mess in the trench."

"What's in the jugs?"

"Gasoline that's been sitting there for maybe twenty years. There might be some oil mixed in, since it looks gunky at the bottom. If the gas doesn't make too much black smoke, we'll burn it. If it does get too smoky, we'll burn it at night. I already told the fire department to ignore any calls about a fire at my place for the next week or so. It all depends on what day the wind isn't blowing."

By noon, the day's warmth was rising but a sky decorated with wispy horsetail cirrus clouds promised a change.

"It's going to rain tonight," she said. "Let's take the stuff off the shelves and pile whatever we can on the floor for now."

They took down a wall-mounted drill and laid it on the floor next to sawhorses, a few gallon jugs, and an old pitchfork, its four rusted tines loose on the desiccated handle. Pigeon feathers and poop and shreds of cigarette butts mingled with the treasure.

"I'm always nervous about this building, like it might fall in on us," she said, "but it has cool stuff." She lifted a wood-handled corn knife off a nail driven into the wall and ran her hand along the wide, eighteen-inch-long rusted blade. To Nick, it looked like a machete.

"There used to be rats underneath the shed," she said, "and we were always watching out for brown recluse spiders. Poisonous spiders. I wouldn't be surprised if somewhere in this mess is a pound or two of DDT."

Laura dangled the knife as she walked out of the shed. Birds chirped in the shelter belt, and flies buzzed around them. The breeze rustled the weeds.

He joined her in the sun, and their shadows stood out starkly low on the shed's wall. She raised the knife to create a dramatic silhouette. When Nick laughed, she lowered the knife and stood there, still facing his way.

This would be a moment to remember, Nick thought. Keeping his eyes on her shadow, he moved a little closer and put his hand on her lower back. Her long muscles tensed and relaxed, and her image merged into his.

As Nick leaned forward to nuzzle, her forehead knocked off his ball cap. She snorted and turned with him as he twisted to pick it up.

"Stop," she said.

It was an urgent order. Laura touched his right hip. She whispered: "Don't move."

The cap had fallen on the mottled back of a rattlesnake.

The snake's rattle, masked at first by the wind and insect noise, took a mean edge. The triangular head was off the ground, pulled back over the coiled body like an arrow waiting to be released.

"What do I do?"

"Nothing. Stay absolutely still. Let the snake decide to leave."

Half a minute passed. Nick was rigid with tension.

When the rattler licked the air, Nick reflexively twisted his left foot.

Laura swung the knife down, burying the end of the blade next to his foot as the snake struck at his ankle.

The snake slid away, disappearing under the shed.

Nick ran a status check of his feet and legs. No holes.

She pulled up the knife, turning it so Nick could see twin shiny trails of venom where fangs had struck the blade.

"First time that's worked," she said.

Nick kept his feet still, unwilling to risk his life with another step.

"That was my first rattlesnake," he said. "Thank you."

He reached for his cap and looked it over with trepidation.

She laughed. "Yep, it's covered in snake cooties."

"Laura?"

"Yes, dear hero of *Wild Kingdom*?"

"If that snake had bitten me, how long would I have lived?"

"A while. There's a clinic in Bull Creek, and a hospital up in the county seat. Or I could've driven you to Hutchinson or Wichita. That would've been up to an hour for a big hospital. But that might not've mattered, because almost no one has antivenom."

"So a lingering death."

"Painful, too," she said.

"Well."

"If I weren't here, or if I decided not to drive you, you would've died here. Unless you staggered out to the road and someone had happened to come along, but every step you took would've pumped more poison through your body and you'd be in a world of swollen hurt."

"Again, a lingering death."

"By then, not all that lingering."

Nick and Laura, watching every step, finished arranging the shed for its destruction. Dusty, greasy, and tired, they walked across the big driveway to plop into lawn chairs at the house. Laura brought out a six-pack of longnecks.

"You want to watch the speech by Gayfeather?" Laura asked. "It's on in a little bit."

Nick was quiet, reliving every tiny moment of the rattlesnake strike. He startled when Laura touched his arm.

"A speech? I'm not ready for that," he said. "You go ahead, though."

Neither one got up. Songbirds sang. Pigeons cooed. Tree leaves rustled. Ten minutes passed.

"Nick, what about that girl in Sandstone? I read in a report Gayfeather got that there was a girl."

"It's over," he said. "We're in different worlds now. Plus, she told me to stay out of her sight."

"You saved her life."

"And she saved mine. That said, being dumped hurt."

The Cimarron Hernandez in his memory: Her flashing smile, her long legs in the crystalline Arkansas River and then wrapped around him, her anger at how he used her mother's café as cover for his assassination attempt against Senator Gayfeather. He gave her a Kansas diamond—a chunk of clear quartz he found in the river—and she nearly killed him trying to save his life. Two years on, she had become an exquisite sand painting, the friction of each day carrying away a few more grains.

"Earth to Nick!"

He blushed.

"I guess not everything's resolved," he said.

He stretched his arms and legs. The shed work had loosened his muscles, but only so much.

"What about you?" he said. "How's your love life?"

"When we were at the funeral, remember that bad poet boyfriend I mentioned? While I was getting my political career going in Wichita and he was teaching at the university, I'd help his family out on their farm west of town, driving the tractor. He'd hang around in town with his anthropology students in the College of Libertine Arts and Sciences. The grapevine said he was handsy with sophomore girls, but when you're in love you don't want to believe those stories."

Laura walked a couple of strides out into the driveway and scraped together a little pile of sand, then stood up a row of twigs.

"And yet," she said, looking back at Nick, "it felt like he was always looking over my shoulder for a fresh face, a possibility, a step up. I despised him for that, and I hated myself for staying with him."

Seating herself again, she tossed a pebble at a twig, and then second pebble and another until she knocked it over.

"Once in a while he'd skip seeing me for a week and make some excuse about having the flu. I figured out later that it was probably to get cured of chlamydia. During each of those episodes, he'd write what he called his love sonnets. They were awful. Talking fence posts, prairie dogs in love, voices in the wind, that kind of thing. You know?"

Nick nodded. "It's like they're writing to themselves."

"My career was getting some traction and, to be fair, I was out in the state a lot. I'd stop at every new river and sketch a picture from the bridge or, I don't know, a city park, and I'd mail those postcards to him. Not once did he acknowledge this thing that was very personal to me. Twenty-nine postcards. So one day I decided that I'd had enough of him, and that was that."

"He sounds like a jerk," Nick said.

"One hundred percent. I try not to blame any individual person for making my life miserable, but he did a pretty good job of it," she said. "God counts my tears."

"Why did you keep writing to him?"

"I'm sentimental, okay?" She laughed at herself. "I should've dumped him as soon as he described anthropology as 'studying the beauty of history without the nightsoil of politics.'"

Nick church-keyed another couple of bottles. He handed her one.

"Anyway," she said, "rivers are profound. When it rains, the stream becomes more than it was. It's water falling on flowing water. Each drop leaves a memory, a set of ripples riding downstream. Each ripple distorts the reflection, so even though the scenery doesn't change, our view of it does."

Nick thought about that scene. "Your river days were not wasted," he said. "The guy was clearly a rat."

"Yeah, live and learn."

"So you've never brought home anyone from the Trailer Hitch? Nobody with a Ditch the Bitch shirt?

"Never, except for one time," she said. "You might as well hear about it from me."

She laced her fingers behind her head.

"He had moved down here from Salina, up on Interstate 70. One day I looked through his phone, because that's what you do as soon as you can with guys from the Hitch. He was sleeping with someone, of course. Everyone else at the Hitch seemed to be in on the joke.

"Eventually I found out who it was. She was a real cutie. So, when I was in Kansas City, where no one knew me, I had a T-shirt printed. He and I dressed up nice the next weekend and met at the Hitch. When he went to the men's room, I took off my blouse so everyone could see my T-shirt.

"What did it say?"

"'Lover from another mother.'"

Nick thought a second and started laughing.

"He came out of the can a marked man," she said.

"You're ruthless."

"I am tough."

"Was Purkeypyle ever your lover?"

"What did I tell you at Quivira?"

"A half-answer."

She shrugged.

"He was a card-carrying Republican, so we ran into each other at party events: fundraisers, Lincoln Day dinners, that sort of thing. He was tall, dark, and handsome, with gorgeous green eyes, kinda sorta like you but with a beard. We did spend time together, especially after he found the leak in the creek. Despite his atrocious name, he was a nice guy."

"Was?"

"He ghosted me."

25

Eighty miles up Interstate 35 northeast of Wichita and a hundred ten miles east of Bull Creek, the plainclothes state cop sat in his SUV in front of the Radius Brewery on Merchant Street in downtown Emporia. He watched Kelli Ochs sign autographs and pose for a lunchtime selfie with three boys from Emporia State University. She gave each a hug and told them to love their mamas.

She strode in past the silver brewing tanks and chose a wooden table against a brick wall. The ceiling was covered by squares of pressed tin, and the floor was strips of brown wood. When the server came with a menu, Kelli greeted him with a generous smile. He left with an order and returned with iced tea.

She was strikingly attractive, made for the internet. Pretty clothes, the cop thought, and modestly dressed. A couple of bracelets on her right wrist. Her blond hair held back in a ponytail.

The cop, Loren Hornish, thought about how normal she looked, not trying to be a TikTok personality now.

On the seat of his unmarked SUV was a copy of the town's newspaper, the *Emporia Gazette*.

"Who will Kelli kill? Is she for real?" was the headline over a feature story stripped across the top of the front page. Inside, an editorial called for keeping an eye on this threat from western Kansas. No one here in Lyon County should have to fear for their life, the piece noted, yet people posting on Facebook and TikTok had offered plenty of suggestions in this one county of 33,000 people.

Hornish was proud to be part of an ad hoc law enforcement team keeping tabs on people in groups that ranged from western Kansas militias to bankrupted farmers to conflicted schoolboys to Kelli Ochs. There was nothing to hold her on, his team had agreed, but if she did kill someone it'd be first-degree murder and law-enforcement heads would roll if some kind of cop hadn't tried to stop her.

He approached her table and rested his hand on the top slat of the chair opposite her.

"Ms. Ochs, may I join you?"

"Name and department?"

"I'm that obvious? Captain Loren Hornish, Kansas Highway Patrol."

"I've seen you before, in the background."

"Then you can guess why I'm here."

"For the pizza, I hope."

"We have eyes on you."

"You and every other male officer."

"Don't go there. That's not a game to play."

"I'm not making the rules, Captain, just playing within them."

Kelli signaled to her server for a second plate and glass.

"I appreciate your watching over me and the good people of our state," she told Hornish.

"We'd like no harm to come to you, or anyone else."

"Do you really think I'm dangerous?"

"You keep telling us that you are, and we have to take you at your word. I feel like a dad for saying that, by the way," he said.

She laughed. "Sorry, Dad."

"Your posts are bringing out the worst in Kansans. Haven't you made your point, whatever it is?"

"My point and 'the worst in Kansans' didn't come out of nowhere. Look around. I may be the face of it this year, but it's been lurking in the cities and in the fields. It was bred and fed by brutal people. Aggressive stupid people. You know those coiled-snake bumper stickers: 'Don't tread on me.' They'd be honest if they said, 'Don't tread on the rich.' That kind of posturing comes from Washington and the Statehouse, and cruel families, and the very wealthy. People on the bottom want injustice to be corrected, and you're missing out on a lot of anger if you don't see that."

"I do see it, Ms. Ochs. It's a dangerous time, and I'm afraid that you could be the one to light the fuse."

"So I'll be the little woman who started the next great war? Maybe the fuse needs to be lighted."

"God, I hope not."

The server approached with her pizza. Hornish moved the second plate and glass to make room for it.

"You're okay, Captain," she said. "Would you like to join me?"

He pulled back the chair and sat down. "Thanks, Ms. Ochs. This is kind of you, but I can't share a meal with you. It's policy. Do you mind if we just chat?"

The killer-to-be slid a piece of bacon portabella onto her plate.

She said, "I'm not going to kill you. Not yet, anyway."

"Try it," he said with a hard smile, "and we'll bust your ass."

"We understand each other fine," she said, lifting her eyebrows. "To your health."

26

The Gleason Center gym on the Bull Creek College campus was filling with mourners and the curious as Senator Gayfeather arrived shortly after noon in a staff-driven SUV. A college executive escorted her to a padded chair on a low stage built for the occasion of the oilfield workers' memorial.

The senator had been in Bull Creek several times as a candidate, once speaking at an undersized rally in the Warriors' gym with its white walls with royal blue accents and painted lines on the court. This time, the basketball goals were raised on their hinges and no kids were throwing paper wads at the baskets. Just as at her rallies, there were four American flags draped on poles, but this time there was also a white Christian banner. Its red cross in a blue canton was safety-pinned so the cross would always show.

She'd make a brief speech honoring the nine dead workers. Each of the nine was remembered by a framed photograph placed on a black easel before the stage. Four men had been buried that morning in central Kansas, including one in Bull Creek. Two bodies were still being pieced together and their wounds examined for data that would hold up in court.

The gym was quiet but for sobbing and the cries of a few babies, as well as the usual murmur of a crowd. Mourners rustled their folded paper programs listing the victims and the speakers, as well as words to the hymns that would be played by a pianist from the college and led by a high school choir.

Families of the dead men were somber, dressed in pressed clothes but also some in plaid shirts. Immediately behind them were oilfield pals who could walk or make it on crutches or in wheelchairs.

Saltwood's chief executive officer and the Kansas governor flanked Gayfeather on the stage. With them were five clergy representing the nearby congregations of the fallen. Clustered in the audience were members of the legislature, squads of uniformed police and sheriff's deputies, ambulance attendants, federal agents, reporters, and high school students brought in for this historic occasion.

Armed and armored officers were stationed outside the gym on scissor-lift platforms and the roofs of campus buildings. Uniformed and undercover officers moved through the aisles, and the event was recorded not just by police agencies but also by politicians' staffs and families streaming on Facebook Live.

The TV networks were represented by camera operators. Local anchors would provide material for the overviews leading into ponderous discussions by pundits.

Magnetometers had been trucked in from Wichita and set up under blue tents at the building's entrance. All but police officers and VIPs, who assembled separately and entered from the side, passed through them. No backpacks or large purses were allowed.

To open the service, three Protestant ministers and a Catholic priest prayed, one in Spanish. The governor promised all the resources of the state in helping track down the bomber. Saltwood's chief executive officer promised six months' pay to the families of the dead and wounded.

Gayfeather, wearing a navy suit and a double string of pearls, followed Saltwood's CEO. She had been told, she said, that the deceased victims were fine men, and as she spoke their names and looked each family member in the eyes her voice broke and she stepped away from the microphone for a moment.

"They were patriots performing good work for a stalwart Kansas company, and it was to commemorate their lives—and to protect men like them—that I introduced the Petroleum Extraction Act. I know hard work in mineral extraction," she said, reminding the audience of her upbringing in the coalfields of southeastern Kansas.

She spoke for three minutes and fifteen seconds, and drew applause that might have been considered weak even under the solemn circumstances.

The fifth clergyman, another Protestant minister, called upon God to grant understanding to the families. The high school choir came to life with two verses of "Amazing Grace," accompanied by a bagpipe band from Wichita that specialized in funerals, and the crowd slowly emptied out into the pleasant quiet of the parking lot.

Two Gayfeather staff members waited just outside the gym with the office's SUV. The senator moved slowly, offering an unspoken invitation for constituents to hug her or shake her hand. Inside five minutes, with three hugs recorded by the TV cameras, a staffer took her elbow and suggested they leave. The service was later described on TV as the biggest peaceful gathering in the state not involving a sports event or church service since the presidential election.

•　　•　　•

On her way back to Wichita, Gayfeather texted to remind Laura to send Nick to Wichita for a dinnertime meeting about his duties.

"The master wants, the master gets," said Laura to Nick.

With a pencil and legal pad, she sketched a map that had Wichita's main streets, as well as her apartment off Ridge Road and Central Avenue on the west side. Gayfeather's home she put in the North Riverside neighborhood, where the Little Arkansas River bent through the park district before blending into the Big Arkansas.

"Remember your good clothes," Laura said. "She might be taking you to dinner."

Wichita seemed a little on edge when Nick arrived from the ranch late in the afternoon, early enough to drive around a little.

Red-capped pickets paraded in an oval outside a medical office, arguing against the sins of abortion and vaccination. Three blocks down the street, a group calling itself the Almighty Rifles, according to magnetic signs on their pickups, stood guard outside a convenience store festooned with American colors and the Confederate battle flag. Curious, he stopped and filled the truck's tank.

"No infringement of 2A rights!" "Protect women's health! No abortion!" "No terror!" shouted the signs and the middle-aged men and women carrying them.

He thought, yep, the best way to prevent terror is to have out-of-shape men wear Mossy Oak camo pants and reflective sunglasses while they brandish black rifles outside gas stations. They looked like dumplings compared to the militias he had seen in the rebellious neighborhoods of southern Russia.

In another neighborhood, he came across street theatre that was backed by no conspiracies. Driving west on Central Avenue toward the sun as it pushed God rays through a hole in the clouds, he slowed down to watch three middle-school girls, all dressed in white, play on the sidewalk outside a neighborhood church. The tallest one wore angel wings, and the smaller ones laughed and swirled around her.

•   •   •

The evening had turned drizzly by the time Nick, dressed in slacks and a long-sleeve shirt in pale blue, landed at Gayfeather's place. He parked five minutes early at the curb, locked his suitcase and an unused burner phone in the cab, and strode to the door of the brick home.

She welcomed him in with a bottle of beer.

"It's good to see you, Senator."

"Harriet, at home. Please."

The living room was gently lighted, and they walked on an oxblood carpet that felt ankle deep. She gestured at the white leather couch for him and placed herself like a queen in a green wing chair. Nick lowered himself uneasily, unsure whether to sit at attention or in comfort.

"I bought this house before I was elected," she said, waving broadly. "Back during the Great Recession. Look at this 1940s woodwork. I've had to do almost no remodeling, except to add wiring for the internet and security cameras, and bulletproof windows. Also, I built on a dining room and above that I put an expanded bathroom, so the upstairs and downstairs plumbing needed to be redone. A kitchen with two dishwashers, mahogany cabinets, and an eight-burner range. Tile floors, new carpets."

She shrugged. "You know how it goes."

Nick smiled and said, "Absolutely. It never stops." He wondered whether he'd ever own a home.

The living room had the scent of a space that was only for hosting fundraisers, and it felt like he and she were set pieces arranged decoratively. Nick wished he could see her casual rooms upstairs. He wished he'd known about the cameras.

On a shelf near her chair stood a framed photo of a US Army officer. The colors of the uniform were faded with time. The silver oak leaf on his shoulders was the insignia of a lieutenant colonel, a man on his way up.

"My late husband, Steven, just before he went to Iraq," she said. "The only portrait I keep here."

Nick cleared his throat. "My family is Army as well. Intelligence service. My father died last year when his plane was shot down. The FBI told me."

"Oh, Nick. I'm sorry. Syria?"

"Ukraine."

"I see."

Gayfeather stared at her husband's photo. Nick watched motes of dust float across a vague ray of window light.

"One of my honors as a senator is to be invited to say a few words at a Memorial Day ceremony each year. It's a way to honor Steven's memory. On Monday morning I'll speak at the Kansas Veterans Cemetery, south of here in Winfield. You should come."

"I'd like that. I've never been to a Memorial Day."

"It goes back to the American Civil War, when there were a lot of soldiers to honor. The day eventually grew into a memorial to all of the dead. You'll see lots of flowers at cemeteries, and little American flags over the graves of people who were in the military."

"It sounds like a beautiful day."

"We need to remember what our freedom cost," she said. "We just need to remember."

She leaned back in her chair and turned her head away.

"After a while," she said, "all we have is past tense."

Finally, he asked: "Did the Bull Creek service go well?"

"I suppose so. It was somber and patriotic, but there was no way to avoid thinking about the horrible way the men died. I don't have to remind you of any of that."

He touched the stitches in his neck. "I think about it every day."

"I'm sorry you got caught up in this. Laura didn't describe your wound over the phone."

Nick nodded his understanding.

"Laura got banged up pretty hard, too," he said.

Harriet looked like she was trying hard not to be nervous. She apologized for keeping Nick and Laura away from the crowded memorial.

"It would've drawn too much attention to you two specifically, and I didn't want to bring my own surviving heroes to a service in front of families of the dead, you know what I mean?"

He leaned back.

"Also, I didn't want you to be identifiable just yet. For your sake."

"Of course."

"Speaking of Laura . . ."

Here it comes, he thought. Pay attention.

"Tell me how things are going on the ranch."

"Laura is sincere in her work. She understands the workings of the party and is proud of her heritage. She's upset by the well explosion, as you know, and by your demanding to know why she was there and not asking whether she was hurt. She feels slighted by not knowing in advance that you were creating the PETRO bill. She's pissed that she wasn't involved."

"I'd feel the same way," Gayfeather said. "Everything I did was expedient but also necessarily secretive. There's a lot more to it than she knows. You should know that I didn't plan for you to come out here and be hurt at an oil well." And, "What has she said about her finances?"

"She said she's keeping the lights on with oil money, which I think understates her income. I haven't heard her complain, but I don't think she's taking outside money."

"Party beliefs?"

"She seems to have what I imagine are common frustrations. She's not MAGA and not liberal, but neither are you. She's pragmatic."

"Other nations?"

"The only thing I can think of is that she pointed out some things from China. Literature, souvenirs, money, that sort of thing. That, and like you she doesn't trust Russia."

The senator crossed her arms. Her fingernails were manicured with clear polish. "Has she said anything derogatory about me?"

He smiled at her question. "No, even when you hang up on her," he said. "She lets water go under the bridge."

Gayfeather paused, as if she were working up her nerve.

"Are you sleeping with her?"

"No. We have separate rooms."

"What if I wanted you to spend the night with her? What about with me? Would you do that? Could you do that and still solve my problem, if there is one?"

"Is it part of our deal?"

"No," she said with a laugh, finally relaxing. "It might be nothing more than lust and the challenge of seducing the man who decided not to kill me."

"Tonight?"

"Let's try tomorrow. My life in Wichita is mostly fundraisers, and this is a big week for the oil industry."

She stood and took an envelope from a drawer in a side table.

"Take this and have a fine celibate time tonight. Eat well, sleep well. Fill Laura's truck with gas. Do whatever you want to do. Come back here about 7:00 tomorrow night. And listen, park the truck down the street."

He expressed his thanks.

"Do you know where you'll go?" she said. "Do you have friends in town? Did Laura introduce you to any of hers?"

Now we're getting into paranoid territory, he thought. Gayfeather didn't want witnesses to his being here, or she didn't want there to be any connection to Laura. Or both.

"I'm not meeting anyone," he said. "You're the only person I know here."

At the door, she said, "Keep your options open regarding our friend."

As Nick started the truck, he wondered why he had passed up another chance to kill Gayfeather in one of her homes. And then he wondered whether he was invisible to the Russians or the FBI. Maybe she was working with the FBI to ensnare him in a federal plan to embarrass the Russians. By parking in front of her house, had he blown his chance to escape cleanly?

Again, he wished he had known about her security cameras before he knocked on her door.

Gayfeather had ended the visit by toying with his sex drive. He wondered whether he was the only man who ever gave a cautious thought to her bargaining chip.

He had arrived nervous and was leaving anxious.

•   •   •

Gayfeather had two bourbons with her dinner of chicken salad with an apple. For dessert, she called Laura.

"I don't know why I keep you on the staff," the senator said. "You argue with me over everything."

Taken aback, Laura said, "I stand in the background holding your purse and remember the names you need to say, and I know your secrets."

Gayfeather, after a thoughtful pause: "You're right. Your job is safe; don't worry. I'm on edge the worst I've been since Great Bend."

"I'm not your enemy," Laura said. "And I'm upset also about the bombing."

"I know," Gayfeather said, pouring the tiniest three ounces more into her glass. "I'm sorry." She took a sip before saying, "I know that makes me the first Republican to apologize for anything."

27

Darkness was at hand when Karlton Cooper nudged his Corolla through the matte-black pickups and chromed-up glare of motorcycles outside Emil's Bar on Pawnee Avenue near Wichita's big airport. The parking lot seemed to be made of potholes, broken bottles, and car-window glass.

Karlton debated whether to lock his car because it was Saturday night in south Wichita. He decided not to because he didn't want to start off by being a wuss. He just wasn't sure what to do. This was the first time he had been invited to a bar, or to any party that wasn't given by his job or his mom on her own birthday.

He tugged at the bungee cord holding the trunk shut, just to be sure, and patted the spoiler for luck. No one here would grouch about his having the ugliest car, and then he apologized to ODIN for even thinking that. He touched his back pocket, reassured by the thickness of cash in his billfold. He made sure that his buckle was squared away, that his pale blue shirt was buttoned except for the one at the top, and that the placket was flat where it disappeared into his almost new Wranglers. The laces of his New Balance sneakers were tied, but in this parking lot he second-guessed his decision to wear white shoes.

But what the heck. He was now an outlaw. He had cash and could buy a new pair anytime, if he wanted to.

Warren Snarr, the guy who had escorted him out the Walmart door after his firing, waved from the smoking porch. He had traded his blue vest for one of black leather, and his sneakers for black lace-up boots. He stuck out his big hand. Four heavy rings together looked like brass knuckles.

"Cooper! Where the hell you been? Get your ass in here. Glad you made it."

"Hey, Warren. I'm not too late?" Karlton winced in Warren's grip, but the big guy was so used to inflicting pain that he didn't notice, or maybe he just liked doing it. He was pretty intense tonight, not like at work at all.

The space outside the bar smelled like piss. Inside, the sawdust-covered floor and paneled walls smelled like nothing Karlton had confronted before.

"Shit, man. The meeting won't start till everybody's here. Let's get you a beer. What'll you have?"

"I guess . . . I'll have what you're having."

"Monica, babe! A Coors for my friend, on me."

Monica the barback put a brown bottle in front of each. She winked at Karlton when she caught him staring at her tattoos, which ran from the back of her hands to her neck and down into the folds of her cleavage. Like everyone else except for Karlton, all she wore was black. Her brown hair, streaked with pink and green, hadn't seen a pair of scissors in months. He was mesmerized by how it slid across the spaghetti straps of her low-cut tank top.

By the second bottle of beer in his life, Karlton was swinging his hip back and forth against the bar. When "Rockin' in the Free World" came up on the jukebox, he joined the guys in singing without knowing the words. He was a rebel; he had joined the New Resistance. He was proud.

"Why'd you go bald?"

Warren's question caught Karlton off guard.

"I'm a new guy now," he said finally. He ran his hand over his scalp, still getting used to the idea.

"Won't be long before you get your first tat."

"Maybe so."

Warren took a solid drink. He looked over at Karlton, then tipped the neck of his beer toward the wall decorated with heavy fabric: thirteen white stars in a blue X on a field of red.

"The battle flag of the Confederacy, man," he said. "Each one of those stars means something. The whole thing means something. You know what that is?"

Karlton shook his head. The music was too loud for thinking.

"State's rights, man. The right of each state to make laws that suit it. The right of every man to live where he wants, and with who he wants for neighbors. You know what I mean?"

"Uh-uh."

"It means we get rid of the blacks, the border crossers, the gays. We live for Jesus, man. No one takes our guns. It means no one steals our jobs."

Karlton's brain perked up.

"Can you help me find a job?"

"Listen, Cooper, when we're in charge, you'll get your job back. We'll kick their asses."

"I need work, man. Rent's always going to be due."

"Sure, bro. You hang with us, we'll get you your job back. Maybe find you something that pays better."

"Pastor Luke at my church is helping . . ."

"Listen to me, man. Damn. Monica, two more! Listen, you see church as a place for miracle money from God, and we here see it as a source of power. Your preacher has three paid-for houses and a wife he can stand to look in the face during sex, like real missionaries, and a mistress, and a boatload of investments. The Mercedes he drives to church has a tag that says YAHWEH. What do you have?"

Karlton stuck out his chest.

"I have faith in my personal savior, the Lord Jesus Christ."

"It's not a miracle that your preacher has all that money. He earned it by preaching against the mongrel races, the abominations, the socialists, the media hoaxes, all sugared up with miracles if his suckers just believe hard enough. People donate offerings because that's what they want to hear. They know the truth when they hear it."

The outburst stunned Karlton.

Warren asked, "Did he offer you the right foot of fellowship?"

"Yeah, but it didn't make sense," Karlton said.

"It means he's kicking you out on your ass. Sink or swim."

Karlton looked morosely into his beer. Warren lowered his voice.

"Between us guys, I got to let you know something. I heard you had the hots for the preacher's kid, that cheerleader with the hair. Be careful, man. Misery loves company, but with her it'd be misery loves legal company."

"She's cute. The Bible in First Corinthians says girls can get married when they're past 'the flower of her age,' like ripe, after"—he wasn't sure the next word was polite, so he said it softly—"puberty."

"Stay of jail, dude. The Bible will send you to prison. Wait until she's sixteen, at least."

Karlton drank, each gulp a thank-you to Jesus for sending him to Warren.

Warren interrupted the conversation to chat with Monica. She nodded and went down the bar. Warren pointed over his shoulder with his thumb.

"Look at that poster there, by the Coors sign. What do you see?"

"A footprint with crosses."

"Half right. A bootprint with crosses and swastikas. That's white power. We're soldiers of the Lord, armed and ready."

Karlton liked the idea of being a soldier. His dad had worn the dead cousin's hard-ass coat from Vietnam and had gone to Honduras himself, and now the son was just like the old man.

"Cooper, drink up."

Karlton sipped with pride.

"You know what it takes to succeed in this fuckin' world, Cooper? You got to be your own man, joining with other men like you. We're pebbles in the boot of society. Me, I cut through the bullshit."

"You sure the fuck do," Karlton said. He said that word again, and it was okay.

"Check out this tat." Warren pulled up his T-shirt sleeve over his right arm.

"Eighty-eight?"

"Eight is for the letter H. You know: Heil and Hitler. I went to a half-dozen shops before I found someone I trusted to ink me. It had to be done right."

One summer Karlton had gone to a revival given by a Bible church down the street where he lived. Like he did then, tonight he was hearing more of the truth than he could handle, and he didn't really know anything about Heil and Hitler. But Warren kept talking.

"Remember how crappy the boss made you feel back at the store?" Warren said. "He does that to somebody twice a week. So, drink like a man. You earned it."

Karlton raised his bottle and drank deeply. Things were falling into place. He thought of how the Norsemen drank, and he felt secure with his place in history.

"Coors, man," Warren said. "Did you know Coors was run by a guy born up in Russell? Anschutz. Big-time conservative thinker."

"Didn't know that, man." Karlton was learning the right way to say things.

Warren, elbows on the bar, leaned over. It was funny, Karlton thought, that Warren looked so much taller at the store.

"You like guns? I know you bought one at the store."

"Yep." Karlton thought, suddenly conscious of his sore right wrist. He hung it at his side and twisted it around. "I like to shoot. I'm a good shot. Forty-five, .44, 9 mil, .22. Whatever you got."

Warren turned away, now staring into the liquor shelved behind the bar.

"That's power, Cooper. Power comes with a gun."

Karlton squared away to the bottles too.

"Fuckin' A," he said. He could bear the weight of the world.

The door opened, and the smell of rain came in.

"You ever shoot anybody?" Warren asked, slyness in his voice.

Karlton's knees went weak, and he clung to the bar.

"We heard about what happened down at that pawnshop yesterday," Warren said. "Ol' Wayne, shot right through the heart. Sounds like you, all right."

Karlton pushed out a denial.

Warren laughed. "I'm just messing with you, bro, but now I think maybe you know something. Maybe you're our kind of guy. You got the haircut for it."

Karlton chugged the last of his beer. For as woozy as he felt, life was becoming clearer.

"Hey," Warren said, as if he just thought of it. "You know, Harriet Gayfeather's in town this weekend. She did that service today for the dudes up in Bull Creek, and then all this Memorial Day stuff Monday. She'd be a sweet target for a stone-cold killer."

Karlton blushed and his mind raced ahead with that vision.

Warren caught the bartender's eye.

"Monica, babe. Two more, and play our song for Mr. Cooper."

Warren laid a fifty on the bar and spoke into Karlton's ear: "Don't tell nobody what we talk about here."

On his way to the can, Warren called over his shoulder: "Enjoy this night, Cooper, 'cause you ain't getting free beer forever."

By the time Warren came back, the gang was singing to a video segment from the movie *Cabaret*, the scene in which a brown-shirted Aryan boy leads a German guesthouse crowd in "Tomorrow Belongs to Me."

Karlton Cooper was joining in on the refrain.

28

Nick pulled into a Dillons grocery on West Central Avenue, just a little east of Cowskin Creek, and bought that morning's slightly aged *Wichita Eagle,* a couple of apples, and a thick slice of smoked Gouda cheese. Then he thought better of picnicking and headed to the Log Cabin Diner, closer to Laura's Ridge Road apartment.

The three aproned servers, two more than were needed this time of day, were clustered at the register and laughing as Nick walked in.

"Wherever you want, hon," one said, gesturing with a nod.

He settled into the far side of a corner table and opened the newspaper, skimming the headlines. The lead story assessed the proposed PETRO Act, finding widespread support in oil country and the stock market. "No surprise there," he thought.

A photo and feature story previewing the day's Bull Creek memorial service focused on the point of view of the oilfield worker with whom Nick provided first aid after the explosion. As Nick suspected, the worker did have battlefield experience, and as Nick hoped, the worker didn't provide any identifying details about him other than he had a minor wound of his own. A sidebar discussed the rifle found at the base of a nearby deer stand and the rifle's owner, who now was described as the likeliest suspect.

A brief item at the back of the news section said the Justice Department had ruled that the collision and arson that had killed two of its FBI agents earlier in the week in Washington had been nothing more than the work of a disgruntled city worker with psychological issues. He remained at large.

Nick ordered iced tea while he read the menu. Even though the uncertainty of his situation had reduced his appetite, he'd feed himself because he needed to be at peak mental performance this weekend.

He'd been set up but came willingly to Kansas, like the old story of the Iraqi who saw Death in a Baghdad marketplace and fled to what he thought was safety in Samarra.

Death had always intended to meet him in Samarra.

•　•　•

Kelli Ochs was tired of the highway, of road food, of her suitcase. Tired of the police hassles and autograph seekers. Tired of putting a happy face on her plans to kill someone. Tired of feeding the internet.

That afternoon, before she pulled out of Emporia and headed southwest toward Wichita, she braided her long blond hair, a tactic she had developed as a calming technique. Nevertheless, her spirit was on empty. Her car's wipers, as worn out as she was, streaked the windows as she drove through Wichita at sunset and registered at the Western Holiday Motel, under the sign of a lounging cowboy.

The weight of her thoughts exhausted her. Every day: Is there a God? Had she offended God, or was she doing his mysterious bidding? Maybe hunger and self-help CDs encouraged borderline hallucinations, so she went to look for food.

Kelli dragged herself back into her car and drove east on the access road as far as Airport Parkway. She turned north and parked outside the Log Cabin Diner, where she had been before and felt anonymous. Maybe God would let her die of food poisoning, or from slipping on an ice cube. Something.

She waved to the cashier, who smiled and gestured grandly that any seat was hers. The most fascinating woman in Kansas got ready to pull out a chair that faced away from the door.

But there he was, Nick from before.

Nick was unsettled that he had come all this way just to be met by the woman who could become his killer, a woman who walked in out of the rain. Their re-introduction was warm but nervous.

He moved to a booth, where they sat facing each other with their hands on the tabletop. He complimented her braids, which were tied off with tiny pink bands.

This time he knew her significance, but they didn't dwell on it. She still asked, "You do know who I am by now, right?"

They chatted through their meal—a burger for him, a pork chop for her—about life, love, killing, and the power of the state, religion, and family. Every subject added depth to what he knew of her public persona, but guiding his lizard brain was a kind of sexual tension.

"I saw you on TV a couple of days ago," he said. "The Killer Kelli thing."

"Does it bother you?"

"I don't know whether you're playing or you're serious."

"What if I am just playing?"

Nick shook his head. "Assassination is a rotten game."

"What if I'm serious?"

"Then we have something in common."

She put her fork down and wiped her lips.

"Last time," she said, pointing at the table where they had eaten three days earlier, "you didn't tell me what you do for a living."

"I'm an aide to Senator Gayfeather."

"With a résumé that involves killing people?"

"I had a previous career. I removed people." He paused and tried again. "I killed people. Often very bad people."

"And the ones who weren't very bad?"

He shook his head and shrugged. "I served a different country, a different set of rules."

"And now you work for Gayfeather."

"Who hired me because I refused to kill her once when I had the chance."

"Good choice."

"Mine or hers?"

"Yours, definitely. Probably hers, too. It's a fascinating situation. Shall we get pie?"

Twice he asked how much time she had, and she put her hand on his and shook her head. She quoted the Bible—"There's a time to be born, and a time to die; a time to kill and a time to heal"—the first time he asked, and later she said dismissively, "Until I'm ready."

"We're the same," he said. "I know what I'm to do when the time comes."

·   ·   ·

She was exhausted from being a one-woman show. That very day, she said, she'd been rousted by a state cop in Emporia. "He lectured me and then refused to split a pizza with me."

She had learned to check not just the streets but also the sky when she left her car, having once been buzzed closely by a police drone. She waved to it and pointed the aircraft out to people around her. Someone videoed it and put it on TikTok. When she mentioned the event later to students at Kansas State University, a student pulled her aside and showed how to use a small mirror to reflect sunshine and blind a drone's camera.

She complained that she often had a hard time finding a place to stay. Hotel clerks, she said, told her that "you make our other guests afraid."

With Nick, she smiled awkwardly when he asked whether she'd try to kill him.

"That's some ego of yours," she said. "A few days in the state and you already think you're my target. You're the stranger, bud. For all I know, you've been sent to stop me."

"Is it Gayfeather? She's in town."

"If she is, I promise you'll be the second to know."

•   •   •

Kelli leaned forward over their pie crumbs. In a whisper: "Will you spend the night with me, somewhere private? We don't even have to have sex."

Nick realized he was making a crazy smile.

She leaned back. "Some people have suggested that I'm an ax murderer."

He placed his fingers on his fork, a defensive gesture, and she noticed.

"Kidding," she said between giggles. "I'm not that kind of killer."

"You look tough enough," he said. "But I'll take a chance."

"There's one catch. You have to take me to church in the morning."

Nick hadn't gone to church twice in a week since he left his mother's home, but it seemed necessary now. He described the angels he had seen from the pickup.

"It's an omen," she said. "Obviously. But the trouble with omens is that you don't know whether they were good or bad until the thing's over."

"And then," he said, "not two blocks down the street, there was a man walking a little dog that looked like a bundle of shag rugs. The dog stopped to pee, but not like a regular dog. She balanced on her front legs and danced in a circle while she peed."

"I don't know what that could mean, but we shouldn't get close to that dog."

•　　•　　•

Kelli asked Nick to follow her back to her motel a mile to the west. She went in alone, and came out with her beaten-up suitcase and plunked it into the wet bed of Nick's pickup.

"My car's going to stay here so people will think they know where I am," she said.

"What about tracking your phone?"

"I left the only one that works turned on in a dresser drawer."

They drove to Laura's apartment, taking a route so circuitous that Nick got lost while checking for tails. He carried her suitcase up the stairs, then dashed back out for his groceries.

Kelli pulled Nick through the sliding doors onto the balcony. She put her arm around his waist, and smiled when he put his around her shoulders.

"Smell the awakening earth, even that little patch of grass down there," she said. "Do you hear the raindrops splash on the balcony? The hiss of cars on the road?"

Nick thought they might've gone to bed then. Instead, he rummaged in the kitchen until he found a corkscrew for a bottle of pinot noir while Kelli put her scraped blue suitcase in the bedroom.

Kelli lit a candle she found on a shelf. They walked around the room, checking out Laura's books and photos and describing their own memories and families.

"Thanks for not making a big deal out of my fame," Kelli said. "Even though I worked hard to become the boogeyman of every two-bit preacher, do-gooder, and sheriff, I like to imagine that I have a little life on the side."

"Notoriety might've kept you safe," he said. "Requests for ignored justice aren't usually well received by the police."

"They say I'm a socialist. Or I'm a lesbian Jewish trans feminist, like those are bad things. Or I'm a renegade operative kicked out of the Special Forces. I'm both a disgraced sheriff's deputy and a convicted felon living off the kindness of internet strangers. Imagine the stories they'll tell about me when this is over."

"Does being so many things make you unpredictable?"

"I think it's more that I'm everybody's fears wrapped up in one skinny body. The kids get it, though."

Nick nodded and refilled her glass.

She raised a toast.

"I'm twenty-nine years old, living a masquerade. I wasn't even overweight, but I lost almost twenty pounds before I started this because otherwise all the haters would dismiss me for looking fat on camera. I lifted weights more often. I started wearing push-up bras. I bleached my hair. I'm tender, slender, and tall. Now that I'm a ghost of my old self, I'm a star."

She patted her hollow cheeks and broke out a happy face that quickly dissolved.

"This isn't even the real me anymore. I'm an actress playing a mysterious role. At least one reporter or blogger calls me every day, reinforcing the public's idea that I'm a reality-show actress. You know the old movie line from *The Man Who Shot Liberty Valance*? 'When the legend becomes fact, print the legend.'"

When the conversation lagged, Kelli lifted a scratch pad and pencil off the kitchen counter. In a few minutes she handed Nick a caricature of himself.

"I'm not just a crazy person," she said. "I'm also a bad artist."

Isn't it odd, Kelli said, how a person can dedicate her life to killing someone? It's like a wasted life. Or to spend your life fighting others instead of trying to make yourself a better person. It's the difference between focusing inward and outward.

"I've listened to a bunch of self-actualization downloads," she said with a laugh. "I learned that the battle isn't with others but with ourselves."

"I was in FBI custody for a couple of years," Nick said, "and I couldn't agree with you more. When I realized how little control I had over my life, I promised I'd make every day better."

"You were in prison? For killing people?"

"I helped put some bad people away, which is good," he said, "but my background also was a little iffy. The government didn't quite know what to do with me, so I wasn't in prison but I also wasn't free."

"You're cut and bruised, and that happened after we met. You've been in a war." She thought about it. "Are you the missing hero from Quivira?"

He motioned for her to lower her voice.

"You're all over the internet," she whispered, "but not your picture."

Her eyes opened wide.

"Oh my God, you're also the guy from Sandstone!"

Nick pushed back from the table.

"No, not me," he said.

"Sure it's you. Am I the only one to make the connection?"

"How's that?"

"Don't you know there are books and podcasts about what happened in Sandstone? I've been through there dozens of times. People love what you did for those girls."

Nick was relieved. Kelli, and apparently most everyone else, didn't know the whole story.

"You're a hero, Nick. One of my heroes."

Nick looked down at the tabletop and shook his head, then at Kelli when she stood with resolve.

She walked into the bedroom, fiddled around with her suitcase, and came back with a hinged tin box that once held Altoids mints.

"Remember I told you I was from Hays? That's where I was born in the hospital and where I lived after I turned eighteen. My mom's family lived in Victoria, a few miles east of Hays. Very traditional Catholic town."

She carefully opened the lid and lifted out a scratched, cracked photo of a newborn nestling in her mother's arms.

"This is me and Mom on the day I was born." She laid the image on the table and, after a moment, turned it toward Nick.

"Mom died of complications from my early delivery. She had very high blood pressure, and her parents were so embarrassed by her out-of-wedlock pregnancy that by the time it was diagnosed there wasn't anything that could be done. My aunt, her sister, kept the picture for me. She gave it to me when she came up for my high school graduation. Little Kelli Katherine Ochs."

"That's so sad, Kelli."

"My birth father was disconsolate." She pushed back her chair and walked to the window. "Mom's family got the priest to prevent him from having custody because they weren't married and he wasn't Catholic, and a day after the funeral he drove into a bridge support up on the interstate. With nobody left to punish, my grandparents fostered poor little Kelli out to some other folks in Victoria. My foster parents refused to adopt me or let me use their name."

"How do you recover from that?"

She tapped the little box, a tick-tick-tick of her fingernail.

"A couple of days ago I pulled off the highway out in the Flint Hills and parked out in the open range. There was a cow path, so I followed that." She closed her eyes.

"I walked to the top of a hill, and it was a wonderful day. The breeze was blowing warm and the sun was out, and there was fresh clean grass. I took off all my clothes and lay down where the grass was thickest. The earth smell was so rich that I wanted to be part of it. Even the cowpies smelled fresh. The grass was lumpy and rough, and the ground was kind of rocky. I knew I'd get a million chigger bites, but that hour was worth it. There was nothing but earth, wind, sky, grass, a bunch of birds, and me. I'd be okay with it if that's my last happy day."

He said, "That's depressing and beautiful at the same time."

She shrugged.

"A path is a promise made that the footsteps you take are on safe ground, that someone has trod this soil before you and lived to tell others about the route." Her eyes focused far beyond the room. "It's a promise that you will get somewhere. The choice of path is yours. . . . Forgive me—it's those self-help recordings."

When Nick picked up the wine bottle, Kelli flattened her hand over her glass.

"No more wine, Nick. I want you to shower and shave and go to bed with me. We can sleep as much as you'd like. I just need to be close to you."

"Do you leave town tomorrow?" he asked. "I'm afraid for you."

"It's what people know about themselves that makes them afraid, my dear Nick. As long as I can love, I'll live."

•　•　•

Nick hadn't been in bed with a woman since Cimi, and after the past week he was as anxious as he was eager. The anxiety was winning, and it wasn't a good look.

Kelli lifted the sheet and climbed off the double mattress. Naked, silhouetted by the streetlight, she stood before the window and slid it open so they could hear the rain and all the sounds that went with it: the drumbeat on the carport's metal canopy, the tiny taps when the wind blew drops against the window glass, the honks of cars on the four-lane, the wind shushing through the property's trees.

"Better?" she said.

He leaned over and put his hand on her hip, drawing her close. She bent down and kissed him, then slid her legs under the sheet and lay half on top of him. She pressed her cheek to his and whispered: "Give everything to yourself first. Think dirty. Imagine how glad I am to have you in me."

29

Kelli walked into the living room wearing a long-sleeved yellow dress, a bright confection that matched the bounce in her step. It was gathered under her bosom, and fastened loosely with tasseled ties at her neck.

"It's Bohemian," she said. "Boho. Do you like it?"

Nick knelt before her, his hands on her hips. Then he rose, gathering her in a hug, and kissed her passionately.

"Easy, tiger," she said. "We're going to church."

"A church is full of people who make love," he said.

She laughed. "Or at least have sex."

She carried a soft-cover Bible, worn at the cover and well thumbed in the New Testament. A loose bracelet of yellow plastic bands decorated her right wrist.

"You are sunshine," he said.

"I always dress for church," she said, lifting her skirt a little. "See, even church sandals."

She hugged him close, then broke away to pop a couple of tablets. "Pain preventers."

He took her hands, and with his thumb rubbed the thick bands peeking out of her sleeve.

"Zip ties?"

"It's a style I picked up," she said. "Fetching, right?"

As he was leaving, he noticed that her baby photo and little metal box were still on the table. He placed the photo in the box and held it out to her, but she asked him to stick it in his pocket for the moment. He folded her sketch of him and tucked into the box as well.

Nick brought the truck to the sidewalk, holding the door open for her in the cool air, and she dashed out with her Bible and a plastic water bottle. He wore Walmart—his surviving pair of dark slacks, a white western shirt snapped to the top, a blazer, and running shoes.

"No coat?" he asked.

"I forgot."

He draped his jacket around her shoulders. She felt the little box and said, "Thank you."

When she found more than that, she looked into the pockets and found thin bundles of cash, all Nick had besides what was in his billfold.

They kept their thoughts to themselves as they drove east through Wichita to the River Jordan Cathedral. Why that one, Nick asked, and she said, "I've seen it on TV."

Nick felt nothing about going to church; he had no religious upbringing. His credo was that life was life, and there was no religious mystery to that. Maybe someday he would have a religion, he occasionally thought.

His mother, the ruthless Russian Army intelligence officer, had suggested that there was a oneness in all life, and all humans had a little spirit that went in and out of human physical existence. That was as good as it got, she said.

His mother never mentioned seeing angels dance in the street.

•   •   •

Karlton Cooper drove his Toyota Corolla off Kellogg, choosing a space right in the middle of the River Jordan lot. The wind hadn't come up yet, and the Stars and Stripes and the Star of David flags hung without enthusiasm even though it was almost 10 A.M.

His car still bore its ODIN tags, because buying new tags would take money. He might have a thicker billfold now, but ODIN had done just as much for him as Pastor Luke had. Besides, he wasn't in the mood to do anything Pastor set as a condition for aid from Jesus. He certainly wasn't going to make his teal car invisible to Pastor.

Karlton twanged his trunk cord and patted the spoiler. He thought he looked better than he felt, which was nauseated and weak. His head hurt behind the eyes. At the glass doors, Karlton caught his reflection. He was wearing what he wore the night before at the bar with the guys. His jeans and blue shirt smelled like cigarettes and beer. They stank, even he could tell that, but they were the only dress-up clothes he had.

The front-door security minister, the one who carried his pistol in an underarm holster, glared at him. Karlton reminded himself that he himself had grown into a killer. If he had to, he could do it again even if it meant another sleepless night. So watch your manners, Mr. Security Minister guy.

He pulled his shoulders back and strutted down to a middle pew, where he sat along the aisle for five minutes listening to canned music—"We are the chosen generation," again and again—until a spitty woman in his mother's White Shoulders perfume and swishing pantyhose hissed at him to get out of her seat. After he slid over, she made a show of wrinkling her nose at him.

• • •

The Sterretts chose their usual seats on the side of the sanctuary, where they would have a clear view of Pastor Luke. As always, Joyleen and Lance had stood in a long line at the coffee stand for her mocha something or other—Lance had long ago stopped paying attention— and he listened to her sucking coffee up the straw from the closed cup required by the church's janitor.

Joyleen and Lance smiled at their neighbors and shook a few hands. She spoke kindly to fellow church workers.

Lance nevertheless was uncomfortable. Joyleen had insisted that he leave his handguns in the truck.

• • •

Christmas and Noelle glided down the aisle like royalty, mother first, and paused at the second pew right in front of the pulpit. A half-dozen folks already seated there jumped into action and with abject apologies stood to let the pair crabwalk to their customary position in the center of the row.

Christmas whispered into Noelle's ear, "The one next to me is the kind who'll wear her hair long far too late in life." The girl bent forward slowly to peek, then covered her mouth and giggled.

• • •

Having arrived early in his own car, Pastor prepped in his office.

He stood before his mirror, adjusting his hair just so and placing the over-the-ear microphone a couple of inches from his right cheek. Every Sunday he did this, and each time he was reminded of a profile that appeared four years earlier in the *Kansas City Star* newspaper. It described him as charismatic, a natural leader, but also preening, pandering, and unctuous.

The profile described how, for example, in front of the reporter and photographer, he bent down beside an old woman and took up her hand. "Your class ring's pretty, like they used to be." The woman told the reporter that she hadn't looked at other class rings for the past sixty years and wondered why Pastor Luke was making such a big deal out of hers.

After the profile appeared in a Saturday edition, Pastor Luke looked up *unctuous* and quickly adjusted the next's day sermon to include the heavenly joy of being handsome and nostalgic before the Lord. The *Star* article was the one clipping he refused to let Christmas paste into the family scrapbook.

He skimmed the announcements he would read from the pulpit, glanced again at the welcoming prayer, and made sure every large-print page of his sermon was in order in the leather folder embossed with his initials. On such a patriotic occasion as Memorial Day weekend, he'd normally lavish a paragraph of praise and prayer on the military and police, but a rival Bible church across town was throwing a highly publicized first-responders celebration and military worship service. On this pretty Sunday morning, he'd be lucky if any of them showed up at the Cathedral.

He used to pray from his heart, but these days the prayer had to be written so that he could read it while casting his eyes down. Pastor was a big believer in prayer. Let people give their faults and worries to the ether and thereafter take no responsibility for their actions. He understood that this wasn't a common understanding of the goal of prayer, but it worked for him. "In thankfulness of heart," indeed.

Unless there was a reward in it for him, Pastor didn't want to get splashed with anyone else's problems.

The sermon he wrote was more of an outline than an organized lecture. He realized years earlier that he was going to wing it every Sunday. Some of it was God's truth, some of it was repetitive nonsense, but what mattered was that he spoke it with conviction.

His suit today, in consideration of the season beginning with this weekend, was a medium gray of summer-weight wool. It suggested prosperity. His shirt was a softer gray, and his tie was garnet red. A rich red. Like the riches of heaven.

•   •   •

Captain Loren Hornish took an aisle seat near the rear of the sanctuary. As a task force officer assigned to track political malcontents, he found much to think about in the Cathedral's militant congregation.

Take that guy in the eighth row, for example. His pale scalp gleamed—a new skinhead? He didn't look like much, but sometimes they didn't.

Churches provide a good sense of rightwing politics, Hornish had advised rookies. Know your enemy, he said, despite knowing that some troopers found nothing wrong with white supremacy and political violence. He'd seen the tattoos and heard chatter approving of the January 6 insurrection and the deportations.

A few military haircuts were sprinkled around the sanctuary, and he recognized a couple of retired city cops. There were unsettled babies and a lot of bland songs as the room filled. In a front pew off to the side, costumed children were being arranged for what likely would be a heavy-handed skit. A video camera was positioned on a wall behind Hornish, another was fixed to the wall high to his right, and a third was above the stage and aimed at the congregation.

Hornish was surprised when Nick Deveraux and Kelli Ochs walked past him, her yellow dress floating in pools of light. What would she post during the service?

The couple smiled warmly at each other and graciously to the worshipers in a pew a third of the way down the aisle.

Nick recognized Lance Sterrett across the sanctuary. It took Nick a moment to put him in a religious context instead of the Hitch and the Saltwood explosion. In a split second, Nick figured out what was stuck in his mind. When Sterrett walked up to the Saltwood men after the blast, he pulled hearing protectors out of his ears. Why would he be wearing them?

But the big event was the arrival of Kelli. Whispers steamrolled across the congregation as she was recognized. Text messages flew out of the sanctuary as the choir started singing and Pastor Luke entered from a stage door to the left of the pulpit.

As Pastor worked his way through the announcements and asked his congregation and the folks at home to bow their heads, Kelli pressed close to Nick and squeezed his hand.

"Whatever happens," she said, "let things play out."

Kelli edged out into the aisle, Bible in her left hand and water bottle in her right. After a long beat, as the prayer ended ". . . in thankfulness of heart," she stepped toward the front of the sanctuary.

30

Late arrivals often had to sit near the front of the sanctuary, where more seats were open, so Pastor paid no attention to the woman in yellow coming forward until she stopped in the aisle, ten feet in front of him.

"Thank you for coming," he told her. "Please have a seat."

Maybe it was his subconscious hearing that picked up on a word floating above the congregation. He smiled broadly and said hello.

"Pastor Luke," she said. The congregation had gone quiet. "My name is Kelli Ochs. Do you know who I am?"

"Yes, my child. You've become quite famous."

"I've made mistakes, and I'd like to repent to Jesus in front of the congregation of River Jordan Cathedral. Will you hear my prayer?"

His nostrils flared. She ascended the three steps, set her bottle and Bible down at her toes, and stood alone before the world.

To a chorus of "amen" from the audience, Pastor stepped up to her.

She found that he was no taller than she. He had seemed larger than life on the TV screen.

"I'm scared, Pastor. I have sinned." Her voice was picked up by Pastor Luke's headset.

She began to cry, leaning into his suit jacket, and he wrapped his arms around her and smiled indulgently.

"I need to know Jesus still loves me," she said.

He glanced over Kelli's shoulder at Joyleen, who wore an expression of concern. Pastor was amused by that. Without looking, he also knew the expression on his wife's face; she had seen him work his magic on spiritually needy women, and she would be bored.

His moves were familiar also to Kelli. A closeness that was too close, a predator's smile, his right hand grasping hers as if he sensed this was a big professional moment that could not be allowed to slip away.

As they separated, she spoke her thanks and took his left hand in her right, hoping that her strength wouldn't frighten him too soon. With her left hand, she gently pulled a loop of zip tie off her right wrist and with a deft move tightened it around Pastor's wrist, tethering them together.

His eyes flew open, and he tugged against the zip tie, which was looped through one around her wrist. She dropped to a knee, keeping her eyes on him. Her hand searched for the Bible. She flipped it open with her left hand and pulled an icepick from a cutout in the pages.

"The Devil has come to our church," Pastor cried into his microphone. He raised his free hand and turned to face the audience.

Amid the wails and cries, the good folks raised their straightened arms, palms toward the altar. Some of the hands held cellphones. Using the camera high on the back wall, the audio-visual operator zoomed in so that Pastor and Kelli filled the screens at home.

Two security ministers strode heavily up the aisles, hands under their blue jackets.

Kelli stood, the icepick's wooden handle in her grip. She closed on Pastor, bending his handcuffed arm behind him, and jabbed the point of the five-inch-long silver spike against the flesh just north of his Adam's apple. He arched his chin back.

"You move, and you die," she said. Her words boomed through Pastor Luke's microphone. "This is long enough to reach your brain."

The security ministers were close now, their handguns drawn, their footsteps small, and their knees bent.

"Drop the weapon," they yelled. "Now. Drop it now, or we'll shoot."

Kelli kept her eyes on Pastor.

"You and I are going to have a talk," she said. "Tell them to walk away, back where they came from."

"Boys, do it." He stiffened his back and spoke sternly with more confidence than he owned. "The Lord is with me."

The Lord, the churchgoers thought, wanted them to draw their own firearms. A rustling of purses and pockets, not just from the first few pews but also from far beyond reasonable range, produced a dozen automatics and revolvers: Glocks, Rugers, Smith & Wessons.

Someone in a hurry dropped an outrageously powerful—for church—revolver. The sound startled the adjacent worshiper, who inadvertently kicked it across the wooden floor. The gun spun to a stop with its four-inch-long barrel nudging Karlton's foot.

Karlton picked it up.

•   •   •

Kelli addressed Pastor Luke face to face.

"You know my name is Kelli Ochs, but you don't know who I really am. You don't know the name of my mother. I know you, though. You got your start here after you appeared in a newspaper picture with her."

Pastor's face was blank, not resigned but lost. The audience had gone silent.

"In 1994, like Operation Rescue, you stood outside an abortion clinic and berated her for trying to get treatment. A newspaper photo of that made you famous. I read that you have a clipping of that on your office wall. You sent my mother back to good ol' Catholic Victoria, where she lived the rest of her life in humiliation.

"She developed pre-eclampsia. Because she wanted an abortion, because she wasn't married, because of what she had tried to do, her mother and father wouldn't allow her the right medical care. Her punishment was that she died two days after giving birth to me.

"She was a student teacher who was one class short of graduating from Wichita State, and you know that no Kansas school district would hire a pregnant woman. But you, and people like you, like my grandparents, gave up a sure thing in exchange for me."

Pastor Luke tried to jerk Kelli off balance, but she flexed and pulled him back.

"She got knocked up by her boyfriend, who she had dated for a couple of months. But she was turned away from the clinic by bullies. So she went home to Victoria and died. Her parents found out my father wasn't Catholic, so they fostered me out to another family. Because who wants to adopt a baby born of sin, right?

"The fosters said they loved me, but you know what? In the winter when I was thirteen, one of my foster brothers tied me to a post in the barn and beat me seven times in two days while his parents were in Salina buying a tractor. He took me outside and made me wash off in the stock tank. When I was sixteen, he and his friends attacked me. He said he'd kill me if I told anyone.

"Well, James Michael and Frankie and Billy, here I am. Come and kill me."

She stepped behind Luke, wrapping his arm behind him until he winced. She leaned around him and pointed the icepick at the congregation.

"This is the life you gave me. You played God years ago and made my mother take the path that killed her. But where were you when this born girl needed help?

"Today, I get to play God. It's my birthday, and you have to do what I say."

Joyleen Sterrett's hand flew to her mouth, and she jumped up. Lance gaped at her, then took her forearm and gently guided her back down. He wasn't stupid, and now he understood why his wife had started wearing high-dollar bras.

Eight rows out, Karlton looked at the revolver in his hand. It looked like his, the one he used at the pawnshop, when he played God. The real God was back with a message. This .44 had a shorter barrel, so maybe it'd be easier to use.

Kelli continued: "Now you all know the answer to the big question. I came to kill Pastor Luke Meriwether, in front of Jehovah, you folks and all the folks at home.

Pastor shouted: "Get my goddamned rifle!"

The two security ministers glanced at each other and came to an unspoken decision. The one closest to Karlton holstered his sidearm and raced out of the sanctuary toward Pastor's office.

The congregation erupted in confusion. Captain Hornish slipped his hand under his jacket and made sure his weapon was ready, but when he assessed all the other handguns being waved around, he chose discretion.

Kelli ignored the hubbub. "Kneel with me, Luke."

She twisted him sideways and kneed him in the thigh to make it happen, then got on her knees beside him. He squirmed, the icepick drawing a little blood, which ran in a thin streak down to his light gray collar.

Pastor Luke was crying as he tried to swing his tethered arm. "Let me clap," he begged her. "O golden dog, let me make you go away."

She winked broadly at him. "Sorry, Pastor. I don't do magical thinking."

Bending close to the microphone, she addressed the congregation.

"You all might even cheer me on, because you've wanted to see who I'll kill. You wanted to see someone die. You love someone else's misery. But here's the big surprise," she said. "I'm going to let this corrupted man live. In exchange, he's going to watch me die."

The video cameras stared.

"All of you: Think of my mother, who your kind sent to her death. And now you build churches like this and honor men like Pastor Luke because you're so smug, so sure that you alone hear God's word. And none of us dirty people can be in your club."

Kelli was shouting now.

"Where were you for the past twenty-nine years? Sitting here congratulating yourselves for bullying women and humming along to that god-awful music. You can call the police or you can run away, but I'm not going to hurt you. You'll just have to live with your dark secrets."

A woman stood up in the third row. She shook her Bible at Kelli and shouted, "You got your state amendment to allow killing babies. You remember that?"

Kelli leaned closer to Pastor's microphone. Her eyes were on his.

"Yes, and I voted for it. But in 1994 we already had a national law allowing abortion, and you—*you people*—got in the way." With each word, she pushed with the icepick.

She moved the pick to her right hand and pushed it through Luke's coat and shirt below his ribs just hard enough to make him cringe. With her left hand, she reached for her water bottle and braced it between her legs. She unscrewed the cap, lifted it, and guzzled.

Pastor stared at her.

She burped, tossed the bottle aside, then in a flash put the icepick back at Luke's throat.

"Stand up, you self-righteous son of a bitch. This is a moment of dignity."

He rose, his head leaning away from the pain. Blood dribbled down the icepick and dripped from Kelli's wrist.

"Pastor, do you want to say anything?"

"My Lord, deliver me of these wicked hands!"

"Good luck. God brought us together. I'm giving up the life I never should've had," she said, her diction beginning to slur. "You can pray for my soul or damn me to hell, but at least now you all know who you are. And who I am."

She accidentally stepped on the empty bottle, which squawked plastically, and she stared at it for a moment. When she spoke again, she had mellowed.

"I've lived my whole damned life knowing I shouldn't have had one at all."

She maneuvered Pastor so that she could face more of the congregation.

"What right did you have to choose me over my mother?"

In a dreamy voice, her body wavering, she called out: "Remember what I told you, and what's in Amos, chapter 5: Let justice roll on like a river."

Sensing his moment, Karlton tried to push past the uptight woman at the end of his pew, but she had grabbed the pew in front and wouldn't let him by. He stepped up behind her onto the pew and leaped into the aisle.

In four pounding steps, his face and scalp flaming, he was standing before the stage, extending the heavy revolver at arm's length in a two-handed grip. As cries of "Oh my God" filled the sanctuary, the gun's front sight wavered between Pastor and Kelli.

Joyleen was standing again, her fists at her face, afraid for being discovered, afraid for her lover, afraid for the hundreds of thousands of dollars that a dead Pastor could never pay.

"Don't shoot," Joyleen shouted.

The security minister glanced at Joyleen and determined that she wasn't armed. He edged down the aisle behind Karlton.

Her soprano cheerleader voice carrying over the ruckus, Noelle begged, "Shoot him. Shoot him."

"Drop your weapon," the security minister shouted again and again, now at Karlton, now at Kelli.

"My Lord Jesus," Pastor Luke cried. "Put down your goddamned gun!"

Karlton bellowed at the stage: "You will not blaspheme in the house of the Lord! Sinner!"

He had never felt fury like this before. He could finally say what he had bottled up.

"You lied to me!" he shouted. "You said Jesus would help me find a job, and I got nothing. You said you loved your wife, but you walk around in God's house with your arm around Miss Green Dress. Where is Jesus?"

Joyleen cried, "Luke! No!" and vomited onto the back of the woman in front of her.

Karlton's scalp flared like an ember.

"And you! Kelli Killer! You are an uncorrected woman." She slowly turned her head toward his voice. "You said I was cute, but you never came back, not once! I lost my job because the boss said Walmart couldn't afford me. Where's my justice?"

Nick leaped out of his pew at the back of the sanctuary and sprinted forward, his jacket flying open. He shoved past the security minister, who stumbled against a pew and inadvertently pistol-whipped a man leaning out for a better look.

Lance Sterrett recognized Nick immediately. He appreciated Nick's military-quality action, but he had to care for his wife and later get the real story out of her. Knowing what was coming, he slapped his palms over his ears, not hers.

Nick was nearly there, five steps away, as Karlton yanked the trigger.

The cylinder rotated, putting an empty chamber in front of the hammer before it crashed down.

The congregation relaxed. The gun wasn't loaded.

Kelli wobbled on her feet. Her eyes were closed.

Pastor Luke drew away from Karlton. He reflexively pulled Kelli hard into his chest.

Furious, Karlton pulled the trigger again. The cylinder rotated again and the hammer came back. It tripped forward to slam the firing pin into a live cartridge.

The Magnum's instant kick threw Karlton's hands back over his head.

Time stopped.

The pressure wave of the muzzle blast, thunderous on the open firing range and abusive indoors, clawed at the congregation's eardrums.

Nick grabbed Karlton's right arm, driving him to the floor. He twisted the forearm until the shooter's elbow snapped and the .44 shook loose.

The security minister stood in deafened silence, holding his empty hand against an ear.

When everyone looked up, Kelli lay crumpled on the carpeted stage, her yellow dress soaking in a dark pool of blood, her sandals fallen from her feet. Pastor Luke huddled behind her. He had tripped and fallen, his body pulled down by hers.

Karlton's bullet had entered between her shoulder blades. It struck her spine, shattering the third and fourth thoracic vertebrae, then deflected over Pastor Luke's shoulder into the wall below the big wooden cross.

Except for babies and adults crying, the church was silent.

As he sprawled on the floor, Karlton looked at his shooting arm and how it bulged out at the elbow. He rolled awkwardly to pick up the revolver lefthanded. Using the gun as a short crutch, he lurched to his knees and screamed, "I have the right! They lied!"

He fired wildly at Nick, who was barreling out past the security minister, who was trying to wedge himself into the pews. Nick flinched as the wild shot shattered a fake window above his head.

"Garmr!" Karlton yelled.

No one in the sanctuary understood his screams, because they couldn't hear it. Four video cameras, however, recorded everything. Almost.

The security minister heading for Pastor's AR-15 had broken the office's glass door and crashed through the wooden door to the inner sanctum. He climbed onto the credenza and pounded on the shadowbox with a stapler until the plexiglass cracked. He lifted out pieces of plexi and then the AR-15. Even before he jumped to the floor pulled back and released the charging bolt, pushing a .223-caliber round into the chamber.

Without delay, he sped toward the sanctuary door and took up a soldierly position, back against the wall. As he listened to Pastor's frantic talk from the stage, he caught his breath. He checked the firing selector and chose full auto. This was war, and he had a mission. Two slow breaths, and he peeked around the corner when he heard a girl scream, "Shoot him!"

Startled by the blast of Karlton's .44 Magnum, he reflexively pulled the rifle's trigger. Shots sprayed through the door, up and to his right into the sanctuary's ceiling, and then erratically down the church's foyer before Nick and others burst through. The rifle cycled through the magazine's thirty rounds in three seconds, so quickly that almost no one heard the burst.

On the stage, Pastor rolled back from Kelli's body and with his free hand checked for bleeding on his neck. He tugged at the zip tie and glared with fury at Kelli's body.

The other security minister used a tactical knife to slice apart the tie. Pastor stood up, staggered around the body, cursed it, and spit into her blood.

Members of the choir looked at one another. A soprano reached up hesitantly to wipe a bit of Kelli off her neighbor's face, and fainted.

A nurse emerged from the blue cloud of gunpowder smoke to examine Kelli's body for a pulse. When she noted the time on her watch and shook her head, a tenor handed over his blood-spattered choir robe and the nurse spread it gently over the body.

Men from the congregation pinned the writhing and howling Karlton to the floor. A couple of them beat him in the face, and another kicked the revolver loose and stepped hard on the broken arm.

Christmas and Noelle waited until their pew cleared out before walking toward the stage. Christmas alone climbed each step with care, her eyes never leaving Kelli's body.

Christmas accepted Luke's stiff hug with her arms folded before her chest, trying to avoid getting blood on her dress. She twisted loose, to look again at the body.

She said, "She died for you."

She said, "She was the age of our lost child."

She said, "You spit on her."

The organist began the first song that came to mind, which was "Doxology." As the choir took its cue and staggered into "Praise God from whom all blessings flow, . . ." Christmas stepped off the stage. She glanced at Joyleen. Without a word, Christmas gathered up Noelle and they walked arm and arm past the crowd around Karlton Cooper and out of the church.

Pastor Luke didn't watch them leave. He didn't notice when the organist stopped and the choir members took off their robes and walked away.

"Miriam," he whispered to Kelli's body. "Her name was Miriam Ochs."

He then busied himself removing his headset, turning it off and collapsing it so it would fit back in his suit pocket.

Within a minute, after the first screaming police car skidded up to the dazed crowd outside the Cathedral's smoked glass doors, the audio-visual guy turned off the feed to Facebook Live.

Not knowing quite what to do after an actual shooting, the security minister with the rifle walked outside. Six police officers pointed their own shotguns and rifles at him, and a seventh bull-rushed him to the ground and beat him even as he wailed, "I didn't do it."

31

Nick drove north on Interstate 135 out of Wichita, not afraid but telling himself he needed to avoid being further involved. He was shaken by the murder of Kelli Ochs. It wasn't the sound of the handgun or the taking of a life; that was his trade. It was that Kelli had been so close to fulfilling her mission, a secret that took even Nick by surprise.

The night before, he had told her, "Killing is best left to the professionals."

Kelli said, "But what if an amateur needs to do it to cleanse her soul? She can't involve anyone else without soiling them. What if it's a personal matter? That'd be important too."

Nick admired her search for meaning in her life. Why had hers been so screwed up, what problem was hers to fix, and most of all why had her life been so full of injustice?

"My only purpose is to live in sorrow," she had said. "God made me, knowing what I would have to do."

It bothered Nick that Kelli had been cheated out of her basic goal—to disrupt the received truth that only governments and religious institutions had the right to decide who lives and who dies. But then he understood that she had made her point.

Nick was also upset that he had given up more of his privacy by not heeding Kelli's admonition to stay out of it. As a result, his image might well be on Facebook pages and TV screens worldwide, and surely some of those screens belonged to the FBI and Russian mobsters.

Beyond Newton, a half-hour north of Wichita on I-135, he was enticed by a two-lane highway where there would be fewer law enforcement officers. Kansas Highway 15 delivered him to a farm town called Goessel, where a sign advertised the Mennonite Heritage

Museum, honoring German-speaking Russian immigrant farmers who brought their wheat to the prairie in the 1870s. In a corner of town he found a small park. Now that the rain had abated, a man and a young girl were kicking a soccer ball at the far end. A purple-roofed shelter offered cover near the strip of parking.

Nick had just edged his bottom down on a picnic table when a dark SUV pulled up perpendicular to Nick's pickup. The driver rolled down his window and waved.

"Don't run," he called.

Arms out from his sides, hands open, Highway Patrol Captain Loren Hornish approached until he stood six feet in front of Nick. Hornish spoke first.

"Are you carrying a weapon, sir?"

"No."

"Turn slowly and place your arms on the table."

Hornish stuck one foot inside Nick's left foot and with his hard hands frisked under the jacket and down from the belt.

"What's this box in your pocket?"

"Something I picked up."

"May I take it out?"

Nick nodded. Hornish peeked into the box and closed it. He put it on the picnic table, and Nick returned it to his pocket.

"You're good. Turn around, sir."

Nick didn't say anything, but he looked for an inside move.

"Do you remember me, Nick? From Bull Creek, and before that from a ride I gave you into Great Bend a couple of years ago?"

Nick nodded. "Yeah. Thanks for the lift."

"I want you to know, I'm maybe the reason you have those shrapnel scars on your face. I shot at you on the elevator in Sandstone."

"I wondered where those came from. The FBI didn't give me a lot of details."

"Goes with our jobs, I guess."

Hornish shuffled his feet against the grass.

"I wanted to kill you then because I thought you'd snitch that I helped you. I regret that, and I'm grateful you didn't tell anyone, as far as I know."

"It remains our secret."

Hornish exhaled.

"As it turned out, I got a promotion for tracking you from Great Bend to Sandstone and then nearly killing you. If anyone had known I drove you to Great Bend even without knowing who you were then, well, you can imagine how that would've looked. I was going to retire, but the state gave me this sinecure, which lets me use my judgment and go after really bad people."

Nick nodded his thanks. "You had a son in Afghanistan."

"He's back. With a Purple Heart, but he's walking again. I appreciate you for remembering."

Nick gestured toward the bench, and they sat.

"I was in church behind you," Hornish said, "and I saw what happened. I didn't know you knew Kelli. Did she tell you I sat with her yesterday?" He held up for a moment. "It seems like a week ago already."

"She said she was tired of being hassled."

"If you mean by me, I had to be gruff. But I admire, admired, her. We chatted for a half-hour or so while she ate. She was strong."

"She and I met accidentally twice. We were comfortable together."

"I'm sorry you lost your friend, and I'm glad you did what you could for her. The preacher is a schmuck. You're a decent guy, a professional."

"I'm just trying to start a new life," Nick said.

"In Kansas? Anyway, until I saw you in Bull Creek, I thought you were dead. After Sandstone, everything went hush-hush. The corpse of the guy trying to kill you disappeared behind the federal curtain, and we never heard another thing. Most of all, thanks for shutting down the kidnappers. I wish we had been as good at our jobs as you were."

"It was luck, and Cimi Hernandez."

"What are you doing here now?"

"Senator Gayfeather hired me to be her aide, believe it or not. She was impressed that I had a chance to shoot her and didn't. She said she wanted someone trustworthy."

Hornish raised a wait-a-minute hand. He walked back to his SUV and opened the front passenger door to reach under the seat. He returned with a small bundle of rags.

"I've been keeping this for a special occasion," he said, "and I think you might need it." He placed the bundle on the table between them.

To Nick, when he put his hand flat on it, the bundle felt like a handgun.

"Are you planting this on me?" Nick said.

"You found it on the table. That's all either of us knows about it," Hornish said. "It's untraceable and unrecorded. Given different circumstances, it might've been found in a ditch next to your body."

"You're a good guy, Captain."

"I've seen a lot of people. Hell, once I arrested a shoplifter dressed as a teddy bear. But Kelli trusted you, and I trust you."

"Is anyone looking for me?"

"Wichita police and Sedgwick County deputies are chasing their tails and don't have an ID for you. As for your truck—I know it's Ms. Eisenhauer's truck and you're borrowing it. There were so many vehicles leaving that no one noticed anybody else."

"Yeah, I don't even remember seeing you," Nick said.

"They know you didn't shoot Kelli but they also don't know how you're involved or that you were the guy in Sandstone. Right now you're considered a concerned citizen. That might all change if you get found."

"What about the shooter? I'm pretty sure I've seen him before."

"He's under guard in a hospital by now, and he'll be arrested after his release. The feds will probably take over, since they're in town for the explosion and a lot of them are bored with that already."

"I'll try to stay out of their way."

"If you stay out of Wichita," Hornish said, "your biggest worry's going to be a retiree or somebody at a gas station, somebody who's in front of Fox News all day."

•   •   •

Nick left Goessel, again driving up K-15, past the courthouse-size Alexanderwohl Mennonite Church, to where the highway joined US 56 for a few miles, and then north again on K-15 at Hillsboro. He detoured when he saw a sign to Hope, a town where another sign promised "There will always be Hope in Kansas."

Yeah, thought Nick, but would there ever be hope *for* Kansas?

He crossed Interstate 70 at Abilene, where he paid cash for a couple of burner phones and a pair of grocery-store sandwiches, and spent the afternoon driving and trying not to think as he followed the Saline River upstream. He listened to radio stations for news about the shooting until they went to fuzz.

From a farm road leading off a paved county road, he called Barb Pellen at the FBI. She answered after two rings.

"I didn't kill anyone," he said. "Don't send a team after me."

"I know," Pellen said. "We saw the video. You did what you could. We wonder, though, why you were there."

"Accidental friends," he said. "Kelli needed a friend, and apparently we had things in common."

Pellen said, "I'm sorry for your loss."

There was a moment of silence.

"Are you going to tell me where you're calling from? We'll have it traced soon enough if we need to."

"I trust the FBI to have it already pinpointed."

"Touché. But now listen. You may not remember the agent I was with in Sandstone, but you met him later. Fred Snike, about fifty, an accounting specialist from Topeka."

"He was in every interrogation about the Russians and the Ukrainian. He laughed like a woodpecker."

"Exactly. He was promoted to your case within a week. It took me two whole months to be promoted to DC."

"He didn't fit in with the other agents. Why was a cow-state agent put on my case?"

"I hate to speak ill of a colleague, and I'll deny saying this, but I've found links between Snike and your buddy Gregori Orlov. It turns out they were playing chess while the rest of us were playing NASCAR. Snike has been promoted twice since the administration's purge of the Bureau."

Nick's thoughts drifted back to Snike's repeated questions about his loyalty to Russia and Orlov.

"Is Snike the one who pushed me out the door?"

"His recommendation that you be furloughed carried a lot of weight."

"Why would he do that?"

"The easy answer is to finish the job on Gayfeather. My secondary guess is now that you know more about the Bureau, you'll be more valuable to the Russians. Like a mole or a defector."

"And completely disposable by either side."

•   •   •

Hornish's gift was a blue-plated .22-caliber Smith & Wesson Model 32 revolver. Nick twisted it this way and that, looking for imperfections. The weapon was small in his hand.

The serial number had been scratched out, scarring the steel frame at the bottom of the grip. He slid the thumb latch forward and let the six-cartridge cylinder fall open, revealing three rimfire rounds. He wished there were more rounds so he could test the gun's accuracy and reliability.

Using part of the rag to hold the gun by the barrel, he rubbed it and each round to make sure it was free of fingerprints. Ten minutes of that, and he wrapped it up again and stuffed the bundle under the passenger seat.

32

Harriet Gayfeather's phone buzzed as she was scrambling eggs for a late Sunday breakfast with Kevin Perdue, who was in the shower. She ignored the first text link from her aide in the Wichita office, and the second, but she gave in when the aide called.

The aide talked quickly. "Check the River Jordan Facebook right now. Kelli Killer is making her move against the preacher."

Gayfeather opened the page just as Kelli Ochs was saying, "What right . . ." and a man from the congregation jumped into the aisle and pointed a handgun at her and the preacher.

The senator watched the gunshot, the collapse, the blur as the gunman was attacked.

Gayfeather sank to her knees in nausea as memories of the attempt on her own life swept back. As Kelli Ochs died, that's how she would've fallen, a sack of blown-open flesh, humiliated, spit upon.

Kevin found her on the floor, crying beside a puddle of vomit. He knelt beside her and dried her face with a dish towel.

"Murder," she said. "In the church. The girl got shot."

She handed her phone to Kevin. As he watched the replay, she pulled herself up with shaky arms and went for paper towels.

The phone buzzed again, Laura Eisenhauer now.

"Nick Deveraux was at the church shooting, apparently with Kelli Ochs. You saw it, right?" Laura was shouting. "Why? Are they a team? Do you know anything about this?"

Gayfeather skipped through TV channels until she found a Wichita station that had broken into another church's service with the news. The whole episode, already larded with sensitivity warnings, had been downloaded before Facebook could hide it, and it was being replayed and discussed.

And there Nick was, only a flash of her nightmare tormentor.

She flipped to CNN, to Fox, to another Wichita station. No one identified Nick Deveraux. No one could identify the bald man being beaten in video clips taken off TikTok.

Her thoughts became more composed as her pulse relaxed. Of course no one would think of Nick. He was old news, and the FBI had made sure his face hadn't been seen for two years. His appearance was out of context.

Gayfeather wasn't involved in this case. Officially, she and her office would know nothing about it.

But why was Nick there? What, or who, would get him into a church?

•   •   •

Facebook and TikTok, X and Instagram lit up with news of Kelli Ochs' slaying.

> Oh, no!! I'm so sorry you're dead! [Crying face emoji x 10.]

> Paster Luke and family I lift you up in prayer.

> Church gunman was a Marxist Fascist Democrat! Beautiful woman Shot dead. #2A

> Way to go Kelli! Tell your story!! #justice #abortionrights #womenshealth

> Go to hell stupid bitch!!! You shd of never been born!!!

> Praise the Lord!

> Sad! Hateful woman, corrupt Democrat abortion Promoter, deserved to die. Donate to Protect our Beautiful Strong Second Amendment. #MAGA #2A #donatetoday

> Concealed carry could've stopped church assault sooner! #goodguywithagun

> Wichita Church shooting protected USA's Beautiful freedom of Religion! Nasty democrat woman got what she Deserved. #MAGA #2A #comstock #donatenow

> God will not put up with aboriton!!

God bless OUR Godly President, a True Christian!
   #liftingupinprayer

Center body mass shot is good, but at that range gunman
   should've hit her head. Anyone confirm yet what caliber
   and weapon he used? #patriot #ArmyOfGod

•   •   •

No one seemed to know whether the supposedly heroic man who flashed onto the screen had a gun, although many commenters stated flatly that he did. He fled and therefore was guilty.

If the clamor over religious freedom weren't enough, Karlton Cooper was praised widely for his personal self-defense and his protection of a man of the cloth against a hostile intruder.

As soon as she got home from buying breakfast chicken at Walmart, Karlton's duplex neighbor, Braylynn Huckstep, posted on Facebook and Nextdoor how she knew he was no good and had cursed at her. As the situation evolved and producers asked her to appear on their outrageous TV shows, she began saying Karlton was her boyfriend. She was offered a book deal.

Joyleen Sterrett Instagrammed her gratitude to #FatherGod and #Jesus that #PastorLuke was #alive.

After a few moments to compose himself after the shooting, Pastor Luke called three Wichita TV stations and offered his account. Soon enough, he was answering calls from Fox, Newsmax, CNN, CBS, ABC, and NBC.

Luke didn't think to call his beloved wife, Christmas, and ask her to comfort him, or to comfort her and Noelle for what they'd seen and felt. The world, however, knew everything he knew or imagined about Karlton Cooper and Kelli Ochs and the mystery man who, Luke said, had saved his life.

Christmas told the first reporter who called that the gunman had aimed at both Luke and Kelli before he fired. Twitter and Facebook posters accused her of covering up for the missing second man. At that point, she turned off her phone.

Christmas was relieved, of course, that her husband had been spared a humiliating death by icepick. But Lord, what if he had been merely mutilated and required her care for the rest of his life?

Just as stressful had been her daughter's reaction at the moment of the shooting. Noelle's face had burned with fury and then with disappointment.

•　　•　　•

By midafternoon Sunday, as law enforcement officers conducted their investigation inside River Jordan Cathedral and loaded the teal Corolla onto a flatbed hauler, mourners gathered in the parking lot to lay bouquets in Kelli Ochs' memory. Most of the participants were women and girls, a few carrying infants strapped to their chests.

It wasn't long before Pastor Luke had the Security Ministry assemble the Almighty Rifles—fifteen camouflaged, armored men carrying carbines and sidearms, their faces hidden by masks and neck gaiters—to push the women and their flowers away from the Cathedral and onto the sidewalk.

Anti-abortion and pro-gun crowds soon appeared and were encouraged to gather in the church's parking lot.

At Laura Eisenhauer's suggestion, Senator Gayfeather was driven to the church. She hoped to address the crowd and call for thoughtful conversation about the issues raised that day, from her perspective as a one-time assassination target.

The protesters weren't in a mood to be consoled. They answered by chanting, "Church and state, greed and hate."

The church crowd also would have none of Gayfeather's opinions. "You're next," one shouted, and soon the senator's bullhorn was drowned out by chants of "Lister missed her. Try again."

After the church group shoved its way onto the sidewalk, police officers began to pin down and arrest mourners.

Gayfeather took back the bullhorn and encouraged mourners to go home for their own safety. Even that was outshouted: "Lock her up! Lock her up!"

The chorus echoed that night on TV screens across Kansas to video of Gayfeather being hounded back to her vehicle.

•　　•　　•

When it appeared that Nick wouldn't—shouldn't—come back to her home Sunday evening, Harriet Gayfeather draped her silk gown over a chair and slid into the bathtub. In a few minutes, she phoned her paramour.

"Booty call," she said. "One hour."

"What are we drinking this evening?"

"Wine. Red."

Fifty-five minutes later, Kevin Perdue leaned over the edge of the tub, offering a randy kiss and a bottle of moderately expensive cabernet. He handed her a home pour in fine Romanian stemware with the volume of a small pumpkin.

She kept a set of those glasses on a tray between the bathroom sinks. That convenience was a challenge to the housekeeper, but it wasn't Gayfeather's problem. In this room, she didn't have problems. She had a relaxation tub, a doorless walk-in shower, a toilet and bidet, a large closet, and completely adjustable lighting.

"Your date fall through?" he said.

"No. Also, that'd be none of your business."

"What's on your mind? Is it PETRO? Or is it that guy you brought in on my plane?" He waited a beat. "Are you seeing another lobbyist?"

She climbed out of the tub, stepping lightly onto the bath mat. Enclosing herself in a robe, she stared at him in the mirror.

"I just don't like his showing up and being hired right now," he said. "Where did he come from? Is he from the military? The FBI?"

"Your security office is going to make the connection sooner or later," she said. "He's Nick Deveraux. Remember him from a couple of years ago, the guy who didn't shoot me?"

"My God! You hired your own assassin?"

"I need protection," she said. "I surely can't have a squad of oil-company bodyguards, and neither of us wants the FBI nosing around. You know this state's full of lunatics. PETRO's already drawing the conspiracy crazies out of the cottonwoods."

"So he's just going to kill you this time?"

"He's had his chances."

"So then what? He's hiding under your skirt and looking for a bigger, better target?"

"Better than me?" Her voice was soft, a trap.

"You know what I mean. The president. The House speaker."

"I'm not worried," she said. "I've spent much of my life with scurrilous men. My father. The Senate. You."

"This scurrilous mess was your idea," he said. "Can he protect you if he doesn't know what you've done?"

"You will not spread this around. I don't need any more hyenas snapping at my ass, and you and Saltwood don't want any glamour and mystery getting in the way of PETRO."

"Were you ever going to tell me that you put a killer on my plane?"

"No."

"You don't tell me things like you used to."

She stepped right in front of him, her nose three inches from his chin.

"You should be glad you have a bed partner who's getting senior enough in the Senate that she can be trusted with secrets and have a few of her own . . . and trust you with a few too. When you need to know them."

In that moment, Gayfeather realized that she'd never tell her patron, her lover, about her hideaway forty miles west of Wichita. It was a Cold War missile silo, bought through intermediaries and remodeled discreetly after careful withdrawals of a couple of million dollars from her campaign funds. None of the contractors had the whole picture. A hundred-foot-deep installation that once housed an intercontinental ballistic missile, it was already hardened against an atomic attack over Wichita's Boeing plant and Air Force base, as well as against a biological attack carried by the state's sweeping winds.

There was no one else in her life whom she cared to save.

Gayfeather held Perdue at arm's length.

"My letting you into my bed is your top qualification for remaining executive vice president for governmental relations," she said. "You screw that up, and you'll be living with your wife in a two-bedroom apartment next to the railroad tracks."

"Seriously, the boss keeps asking me where else your money's coming from."

"If he wants to know that, he'll have to double his donations and be better in bed than you are."

"I'll tell him. He'll probably imagine it's China."

She thought, I'll ruin you if you push that any further. But she said, "Probably. Anyway, he's in too deep with PETRO to rock any boats now."

Gayfeather squeezed Perdue's bottom and made up her mind. Laura Eisenhauer was playing close to the edge, and she's paying too much attention and thinking about it. She knows about China. It's an exposure that'll have to be taken care of.

"I love you," Kevin said. "I have since we met."

"If you want to say you love me, the price is that you have to be handsome, be horny, and be silent," she said, putting her hand over his lips. "Can you be all that, big boy?" She gently shooed him out and watched him stride into the bedroom.

Gayfeather turned before the full-length mirror by the walk-in closet and stared into her soul. For a moment, she thought she'd cry, but then her face tightened, her upper lip furrowing with frustration.

She flung her wine glass across the floor. Like furtive silverfish, shards of thin glass skittered up against the toe kicks and under the chairs, leaving cabernet trails pointing back to the senator.

• • •

At dusk Nick pulled up in Russell, a county seat along I-70, and chose a highway-adjacent hotel that wasn't as busy as its neighbors. He talked the clerk into accepting cash for the room and a damage deposit of two hundred dollars.

If there was any damage to be found, Nick thought, it would be all inside his mind.

Having not eaten for hours and exhausted by tension, he used the room phone to order a pizza from the place next door. On his way over, he used one of the hotel's hand towels to wipe down everything he had touched in the pickup. Good tradecraft suggested cleaning up fingerprints when you had the chance.

Laura's dinged and dirty pickup looked absolutely proper in the back of a second-tier hotel lot, but there was always a chance the pickup's out-of-county tag would be noticed by some cop or patrol service overnight and matched up to a possible be-on-the-lookout bulletin from Wichita.

The TV in the pizza parlor was turned on to Fox News, and the killing of Kelli Ochs was the main story. Nick spent only a minute there, paid cash, and was polite. He walked back casually, doing nothing that would make him memorable. This used to be his normal life. Prepare, kill, lie low.

Even Nick's benefactor, the Highway Patrol's Captain Hornish, could have second thoughts—if he was on the level to start with—and now Nick had in his room an illegal handgun that by itself could get him jailed or shot.

·   ·   ·

After watching CNN and Fox repeat their borrowed footage of the church shooting, followed by wild guesses from the networks' pundits, Nick was sure he'd never sleep. A twelve-inch pepperoni pizza, comfort food on most days, felt like a bag of dirt in his belly, and even a Dr Pepper and three bottles of vending-machine water didn't help.

A mugshot of the bald church shooter played again and again, but it wasn't until the man was identified as a laid-off Walmart clerk named Karlton Cooper that Nick realized he had met the guy on his first day in Wichita, an hour after he had breakfast with Kelli Ochs.

"How do I find such unfortunate people?" he asked the TV.

The news reader said the Wichita police would like to speak with the man who interrupted the shooting.

From Nick's time with the FBI, an observation by a Bureau psychiatrist in her sterile beige office slipped into his groggy world.

"I've watched you walk around the campus," she said, "and it reminded me of what I saw once at a family's yard party. Some gentleman, a nice enough guy, was a friend of the family, so he got to help in a vague but important way, I don't know, watching over the portable toilets or something. He wrapped himself in a common defense mechanism: an air of mystery. He never was *without* anybody but also never *with* anybody. Just not fitting in.

"I see a bit of that undefined self, a vagueness, a disguising of your true being," the psychiatrist continued. "How I interpret that is this: Your fear isn't that when trouble comes that you'll stand there and do nothing. It's that you'll see what I surmise is your real nature. You'll rob, betray, and kill, and you'll like it."

When trouble had come in the church, Nick stood in place a second too long. Kelli Ochs wasn't his to protect and she wasn't performing for him, but even so he felt like he had failed her. His indecision had meant the murder of his friend. She had injured and threatened to kill the preacher, but it was also clear she was going to kill only herself after making her grievance public.

The night before, Nick and Kelli together were kind to each other, as killers might be. Hand in hand, face to face, compliments, eye contact. He knew at the time that he wasn't going to fall head over heels for her. He wouldn't catch the thunderbolt as he had with Cimi Hernandez. But for all of Kelli's deception in public, she was honest to herself and to her mission.

All of Kelli's travel, all of her Facebooking about intending to kill someone, was a performance to ensure that she got on the church stage. She made herself into catnip for the preacher. How could he resist the lure of this most publicity-worthy repentance of the hardline era?

She was no pushover. She had transformed herself into a different person. She was tough, a fact that followed from her childhood, and she could be gentle because of that inner strength. She was what Nick imagined himself to be.

Nick, as he had the previous night, fell asleep then, drifting away to the hope that Kelli Ochs' last thought was of lying atop a hill, breathing the aroma of spring grass.

33

A.B. Abbey, the *Wichita Eagle*'s metro columnist, dug into the newspaper's archives and found the photo Kelli Ochs spoke of, in which newly arrived Pastor Luke Meriwether berated a woman outside a clinic in the autumn of 1994.

The caption quoted him: "That young woman from a small town, I just saved her soul and the life of her unborn child. Hallelujah!"

Abbey used the photo above her column, written for Monday morning's newspaper and published online late Sunday.

What's the Matter with Wichita?

As echoes of the revolver faded, most of the crying stopped and the sanctuary fell silent as members of the River Jordan Cathedral faced the enormity of what had played out on their stage.

Pastor Luke Meriwether stood up, tried to wipe the blood off his lapels and sleeves, and spit on Kelli Ochs' body. He called her a whore. He lifted her by the plastic handcuff that bound them, and he kicked her. It's all there in the Facebook video.

Led by members in the back rows, the congregation filtered away, and within minutes you could hear the pastor on the phone with a television network even as police officers swarmed into the church. The service was abandoned; the teaching moment was lost.

But for those of us who are not Meriwether, what did our moment with Kelli Ochs and Pastor Luke leave us? For five weeks, she had playfully teased Kansans that she was going to kill someone, and it made her famous nationwide.

Many people, especially young adults but also goths, skinheads, and even churchgoers, her fans and the merely curious, swarmed to her side for a shared selfie. Tabloid TV loved her. Before yesterday, the *Eagle* had published six stories about her.

We as a people were excited about death being dealt to an unlucky stranger or a familiar person—even in a monstrous month in which nine oilfield workers were killed by a terrorist strike near our home.

The dark angel is always among us and we've accepted that reality, but Kelli Ochs hinted at a violent death and a public one at that, and we hungered for it even if we didn't know what could possibly justify it. It was the worst of times, and it was the most entertaining of times.

Ochs chose her final stage well. We in Wichita admire violence and intensity; our heroes willingly strap a chip to their shoulder. Many in our community welcomed the anti-abortion movement when it arrived and tore apart our city in 1991, and those people and their spiritual descendants still draw power from the hatred it begat. Our university basketball team once had the motto "Play Angry," exchanging "chip on our shoulder" for "we're martyrs," and we made a bumper-sticker religion out of that idea.

Perhaps we secretly hoped Ochs' target would be someone we knew: a public person, maybe a politician or a teacher or an athlete important enough for us to gossip about. Her quest became a game, and we wanted to be there for the last shot.

In the end, we *were* there in the pews and on the internet, and the game turned out like no one expected. This woman was on the verge of killing her mother's tormentor, but with either compassion or cleverness did not.

"Who will Kelli kill?" the come-on line of so many news outlets, has been answered. She wanted to make her point and then conclude her own tragic life.

When the sanctuary was so quiet you could hear a feather drop, a man with a gun shot her, whether he was aiming at her or not. He stole her last bit of self-agency, just as Pastor Luke had robbed her mother.

The gunman spared the preacher, whose blasphemous scream drew his wrath, but only because he was apparently a bad shot. It was the preacher who the gunman said had promised to ask Jesus to find a new job for him, and whose guidance—or misguidance—had encouraged the former discount-store clerk to become the man he turned out to be. To be fair, the gunman also felt slighted by Kelli Ochs, calling her "an uncorrected woman" and conflating his unrequited feelings for her with his job loss.

We apparently have learned little from three decades of polarization, preferring instead to poke our neighbors in the eye for the sheer angry joy of it. The aggression against mourners and women's-health advocates outside the church yesterday afternoon is a fuse that didn't have to be lit.

A simple idea:

Let's step back from the brink. Let's take a month and look for the good in our neighbors. With everything else that's going on, we don't have to keep making ourselves crazy.

34

Nick woke at 3:00 in the morning, groggy and ill. He dreamed he had shared the bed with Gayfeather and was overwhelmed by her body heat.

He showered and felt better enough, so he laid a dry towel on the carpet beside the bed and did a hundred situps and fifty pushups. He wiped down the motel room and left the key card on the dresser with a ten-dollar tip for the housekeeper. The front-desk clerk would no doubt keep the deposit for damages, cash in hand to forget Nick.

On the way out of Russell, he stopped at a convenience store along the interstate for gas, coffee, water, and meat sticks. The pickup and his face would probably be recorded on a security camera, but he had to take the chance. As he checked out, he casually mentioned that he had to be north, up in Omaha, Nebraska, by nine, and it was going to be tight.

Maybe that'd be enough to throw the cops off, if any cops came to the store with questions. He immediately headed south on US 281.

Heavy on his mind was the realization that he had been so wrapped up in spying on Laura, the Kelli Ochs adventure, and the aftermath of the wellsite explosion that he had missed the big picture. He had to put his memories of Kelli in a compartment now.

Gayfeather and the Russians, he was sure, were at the center of the present universe. Tapping his finger on the steering wheel, he ticked off his reasons:

1. The FBI released him without preparing him—not even setting up an exit interview with its lawyers—but with basic credentials. Why? It was a pure handover.

2. He was dumped into a trap operated by the Russians, who were waiting at Dupont Circle.

3. The Russian, Orlov, had a plan. Why was a gangster connected inside the FBI? Had the Russians infiltrated that part of the FBI? Maybe the deal had been arranged between governments.

4. The US and Russia had developed overt and backdoor cooperation during the president's first term. The Russians could do dirty things using Nick as their cat's paw, and the FBI would have deniability.

5. Part of the deal must've been that Nick was disposable. The FBI could say he escaped, and the Russians could score points after his mission by turning on him. Both sides would eventually want him dead.

6. The FBI clerk who saw him off was new on the detail that day. The two agents who ferried him from his installation were killed minutes after dropping him off.

7. The Russian mob wanted Gayfeather dead. Her death used to be important to the mob, but the perspective had changed. Now it's a game to Orlov. Was Russia handling the FBI's rogue wet work, or the administration's? Additionally, would her death benefit Russia in a way hidden to the US? Gayfeather sat on the Energy and Agriculture committees and was the sole remaining Republican moderate in the Senate.

8. The well explosion was another plot in which Gayfeather and Kevin Perdue seemed to be involved. Russian oligarchs would have no interest in seeing the US oil industry strengthened, but creating a martyr of her would likely widen America's political divisions. That could upset aid to Ukraine and other countries pressured by Russia, if the US was interested in doing that anymore.

9. The China connection was still a mystery, although discovering that Gayfeather had an underground deal with Beijing might've induced the Russians to fund a third-party jab at China. He thought of a James Bond movie, *From Russia with Love,* in which the unaligned SPECTRE crime organization created a plan to let the Soviet Union

and the United States battle to exhaustion or death, and then take over. In real life, what if that patient organization were China?

10. Unlike other senators who could become vulnerable to pressure from Russia, by being blackmailed because of financial or sex crimes, Gayfeather was neither an overt political threat or a pansy to Russia and the mafia. Her replacement might be more susceptible to blackmail. Nick wouldn't put it past a domestic sponsor to want to install a pliable MAGA senator in her place. For example, culture-war sponsors and high-tech American oligarchs might demand her replacement.

11. If Gayfeather came up dead, Nick would be the obvious scapegoat. Indeed, he had followed her to Kansas. There was no proof she had hired him to protect her.

And then there was Laura, whose situation occupied a dozen highway miles of thinking. There were many ways to remove a person who lived alone in rural America, so "how" and "when" weren't concerns. But what about the "would"?

Would killing her be at all justifiable morally, or would it be nothing more than murder for hire? Would it be Gayfeather's price for helping him stay in America, or her way to have him removed? Would he even want to stay in America, considering the government's apparent ties to Russia?

He asked oncoming drivers: Who gave him permission to wander in and out of lives, bringing death?

If he killed Gayfeather, she'd become a martyr and her secrets likely would die with her. If he killed Laura, who besides a single senator would benefit? Which is the greater good, or the lesser evil?

He was tired, hollowed out by Kelli's death and by the bombing. He'd seen Laura's sunken, searching eyes. Life hadn't been any easier on her.

Would it be unfair to kill Laura first if he knew he might kill Gayfeather? He liked Laura, he admitted, and didn't want her to die.

Too many questions. How could he decide with confidence?

•　　•　　•

Nick turned off the highway onto a dirt road and drove west a couple of miles. He let the pickup coast to a stop in the predawn darkness without touching the brakes. No sense in giving farmers any unusual red lights to wonder about.

On a clean burner phone, he texted Pellen's cell—"Anything new in Kansas?"—and turned the phone off.

Eleven minutes later, he turned it on. A single text awaited him:

One-time prey arranged for your release. Using you for something?

.   .   .

Nick slipped his .22 revolver into a jacket pocket, then thought twice about showing up at the senator's house with a firearm. He wrapped it back up in the rag and shoved it under the seat.

At 6:00 A.M., as the sky was brightening and sparrows were chirping on a cloudless Memorial Day, he walked a quarter-mile south through a tree-heavy neighborhood and across a bridge over the Little Arkansas River to Gayfeather's house.

She answered the door wearing black and gold running gear with her hair tied back. She held her index finger to shush him.

"Where the hell were you last night? You show up at my house today looking like unshaven shit?" she hissed. "And playing hero in church? What the hell was that all about?"

She let him step into the foyer.

Hands in his jacket pockets, he said, "I thought I should get out of town yesterday. Too much exposure."

Gayfeather walked away then turned and glared. She said, "I'm going to assume you were there to keep that TikTok girl from killing me."

"That's pretty much it," he said. "I didn't know who she was until a couple of days ago."

"It's a relief that I won't be asked to perform some eulogy for that slimeball preacher. My God, his sermons have more sulfur than a bowl of asparagus. But now half the city is chanting 'My body, my choice' and the other half is strutting around with guns. Angry people don't like the status quo, and I'm the status quo."

"You sent me away," Nick said. "There was a fluid situation."

"We can talk after I get home and take a shower," she said. "You seem upset and I get that. Still, I wanted you as my bodyguard and enforcer, and you weren't available. And given your emotional state after what you had a hand in yesterday, you obviously aren't up to the job."

"I am capable of many things, but I can't be in two places at once."

"I hire people who live on the cutting edge. They're used to handling problems. One of those problems is Laura."

"She isn't your enemy."

"That's the same line I heard from her. Did you plan this?"

Nick shook his head.

"Go clean up my problem," Gayfeather said. "Our problem. Because if she gets out of this alive I'm going to give you to both the FBI and the Russians, and the Chinese can have what's left."

"The Chinese?"

"Cooperate or get sent to Guantanamo, Deveraux. Don't fail to shoot again. I so wanted to trust you." She guided him out onto the porch. "You have a hard time remembering who owns you."

He paused, struggling to hold his temper.

"I own myself now," he said. "I was hired by you, and you're the only one I'm working for. But I have to know: Why did you hire me? The truth this time."

"Fair enough," she said. "There's trouble coming, not just from Laura Eisenhauer, and it wasn't from that dead girl. I need you to think like a killer and stop trouble from happening to me. I'm not going to be anybody's loose end."

"I need to know more," he said.

"When I'm done with my run, we'll have a few minutes before I leave for my speech at the veterans cemetery. Now scoot."

Sotto voce, she added: "And be careful around your little friend. She'll cut your heart out."

•　•　•

Nick was trained to keep his wits, but solving the problem of how to kill Gayfeather focused him in a way he hadn't felt since the last time he meant to kill her. Would slaying his employer—the one who provided his ticket out of the grip of the FBI and the Russian mob—make him a terrible person?

But the rules were different now.

On the way back to his pickup, Nick walked the perimeter of the house because he was curious. He tested the knob of the wooden side door into the garage. A little pressure back against the hinges, and the latch slipped out of the strike plate. He twisted the thumb turn in the middle of the indoor knob and locked the door behind him.

Two bays were separated by painted steel supports. The floor was polished concrete, and it gleamed with dawn's light coming in window slits in the bay doors. The garage looked twenty-five feet wide.

A dark-blue Tahoe, Gayfeather's apparently, occupied the near spot. Beyond that sat a white Saltwood crew cab pickup, a Ram that was probably Kevin Perdue's, which meant he was in the house. The truck was so large it barely fit between the back wall and the rollup door; the hood itself was almost five feet above the floor.

Nick found a flat box of blue nitrile gloves on the workbench next to a spray bottle of windshield cleaner. After pulling on a pair, he opened the driver's door of the pickup. The key lay on the dashboard.

He flipped the visors and searched in the console for a garage door opener. In the glove box, he found nothing but the registration and an amber bottle of sildenafil pills: discount Viagra. He finally found the opener velcroed under the steering wheel column.

With care, he backed the long pickup out of the bay, lowered the door, and cranked the wheel around to drive around the corner. The truck rode like a bus and filled the middle half of the street.

Gayfeather had taken off to the west, so Nick started off to the east, into the slanting sunshine. He took a Tallgrass Country Club ball cap off the passenger seat and pulled the bill down over his eyes.

She had an eight-minute head start, heading into the riverside parks. Assuming she ran slowly as she warmed up, he turned south for three blocks and then west to enter Oak Park on a street that curved along the Little Arkansas River.

Nick was on the hunt. There was no special thrill to it. Gayfeather was at the center of something horrible. Good things happen to good people, he thought. Bad things happen to people I know.

He hoped he could deflect blame with an alibi he'd need to invent. If he got out of here alive, maybe he could let himself be videotaped in a Walmart in some small city north of Wichita. From there, it'd be a short step to Nebraska and on to the Rockies or Canada.

• • •

Gayfeather breathed deeply as she loped along the left side of the road through her favorite part of the city, Oak Park, facing traffic should it come, smelling the mossy mud of the dammed-up Little Arkansas; the stream slinking out of central Kansas was low even after the recent rain. The redbuds and oaks were leafed out, and the resident Canada geese were feeding on young grass. When she saw Perdue's truck turn onto her road, she frowned because of the interruption, then smiled as she remembered arching her back in his arms. She started to cross the road so she could be at the driver's window.

Her expression went blank when she realized that Perdue wasn't behind the wheel, and in a flash she recognized Nick Deveraux and knew he meant to hit her.

Her lifetime of regret and anger coalesced into a ball of fury and relief.

• • •

Gayfeather raised a hesitant wave. Any other person in the park might've thought she had seen a friend and was crossing the street to chat.

Nick gunned the engine. The big truck coughed once and roared forward.

Gayfeather's features gathered in determination, and in her final steps she moved not away from the truck but toward it. The front bumper and left headlight struck her abdomen, and her face whipped down into the Ram's shoulder-high hood.

Her body flew thirty feet across the road, landing hard at the base of a middle-aged oak. She bent backward around it, snapping her spine at the waist. She lost consciousness but regained a ghost of it, enough to hear vague voices from a blur of people gathered around her. None of them made sense.

She whispered a prayer to Steven, her dead husband, her one true love.

"Care for me in . . . heaven," she said.

At the end of a shallow exhalation, the senator died.

35

Nick used the remote to open Gayfeather's garage, which wasn't all that far up the street from Oak Park, and parked the Ram where he had gotten it. He'd been wearing gloves the whole time he was in the truck, but he took off the Tallgrass cap and ran his hands around its interior in case he'd left any hairs.

As he stuffed his blue gloves into a pocket, he looked over the damage left by Gayfeather's body.

The hood was dented where her head had snapped downward, and the left headlight lens was cracked. There was a bit of blood from the momentary impact and a spray of drops created when her head whipped away.

He was glad it was all over, but soon someone would find her. The police would come to the house, and he had no more time to look at details.

He had barely stepped away from the truck when Kevin Perdue surprised him by keying open the garage door and striding in with a golf bag over his shoulder. He was dressed in loose burgundy slacks and a white polo shirt. He was gym-muscled, something Nick hadn't noticed when Perdue led him through the fixed-base operator's terminal at Dulles International.

Perdue was just as surprised. He set down his bag and leaned it carefully against the workbench.

It was the first time Nick saw Perdue's thin smile. It wasn't a welcoming expression, but Nick chose a forthright approach. "You're Mr. Perdue, right? Thanks for the great ride to Kansas you gave me last week."

"Nice to see you again, city boy. How's it going?"

"The senator asked me to wait while she went for a run," Nick said.

"Not in the garage, I bet."

Nick plunged ahead. "I'm driving her to Winfield this morning. She asked me to get her ride ready."

"Uh-huh. Sure she did."

Perdue lifted a club out of his bag and lightly poked the head into Nick's chest. "It's my six-iron. Drives a ball 155 yards, no hook and no slice."

Nick stepped back from having his explosion bruises jabbed. He bumped into the truck's fender and could go no farther.

"Were you out here before? Your engine is ticking," Nick said, pointing at the hood, "and there's some damage."

Perdue pushed Nick out of the way and ran his finger through a blood spot.

"You did this?" Perdue was pissed. "You messed up my truck?"

"I found it," Nick said. "If this is what it looks like, we need to hide the truck right away. Whether it's your accident or not, you don't need to be answering questions about it."

Perdue toyed with Nick, asking, "What's it look like to you? A deer?"

Nick edged toward the workbench. He pulled a new pair of blue gloves out of the box. He felt around the creased sheet metal.

"Maybe. But a hot engine and fresh damage says it happened not in the country but in Wichita to a human. Where can we hide it?"

Perdue brought the head of the club up to Nick's ribs and poked him again.

"I think you did it," he said. "Who did you hit? Why are you so helpful?"

"I'm the senator's aide," Nick said. "Everything affects her."

"Yeah, maybe." Perdue waved his left hand, the one without the six-iron, at the truck. "Step into my office."

They sat for a moment, Perdue in the driver's seat, holding the club across his lap. He wore cologne. Polo, Nick decided, and a splash too much of it. They looked out over the dented hood.

Perdue cocked his head and said, "You're with Laura Eisenhauer, right?"

"I've been investigating her for the senator," Nick said.

"Sleeping with her? You know her that well?"

"What?" Nick was surprised. "No."

"What do you know about that friend of hers named Purkeypyle?" Perdue said. "Can you imagine how rough his childhood was? Kids every day calling him Turkeypyle."

"Laura said a guy by that name is missing."

"He's a scientist."

"Really. Weather? Birds?"

"Hydrology, dumbass."

"Why're you looking for him?"

"He's digging up trouble for Saltwood."

"Laura never said."

"I think they have a thing for each other and against Saltwood," Perdue said. "They're together a lot out at Quivira, makes me think there's something weird about you staying out there too."

"So that's why Gayfeather was afraid of Laura?"

"She is? Hell, I didn't know that, and I'm not sure you do," Perdue said. "Are you here to ride herd on Eisenhauer? Well, Harriet's wasting her money on you. Sterrett's going to catch Purkeypyle and hang your Miss Laura out to dry."

"What's going on with this Purkeypyle?"

"We were adding waste chemicals to the down-hole mix, and the mud contractor decided it'd be a great place to pour eight and a half thousand gallons of perc."

"Perc?"

"Discarded dry-cleaning fluid. Stinks worse than a hog farm at a New Jersey factory. The contractor somehow broke the pipe, and the perc and other chemicals leaked out and found their way to the river. That's where the hydrologist sniffed it, and now everybody downstream is fucked for years."

"No wonder Eisenhauer is pissed."

"Of all the wells in all of Kansas, why the contractor picked this well on this semi-pristine stage is just dumb luck. He's dead now. But now we have the PETRO Act built on a tainted well, and we have to clean up the mess in secret while we're coasting to victory. Otherwise, it'll look like the bill was created for the spill and not for national security, and there's no way we can win that publicity war."

"Was the senator always in on it?"

"In on it?" Perdue said with a sneer. "Hell, PETRO was Gayfeather's idea."

"No shit," Nick said. "How'd that work?"

"The bombs also were her idea, you know, so the act wouldn't just come out of the blue," Perdue said. "She didn't know how we'd do it, and boy howdy was she pissed that we chose her state to do it in. She thought nobody would get hurt."

"She's very smart."

"It's almost a counterintuitive move to put her on point," Perdue said. "She gets to be the hero and the goat. The Republicans here hate her, but outside Kansas she's the most believable politician in the state."

"You shouldn't be telling me this," Nick said, "unless you want me to work for you. Or am I already?"

"It's something like that."

Perdue put his left arm over the steering wheel for leverage, turning slightly in the seat to assess Nick's interest.

"PETRO will make our oil more competitive in the big markets— here, India, and China. We'll do well, and the Asians'll do well, and the Russians and Arabs will be frozen out of the market unless they cut their prices deeply."

"You must have a new field somewhere. I thought they'd all been found."

"Now they have. A honey hole in the 1002 area of the Arctic National Wildlife Refuge in Alaska."

"That's bullshit," Nick said, his eyebrows high. "You've found a super field in ANWR, where no one's buying leases, where surveys have been run for decades?"

Perdue chuckled.

"Well, ain't you the brightest kid in your class," he said. "We're building the narrative around national security. People will believe anything about national security, and then they'll be willing to die rather than admit they were suckered into giving up every environmental protection. In the meantime, we'll have immunity to do whatever the hell we want."

When Nick looked away, Perdue used the head of the six-iron to pull Nick's chin back around.

"We have interests in Alaska other than ANWR. You must know that, if you're working for Harriet. It's expensive to produce up there, even though the state's throwing money at us to do it. Look who'd benefit: Army, Navy, Air Force, Space Force, merchant marines. The Anchorage airport with its cargo traffic. The rocket site in Kodiak. Artificial intelligence server farms, if the governor's wild dreams come true. Plus, we really did find a couple of square miles that's above a passage into the biggest pool of oil anyone's seen in years. It's out under the Arctic Ocean, out there with the polar bears and seals and whales, and we'll drill laterally from the coast and run pipelines wherever we need to."

Nick interrupted. "And everybody's just going to let you do this."

"Even if our investment fails, what have we lost? A few billion dollars, a few lives that we'll expense, a hundred caribou that'll never be born. Look at what we'll have gained with PETRO."

Nick started to respond, but Perdue held up his hand.

"Remember when the president asked the industry for a billion dollars? Profits after PETRO will make a billion look like chump change. We have some things in the works with China. Now we refine Alaska oil on the West Coast. But with PETRO, we can ship out crude or put in a new refinery on the North Slope, right up on the Northwest Passage. Easy access to Asia and Europe. No messing with Canadian pipelines. The tree huggers and caribou lovers won't be able to do a thing about it."

"The senator must've liked this to have her name on the bill," Nick said. "It's hard to believe you're taking this risk to serve the Chinese market."

"The plan's got some problems, but Jesus, for some reason she respects the Chinese," Perdue said. "She'll never say a bad word about them, which is odd in a government that seems bent toward licking Russian boots. Anyway, Gayfeather understands economics and practical politics, and this'll work because it's counterintuitive."

Nick couldn't keep the sarcasm out of his voice. "What's the matter with the United States?"

"We wanted to pull the teeth out of the Environmental Protection Agency, but the president's blunderbutt administration in his first term couldn't pull that off because the election was coming and it was already in bed with the oil and coal companies, thank you very much. Now that he's the prez again, he said to do what we want, so we're going around the EPA, for what the EPA is worth anymore."

"Even a broken idiot is right once every four years, right?"

Perdue laughed with him. "Not just an idiot. A real tool. Anyway, we went for immunity instead, and now everybody's so scared of the economy that we'll get whatever we want. The Supreme Court will give us anything. We're indebted to Harriet for coming up with a series of false flags that even our evil spirits hadn't thought of."

"So you all are responsible for setting off the bomb and for everything else?"

"The chick at the church? Not that, but for example Harriet and that preacher have kept the abortion issue alive, that preacher and his goddamned Almighty Rifles. And that's why the bomb was detonated, and why we keep Harriet in office, and how we're going to screw the Russians on what they think is their entire arctic shelf. People are going to piss their pants so hard later over the environmental risks that nobody'll be looking closely at what we do with the money."

Perdue's phone buzzed in his shirt pocket. He pulled it out, held it up for face recognition and read the text. He replied, then laid the phone on top of the dashboard and watched it for a moment.

Nick said, "You've spent years working on this."

"For PETRO, more than a year. For the big plan, decades. Some of the execs had family who worked with the Soviet Union and Germany before World War II. Now we're doing a deal that'll make us thieving rich, and it's at Russia's expense. The Russians think they'll ruin our country with blackmail and bribes and memes, but we have 'em lined up like bowling pins. We're going to drown them in their own oil until the place goes up in civil war. Ukraine's going to look like a high school fistfight."

Nick shifted in his seat.

"Do you know who I really am?" he asked Perdue.

"A hack retired military operator who Harriet dragged off the street? By the way, she said you're a lousy lay."

"She lied to you," Nick said.

"Not just about you, it turns out. It's part of the game."

"Also, I was born and trained in Russia. The Russian mob sent me to kill her, but now you're saying you might do it," Nick said. "You'd probably screw it up, and the Russians aren't going to be happy with that, so I had to do it for you."

"Screw you." He jabbed Nick's ribs.

"Everything you've done has been a waste," Nick said.

"You know what?" Perdue said. "It'd be okay if the Honorable Harriet Gayfeather got dead. It'll give us a head start on propping her up as a martyr for PETRO."

Nick recoiled. He had performed the work of both the Russians and Saltwood.

"And we're going to kill you like a bug," Perdue said. "We own this state. We own the cops, the governor, the House, the Senate, the Supreme Court, the last president, the current president, and the next president."

With one wrist, Perdue short-swung the club into Nick's gut. Nick retched.

"You little prick," Perdue said. "I'm giving a US senator orgasms and you're at best dicking around with a psycho farm girl."

Perdue laughed as Nick squirmed into a position that hurt less.

"Harriet hired you out of pity for some job that's so low she won't even discuss it," Perdue said. "I, however, am helping America remain the strongest country in the world."

Perdue again jabbed Nick's ribs.

"I thought maybe you'd want to work with us, but you're just a cheesy little mobster. You don't have any idea about our reach."

"Did she know how you used her?"

"Don't know, don't care," Perdue said. "I like her, just so you know. She's a great lay. But she's also my job."

He wiped sweat from his forehead. "And anyway, we're going to let her go in the next election, if she lasts that long."

Exasperated, Nick said, "Are you not listening to me? She's dead. And now that she's dead, what good will you be to Saltwood? The bosses will have the PETRO Act and the money, and you'll be rotting somewhere with a black bag tied over your head."

"It's politics. It's business, and we've paid her for her service. The bosses are paying me too, but I have my own little counterforce. We'll see how the chain of command holds up."

Nick waved his hands. "You against a thousand mercenaries?"

"All I need is the right one. And you know what? He set off the bombs, and you didn't know that, did you? He's out at the Eisenhauer place now waiting to blow your girl's heart out. When the time comes, the CEO is next."

Perdue coughed into his fist, then cleared his throat.

"Harriet knew what she was stepping into," Perdue said, "and that she'd be a loose end. The fact that we blew up a site in Kansas should've made that clear. Maybe it's worth it to her. Maybe she's got an escape hatch. Maybe she hired you to protect her, for all the good that's doing her."

"Maybe," Nick said, "she hired me to kill you."

While Perdue swore at him, Nick slid his hand forward to the door latch. When he thought Perdue wasn't looking, he pulled the handle and pushed out with his shoulder.

Perdue smirked. "It's locked."

Perdue opened his own door and let the golf club clatter onto the garage floor. In the same motion, he pulled a pistol from under his seat and worked the action.

"By the way, I do know you, Nikolai Fyodorov Deveraux," he said. "You're the guy who was supposed to shoot Harriet a couple of years ago. Why else do you think we've been paying you any attention at all? You're going to fail again."

Perdue emphasized his points by waving his .38-caliber semiautomatic and holding it flat, a TV move. It was silver-plated with mother-of-pearl grips and looked new out of the box.

"We're going to get even today. I'm going to put an end to your interference, and my man Sterrett's going to burn your farmgirl's place to the ground if she doesn't cough up Purkeypyle or what he stole from us."

Perdue grabbed Nick's hair, pulled him closer and then shoved him back against the door. Nick settled in, watching Perdue from the corner of his eye.

"Say your prayers, Fyodorov. Voz'mi menya za ruku, Isus, ya idu domoy." Take my hand, Jesus, I'm going home.

"Go find Jesus yourself," Nick said. "I'm going to kill you."

Perdue wouldn't shut up.

"And then Sterrett's going to have a beer with his wife, who is one of the nicest sexpots you'll never meet," Perdue said. "The world will close over you, and nobody will notice that you're gone."

He jabbed his finger into Nick's cheek. Nick snapped at his hand.

Perdue snatched his hand back. "And in a couple of weeks," he said, "no one will even remember you."

Perdue pointed the pistol at Nick's chest. "Cocked and locked, you stupid boy." He twitched his thumb against the safety. "Not locked anymore."

Nick laughed. "Rookie."

Perdue sneered. "Russian khuyesos." Cocksucker.

"Scream or be a man," he added. "It doesn't matter. No one's going to hear you. No one questions what goes on at this house."

"What about the cameras? Someone will see those."

"Cameras?" Perdue scoffed. "Those are fakes. My guy installed real cameras but they don't do anything but swivel around and blink red lights. You think Harriet really wants there to be a record of people like me and you staying the night?"

Perdue pushed the muzzle against Nick's chest. The gun didn't smell like it had been cleaned and oiled recently. He's an amateur, Nick realized.

Nick fixed his eyes on the pistol and quivered. Perdue thought it was because of pain, but it was with anger, and the slight movements braced Nick's back and loosened his arms.

Nick coiled around and slammed his gloved right palm down on the .38, pushing it down toward his hip. As he did that, he slipped the web of his left thumb between the hammer and the firing pin.

Perdue pulled the trigger. The hammer pinched Nick's flesh through the thin blue latex, burning his hand like fire but not striking the firing pin. Nick turned hard toward Perdue and grabbed his wrist.

Using both hands, Nick twisted the pistol around. Perdue's right hand awkwardly gripped the butt and his finger remained inside the trigger guard. The oilman's back was now against the truck door, and Nick nearly was kneeling in Perdue's lap.

Holding the gun at Perdue's lips, Nick jerked his left hand away and let the hammer fall the safe distance to the pin. And then with his aching left thumb, and with Perdue's finger still on the trigger, he pulled the hammer back.

At the sound of the hammer locking into place, Perdue's body went taut, his lips drawn back with anger and fear. With his left hand, he jabbed awkwardly at Nick's throat, trying to get around Nick's protective forearm.

"Here's some news, pridurok," Nick said. You shithead. "You did all this for nothing."

Perdue's face scrunched into a mask of fury. His words were garbled.

"Go ahead, you fucking enemy of the people," Perdue seemed to say. "You're going to be dead by dark."

"You first, big man," Nick said.

It was over in two seconds.

Nick stomped on Perdue's foot, and the reflex opened Perdue's jaw enough that Nick could shove the muzzle in.

Nick tightened his pressure on Perdue's trigger finger, and the gun fired.

As Perdue's body went slack, Nick dropped his arms and pulled away. The pistol fell out of Perdue's fingers and bounced off his thigh. It slid to the floorboard, where it pointed at Nick, cocked for a shot that would never be fired.

• • •

With his blue-gloved hands, Nick picked Perdue's phone off the dashboard. He quickly went to Settings and changed the auto-lock time to "never." He slid through the contacts list, seeking two particular accounts. He texted an apology to Gayfeather and sent an order to Sterrett:

Wrap it up.

Now Nick was on the clock, having put himself in competition with Sterrett. He thought he might have two minutes left before someone came knocking.

He put the phone back where he found it. If it wasn't perfectly placed, it wouldn't matter. The first person to open the truck to check on Perdue's body would jostle it enough to create a margin of error.

First things first. Nick had to make Perdue's death look enough like a suicide that the police wouldn't go looking for another suspect. With luck, the police and the FBI would settle for a quick, plausible wrap-up to Gayfeather's death.

With his knuckle, Nick touched the driver door's unlock-all button, and backed out of the truck through the passenger door. A close examination by the crime scene folks might find a shadow in the spray of minute blood drops and smears on the cell screen, dashboard, and seats, and Nick had to hope that he wouldn't come to mind.

On the way past the workbench, he lifted another pair of gloves and a paper towel. Outside, he peeled off his bloody gloves and tucked one inside the other, put on the second pair and wiped the doorknob with the paper towel. When he finished, the towel and all the gloves went into his pocket.

He strolled along the sidewalk casually for a man in a hurry. He got upstream and across the bridge to his pickup. Neighborhood traffic was flowing early, even on the holiday. He fit right in, just another guy going to his job at Home Depot.

He drove out 13th Street to cross the Big Arkansas and connect to Zoo Boulevard, which took him to the I-235 bypass and on up to K-96. He'd follow K-96 and the Arkansas back to Quivira.

Had he committed any sin? Like the one about not warning Laura that he'd given Saltwood's troubleshooter the go-ahead to attack?

He couldn't leave a digital record that he was at Gayfeather's house this morning without putting his own life at risk. He was now the only one who knew the bones of the whole conspiracy, and he had to stay alive. For himself, for Laura, for the nine dead men of the Saltwood crew.

He'd think about his sins when this was over. Maybe. Now he had to cover eighty miles to stop Lance Sterrett.

36

On Monday morning's episode of *Fox and Friends,* Pastor Luke cast his near martyrdom in harsh terms. He had high praise for Karlton Cooper, calling him an innocent hero who Jesus was going to help in his struggle to achieve religious freedom and support the Second Amendment.

After making a deal to reappear later on Fox News, Pastor Luke had no comment for the local stations or the newspaper.

Karlton, meanwhile, sat in the Sedgwick County jail, digitally fingerprinted and awaiting arraignment on state and federal charges. His arm hurt where the church assailant had broken it, and it was in a cast and he was on painkillers. Cooper, however, was respected by other prisoners. He was reported to have yelled "On to paradise," which was discovered to have been an old Norse dying cry, and "Tomorrow belongs to me."

Kelli Ochs' body had been taken to the morgue for an autopsy. Early toxicology reports found an extreme load of lorazepam and alcohol in her blood, matching the potent anti-anxiety cocktail of Ativan and vodka in her water bottle. The medical examiner said there was no evidence of her having been in an altered state before she drank on camera. The examiner speculated that Ms. Ochs, who he said had obviously researched Luke Meriwether and the church, may have counted on being shot to death by the Security Ministry.

Two people from her past were willing to talk to reporters.

Her foster father spat out that Kelli had been an ungrateful troublemaker and that his son, identified by Kelli in church, never sexually assaulted her "when they were just playing around." The son, now thirty-one years old, didn't make himself available to reporters.

Kelli's aunt, on her way to Wichita to claim the body and arrange for cremation, simply wished her niece well on her journey.

• • •

Back at home, Joyleen Sterrett was coming up from her self-anesthetized night, afraid for what she might've admitted to Lance. She was worried that he'd gone to the police. No, it was Monday, Memorial Day. He probably was fixing something for Saltwood while the bosses took the day off, or driven to sit at his parents' grave.

She felt the need to lie low, not knowing how Sunday's events would affect Pastor Luke and especially his wife. She didn't pray often on her own, but she did ask God that the harsh words by the Ochs woman and that crazy Karlton Cooper wouldn't inspire members to ask for their gifts back.

You know what, she was already tired of Pastor Luke. She shouldn't have agreed to let him delay payments on her finder's fee. Last night, had she told Lance about that arrangement? If she explained it the right way today and if Lance were in a forgiving mood, he could put some teeth into her demand for full payment.

• • •

A young couple walking their retriever mix along the park road early Sunday morning had found Senator Gayfeather's body at the base of a tree. They hesitated to approach her, thinking the woman was a drunk, but their dog insisted.

Her face had flattened features and was purple with bruising. Her bowels had released. Aside from the gray-blond hair, there was nothing familiar or welcoming about her.

"Don't touch her," the wife said after she called 9-1-1. "There might be spinal damage."

"Look, she's saying something. Can you record it?"

Gayfeather was recognized by city cops who had served on her security details, but her identity was withheld for a couple of hours. The FBI showed up quickly, however, and the fact that the FBI was involved in a hit-and-run stirred up further attention among the neighbors, who reported it on Facebook. Their streets had been blockaded, and officers swarmed over the park and the senator's property.

Police tested all the doors of the home and garage, then requested a warrant. An officer peering into the garage saw what looked like probable cause, a slumped body and blood spatter on the window of a white pickup. A tactical unit burst in and found a dead man seated in the driver's seat. He apparently had been fatally injured by deep-throating a .38-caliber pistol, which was found under the brake pedal near a spent cartridge.

The entry team also found truck-body damage consistent with Gayfeather's injuries. Samples of the blood were taken for matching against a sample from her body.

Within twenty minutes of finding Perdue's body, a forensic investigation of his phone brought up a text sent to Gayfeather. It was time-stamped a few minutes before the couple reported finding her body.

Harriet, I know I hurt you bad. We did our best. Love you always.

Less clear was a text sent a minute later to a number belonging to a Lance Sterrett, who was that afternoon described by Saltwood as a field manager. Police used the text to establish Perdue's time of death.

FBI agents traced the number to cell towers across several counties in south-central Kansas, pinning it down to a tower near Cheney Reservoir a half hour west of Wichita, but the receiving phone had apparently been turned off by the time police checked for it. A search of Sterrett's home turned up nothing but his distraught and deeply hungover wife.

When the news of Perdue's apology was played on TV, the witnesses with the dog figured that what they had recorded might be important. They posted the recording on Facebook, writing that to their ears Gayfeather's final words were, "Carry me . . . Kevin."

When the Wichita office of the FBI called Gayfeather in dead, the suits at FBI headquarters in Washington and assorted vacation homes went crazy. The promise of a thorough investigation was delivered with sound and fury, even though officials at lower levels were already walking away from the case.

By midafternoon Washington time, the FBI accepted as truth what it knew about the deaths of Gayfeather and Perdue. Nothing more was wanted, and nothing more was done.

Evidence was being collected, however, for a quiet federal investigation into the financial and personal relationship between Gayfeather and Perdue.

Sarah Perdue, who had hugged her illicit lover goodbye only a few minutes before the police arrived with somber news about her husband, asked the public through Saltwood for privacy as she, his only family member, searched for closure.

Her pro-patriotism group called an emergency meeting without her to discuss the deep-state conspiracy against Saltwood. Those who had an inkling of Kevin's infidelity spoke the loudest, intending for their vociferous support of Sarah to get back to her.

Saltwood Exploration itself expressed shock and sadness about what appeared to be an action by an employee on his own time.

"Case opened, case closed," was how a TV reporter described company's attitude.

In Washington, members of the Senate spoke of thoughts and prayers but also of gratitude for Senator Gayfeather's service and bipartisanship. They promised to continue pushing for her landmark PETRO Act bill after a proper period of mourning.

"Harriet Gayfeather's life was tragically ended because of a personal matter, but her belief in energy superiority was strong, very strong," said a Republican from Louisiana. "She shall not have died in vain."

•   •   •

When Captain Loren Hornish heard the double-fatality news on the Highway Patrol radio, he hustled into Wichita from his home in Derby, a suburb downstream from Wichita. His presence should be noticed, he thought, just in case radicals were involved.

Hornish had his suspicions about what Nick Deveraux was capable of but, as far as he wanted to believe, the young man had not returned to Wichita. Most of all, Hornish was relieved that neither Gayfeather nor Perdue had been killed by a .22 slug.

37

Lance Sterrett was loading his tackle into a rented fishing boat at Cheney Reservoir, west of Wichita, when a text from Kevin Perdue woke up his phone around 6:30 A.M.

It was succinct, but in Perdue's style it was complete:

Wrap it up.

Maybe things were getting desperate. Maybe Perdue had had a bad night in the bedroom, or maybe the political situation had changed. Possibly Perdue was also just tired of this pursuit.

Sterrett was more than ready to bury everything. The further he could get away from the whole Quivira mess, the happier he'd be.

Sterrett deleted the text and didn't reply. Mission secrecy and deniability, and all that. Reindeer games.

As he always did when he was going covert, he turned off his phone and slipped it into a wire-mesh bag. He became invisible to the cell network.

He returned the rented boat's key to the marina master and immediately left the Sailboat Cove parking lot. In his Saltwood Exploration pickup, he drove west on a county road through Pretty Prairie and Lerado, a town whose population now resided in a cemetery, then north on another paved road through Langdon and eventually across the North Fork of the Ninnescah River. Through Huntsville, another defunct settlement, then Kilbourns Corner, which wasn't even that much, and finally across the Arkansas River south of Alden. When he met traffic on county roads, he gave the other driver a hand-on-the-wheel two-fingered wave, an instantly forgettable gesture of social camouflage that suggested that he was a local and not someone to track in the rear-view mirror. He had driven these back roads often enough to feel like a son of the pioneers.

On the north side of the Arkansas, he took a series of gravel roads until he was a half-mile from the hunting blind he used when he spied on the Eisenhauer ranch. The drive from the reservoir had taken a little more than an hour. If all went well, he could take care of shooting and disposal, then be back at the lake by late afternoon.

He pulled off onto a two-track lane leading around an alfalfa field and nestled his truck in among the trees and brush near a small bend on the east side of the river. Deer hunters and target shooters frequented the area, so someone zeroing in his scoped and suppressed rifle would hardly get a second look.

It was a holiday weekend, and the riverbed runners would come out in their off-highway vehicles as the day progressed. There'd no doubt be plenty of meaningless shooting to cover whatever he needed to do.

Sterrett clambered down the silty bank onto a sand bar inside the bend. Once around a puddle of muck and bright green cattails, he crossed the packed gravel and soft sand to the downstream end of the sand bar, where the channel was broad and shallow, knee deep at the most. Even burdened by his backpack and rifle, the former combat soldier had no trouble fording the clear water and scrambling up the far bank.

He climbed the rudimentary pipe ladder to the platform of the deer stand. With his feet on a floor eight feet above the prairie, he had a clear view over the brush into the driveway.

He wondered what pushed Perdue to make the execution call. Whatever it was, the clock was running and it was about 9:00 o'clock.

Perdue might have his own issues to worry about, Sterrett thought, but they were minor. Perdue hadn't had to sit through a church murder the day before and then talk his sedated, cheating wife down from her shock while she rattled on about some church deal that'd bring her boatloads of money.

Sterrett was glad he was out of the house for the day. When this was over, he'd go fishing for a month. Put all his shares in a trust inside a shell company. Sell everything else and buy a place in Alaska, get off the grid for a few years. Let Joyleen have her preacher, if she could keep him. The only living person he believed in had betrayed him, and he was angry. Angry at her, at the world, at this horseshit Quivira situation.

Sterrett's rifle was his truest friend. After he left the Army, he bought two M24 rifles identical to the one he had used in uniform. This one was a lovely piece of machinery, forty-three inches long and weighing twelve pounds, mounted with a 10x40 mm fixed-power scope. To the muzzle, he screwed in a long suppressor, which wouldn't silence the shot but would knock the report down from an eardrum-rupturing 160 decibels to 130 or so. He'd still need his ear protectors.

He laid the rifle on the platform and set out his three ten-round box magazines, two of them with regular rounds. The third, marked with a dab of orange paint, contained regular rounds interspersed with orange-tipped M25 tracer rounds. The tracers had recessed tails contained a mixture of strontium, magnesium, and chloride, which would be set afire by the gunpowder's ignition.

When he was sure of everything, he positioned his weapon with a magazine of regular rounds on a sandbag resting on the platform's chest-high railing of 2 x 8 lumber. The rifle was equipped with a bipod, but on the stand the sandbag was a better gun rest. He flipped up the scope's forward and rear caps. He raised the bolt and pulled it toward him, opening the chamber. Into it rose a 7.62 x 51 mm cartridge, and gently, firmly he pushed the bolt forward and rotated the handle down to the right.

In the millisecond after he pulled the trigger, a bullet a third of an inch in diameter and weighing half an ounce would rush through the barrel's five lands, picking up a right-hand twist that would allow it to spin reliably through the air at 2,850 feet per second.

Working the bolt quickly and re-aiming through his scope, Sterrett could empty his ten-round magazine in sixty-three seconds on the firing range, a little bit slower in combat. A small mound of corpses in southwestern Asia attested to his dexterity.

•   •   •

Sterrett's first shot—he flinched when a pheasant flushed right in front his tower as he squeezed the trigger—thwacked high into a honey locust where Laura Eisenhauer had been trimming away suckers at the base of the trunk. She attributed the sound to branches scraping in the wind, even though she heard a gunshot a moment later.

She had gotten up early for this, a job delayed for almost a week by Nick Deveraux's arrival. The loudspeaker by the running track had been playing Beethoven's *Sixth Symphony,* which she thought of only as the *Pastoral,* and was about to begin Bizet's *Carmen,* an opera about an amoral doomed Spanish gypsy. Then would come French icon Mireille Mathieu, singing "Hymn to Love," and the mesmerizing second movement of Beethoven's *Seventh,* the "Allegretto." Laura thought of it as a valediction after first hearing it as a soundtrack during a scene in the 1974 movie *Zardoz,* in which warriors played by Sean Connery and Charlotte Rampling age peacefully into their late years.

Laura had just stumbled over an exposed root when the second bullet cracked into the tree trunk right above her. One second later, the muted pop of a rifle shot arrived in the humid air. She ducked and ran around the house and in through the front door, protected from the river trees she thought the shot had come from.

A hunting rifle's bullet would travel that distance in a second; the sound would take two seconds.

Her 12-gauge pump shotgun and .22-caliber semiautomatic carbine were in the closet, always loaded. She pulled them out and checked the chambers and magazines. The Remington 870 shotgun, seven and a half pounds of steel and carved wood, held four rounds in the tube under the barrel and a fifth in the chamber. It was good for about sixty yards.

The Ruger 10-22 held a rotary magazine of ten long-rifle rounds, hollow-points good enough for varmints but too light to address an intruder a half-mile away. Laura had once set up an informal range of big cardboard boxes and found that only one in ten of her .22 shots made a hole at a quarter-mile. That distance could reach the river at its nearest point, and her subconscious mind knew that to be the distance from the river-facing exposure of the locust. Given the susceptibility of little bits of lead to wind, though, she'd be very lucky if she hit what she aimed at.

She had to assume the incoming bullet was meant for her and was not the errant shot of a deer poacher or a teen test-firing his first black rifle on the holiday. The whole Saltwood mess, followed by the shooting of Kelli Ochs, weighed against coincidence.

She barricaded the doors, switched off the lights, and closed the blinds and curtains.

Lying beneath a window and holding a hand mirror between the curtain and the glass, she watched for anyone approaching the house. Finally, her adrenalin subsiding, she moved to the hallway, where she sat with her back to the wall so she'd have a clear shot at anyone coming through the kitchen door. If she wanted to run, she could dash out the front door, slink around the side, and crawl to her Flex, which was parked directly in front of the kitchen door. It'd offer some protection if the shooter was some distance away or just not watching for those ten or fifteen seconds.

She could call the sheriff. Half the department was six miles from her house, guarding the oil rig. Was she too self-sufficient? Too angry? Too afraid of causing trouble? Was she being stupid by not calling? Absolutely.

Did she want Nick or not? As far as she knew, he didn't have an active phone, unless he had turned on a burner that she didn't have the number for. Or maybe that was him shooting at her. She couldn't remember whether he said he'd be back, but he wouldn't need to shoot from a distance when he could walk right up to her.

The phone buzzed in her hand, and she yipped in surprise.

It was the office manager in the senator's office in Wichita.

"Oh, Laura," she said, sobbing. "It's so sad."

"Darla, what?"

"Harriet's dead. A driver hit her while she was running."

"Oh my God."

"It was just two hours ago. It's all over Facebook and TV."

"Does everybody else know?" She crawled to her room and turned on a Wichita news station.

"Can you come into the office or be available for Zooms? Or at least take some calls? We're already getting an awful lot of inquiries from the press and the party. And you've been with her since the beginning."

"I'm dealing with a trespasser right now," Laura said. "I'll be back in touch as soon as I can."

Sitting on the floor and keeping the bed between herself and the window, Laura monitored TV, Facebook, and X for the next half-hour.

About the time Laura concluded that Nick Devereaux must've killed Gayfeather, up popped the hot takes saying that an oil-company executive had been found dead, apparently a suicide, in the garage of the senator's home. That development didn't rule out Nick's involvement, but now it was plausible that other people had a hand in it. Was it a coordinated attack against Gayfeather's people?

She didn't know what to think, what to do.

Maybe nobody trying to kill her. She'd had wild gunshots before on her land.

But Nick was coming for her. She knew it.

Maybe Gayfeather's killer was a nut job from the rally yesterday at the church. Maybe it was someone who thought a deep-state version of Gayfeather had bought oil futures and oil-company stocks to make herself rich. There had been stories of senators doing that.

Perhaps Harriet had outlived her usefulness after introducing the PETRO bill. Kevin Perdue, that sleaze, could certainly have been the point man in her death despite his liaison with the senator.

Laura took a deep breath. She would mourn the senator's death when she could. Today was for not being killed herself.

Who was after them? Did some thread link them all? The oilfield workers, Kelli Ochs, Gayfeather, and Perdue. And now, apparently, her own lonely self. Or was it just a whipped-up panic fertilized—fostered?—by new radicals?

She could call Orion, but he'd be walking into trouble and probably get killed.

She could call the sheriff, but she had her own reasons to avoid contact with the legal system.

The only person who could help, her only supposed friend with experience in this kind of thing, was Nick Deveraux. She prayed he wasn't the one shooting at her.

•   •   •

Having despaired of anyone coming to her rescue, Laura decided to save herself.

She tucked her loose hair under a ball cap and double-checked the knots in her shoelaces. Her car key and fob were in the right pocket of her roomy work jeans.

Five red shotgun shells loaded with buckshot and a spare rotary magazine were in the left pocket, to go with the five shells already in her 12-gauge and with her loaded Ruger. She texted Orion: "I'm heading to your place. Call if you don't see me or hear from me in 30 minutes."

She made a recon circuit, peeking out each window and seeing nothing out of place. The back door was open but exposed. With care, she opened the front door and its storm door, propping the doors open in case she had to retreat inside.

With the shotgun in one hand and the rifle strapped over her back, she crept close to the foundation around the side of the house away from the river. As she crawled through the little bed where she expected to plant purple and yellow irises in the fall, her knees pressed into the damp soil.

She felt confident until she reached the water tank. Once she committed herself, she'd have to cover fifteen feet—and then open the car door, slide the key into the ignition, start up, and drive out. She could awaken the car with her key fob, but the beep and flashing brake lights would alert anyone within two hundred yards.

Laura pressed the button, and the Flex unlocked its doors.

•　　•　　•

Despite closing in on a kill, Lance Sterrett was in a mood getting sourer by the minute.

As soon as he fired his second shot into the trees, he ran toward the ranch house, splashing through Salt Creek and taking a position behind the machine shed blocking Eisenhauer's view from the house. His trail through the grass was obvious but unimportant now. From there, he scoped the house's windows and saw nothing. He slid around to the shed's open front and ducked inside to a nest of shadows.

Now he was lying on the machine shed's nasty dirt floor putting an end to the senator's aide. Once, she was sacred because she was the key to finding the scientist. He wondered what had changed.

From his point of view, the one person who needed to be shot was at home mooning over her obsession with Luke Meriwether.

Maybe Joyleen was screwing Meriwether right then, consoling the flag-draped scumbag in some motel out near the city limit. He imagined his wife's body knotted up with Pastor Luke's vague shape, and he hated the world.

Sterrett had nothing to live for except to show Joyleen that he didn't need her. He'd dump her, maybe have her killed the next time he was out of town. There were enough people around who'd do it and shut up for the money he could afford. He had been gone for several days just before the bombing, tracking down that North Dakota nut he'd found on Facebook. Had he known then about Joyleen's faithlessness inside the church, everything could be solved by now.

A Saltwood pilot had given Sterrett a lift a week ago Thursday on a nondescript Cessna 152 as far as Rapid City, South Dakota. Sterrett told the pilot he'd catch a ride back to Wichita with a friend, and he masked his visit by attending an industry conference on Friday. But Saturday, he borrowed a pickup from a Walmart parking lot and drove north 280 miles, almost six hours in a smelly Chevrolet, to the Williston oil play of the Bakken formation along the Missouri River in northwestern North Dakota. Using an alias, he rented a room for less than a hundred bucks near the city's airport.

When most people in this farming area were home eating dinner Sunday, Sterrett explored several oil-tank farms and pump jacks lining a road he had picked out on Google Maps. When he felt lucky, he pulled in behind a trio of 5,000-gallon tanks and their protective berms. It didn't really matter which set of tanks he chose, as long as it had a dirt berm instead of gravel, which was annoying to dig into.

With a small shovel, he dug a couple of feet down into the backside berm. Into the hole, he placed a gallon paint can containing shrapnel and a kilogram of C-4 plastic explosive, breaded in Tannerite like a slab of catfish and jabbed with a blasting cap. He set the timer set for 11:45 Wednesday morning.

Waiting until a pickup and two cars rolled past, he tucked the soil down gently and trailed a length of bindweed over it. The disturbed soil would blend in after an hour in the arid wind. Day in and day out, inspectors might look for leaks and the theft of crude by drivers of rogue vacuum trucks, but they'd never notice an explosive device strong enough to blow pieces of the tanks a quarter mile.

At noon the next day, Monday, just a week ago, Sterrett ran into his mark, Ray Brehm, at a bar—he knew which one to hang out in from reading Facebook—and ended up buying the husky fellow lunch and a couple of beers. After an hour of joshing and commiserating about politics, he allowed Brehm to offer him a Remington 700 rifle with the serial numbers ground off the receiver.

Out at the Dakotan's isolated farmhouse near West Bonetrail, Brehm loaded the rifle with a single round and let Sterrett fire it into a berm on a makeshift range. Sterrett handed him back the rifle without ejecting the shell. Then, with a handgun, he put three quiet subsonic hollow-point bullets into Brehm's chest.

After slipping into gloves, Sterrett took the sale cash out of Brehm's pocket and wiped down the rifle. With effort, he lifted Brehm into a sitting position and bent his fingers around the stock, barrel, trigger, and bolt, and awkwardly rubbed the stock against Brehm's cheek for a load of skin cells to make the eventual DNA testers happy. The rifle went into a case in the cab of Brehm's truck. From the berm, Sterrett dug out the round and put it in a baggie. The expended shell stayed in the rifle.

The stolen pickup, its South Dakota tags stripped, went onto a five-ton repair lift in Brehm's workshop. Sterrett knew all of this was possible; he had seen pictures of Brehm's rifle, pickup, and lift on Facebook.

He positioned two nearly empty containers of Tannerite, which he had brought in his suitcase, and a pile of scrap metal on the workbench. The Tannerite didn't really matter when combined with the plastic explosive, but a spectrographic analysis would link crime-scene data to Brehm's containers and the evidence at Quivira.

After that, everything was easy. Sterrett encased Brehm's body in a body bag and pushed it into the camper in the bed of Brehm's Chevy Silverado pickup. One of Brehm's shovels went in with the bag.

Around 9:00, after six hours of driving down US 85, Sterrett buried the machinist at dusk in a recently plowed field in South

Dakota, a tedious state he had driven across so many times for Saltwood that he considered it the scar tissue of the northern plains. The shovel was stuffed into a ditch culvert five miles down the farm road. A couple of hours later, he allowed himself a few hours of sleep in a creekside pullout.

And then, wearing leather gloves the whole way, he drove at a safe and sane fifty-five miles an hour on US 18 and 281 to central Kansas. He parked late Tuesday night behind an abandoned farmhouse in Stafford County and cleaned Brehm's truck of paperwork, fingerprints, and the rifle. He left the gun case and Brehm's phone in the camper and laid the keys on the dashboard.

In Wednesday's predawn darkness, he strolled to his own Saltwood truck, parked a week earlier a mile away in an old outbuilding. Once on the county road, he walked back and swept away his treadmarks from the driveway.

Inside his pickup was a sealed five-gallon steel bucket of shrapnel plus twenty pounds of mixed Tannerite, the equivalent of ten or twelve pounds of dynamite. In the semidarkness, before the day crew came to work at the Quivira well, he drove into the site and parked in front of the office trailer. He lowered the bomb into the trash barrel and placed a few pieces of scrap lumber atop it. With a pencil, he drew a small circle on the outside of the barrel; he'd use it as his bull's-eye. He knew that no one on the rig would give a second thought to a Saltwood truck making its rounds early in the day.

He flung the lightly mushroomed rifle bullet he had dug from Brehm's berm far out into the pasture. The prep finished, he drove fifty-five minutes to a shop in Great Bend to establish his alibi by buying a breakfast burrito and a large coffee, just as he had done every Wednesday morning for the past month and a half. By 9:30, he was set up in his sniper position at the old school near the wellsite, waiting for the boss to arrive.

·   ·   ·

He had been away six days. That part of the plan was a success. Now he had been back six days, and everything in his life was going to hell.

How many times did Joyleen screw her sleazy boss in the six days he was gone?

And that fucking Purkeypyle. He caused this whole mess. Sterrett had been ordered to keep the Eisenhauer chick alive until she gave up Purkeypyle. She was another woman sleeping with a married man.

Sterrett squirmed into a slightly less uncomfortable shooting position next to a stack of mildewed furniture, trying to find a posture that didn't have him lying face down in years of crap left by rats and pigeons. Several gallon jugs had been moved from shelves onto the floor next to a pitchfork, and now they restricted his view. It was camouflage, though, for him and his bipod-mounted M24.

The swoosh of a rapidly approaching vehicle rose and fell as it passed over little rises in the sand hills. Better get this over, he thought. Help for her might come soon.

The Flex beeped and the brake lights flared against the glare of the morning sun.

He scanned the car and house through his scope. There, sticking out from behind the water tank, was a hand holding out a key fob.

He shifted the rifle, the legs of the bipod leaving trails in the dust. He fired once, worked the bolt methodically, and fired again, in time with the beat of Carmen singing the "Habanera."

38

Nick turned onto the washboard road at highway speed and nearly lost control of the pickup. At this point, however, he could live with the pounded kidneys and the mess of papers and small tools that bounded out of the glove box.

Two more miles, one more, and there was the ranch house's shelter belt and long driveway.

Water was squirting hard out of a ragged hole in the tank two feet off the ground, washing into a puddle in the driveway. The truck splashed through it, a slurry of sand and water widening out like wings. The splash fell on Laura, who was lying at the base of the tank.

He braked and spun the wheel hard right with the suicide knob, skidding backward onto the parking area as he watched for trouble. The truck slid to a stop on the outbuilding side of the Flex, the front of the F-150 jutting two or three feet in front of the Flex's grille.

The battle was underway. Nick hoped he wasn't too late. A quick look around didn't reveal the enemy.

The truck's steel door wouldn't provide a napkin's protection if the marksman used a high-powered rifle. Sterrett had already proven he did, using one to blow up the Tannerite bomb at the well. Nick had no doubt that Sterrett was a cold-blooded killer.

Nick opened his door and shoved himself out. He fell in a clumsy pile onto the sandy driveway.

"Nick?" Laura shouted. "Shed. Rifle."

"Give me room," he shouted. It'd be a long dash to her side, with the vehicles providing some protection.

The next shot came quickly, ripping a trench into the gravel under the truck and blowing out the tire beside him.

He hunched over, zigzagging until he dived hands first into the grass and rolled behind the tank.

"Welcome home," Laura said. "Thanks for not being the one shooting at me."

"Glad to be here," he said.

She held her key fob out to him. "He shot the key off and then put a hole in my tank."

"You okay?"

"Dandy," she said. "What's your plan?"

"It's Lance Sterrett. We need to make his world fall apart."

"How do you know it's him?"

"I sent him."

She rapped Nick in the temple. He looked at her in surprise. She looked at him with disappointment. He thought it was anger.

"It seemed like the best way to get a shot at him," Nick said. "Put an end to all of this."

Her phone rang. They both jumped.

She answered. Nick saw "Orion" on the screen.

"Yeah, dang it, I can't talk now. Give me another hour. . . . Hey, do me a favor and call 9-1-1 and remind them we might burn some stuff today and not to send a truck unless I call again."

Another shot ripped into the tank, splashing the water high.

"That was my water tank. There's some asshole shooting toward the farm. . . . Uh-huh, Nick just got here. . . . We'll be okay. See you soon."

The holes in the tank let in enough sunlight that the sides were becoming translucent. They watched the shadow of the water as it sloshed back and forth.

"If I live through this, that guy and you are going to pay for my tank."

"If he lives through it, take the cash out of my pockets and run."

He tossed his jacket behind him.

The next shot jolted the stock of the shotgun at Laura's side. She pulled it back in.

"Where is he?" Nick said.

"The shed, I think. Thirty yards."

"Do the car and truck block his view anywhere?"

"Yes, but he can move around in there and we won't see him," she said. "We can go around the house, but we won't have a view of the shed without exposing ourselves. I know he can shoot low enough to hit us here. I can't believe he's wasting all my water."

One ear to the ground, they faced each other, inches apart.

"You hear about Gayfeather?" he said.

"And Perdue," she said.

The next shot skipped across the water just above their heads. It ricocheted obliquely into the house's wooden siding.

"I have ideas," Laura said.

On the loudspeaker, Carmen was dying from being stabbed by her lover.

•   •   •

The plans were simple and suicidal.

The first alternative was to use the house as cover and run the other direction as low and fast as they could, trying to stay below the sandhills' low horizon. They'd probably live, but so would Sterrett, and he could chase them forever.

The good part of that was that the sheriff's deputies could pen Sterrett in unless he got to the river and escaped. The bad part was that without a positive identification of Sterrett as the gunman, police officers would have no reason to hold him. Sterrett could spend all his time hunting them like an angry bear.

The second alternative was more direct and likely to hurt.

"There's a box of highway flares in the truck," Laura said. "They're in an ammo can behind the passenger seat. You can get it for us."

"And where will you be?"

"I have twenty rounds of .22 long rifle. I'll lay down covering fire, every second or two. It won't tear him apart, but he might pull back into his hole long enough for you to run up there and bring back the flares."

"Everybody's got to die sometime," he said.

"Let's make it today for him," she said.

Nick chose his path. He'd dash toward the Flex, which was slightly offset from the pickup and separated by five or six feet. From there, he'd get to the pickup. Considering the length of the overlapping vehicles, there was more than twenty feet of screen, but any shot under the vehicles could take him out if it hit his feet or legs. With luck, Sterrett's view of Nick's feet would be blocked by the tires, and the rest of Nick should be protected somewhat by the metal sides and engine blocks of the vehicles.

Laura said she'd fire a couple of shots from just above ground level into the shed. Maybe the rounds would skip up and do nothing more than get his attention, but at least Sterrett would know the enemy had teeth. When the first ten bullets were gone, she'd press a release under the receiver to drop out the first magazine and push the second one in.

Once Nick was set, she'd run around the house and fire rounds from that side. Nick could deliver the flares to either location.

"I'm ready," he said. "Count down from three, and I'll run on your shot."

Without either one of them thinking about it first, they kissed lightly on the lips.

She pulled the spare 10-22 magazine out of her pocket and held it in her left hand.

"Three. Two. One." Laura squeezed off the first round.

Nick was six feet into his run when her second shot spat past him, and he opened the truck's driver's door and slid into the rear footwell as Laura's third .22 round whispered by. He found the flares in a sturdy olive-green steel box and fished around under the front seat for the .22 revolver wrapped in rags. He stripped away the cloth and made sure one of the three live rounds would rotate into firing position when he pulled the trigger. He stuck the gun in his pocket.

The truck rocked with the impact of a large round through the bed. The rifle's thunder was suppressed but still barked of death. Nick waited for Sterrett to guess where he was hiding. The answer came quickly: a round through the side panel sprayed metal splinters into his slacks.

"Nick, go!"

Laura had reached the far side. She held the .22 around the corner and fired blind. Small brass casings flipped out the right side of the receiver.

Sterrett, in the darkness of the shed, fired three of his own into the house. It seemed that he hadn't spotted Laura.

There was a pause. Was he reloading?

Laura's rifle spoke. Pop, pop. Pop, pop. Metal rang out dully in the shed. And then there was no more from Laura.

"Nick," she yelled. "I'm jammed."

The truck rocked again, the bullet piercing the door and creasing Nick's arm. He gasped and pressed his hand over the wound.

The next round ruptured the truck's gas tank, and a dozen gallons of regular poured into the sun-warmed gravel. Vapors shimmered around the pickup.

Laura shouted: "Get out now."

Nick jumped out with the ammo box, but the revolver fell into the sand. As he reached for it, Sterrett fired twice; it seemed to Nick like they were unaimed grabshots. Unharmed, Nick stretched, got the gun, and scrambled around the Flex as Sterrett fired again.

It was a tracer round, an unimaginably rapid transit of red fire that splashed into the gassy sand and richocheted beyond the house. The vapors ignited, and after the briefest moment a flame shot like a torch out of the punctured tank, and the tank exploded.

The truck elevated then came down hard, blowing out its overheated tires and settling a few inches lower than before. Four feet separated the two vehicles now.

A two-second-long fireball, pulled in and pushed out by the truck's flight and rising gases heated to fifteen hundred degrees, washed over and under the Flex. Squatting behind the Flex's front wheel, Nick patted his hair and scorched clothing in case any of it was on fire.

Oily smoke drifted toward the house. Nick felt the radiating heat, gasping for clean air and holding the box of flares in his lap.

Five pops came from the far side of the house, then two booms in rapid succession. Laura had announced the shotgun. The gun's twenty-pound recoil staggered her strides toward the Flex.

She sat on her haunches, leaning back against the other wheel.

"I know what we can do," she said. She was speaking loudly, a little deafened despite wads of tissue stuffed in her ears.

Nick asked, "How bad are you hurt?"

"Twisted my ankle, caught a bit of full metal jacket in my other calf. Both legs hurt. You all right?"

"Singed but not bleeding much."

Nick scanned her leg and frowned. He pulled out the folded Russian knife and tossed it into the sand beside her thigh.

"You're bleeding too much," he said. Nick popped the snaps of his bullet-torn white shirt, wadded it up, and tossed it to her. "Make the bandage out of this, and then let's get him."

She opened the knife. "Are you up for a little more fire?"

"Hell, yes."

"How far can you throw a flare?"

"To the shed, I'm pretty sure."

"It means you have to stand up," she said. "You're bleeding, too. Are you okay?"

After she cut into the shirt and ripped out a wide strip of fabric, she wrapped it tightly around her calf twice and made a square knot.

"Good to go," she said.

Laura pumped the shotgun to put a round in the chamber, then refilled the magazine from her pocket. She looked at him and raised her eyebrows as a question.

He said, "I'm here for the adventure."

"You're here for the sex." She grinned without joy.

"Yeah. Don't get more hurt."

"How many flares are in the box?"

The Flex shook. Sterrett had found an angle.

Nick held up three dark-red flares, each nine inches long, about an inch thick, and topped with a removable white cap that was rough on one end. He set them back in the box, beside the tire.

She frowned. "It'll have to do."

He turned toward the shed, kneeling as he hefted the first flare. "I'm ready."

"When I say so, light it. Get a good grip. See the shed in your mind, then stand and fling that stick at the door."

She checked and double-checked that the shotgun's safety was off.

Nick pulled off the plastic cap and reversed it in his grip. When he scraped it hard against the end of the flare, the stick erupted into a hissing red flame.

"Twenty-six hundred degrees," Laura said. "Watch yourself."

He slid his throwing hand to the bottom of the flare and concentrated on the shed's location.

The Flex rocked again with a gunshot punch. And again.

Nick stood quickly and hurled the flare. It went high in the air, turning end over end, and fell to the sand ten yards short.

"What was that?" Laura, crouched on one knee, peeked around the front of the Flex.

"I slipped."

Nick brushed sand away from his feet before picking up the second flare. He struck the top again and again, then tried using the first cap. Nothing. He tossed the flare aside, out of the way.

The Flex was heating up. The pickup's flames were bubbling the paint off the car's hood.

Black smoke and heat waves made it hard to see the shed.

Sterrett hit the ammo box beside Nick's knees, skittering it away.

"I'll count from three," he said. "Fire somewhere in his direction and I'll get the flare."

She did and he stretched out for the box, but he misjudged his balance and fell awkwardly onto his side.

Sterrett's next shot nibbled a piece out of Nick's throwing forearm. Laura answered two times with the shotgun. Nick retrieved the box and returned to his wheel.

"In the door, Nick," she said. "Do or die."

"Three, two, one."

He stood and turned, and the fire's heat made him recoil. The smoke and flames blocked his line of sight, but they blocked Sterrett's vision too.

Nick gathered his wits. Rearing back, he hurled the flare with all his strength.

39

In the magic of slow time, Nick's last flare rotated in its long arc, a hissing pinwheel spitting red flames until it smacked the front of the wooden shed above the entrance and fell to the ground. Its smoky brightness taunted him.

"I guess we'd better starting running," he said.

"Sit tight."

Laura stuffed the last shells into the shotgun and worked the action just enough to be sure a shell was in the chamber. She pushed the safety twice to ensure that it was off.

"Five left. Wish me luck," she said.

Extending herself over the Flex's hood, she fired quickly into the shed's doorway. The first shot went straight toward the back, to hold the intruder down, and then two low shots into the shed. Wood splintered. Glass broke. She fired twice more to keep him in place.

She retreated to the ground and turned to Nick. "Hymn to Love" ended, and the "Allegretto" of Beethoven's *Seventh* was beginning: four beats of one chord, then a quarter note, two staccato eighth notes, two staccato quarter notes. The phrasing was repeated by the string instruments, rising and falling, a theme repeated at a noble seventy-six beats a minute.

"Remember those gallon jugs of gas?" she said. "They've gone to heaven."

Fumes wafted from the mess, floating low inside toward the walls of the shed, toward the sniper's nest in the back, and toward the burning flare.

Nick and Laura peeked, their lives riding on the moment.

Sterrett burst out of the shed, blood clearly visible on his face. He carried his rifle by the grip in one hand, and in the other, the old pitchfork.

Just as he stepped into the pool of gas, its vapors reached the burning flare. The fuel-air mixture exploded with a whumpf, pushing the shed's decrepit wooden walls outward, and then the superheated air poofed out the front when the roof fell in. The surge of orange flames and oily smoke created a mushroom cloud that towered briefly over the farm.

The blast rocked the Flex. The heat from above pressed against Laura and Nick, singeing their hair.

Sterrett was engulfed in the fireball. He staggered and fell into the sand, his clothes and hair aflame. Pushing himself up with the pitchfork handle, he dropped the rifle and ran forward screaming as a man possessed of superhuman anger.

Nick stepped out from behind the Flex, drawing Sterrett away from Laura. He pulled the .22 revolver from his pocket and fired from ten feet, then eight and six. The first round missed, the second took a bit of cartilage off Sterrett's ear, and the final shot made a tiny hole in Sterrett's shoulder.

Sterrett, his skin smoking and his body burned free of clothing down to his boots, jabbed the pitchfork again and again at Nick, wild motions as if his vision had been ruined.

Nick dodged, and after the third jab he grabbed the tines and pulled hard. Sterrett tumbled to his knees, losing his grip.

But Sterrett was beyond caring, driving now with the grit of a Medal of Honor recipient. He rose and swung his darkened fist into Nick's ribs, then pushed a step closer so could he wrap his arms around Nick and squeeze. As Nick spread his feet to hold his balance, Sterrett kneed him in the testicles.

Nick collapsed, pulling himself out of Sterrett's grasp. Sterrett booted him in the head as Nick writhed in the sand.

Sterrett grabbed the pitchfork off the ground and raised it above his head. With a bellow he drove the tines down at Nick's chest.

Nick saw it coming and squirmed, but the fork still trapped his left arm below the shoulder. He was pinned to the ground.

Sterrett growled: "Stay." He reinforced it by stomping on Nick's belly, knocking the wind out of him.

Sterrett turned toward Laura, who held her empty 12-gauge by the barrel like a baseball bat, ready to bash Sterrett's skull in with the walnut stock. They circled each other, feinting and edging closer and closer.

Laura rolled her ankle on the second flare, the dud, and nearly went over sideways. A blind kick knocked it under the Flex just far enough to reach the flames.

The dud began to burn, which provided enough new heat to ignite the interior of the Flex. The car filled with smoke instantly. In seconds, the windows blew outward, bringing with the shards the toxins of burning plastic, insulation, and foam. Flames licked at the combatants, but neither gave ground.

"Where's Purkeypyle?" Sterrett said, forcing the words from his ruined lungs through his scorched lips. "Tell me!"

"I don't know, asshole. I don't care."

He rasped in her face: "Purkeypyle!"

"No!"

"Give me data."

"I don't have it."

Laura kept her eyes on Sterrett's blackened and blistered hulk, but she knew her car and her truck were destroyed. The water tank was a wreck. There were bullet holes in her house. She was wounded, and she was furious.

She half-swung the shotgun, not going around with her wrists, and he flinched. When she swung with intent, he stepped into her swing and grabbed the stock, wrenching the gun from her hands.

He pulled the trigger on a spent shell, worked the action, and again aimed the gun at her. When it dry-fired, he tossed it aside.

Laura charged, pushing him over and falling on top. She wrapped her hands around his neck, but they slid off with sheets of his destroyed skin.

In her moment of disgust, he flexed his right leg against the ground and rolled out from under her. From there, he sat on her waist, leaning forward to grind her shoulders into the soil.

She struggled with her pocket, trying to free the knife Nick had given her. Sterrett paid her hands no attention.

"Purkeypyle! Where?"

The knife came out, and she fumbled under Sterrett's arms with the ribbed handle, turning it in her fingers and edging it forward so she could get her thumb on the peg and flip the blade open. When it popped out, she moved quickly. She slid her hand across in front of him, beneath his arm, and the knife became a claw.

Without hesitation, she plunged the blade in and drew it across Sterrett's gut. He pulled his arms in to protect his belly. She raised the knife higher and slashed his neck under his left ear, severing his carotid artery and opening his jugular vein. Pumped by battlefield stress, his rich blood splashed like heavy rain into the sand.

He grunted and scrabbled to gather his intestines. He leaned back and then forward. And then he was gone, lifted off her midsection.

Nick had pitchforked him from behind.

Nick staggered under Sterrett's growling weight as he push-marched him awkwardly toward the tornado of flame spinning above the collapsed shed. Halfway there, Sterrett sagged, blood dribbling from his neck, and his arms no longer held his body together. A loop of his intestines dragged beneath Nick's feet, jerking Sterrett down whenever Nick stepped on them.

Laura rolled away from the burning vehicles and got up on her hands and knees. In that moment, her car's gas tank lit up and she was knocked over by the concussion.

She scrambled to her feet, screaming, "Nick, Nick!" She limped after him until she could get no closer to the inferno.

Nick was a few steps away from the fallen roof, its wooden members vaporizing in flames twice his height. He tilted the pitchfork back and moved his right hand to the end of the handle. With all his might, he shoved the pitchfork and his enemy into the flames.

Nick raised his arm to block the heat from his face, and crept backward. A moment, a minute, two minutes later, he turned away from the fire.

40

Laura sat on the lawn, talking by phone in a casual, upbeat tone with Sam Orion.

"I know there's more smoke than anybody expected. That's the hassle with farm sheds. There was some gas in there, and a lot of oil had gone into the ground over the years. Just tell the fire department we've got it covered. No wind here at all. It'll be all ashes in a little bit. But yes, I still want you right away with your big first-aid kit. Please call it in first."

Orion returned her call four minutes later. Laura laughed thinly.

"I bet they were surprised. There was a lot of oil. . . . Cuts, burns, flesh wounds. . . . Nothing that requires a hospital or the police."

Nick sat beside her, his knees up and his arms on his knees. He reeked of smoke and Sterrett, and he felt like he'd been in the oven too long. Strands of their hair were singed into little balls at the ends. Ashes had sprinkled down on everything, dark rain on a sunny morning. He brushed them off his arms as she ended the call.

"It's not even 10 o'clock," he said. "For what that's worth."

"I'm not hungry," she said.

"Same," he said.

"Good job putting the flare where it needed to be," she said.

"A trained monkey could've done it." His smile lacked humor. "It took me three tries."

"Got the job done."

"How's your leg?" he said. "Can you show it to me?"

"I'm not pulling my pants down."

"Still have the knife?" he said. "We can cut the pant leg open."

"It went with Sterrett, I think."

"It was a good blade. The Russians gave it to me."

"They come in handy."

"I'm glad you're sort of okay," he said.

"We protected my land and our lives. We're a team."

Nick nodded. "You thinking you like this kind of thing, want to give it a try?"

"I might as well. I assume I lost my job today."

•　　•　　•

The shed's flames were almost down to embers when Orion arrived in his RV.

"His pride and joy," Laura said.

The recreational vehicle was a Winnebago Navion, a twenty-five-foot class C motorhome with a three-point Mercedes emblem on the grille. It was dressed up in gray-green livery with white and red slashes stretching from the front bumper all the way back. He parked on the driveway side of the house, well clear of the smoldering battleground.

Orion gave Laura then Nick the quickest of hugs, which was generous given the messes they were.

"My God, are you roasting a cow? And tell me that's barbecue sauce on the ground."

"A rat must've gotten caught in the fire," she said.

"First question: Do either of you have burn blisters or gushing wounds?"

Nope and nope.

Orion, the physician's assistant, waved his flashlight across their eyes and checked their pulses. He scissored Nick's slacks off and tweezed metal splinters out of his leg.

"Your house might be a mess, considering the bullet holes. The RV's got a shower and room for examining you." He nodded at Laura. "I'll get clothes from your room, and you can change in the RV after your shower. Nick, you have any clothes you can change into?"

"All I have is what I'm wearing, plus my jacket," Nick said. "Everything else is in Wichita."

Orion busied himself putting out a bath mat and a trash bag for clothes. He opened all the doors to catch the breeze, which was rising from behind the RV and pushing the acrid air away from the house. From Laura's bedroom, he brought out a loose T-shirt and a pair of shorts, panties, and a bra, and he handed Nick a T-shirt and shorts from the RV's closet.

"You'll have to go commando, bud."

"If there's one thing I can do, that's it."

"Quick showers now," Orion told them. "Get sanitary enough to be treated. If you need a serious cleanup after that, I'll take you to my place. Seriously, this big-ass RV carries only thirty gallons of fresh water, which is just a tenth of what we'll get from what's left of your tank."

Before they showered, Orion used a hand saw to widen a hole in the water tank's fiberglass wall so he could maneuver a gallon bucket down to collect the last two feet of clean water, pouring bucketfuls over them in the yard to wash away much of the battle grime and odor. In the RV's snug shower, they were each to run a bit of warm water, scrub with soap, and rinse off quickly.

After dressing, Laura limped down the RV's fold-out steps, her fresh clothes exposing glistening wounds. After his turn, Nick wore only the borrowed shorts; his chest and arm wounds glared fiercely and seeped blood.

Ushering them back into the RV, Orion cleaned their wounds gently with alcohol and bottled water before applying antibiotics and butterfly bandages.

"Your calf doesn't look so bad," he told Laura. He winked. "You know I'm required to tell the cops about any gunshot wounds I encounter. What you have, it could be any kind of nonreportable injury. Take the pills I give you, but if any infection shows up, get to a doctor immediately. Make up a really simple story about it, maybe a bad scrape on metal out in the weeds. Or say it's from the explosion."

Orion put two stitches in Nick's forearm and wrapped it in gauze and tape.

"I have to know," Orion said.

"It's better that you don't," Laura said. "Don't be the guy who knows too much about this."

"Is the danger gone?"

Nick said, "The guy who shot at us was the guy who set off the explosion at the well. The whole thing was faked for that PETRO bill Gayfeather introduced. Kevin Perdue told me."

That got Laura's attention. "When did you see him?"

"Earlier."

She didn't say anything. When she thought Orion wasn't looking, she smiled, a sad smile.

"Babe," Orion said, "you've had an awful day. It sucks that the senator won't be around anymore, but it's even worse if she was involved at Quivira. It's not actually being abandoned that hurts. Understanding what it's about is what hurts."

"Story of my life, pal," she said.

Orion and Nick each took one of Laura's hands, and the three sat in silence. At last, Laura pulled back and stood at the windshield. Hands on hips, she surveyed the mess that was her ranch yard.

When she turned back, her voice carried a steel edge.

"Here's what happened: Some unidentified vandal shot up my water tank and my vehicles. I burned the shed, rather than tear it down, and leaking gas burned my vehicles. All of that is absolutely true.

"And so is this," she said. "I need to buy a new water tank and new wheels. I don't feel like dealing with insurance or the police, so I'm not going to report the car or truck. Anyway, their value was practically nothing. I loved that car. She looked like a shoebox that wanted to be a truck, but we went through a lot together in six years. I might get another Flex. Cash only."

•   •   •

Laura spent the next two hours on a dinette bench in Orion's RV returning calls to reporters and donors to describe what a wonderful senator Harriet Gayfeather had been and how much the good and upright citizens of Kansas would miss her can-do attitude and attention to detail and principle.

"I've known Senator Gayfeather for ten years, even before she was elected," Laura said again and again, "through some of the most stressful days of her life. And not once did she lash out in anger. She believed in building consensus and asking, 'Where do we go from here?'

"Senator Gayfeather wished the best for all her constituents, even those who disagreed with her. She stood on her own for women's health and for the rule of law. Her words at Saturday's memorial for the oilfield workers were from the heart."

Laura's closing words each time: "Her death is hard for us, but it is God's will."

Nick and Orion made ham sandwiches and brought her a Diet Coke. Laura skimmed Facebook and Twitter.

"Lots of hot air online," she said. "And somebody got a recording of Harriet implicating Kevin Perdue with her dying words."

Finally, Laura shut down her phone.

"That's enough feeding the corporate media. The world . . ." She took a bite and wiped her lips. "The world is a needy place."

She made up her mind about something and moved to the right-hand captain's chair to set things in motion.

"Orion," she said, "can you take me to Dillons before everything in my body starts to hurt?"

• • •

Nick was using a scoop shovel to scrape a firebreak between the machine shed's embers and the barn when Orion brought Laura home at midafternoon with three bags of groceries, four gallon jugs and two flats of bottled water, and a twenty-four-can carton of Diet Coke.

Orion said his goodbyes, and the RV lumbered down the driveway. Nick carried the groceries in.

"Here's a T-shirt and jeans from a giveaway collection box," Laura said, "although you look pretty already snazzy in those leather dress shoes."

"The county's most elegant fire department," Nick said. "My other shoes are in your apartment, but they would've melted this close to the heat. It's still so hot my fire-poking stick keeps catching fire."

He had forgotten about the wadded-up gloves from Gayfeather's garage, the ones misted with Kevin Perdue's blood. He found the jacket where he had tossed it beyond the shattered water tank and collected the packets of cash from the pockets. Kelli Ochs' little metal box had flown from a pocket but not broken open, and he took it to his room. The box reminded him now of a coffin, and he couldn't face the photo of baby Kelli being held by her mother. He put her sketch of him in his billfold.

After a while, Nick walked the coat out to the shed and tossed it onto the embers, wishing he could toss his memories of the day in with it. The coat smoldered briefly, food for the tired fire, and then burned brightly until it was nothing but a shadow.

As Laura shuffled around the kitchen, her eyes seemed unfocused. "I know we need to do something with the remains," she said, "but can it wait until tomorrow?"

"I don't want to think about what's out there while we're eating."

"Tomorrow. We'll talk tomorrow. The scoop shovel and wheelbarrow are in the barn. The only other shed," she said. "Go outside now. My little ranch . . ."

As Nick let the screen door close softly on its spring, Laura's voice quoting Wordsworth followed him:

"Where is it now, the glory and the dream?"

Laura, finally, broke into sobs.

•   •   •

Nick was back at the shed, annoying the embers again, when Laura ran out of the house.

"Call for you," she said. "On my cell. She sounds important."

He nodded his thanks and took the phone.

"This is Pellen," the caller said. "I'm fifteen minutes away from you. We need to talk."

Pellen parked her dark blue rental sedan well short of the vehicle carcasses. She wore navy pants and jacket, and black shoes with low heels. Her black hair was pulled back, but not severely.

Nick walked over to shake hands. Laura stood at a distance until Pellen beckoned her over for an introduction. Pellen looked at them, standing together with damaged hair and fresh bandages.

"Barb Pellen, special agent-in-charge, FBI Washington office." When she reached for her badge, her sidearm was visible at her waist.

"Laura Eisenhauer, deputy chief of Senator Gayfeather's staff."

"Agent Pellen was there in Sandstone," Nick told Laura. "She made sure I was treated okay."

"That was a most difficult day," Pellen said.

There was no hiding the vehicles and burned shed from Pellen's eyes or nose.

"Looks like you had a regular shootenanny out here."

"Busy morning," Laura said.

"You two the only survivors?"

"It was a vandal," Nick said. "Somebody with a rifle and road flares. He's gone."

"That explains the bullet holes on one side of the vehicles and the shotgun shells on the other side," Pellen said. "I hope you're as okay as you can be, given your bandages."

Laura cocked her head. "What brings you to the ranch?"

"I was in the neighborhood," Pellen said. "The bomb, the church shooting, the protest that was almost a riot, the likely hate crime against a reporter in Wichita. And, finally, Gayfeather."

Nick and Laura exchanged a glance.

Laura asked: "Hate crime?"

"You must know A.B. Abbey, right? Before dawn this morning, after she published a Kumbaya piece on the newspaper's website, someone torched her house, a little frame place on Waco Avenue not all that far from the senator's house. She made the mistake of encouraging Wichitans to learn from the shooting. She survived, but with burns. The only thing she asked about, I heard, was her dog."

"Oh my God," Laura said. "She's a handful, but smart. She had a Pulitzer before she came to Wichita."

They were quiet for a quick minute. Across the parking area, a dozen or so pigeons cooed from the roof of the barn then flapped down to peck at the gravel.

"Do you mind," Nick asked Laura, "if I give Agent Pellen a tour of the ranch?"

He led Pellen off toward the shelter belt on the south side, away from the burned shed.

"Good to see you again," he said.

"I flew in late this morning to follow up with the bombing and the senator's death. How am I not surprised to find you here?" She gazed around the yard. "In this lovely corner of hell."

"You know hell as well as I do," he said. "You ever find something like this when you were in Seattle?"

"God, no. But then I was in counterintelligence. Now I work in financial crimes and terrorism. Guess why I'm here."

"Gayfeather and Saltwood certainly had secrets," Nick said.

"One of them was the extent of her contact with you," she said.

"What do you know?"

"Less than I need to."

"As I understand it," he began, pausing to turn toward Pellen. "She got lots of Saltwood money, maybe more than she reported. There's also hearsay that she had a fascination with the Chinese and maybe took the odd donation from them. Even though Saltwood competed against Russian oil and wanted to do business with China, the company was getting tired of her drama. She hated Russia because the Russians used me to try to kill her."

Pellen put her hand on Nick's arm.

"Between you and me," she said, "and you can't repeat this. She had $400 million offshore."

"No wonder she was paranoid."

"Paranoid how?"

"She was certain that Laura was out to get her. She asked specifically what Laura talked about, and the word *China* irritated her, made her angry."

"We're pretty sure she was on China's payroll for her committee work. Their money handlers are good, but our hackers are better."

Nick and Pellen strolled past the barn and toward the chicken house.

"What will happen now that she's dead?" he said.

"Now that we know the process the Chinese used, we'll check out other people."

Nick steered them away from the ruined shed, which still was radiating heat.

"That smells like . . ."

Nick butted in: "Farm chemicals. Maybe DDT. Definitely lead paint. Don't get the stink on your clothes."

They headed back toward her car. Pellen brought up the shooting of Kelli Ochs.

"Our team is almost certain you were the mystery man," she said.

"I was there with her. She caught me by surprise." He told her how they'd met, and he confirmed what Pellen said the church's livestream had recorded.

"That church—armed guards, a black-rifle militia." She shook her head. "There's going to be a lot of lingering trauma over this."

"Welcome back to Bleeding Kansas."

"What's new with the Russians?"

"No contact since I got here," he said.

"I'm not surprised," Pellen said. "They were just an intermediary in your being here. Did you know that?"

"I don't think I'm going to like where this goes."

Pellen took a deep breath.

"Gayfeather herself arranged for you, through Fred Snike, that counterintelligence agent who questioned you, to be released. My colleagues turned Snike two hours ago," she said. "Because the senator had connections in Topeka, where Snike was based before your failed assassination mission, she learned that Snike had taken money from the Russians and wasn't completely on our side. The Russians are the flavor of the month for the foreseeable future, so the covert deal was easily made with them, through Snike, to direct you to Gayfeather."

"Gayfeather hired me to spy on Laura and yesterday ordered me, in deniable words, to kill her."

"You can probably guess why you didn't get a new identity from the cabal."

"No one expected me to live long enough to need one? If Gayfeather was killed, someone wanted to pin it quickly on a known troublemaker with a history?"

"Yes and yes. Plus, the faction wanted to be able to pretend you escaped, without the aid of the Bureau."

"I guess I should be honored that so much thought went into this."

Pellen shrugged. "Everybody wants you on their team."

"Does that mean you can still get me new IDs? An American passport? A credit card?"

"That won't be a problem. I don't think I can get you a firearm."

"In America, that's not a problem. Thank you for the other items." He raised his chin. "There's one thing. I probably should leave in the next couple of days. This wide open prairie is starting to feel tight."

"I'd say so." she said. "If there's a storm in Kansas, you're in the center of it."

"I heard someone say rain is good for the wheat."

"Okay, now, we'll try to get all this done without letting the Russian faction know. You call me immediately if you find out otherwise."

"Speaking of," Nick said, "what'll happen to Snike?"

"I can't discuss that. Protocol."

Nick and Pellen had circled around to the shelter belt at the edge of the pasture.

She pointed south, into the breeze. "The well with the explosion was over there?"

"Just a few miles," he said. He cleared his throat. "Let me tell you some things about the bombing."

When he finished, she asked: "You believe this is true?"

"The downside is that Perdue said it knowing I was Russian, so maybe he wanted to mislead me. Or, he wasn't the brightest guy and maybe wanted to brag, and I was safe to tell because he had me trapped and was going to kill me. It does match up with the senator's distress and all the other circumstances."

Pellen thought about it and came to an acceptable path for discussions back at the office.

"Or," she proposed, "he was distraught over having run over Gayfeather. High stress does funny things to people, and his life had just taken a big left turn."

She asked for a moment alone to make a call, and he stuffed his hands in his pockets and walked on to her car.

She caught up after the call, trying to hide a smile.

"I've got to visit the bomb crater and Gayfeather's house, just to get familiar," she said. "The folks in DC are, let's say, intrigued with where this is going."

"What about the local cops?"

"When they show up, for either you or Ms. Eisenhauer, instruct them to call the number on this card." She took a case out of her jacket and pulled out a couple of her business cards. "Don't answer any of their questions. The Federal Bureau of Investigation, through my office, is declaring national-security jurisdiction over this whole matter. You and Ms. Eisenhauer are persons of national interest, answerable only to the Bureau, in particular to me. This is non-negotiable."

He held the car door as she got in.

"Can I ask for a personal favor?" Nick said. "Laura has lost a lot this past week, between the bombing and Gayfeather. She can't really go public about any of this. Can you . . ."

Pellen held up her hand.

"You'd be surprised how often we have to clean up a scene," she said. "We'll work something out. In the meantime, police your grounds and do something about that item over there that looks like a sniper rifle."

•   •   •

Nick dropped spent shotgun shells and wads and .22 casings into a grocery-store bag. He tossed the whole bag, his revolver, and Sterrett's charred rifle into the embers, where the casings and wads would melt and the heat would disfigure the brass and steel. Using duct tape, he patched bullet holes in the siding of Laura's house and dug two mushroomed bullets out of the kitchen wall and a cabinet, where they had shattered dishes. He cleaned and oiled Laura's firearms.

Late in the afternoon, Laura, who had been nursing her wounds and had remained generally quiet after Pellen left, announced: "Dinner is vegetable stew. You're going to cook it because I can't stand holding a knife right now."

Nick hugged her and sent her outside with white wine.

She warned him: "Absolutely none of your truth serum."

In an hour, he ladled stew—potatoes, carrots, green beans, kidney beans, kale, and onions—into their bowls. Afterward, when the bowls had been washed with jug water and dried, she took his hand.

"Why this all came together, you know more than I do," she said, "but I have things to tell you tomorrow to help you understand."

Nick nodded.

"Tonight," she said, "we'll live in peace. I want you to sleep in my bed."

Nick watched her fall asleep the moment she laid her head on the pillow, three hours before the sun went down. He was exhausted, and all night long he was beset by dreams that he wasn't fast enough, or strong enough, or happy enough.

41

When he awoke sometime after midnight, Nick was holding Laura's hand. As she woke, she cuddled him sleepily. Things went from there.

He finally got out of bed in the foggy half-light of dawn and stood dopey-eyed in front of the kitchen window, intending to fry half a pound of bacon and a half-dozen eggs.

As the eggs began to set, his mind registered a metallic-green Ford Bronco parked out the back door.

The burned vehicles had been disappeared. The gravel was raked over so well that the scorch marks were barely visible. Sterrett's blood had been diluted out of visibility; apparently the FBI had a water truck.

He returned to the bedroom and asked Laura if she knew whose horse had wandered onto the ranch.

"Not another disaster," she said with a sigh as he led her into the kitchen. "I can't keep dealing with this."

It was her first view of the new farmyard: no machine shed, neither of her vehicles. She was relieved to not find a mare loose in the yard, and then she figured it out.

The Bronco's key fob was zip-tied to the inside handle of the screen door. In the glove compartment of the sporty SUV, Laura found the registration and title in her name.

"I think it's a gift from a grateful nation," Nick said. He filled her in with what he knew.

"Confiscated," she marveled, "with only sixteen hundred miles."

She also found a five-inch-thick package wrapped in kraft paper and tape. It contained ten bundles of a hundred twenties each, twenty thousand dollars total in used bills, and an unsigned ink-jet note saying, "With deep appreciation. Never talk about this."

She hugged Nick so hard they fell over. "You did this, you did this," she repeated and laughed.

She dusted herself off and ran inside to change clothes. Back in the truck, she shouted, "On a mission to Wichita!" Spinning gravel out from under the wheels, she disappeared down the driveway. He imagined her being able to raise a cloud of dust on a paved road.

Nick went back to work in his baggy thrift-store jeans and loose T-shirt. The morning fog rising out of the marsh next door was chilly against his sensitized skin.

On the way to the barn to get a shovel and wheelbarrow, he worked on figuring out where Kelli and Laura fit into his heart and mind. Was he using Laura to forget his time with Kelli and her death? But then, after the week he and Laura had, wasn't hooking up inevitable? Two grown unattached people do this kind of thing. It wasn't a real romance, he thought, but it was worth a couple of days of feeling bulletproof—if they didn't overthink what being "bulletproof" actually meant.

He passed the barn's walk-through door, a misfit wooden piece that looked like an item left over from a construction project in the house. It didn't seem wide enough to maneuver a wheelbarrow through. The large door, however, hung on rollers that moved on a rail. He pulled the handle, harder than he expected he'd need to—no wonder Laura was so well muscled—and moved it wide enough to drive a pickup in.

The barn smelled of dust, ancient manure from cattle and fresh poop from pigeons, plus all the smells that went with farm vehicles: grease, oil, rubber, solvent. Nick had never before been in an American barn that had been kept up. Beyond the bay for the truck were a bright-green riding mower dusted with faded grass clippings, shelves, and wall-mounted cabinets, plus a foul-smelling, canvas-draped, waist-high counter that wasn't quite a workbench.

Looking idly for light, Nick twisted a tarnished brass knob on the misfit door, wrenching his wrist as he tried to push it out and let sunlight in. Stepping back, he saw the door was held fast by loops of thin wire wrapped around a nail in the door frame, what Laura had told him was baling wire when she picked up a rusted length of it by the old shed. When he lifted the loops, the hinges complained but complied, and light flooded the end of the barn. Gentle rustling came from rafters under the peaked roof, the sleeping bats explaining the stalagmites of guano.

Out of curiosity, Nick blew a cloud of brown dust off stacks of parched *Grit* and *Capper's Weekly* tabloid newspapers from the 1970s and shoeboxes of letters and postcards. He held the yellowed stacks at arm's length and shifted them to the floor. Pulling a canvas tarp off next, he revealed an eight-foot-long glass display case. In it was a museum of the dead.

Lined up on clear glass shelves in the case were skulls and skeletons. There were two cattle skulls, with and without horns. Two long skulls of horses. A deer head with antlers. A prairie dog skeleton. A coyote skull with spine and rib cage. Whole skeletons of mice and rats, and tubular owl pellets containing the undigestable fur and bones of mice and rats. There was a whole opossum with its ratlike nose and, separately, another opossum's jawbone.

Each exhibit was labeled with a tightly trimmed note in the old Courier face of heavy steel typewriters, the kind a retired lawyer might have kept. It said where and when the specimen was found, whether it was collected as is or was reduced to a skeleton with the help of a bucket of beetles.

He found two more cases. The second had bird skeletons, including ducks, geese, a sandhill crane, meadowlarks, sparrows, and a great horned owl. The third contained skeletons of frogs, lizards, snakes, three kinds of catfish, and several other fish that had come from Salt Creek and the Arkansas River. One snake skeleton carried a frog skeleton in its belly.

•   •   •

With the scoop shovel, Nick awkwardly scraped up what he could discern of Sterrett's imperfectly incinerated corpse and laid it in the steel tray of the wheelbarrow. From the greasy ashes, he sifted out misshapen nails, fragments of thick glass, and the bails of buckets.

The shovel rattled against the tines of the pitchfork. He lifted the pitchfork away from the mess, marveling at how it had both nearly brought his death and then saved his and Laura's lives. But it wasn't a trophy. Maybe someday he would think of it as one, a grim memory of ingenuity, and he flung it back into the ashes.

With the shovel's edge and blade, Nick flattened what he could of Sterrett's charred flesh and bones. He had been around burned bodies before, gagging on the odors of burned blood and poorly cooked organs. Sterrett had lost a lot of blood before his death, though, and his innards had been vented by the knife wielded by Laura and by the pitchfork shoved through his upper chest. It could have been worse.

Nick spat into the ashes of a thousand incinerated weeds, trying to get the taste of the odor out of his mouth. He'd be desperate for a soapy water-bucket shower when this chore was done.

He went back to the barn and searched for a larger tool for the bones, coming up with an eight-pound sledge hammer. He held it directly above the bones and let it drop straight down, again and again, trying to keep ashes and fragments in the wheelbarrow. He shattered the skull, and from it he picked the teeth, cracked and discolored, and broke them further. He pounded the sledge down to shatter the long bones; the key was to put the legs and arms on flat ground and swing the sledge hard.

The Russian knife, the blade extending out of the heat-distorted handle, was near where Laura left it in Sterrett. Nick had missed the details of her struggle, and she didn't want to talk about it. He nudged it out into the open with the shovel. It was warped and wouldn't close, and there was no chance that DNA remained on it. Nick braced the blade against a brick and broke it off with the hammer. He tossed the pieces into the trench, and Nick hoped that everything Russian about the knife went into the hole with it.

The last item on Nick's duty list was to search for Sterrett's weapons, all the metal that could suggest he had been there.

Sterrett's rifle was burned down to the barrel, receiver, scope tube, and bipod. Blown-out cartridges and the bent remains of ammo magazines were not worth sifting from the blackened bits of the shed. The anonymous pieces would be pushed with the ashes into the trench.

Pigeons and sparrows scattered before the squeaky wheel as Nick rolled the assassin's remains past the house and into purgatory among the fragrant cedars and thorny honey locusts of the shelter belt.

Nick wasn't sure why he did it, but having set the wheelbarrow down he stood at attention for a moment. There was no salute, no eulogy, just acknowledgment. There go I, Nick thought, but for the grace of a dozen missed rifle shots and a hastily thrust pitchfork. He didn't know where the grace had come from or why he deserved it. Maybe it was all luck.

The morning's fog had dissipated by the time he snugged the wheelbarrow the last five feet into a passage between two cedars.

Neither Nick nor Laura had said a word about whether to tell the sheriff or anyone else about the man who had attacked them. Adding Sterrett to the mix would open the door to an investigation of why Nick was really on the ranch and would blow his cover. An inquiry would eventually discover that Nick had an association with Senator Gayfeather and might well be part of the Saltwood conspiracy. Furthermore, Nick understood that Laura, for unknown reasons all her own, needed there to be no questions about Sterrett's interest in finding Dr. Cletus Purkeypyle.

He and Laura would decide where to commit the remains.

Somewhere, elsewhere, anywhere but here.

•   •   •

In the final winter of his academy days in St. Petersburg, he visited the ridge where his first love, Anya, lay buried at the base of a fine marble marker behind a fence worthy of her high-ranking father. The hills in the distance were sharp against the solstice sun, a few degrees above the horizon at its midday peak. In the St. Petersburg neighborhoods below the ridge, spruces and leafless birches made a ragged carpet obscuring the streets and rooftops. Above each chimney hung a wisp of smoke, stuck in the still air like a shred of cotton caught on an unshaved face.

The wisps were memories, fading into what was real, reminders of heat that dissipated into nothing, and he remembered the joy and completeness of being with Anya but no longer felt with certainty her lips or her hair or the weight of her body atop his. He knew he had loved her, and he knew that soon enough all the traces of her essence would fade into life's haze.

It had been his fault, letting the dogs get her.

•   •   •

Laura returned from Wichita after four hours, parking her Bronco where the Flex had once had pride of place. She toted in groceries and six cartons of shotgun and rifle ammo, plus a bulky white Target bag of slacks and shirts for him.

"And here's your suitcase and clothes from my apartment. That's where I got your sizes," she said. "I've never shopped for a man before. I brought Kelli's stuff, too, which was really sad to find. It's all of her clothes there, her toothbrush and all that. We can decide what to do with it. Did she drive there? I didn't see any cars in the lot with an Ellis County tag. And just so you don't lose any sleep over it, I washed the sheets and cleaned up after your picnic."

"That was kind of you, Laura." Nick hefted the two suitcases and walked somberly into the house.

In the kitchen, Laura set down her Diet Coke. She kissed him and, with her hands in the small of his back, pressed her hips against his. He wrapped his arms stiffly around her back, and after a moment relaxed them and let his hands lie flat against her.

"Yes," he said. "Later. Definitely."

She kissed him again.

"Not too much later," she said. "I showered for you."

He sidestepped her.

"I need to wash my hands," he said. "Of all of this."

"Is it so bad that you can't have breakfast? Eggs, pancakes?"

"So, then, IHOP in bed?"

"Yes, as a matter of fact."

Over the pancakes, Nick lightened up.

"The mystery guest is a pile of ashes out in the trees," he said. "It's time for him to be tucked away."

Laura nodded.

"I want him off my land," she said emphatically. "My first thought was the trench, but if the cops came that'd be the obvious place for them to look. Or we could use the river, but there's not enough water to hide that much mess. So maybe in Quivira. Either the river or the refuge would be an insult, though, after what Saltwood has done."

Nick lifted another bite of pancake. "Let's think some more."

They washed the dishes and moved to the living room, where they sat at the big window. A sparrow landed on a trellis, picked at a minute insect and flapped away. The upper branches of the trees shifted lightly in the breeze. The letter carrier from Bull Creek stopped at Laura's distant mailbox and rolled on.

Nick and Laura turned to each other and smiled.

He retrieved the wheelbarrow, and she brought the shovel and an orange five-gallon bucket.

Laura stood away, turned toward the house, as Nick shoveled Sterrett's ashes into the bucket. He hefted it, thinking five, maybe six pounds.

Together they limped down the driveway to the mailbox, and there they turned west. They stopped briefly after a hundred feet. She scooped up a half pound or so of ash and bone and dribbled it out over several dozen yards of soft sand where traffic had left tire tracks over the prints left by turkeys and whitetail deer.

And then they moved on, pausing only to eavesdrop on two kingbirds arguing on a barbed-wire fence.

"Anyone asks," Laura said, "we're looking for gayfeather plants to put in my flowerbed as a memorial."

"That's really a flower?"

"Tall spire with purple flowers. I don't think they grow well in the sandhills, and they wouldn't be blooming until real summer. But that doesn't matter."

"I guess not. We see somebody coming, we'll dig up a few plants up and put them in the bucket. A sunflower or two, maybe."

Laura said: "We'll have as good a chance of being right about the flower as we did of getting the senator right. I knew her as well as anyone, and I can't tell you what was breaking her down. Who knows what she really wanted out of the shadows she lived in."

Nick said nothing. No one came by. A quarter of a mile down the road, the bucket was empty of ashes and half-full of wildflowers: yellow stargrass, Indian paintbrush, and a pincushion cactus.

"Hey, speaking of dark corners, tell me something."

"Okay, I guess."

"When I was looking for a shovel and wheelbarrow this morning, I found cabinets of skeletons."

"Oh, that. Grandpa had a hobby. He called it the Evolutionary Ossuary."

"It's a fascinating collection," Nick said. "Was he disturbed?"

"No, just curious. Whenever he found a dead animal or a horse skeleton washed out of the creek, he'd keep the skull or hoof or some other weird part. 'Got to remember our ancestors,' he'd say. 'It was their land first.' It was in his will that I have to keep the collection for as long as I own this property."

"It startled me at first," he said. "It's easy to forget how many things live and die around us, and we don't notice."

"Yeah, the collection is cool," she said. They kept walking.

"Want to hear a true fact?" Laura said. "You saw the snake skeleton, right? The roots of the gayfeather can be made into a snakebite poultice."

He laughed. "So Gayfeather nearly killed me with a bomb, but you could've used that plant to save me from a rattlesnake if you hadn't been so quick with the big knife."

"Well, yeah, if we had the plant on hand. I'll make sure I get some in the garden this summer. For the next time you're here."

The splinters and ashes of Lance Sterrett blended in with the blond river-borne sand. In time, traffic would grind the chips of bone into even smaller pieces. They'd be pushed aside and then back into place by the township's road grader on its periodic sweep. The eroded ashes would be lifted away by winds or washed into the ditches by summer thunderstorms.

"I want to run him over every day," Laura said.

• • •

"You know," Nick said as they put the shovel and bucket back in the barn, "the senator said to watch out for you because, and I quote, 'That bitch will cut your heart out.'"

"She knew me pretty well. Still, she deserved to die just for that. Sharing secrets."

Nick chuckled. Laura didn't.

"Okay," he said. "Tell me."

She sat down on a concrete block, leaning into the barn wall.

"You remember the story I told you, about how my old boyfriend screwed around on me with his anthropology girls? One weekend he came home and went out on the tractor with me and a twenty-bottom disc . . ."

Nick interrupted. "What's that?"

"It's a harrow pulled behind the tractor like a plow, but it has a bunch of notched steel discs that slice into the soil at an angle and work the old stubble into the ground and break up clumps of dirt. This one was red. It was six feet wide and had twenty discs set seven or eight inches apart in two rows."

He nodded.

"This was while I was taking care of his parents' fields. He was being a jerk, grabbing my breasts. I elbowed him hard, and he fell off backward and went under the discs."

"Yikes."

"The harrow weighed more than 700 pounds. He was torn up. Shredded. Sliced, a whole pitiful bloody mess."

Laura plucked a blade of grass and put it between her thumbs. She blew, and it squawked like a goose.

"I was angry at him," she said, "and doubly angry for his causing a mess. So I reached into his chest piece and used my Buck knife to cut out his heart. Some of it, anyway. What I could find of it. There wasn't an autopsy, so no one ever knew. I kept the chunk for a day and then tossed it out for the ants."

"You can be cold," he said.

"Yeah, I guess so," she said. "But I helped his parents and sister grieve. Told them he slipped after reaching into the toolbox. He dropped a screwdriver and rolled his foot on it and slipped off the back, I said. After two days of wiping their tears, I told them I had to grieve by myself and went home and burned his stupid poems and kept my drawings of the bridges. Five girls from his college classes showed up at the funeral. I think four must've shared him at one time or another, and the fifth girl was there to take Instagram photos of the others with his casket. I spent the whole time wondering which ones gave him chlamydia. I don't think any of them knew who I was."

Laura was waving her arms, swimming through her memories.

"So, yes, my parents, my grandparents, my farmboy Romeo—I know a little about death. To make matters worse, his parents still send me Christmas cards and get pissy if they don't get condolence notes on the dates of his birth and death. All this for a jerk I was the last one to see, even if I wasn't the last one to sleep with him.

"On the sad side," she said, "I haven't really drawn any pictures since then."

"There's still hope," he said. "No art comes from happiness, just from the pursuit of happiness."

Her grimace said it wasn't the day for inspirational admonitions.

Nick asked, "How did Harriet find out?"

"We were drunk, and I wanted to impress her."

"You told your boss?"

"She and I agreed that you establish trust by each confessing something awful. It's consensual blackmail but also a way of staying moral, because the secrets have to be balanced."

"What was her secret?"

"That she killed her old man."

"Her husband?"

"Father. He was a truck driver and a drunk son of a bitch. He was beating her mother to death in the kitchen. When the police came, Harriet wasn't home. Her mother was given the blame posthumously. The cops called it an even fight."

"Is that what you promised you'd tell me?"

"Some of it. You tell me something."

Nick spoke softly, as if to himself, then repeated it for Laura.

"I killed Gayfeather with a Saltwood truck."

She smiled a little.

"I figured," she said. "I suppose I miss her, and the country will suffer in some ways. But my God, what she brought out with the PETRO bill. You know what else, something that nobody else will know? Perdue had neither the guts to kill her himself nor the capacity for regret that suicide suggests."

"He bragged about giving her orgasms. A real gentleman."

"Did I tell you he could speak Russian?"

"He offered in Russian to lead me in a final prayer."

Laura laughed. "He was a man for every occasion. But he was also like road salt. You'd call on him only when it's absolutely necessary, and you really didn't want to track him inside."

"The funny thing," Nick said, "is that Perdue was going to have her killed anyway, probably by Sterrett. She was coming untied, a real loose end."

"It's the happiest ending we could hope for, I suppose. At least we know what it was all about."

"Also, I apologize for spending Saturday night with Kelli Ochs at your apartment without your permission."

"I'm honestly glad she had a friend when she needed one. She symbolizes something that the nation needs. So, did you call her, or what?"

"We met at that diner again. A complete coincidence."

"You didn't know what she was thinking?"

"I suspected at the church that something was going to happen, but it was her show."

"I don't mind that you were with her. She was an angel," Laura said. "A tortured angel."

"She was beautiful in that yellow dress. She glowed as she walked to the pulpit. She'd had such a hard life, and such regrets. At the end she was ethereal."

Lost in the distant past—two whole days earlier—Nick kicked at some pebbles. "I tried to protect her," he said. A moment later: "Nobody could save her from her pain."

Laura squeezed his hand. She thought his cheeks might be wet.

"Hey," Laura said. "I have a secret about you. It's from yesterday. Maybe it'll help you feel better."

"What?"

"After you walked Sterrett up to the fire and pushed him in, you went down on your knees. You stuck your arms out to the sides. He was screaming, and you laughed. It made me really afraid of you."

•　　•　　•

Nick and Laura retraced their steps from the barn through the battleground. With a little searching, they found the locust tree struck by Sterrett's long shot that barely missed Laura. And then came the visceral memories: the water tank, the burned-out pickup and car, the hand-to-hand fighting, the shed, the odor of everything. They did it not to savor but to understand.

"A predator was killed," Nick said. "There was never going to be any reasoning with him. He knew it would be that way for us or for him."

Laura put her arm around Nick's waist. "Thank you," she said.

"I think he was here before," he said. "When we worked on the shed, I found a field-stripped cigarette butt back there but didn't think anything of it. Remember at the bar when Sterrett did that?"

"I don't want there to be any memorial to that man."

Five minutes later, after some noisy fussing around the house, Laura brightened up.

"Hey, Nick, want to go for a drive? We haven't been back to the well. I don't want to go without you, and if we don't go now we might never have another chance."

"If you're sure," he said.

At the entrance to the Saltwood 7 lease, a sheriff's deputy got out of his cruiser and blocked their way. No, he told Nick and Laura, they couldn't go in. It was private property and leased to Saltwood, and the feds had taken it over. You can imagine how evidence could be destroyed if everybody got to walk in, he said.

As they turned away from the deputy's outstretched arm, Laura said to Nick: "Or how much evidence could be protected from discovery."

They walked east down the road a few yards, and with a little bit of effort stepped through the weedy ditch. They climbed up to the ledge of flat pasture just outside the five-strand fence, to which families had tied crucifixes, photographs, and bouquets of plastic flowers that were already whipped by almost a week of wind and sun. They stood with their hands on the top strand, fingers gripping twisted, rusty wire between the barbs every four inches.

In the field, a flatbed trailer was being maneuvered to carry away the remains of the Saltwood office trailer. Bits of insulation that had been blown out of its walls lingered in the trees and fence like strips of pink flesh. Small markers noted where evidence of one sort or another had been found. From a distance, the bomb's dispersal of sand and soil was barely discernable.

The drilling rig was shut down, its purpose served. When the investigation was completed, Laura explained, Saltwood was required to fill the well casing with concrete in the layers of permeable rock and with drilling mud elsewhere, and then cap it all with concrete. If investigators hadn't already located the break through which the chemicals had found their way into the groundwater, that clue would be lost forever. Still, the chemicals would remain in the soil, creating a plume that would for years point a finger of liability at the well, regardless of what Congress and the administration did with the Petroleum Extraction, Transportation, and Refining Oversight Act.

The warm southern breeze pressed Nick and Laura's shirts against their backs. Her hair fluttered forward around her face, and finally she stopped brushing it away. He put his left arm around her, and she leaned into his shoulder.

"All the evil they could create came to be born in this place," Laura said. "It'll be generations of sorrow for every family who had someone here."

She put her hand on his and squeezed.

"Oh, Nick, the horrible things you saw, we saw, we did."

Hair matted with blood, shirts and vests glued against caved-in chests. Streams of A and B and O seeping from men, disappearing but for a surface stain into the bottomless sand. Arms separated from the men who had checked their watches ten minutes earlier; legs not just ripped away but also torn and rolled across the sand until they looked like plastic limbs of broken dolls tossed about in a beaten-down yard and forgotten. But for the flies, so many flies.

It was stuck in his mind, the memory film. The field of destroyed bodies. Sterrett's sagging physique riding the pitchfork to his death. Gayfeather's face barely reaching over the Saltwood truck's hood, slamming loudly against the white sheet metal before her body rebounded away. In the last two seconds, she had angled into the truck's path and looked him in the eyes. She knew.

"We did it because it had to be done," he said. "We'll carry these days forever."

42

It became a lazy afternoon of sex, which was not an afternoon of lazy sex, and the sun was low in the clear southwestern sky when Nick took over the kitchen.

Nick scooped stir-fry chicken, peppers, carrots, onions, and zucchini onto their plates. They'd dine al fresco. Laura had set two tall glasses and a box of merlot on a small table in front of the webbed lawn chairs. They quickly agreed that the backyard scenery was awful, so they moved to the front yard.

"Reliving this is like getting back on a bike after you fall off," Laura said.

"Once you fall off, you never forget how," Nick said.

Their plates were cleaned, the glasses refilled. Bats flitted in the blue space between dusk and darkness, and there were fireflies.

Laura pointed toward a pair of redbud trees silhouetted against the stars.

"Grandpa had arthritis. He'd sit out here for hours on his lawn chair, that one you're in, soaking his feet in a tub of Epsom salts. He named those trees Rheuma and Toid."

"Laughter is . . ."

"The best medicine. That and painkillers."

They clinked glasses and laughed. She filled them again.

"I want to tell you a story," Laura said. "I should say, 'Don't judge me,' but I don't think you will."

He shrugged. "I live in a glass house."

"It's about Purkeypyle. He's always in my mind. A lot of complex emotions."

"I wondered."

"Anytime I go anywhere, whether I work or run, memories of him come up like a pack of family dogs, a surging wave of fur and teeth, all demanding to be petted and all waiting for me to sleep so they can slip into my dreams. I pet them, and even when I wave them away they sit just out of reach and wait to come again."

Nick watched her out of the corner of his eye, pretending they were watching the same part of the sky.

"I heard you had a thing about dogs," she said, "that you called yourself the Dog of the Afterworld. Gayfeather said she was asked whether that meant anything to her. Apparently your sweetheart over there in Sandstone told the FBI about that. A dog from hell. You know, like the drawing that Walmart clerk showed you. You heard that Kelli's killer was that clerk, right? Karlton Cooper?"

"I didn't realize it was him at the time," Nick said. "Poor guy. His life was tied up in fantasy, and he played that out. For me, life usually was like a dog *in* hell. That got more or less resolved."

"I'm glad there's hope," Laura said.

"Kevin Perdue said a contractor dumped eight thousand gallons of perc without permission into the well."

"Thank God for the perc," she said. "In a way."

"The contractor is dead now."

"Given what we know about Saltwood," she said, "that's not a surprise."

"So Saltwood is, or was, going after Purkeypyle to bury data about the leak," he said.

"Yep."

"It won't be hard for Saltwood to recruit somebody meaner," Nick said. "PETRO would be worth billions in the short run, and trillions for the short time civilization exists after that. The cost of coming after you would be insignificant."

"OK," she said. "You want more truth?"

"Will it set me free?"

"No. But you'll understand why we're here."

"Go for it."

"I already told you about the study Clete Purkeypyle was doing and how his wife got the money from it," Laura said. "That was fine with me. He was happy living along the river, which was more and more often my house."

She glanced at him.

"Orion said people in town called me Clete's common-knowledge wife."

Nick kept his eyes on the stars glimmering above Toid's branches, but he smiled.

"Now," Laura said, "Purkeypyle's cheating on his wife, which also was okay with me, but he took money from Saltwood to cover up the perc leakage. For $50,000, he gave Saltwood half the spreadsheet data—data on diffusion and fluid dynamics, hydraulic head, porosity, water content, pollution plume, and not just drilling wastewater but also chemical waste, measured isotopes, and so on. The kicker is that he held out for another $250,000 to give them the whole report on a single chip."

"That sounds dangerous," Nick said.

"Saltwood could've replicated all the information with its own hydrologists, and surely did, but Clete's was the only data set Saltwood didn't control. They even offered him a career if he brought the card with him."

"So . . ."

"So Clete cashed their check," she said, "but he showed he couldn't be trusted. He played with Saltwood, creating delays and making excuses for not providing the card. Saltwood made harsher demands, but he wasn't intimidated. He kept saying, 'I'm smart, but not *that* stupid.' Neither of us had any idea that Saltwood was working on a timeline for the bombing and the PETRO Act. So it makes sense that Saltwood would want to get his data in a hurry."

"But didn't he violate your trust too?"

"And his wife's."

Nick leaned forward, then decided to turn his chair so he could see Laura better.

"No," she said. "Let's face the same way, because we're going to the same place."

"So where's this card?"

"He left it with me."

"You were his backup plan? Didn't he realize how much danger he was putting you in?"

"Not exactly, and it didn't matter to him," she said. "Or to me either at first, because I didn't understand how ruthless Saltwood is and how little protection I'd get from the senator. Anyway, now the data can go where it needs to go, as far away from Saltwood as it can get. I'm hoping you can help with that."

"What happened to the money?"

"I kept it as a fee. He left it in my safe-deposit box."

"Shouldn't his wife get it?"

"He was sleeping in my bed, not hers."

"You said he ghosted you."

"I wish this whole thing with Clete would just disappear. He's gone. Pffft. He's why Saltwood kept after me, even after he left, like they thought I'd give them the data. Gayfeather probably was being told by Perdue to can me and make me more vulnerable."

"Want me to ruin your day?"

"Sure," she said, sighing. "Why not."

"Gayfeather hired me to kill you."

"That bitch. You asshole."

"And yet you're still alive and well thought of."

Laura turned her back to Nick.

"That's why you got stuck with me," he said. "I was supposed to find out how you were sabotaging her. She seemed obsessed about China, so I told her you have your grandparents' Chinese souvenirs, and she tensed up."

Laura pounded her fist on the arm of the lawn chair.

"She had something going with the Chinese," Laura said, "but that was the secret she'd never tell me. The money must've been huge."

Nick said, "She told me Monday morning that she was going to hand me over to the Russians or the FBI or the Chinese because I wouldn't hurt you."

"And we hadn't even had sex yet. Aren't you the sweetheart?" She put her hand under his chin and made a kissing sound. "Want more wine?"

They refilled their glasses and sipped.

"What did she call me? What was it? A girl of reduced social responsibility?"

"Something along those lines, but not really harsh."

"The senator had a perfect plan," Laura said. "Get you to kill me to hide China and protect the PETRO Act, and get you sent to a Salvadoran prison or killed in revenge for going after her in the first place."

Laura took a deep breath.

"You have to leave," she said in a rush. "You know that. The cops will come soon, and the press will find out. Your picture will be everywhere, and people in town will talk. People at the Hitch. People at Alice's funeral. People at Kelli's killing and everybody who watched the videos."

He took her hand.

"I know," he said. "I don't want to go, but I can't wait for the next Russian or Bureau or Saltwood gunslinger to find me. It'd be risky for you, and we don't want any more of that."

She squeezed his fingers, lingering with the feel of his skin.

"After the thing before," he said, "I was held by the FBI but not arrested, never charged. Last week, some part of the FBI handed me back to the Russian mob, and the mob ordered me to go after Gayfeather again. I didn't kill her right away when I had the chance and I needed to get out of DC, so when she offered me the job I took it. I'm sorry I ever thought of hurting you."

"You do bring trouble to the table," she said, "but don't give up on me. We could be a team, fighting injustice the world over. I need a job. You know I'm tough enough. We could live here or anywhere you like when it's all over. You'd like Quivira when the birds are migrating through."

He said, "I'll be back."

Under the covers that night, both of them facing the ceiling, Laura had more to say.

"First, I'm not a bad person. I've told you bad things, but I hate to think of anyone suffering. One time I was driving through a county seat south of Hays at night and saw a black cat in the street. It must've been hit by the car ahead of me. It was flopping around. I swerved around it but flipped a U and came back and tried to run over it so it wouldn't suffer any longer. The damned thing flopped out of the way of my wheels. When I looked back, it was still flopping. I was so distressed that this time I just kept driving out of town."

"That's a terrible thing. Did it give you nightmares?"

"Jesus, yes."

Nick imagined the scene. He didn't know what he would've done, and he said so.

Laura took a deep breath and went on with her list.

"Second, everything's a conspiracy theory, but you have to believe some of it."

"We proved that," Nick agreed.

"Saltwood wasn't even looking for black gold in Quivira," she said. "Perdue and his pals did it all for the PETRO Act, the biggest pot of gold in the world."

Moments of the bombing, not the explosion so much as their departure past the Saltwood execs, slipped into Nick's mind. Laura nudged him.

"You fell asleep," she said, "and I wasn't done talking."

"Everything okay?"

"Item three: I've lost my virginity for the last time."

43

I was wrong to make fun of you last week," Laura said at the breakfast table. It was 5:30 and they were dressed. "But those pants really do look like grandpa jeans on you."

"Really? I'm starting to like how they feel," Nick said, heading to the sink.

"You're a fashion plate." She reached sideways and swatted him twice gently on the baggy butt.

"Pattery will get you nowhere," he said, puffing up in a flirtatious way with his eyebrows.

"Lord," she said, "every time I go to the restaurant here I see guys in those pants who forgot to fasten their suspenders. Or buckle their belts under their guts or zip their flies. Now you're an honorary grandpa."

"Fine," he said. "Want me to stop wearing them?"

She made a square with her hands, framing him like a photo.

"No . . . yes. . . . maybe . . ." With a smile: "I guess so."

• • •

An hour later, the rising sun was coloring the ranch's yard. They were dressed again, wearing jackets, and sitting on the back steps. Laura had put Tchaikovsky's haunting *Hymn of the Cherubim* on the speaker.

"Something for you," she said. Pulling it from her fleece, Laura offered him her Buck knife. It had no case, and the handle was worn.

"I want you to take this," she said. "You know its history, so treat it well. It's like a promise ring."

Nick hefted it, half a pound and five inches long with the blade folded in. He stretched his leg out and slid the knife into the front pocket of his roomy jeans.

"Grandpa pants," he said. "And I am glad to see you."

"Don't cut anyone's heart out," she said. "Especially mine."

Taking it out of her other pocket, she put in his hand a tiny plastic case containing a memory card, black and thin and snug inside.

"Make sure the right people get it," she said. "I can't do it, or anything. My cell, mail, and internet are probably being watched now by evil people."

She walked with him to the driveway, where he placed one hand on the small of her back and the other behind her neck. They kissed goodbye and then another squeeze, and Nick stepped back with his suitcase.

"Your ride will meet you at the mailbox," she said. "Come back when you can. Take a chance on me, with me."

• • •

It wasn't the ride Nick expected.

A dually city pickup, dark gray and diesel, chugged around the mile corner a little fast, kicking up sand in the heavy morning air. It skidded to a stop just past Nick, who stood there with his earthly belongings like a college-bound freshman.

"Nikolai Fyodorov," said the passenger in Russian-accented English as he walked over with his hand out. He looked like he wanted to be called Cowboy. He was stocky, wearing a short-sleeve snap shirt, a cowboy hat, and embroidered boots. "So good to see you."

The driver shouted "Dobroe utro," good morning, and waved from inside the cab. When Nick flicked his eyes toward the driver, Cowboy sucker-punched him below the ribs.

Gasping, Nick lowered himself into a flat-footed squat.

Cowboy laughed. "Like Orlov says: Heels on the ground, Russian found. Heels high, American spy."

Nick stood up and brushed the grit off his hands.

"Kakogo khrena, muzhik?" Nick said. "Poprobuy yeshche raz." What the fuck, man. Try it again.

"No, no." Cowboy took a step back. "Orlov told us only way to beat you is to cheat you."

"What else did Orlov say?"

"He said he wants to talk." Cowboy pulled out a phone, pushed a quick-dial number, and tossed the phone to Nick, who caught it with disdain.

"Nikolai!" It was the mobster's voice. "Congratulations on accomplishing your mission."

"Whose mission was it? Yours or the FBI's?"

"We celebrate together, as you were told at Dupont Circle when you accepted this assignment."

"You got your money's worth," Nick said.

"Your performance made proud all your instructors. An oilman dies and it's a self-inflicted gunshot wound, not a long fall from a window!"

"What do you want, Orlov?"

"A little job done in Arizona. Tucson," Orlov said in Russian. "A lovely city with a very nasty man in it, as the hugely popular president would say."

Nick spat in the road and thought of Sterrett's ashes. He looked for bone pieces and saw none.

"Take some time off first," Orlov said. "A few days. We want you to arrive ready to work."

"When?"

Orlov's origins were a well-guarded secret, but to Nick's ear his voice suggested Orlov had grown up south of Moscow; his *g* sounded like an *h*. The only time he had seen Orlov was in Seattle in the company of their old boss, Karp. Karp disappeared after the Sandstone event, and Orlov now was in charge.

"You have been in the contact with the FBI. That is all okay, as long as you still help us from time to time behind the curtain. We will contact you when the time is right. In the meantime, we have living expenses. Please hand the phone back to obez'yana, the monkey, who I hope tried to hit your gut."

Nick whistled at Cowboy and tossed the phone just before he turned around. The Russian made a frantic basket catch and flipped him the bird.

Cowboy listened to Orlov. "Da. Da."

Cowboy reached into the pickup and pulled a bulky white and orange envelope off the dashboard. He waved it at Nick before laying it on the sandy road.

"For you, patriot."

"Thanks, Cowboy. You have a good punch."

Cowboy opened the passenger door and put his foot on the running board.

Nick said, "That was you who shot my canoe."

Cowboy grinned. "Keep you honest," he said.

He raised a two-finger salute to the brim of his hat and climbed into the truck.

After the Russians drove off, Nick picked up the Tyvek envelope.

The heft suggested it held a handgun and a box of rounds. He kneeled and poured everything out on the less-sandy side of the road: a 9-millimeter Glock; US, Argentinean, and Canadian passports and matching driver's licenses with his FBI likeness but new names; a Visa and a MasterCard with a note about monthly deposits that would be made; a new burner phone and charger; and a hefty manila envelope containing used twenties, fifties, and hundreds.

Nick thumbed through the cash and figured it at $40,000. The Russians seemed confident they were taking over his care and feeding.

The phone rang. Nick touched the screen and listened, not saying a word. A woman spoke at a slow, even pace. It was Anastasia, the Russian in black.

"We met at Dupont Fountain, in DC. Remember me? No names. We have work for you. Remove the SIM card from the phone for three days. I will call you. Be alone." In a friendlier tone, "Remember me."

Nick closed down the phone, put it with his own burner holding Pellen's number in the contacts, and stuffed everything into his suitcase. He sardonically hummed the refrain from Aunt Alice's funeral music:

And He walks with me, and He talks with me,
And He tells me I am His own . . .

• • •

Two minutes after the Russians drove off, a beige sedan glided to a halt ten feet short of Nick. The woman in the passenger seat lowered her window and asked Nick to identify himself, and then demanded, "Who sent us?"

Nick suspected that the two people in the car had their handguns at the ready.

"Pellen, FBI in DC."

"Please approach the car."

She handed Nick a plain manila envelope with a metal clasp.

"Please verify the material."

It was Nick's photo on two driver's licenses, one listing a home in Dallas and the other a home in Denver. It was also his mug under the plastic coating on the second page of two US passports. There were two credit cards, one for each of his new names, and each bore a pale sticky note inscribed with "$10,000 limit." The final items, packed into a zip-lock baggie, were a cell phone and charger.

"Do I sign?"

"Sign here." The agent held out a clipboard holding a single sheet of paper. It said "Receipt" at the top and had a line for the signature, but no list of items. Nick knew it didn't matter what name he wrote. The loops and lines of his handwriting would verify the signature.

The beige sedan accelerated at a turtle's pace, not raising a bit of dust or ash.

• • •

Sam Orion showed up five minutes later in his gray and green Winnebago RV.

"Climb aboard, Nick. Stow your bag and state your destination."

"How about Colorado?"

"Wonderful choice, pal. Fasten your seat belt."

"Can I borrow your phone?"

Orion handed it over. Nick googled "diner sandstone kansas" and made the call as Orion put the RV in gear.

The phone rang twice on the far end, which was twenty-five miles to the northwest in Sandstone.

"Clara's Diner." It was Clara Hernandez herself at the checkout counter: cheerful, with breakfast clatter in the background.

"Clara, you probably remember me as a dishwasher who stayed in a trailer, and please don't say my name."

"The guy who saved my daughter?"

"Is she there? I'd like to make up for something."

"I'll see if she's here, even though she's standing next to me."

Cimarron Hernandez came on the line.

"This is Cimi." The bounce in her voice pulled at Nick's heart.

"This is your least favorite ex. Don't say my name."

"Still playing that game? What do you want? They let you make calls now?"

"I'm out. I have data about the river of diamonds, and I'd like you to set it free. Or give it to someone who can."

She sighed. "All right. But no bullshit."

"Can you meet me at the Sandstone cemetery in an hour? It needs to be public but private."

"This is breakfast time. Coffee needs to be refilled. At least we have a good dishwasher now."

"I don't think anybody died from dirty dishes while I worked there."

"Okay, I'll meet you. One hour."

Nick described the RV, as if there'd be more than one arriving at the cemetery, and pleaded with Cimi not to tell anyone anything. She hung up.

"Orion, to Sandstone, please."

"Seriously? Weren't you there before?"

"It's necessary."

As they motored west through the refuge toward US 281, Nick fished Laura's folding knife from his pocket. He pulled the blade out and locked it open. Flecks of dried blood that he assumed belonged to the unlamented anthropologist boyfriend clung tight inside the fingernail groove and the blade case.

Laura had trusted him with her deepest secret, but that cut two ways. He could have her convicted, assuming her fingerprints were on the knife. It conversely could be that she gave him the knife as a reminder that she could have killed him too.

But Laura still had a knife, a figurative one, that she could use anytime against him. He had confessed to killing Gayfeather. If that news got out, he'd be shot dead in the street.

He depressed the blade lock and closed the knife, then tossed it a couple of times from one hand to the other. Finally he felt at ease and pushed the knife back into his pocket.

Laura was safe, conditionally, and so was he.

Orion pointed at Nick's pocket. "She trusts you," he said.

"I gather the knife has a history."

"When she called to have me deliver you out of here, she said I could tell you the rest of the story about Clete Purkeypyle."

Nick raised his eyebrows. "In Kansas, nothing is stranger than the truth."

Orion's laughter had an edge.

"It's a sad story," he said. "This is pretty much what she told me and what I saw myself."

Orion checked the rearview mirrors and shifted in his seat.

"Spring came fast with a heat wave, highs in the 80s. Clete was at the ranch. Laura wanted to start tearing down the shed, and he followed her outside. They had been arguing about the Saltwood money.

"Purkeypyle wasn't watching where he was going, and a rattler struck him on the ankle. With her shovel, she had tried to block the snake, and she came close because the snake had just come out of hibernation and was sluggish. She says her move was instinctive, but in retrospect she wasn't sure she didn't pull her punch. While Clete lay there in the weeds, swelling up like an inner tube, she called me. My lord, she was crying and desperate.

"By the time I got there, she had dragged him into the shed and performed what she called a mercy killing. She stuck that very knife directly into his heart. Then she started taking him apart. There she was, standing amid Purkeypyle's organs, broken down—not with regret but just exhausted."

Nick stared open-mouthed at Orion as he described the woman Nick had been sleeping with. The knife in his pocket grew heavier with every one of Orion's sentences.

"The rest was up to me. I had protective gear in the Jeep because sometimes I have sick people over at the camp. By that point, we couldn't leave him as he was. Even with his probable eventual death by snakebite, Laura would go straight to prison. We had to finish the job. I hacked him apart at every big joint. If you can imagine how long that takes with a sharp ax, double it for the rusty ax I was using."

Orion took his hands off the wheel and spread his arms wide. "Poison blood splashed everywhere. But I was so angry at him for selling out that I didn't need any convincing that it was the right thing to do. When I first met him, I admired the fire in his belly, but he was a sideways talker.

"Anyway," Orion continued, "I was having a new septic tank put in, so I suggested burying Clete beneath it. Laura refused to let me do it. She said there should be no physical evidence linked to me."

Orion said he next suggested disposal in the Arkansas River, but there wasn't enough water to float the parts and not enough catfish and turtles to eat them. Somebody would find a bone and a DNA test would be run. Purkeypyle's body would be identified and traced to her. Besides, she said, Purkeypyle didn't deserve the river.

"So I told her I'd take him down to Cheney Reservoir, about forty miles south of here, and drop the pieces in the deep end. But what I really did was sneak the flesh and small pieces into the ponds and marshes at Quivira. His flesh is probably still being eaten by the microbes he wasn't protecting."

Nick said, "I'm in awe."

"The big bones did go under my septic tank. Sooner or later, maybe in decades, the tank *might* be replaced and those bones *might* be found. Eventually, Quivira will go dry for a spell and the smaller bones *might* be discovered. If either of us are still alive, we'll blame Saltwood for killing him. Plus, now I have as much at stake as Laura—and you—do."

Orion jabbed at the windshield. "Clete was going to run off and hide, leaving Laura to face Saltwood by herself. He was not a good man or smart enough for the game he wanted to play."

Laura nearly had a stroke, Nick said, when she heard that a stray finger had fallen into the bomb scene.

"It's like Laura's tell-tale heart," Orion said. "And that's my fault."

"How so?"

"About a week after I dropped him off, I found that finger loose in the back of the Jeep. It must've fallen out of the tarp. So Mr. Lazy here just tossed it out in the marsh the next time I was there. DNA will eventually tell whose it is. If there's a problem, Laura will say that Saltwood was angry over Clete's discovery and maybe sent the security man after him. Which, as you know, is true."

"Orion, are you in love with Laura?"

"I wasn't jealous when she started to date Purkeypyle, but I grew to hate him," he said. "She and I have been friends for years, and we were lovers after I got home from the war. We evolved into intimate friends. Purkeypyle was using Laura and her ranch for his extortion scheme, and his family life conflicted with the way he was romancing Laura. The man deserved to be bitten by his brother, the snake."

As the RV slowed to a stop before entering US 281 near St. John, Orion pointed out Rattlesnake Creek where it crossed under the county road.

"The Rattlesnake, one way or another, ties it all together," he said. They were heading north on 281 when Orion asked, "Laura gave you the card, right? So now a search warrant will find nothing and she's clean. No card, no Purkeypyle DNA in the shed after that fire. He's a ghost."

Nick chimed in: "And where is Saltwood's security man?"

"Exactly," Orion said. "For weeks, he's been grasping at smoke."

44

Orion couldn't contain his curiosity. "It sounds like your meeting has something to do with someone you used to know."

"It does."

"You're not stepping out already, I hope."

"It's someone who can help move things along," Nick said. "I won't talk to her long."

Orion drove the land yacht slowly across the bridge over the trickling Arkansas River south of Sandstone, while Nick looked right and left at his memories: fleeing a lunatic in the riverside cottonwoods, a night of love. A long mile west, and then north brought them to town, where Nick wanted to cement his recollections in real scenery.

Nick directed Orion up Centre Street past the house where Cimarron Hernandez grew up, past the elevator where he had nearly died, onto the paved portion of the street and past Clara's Diner, and finally up the bluff where Pawnee Rock overlooked the north side of town. Fewer than two hundred people lived in Sandstone, down by almost half over the past twenty years. There was no school anymore in this town of old elm trees, no grocery store; people chose instead to live in Great Bend or Larned, the county seats to the east and west.

"The cemetery's just around the corner. Turn left at the top of the hill," Nick said. A car was parked in the short grass outside the white two-board fence. "Can you drop me off and drive around the section to the north? I'll be ready by the time you get back."

"Short and sweet. Good man."

Cimarron Hernandez, leaning against her white Honda Civic, waited for him to step down and walk over. Cimi was slim and fit. Her hair was shorter now and maybe darker from not being in the sun so much. Her brown eyes still stopped his heart.

She put up her palms, holding him off at four feet. He was surprised that he had forgotten the burn scar on her wrist.

"It's kind of good to see you, secret agent Dog of the Afterworld."

"You too, college student."

"You heard about Gayfeather?"

His sad eyes told her he did. "My being in Kansas is a coincidence. But she and I had a long talk back in DC about what happened in Great Bend."

Her eyes carried the smile now, but wariness remained.

"Cimi, I'm sorry I was an ass when you came to see me."

She frowned for an instant, just a flash of sour memory. "That's the distant past," she said.

His shoulders relaxed.

Rising onto the balls of her sneakers, Cimi declared, "I graduated from the University of Kansas two weeks ago. Geology and pre-law."

Nick grinned. "Congratulations. Did you get into law school?"

"KU Law in the fall. Then, I hope, the FBI."

"You'll do great. I know it."

They both blushed, remembering the gentleness of their relationship. To avoid looking at each other, they both turned south toward town, into the sun and wind. Pawnee Rock, the historical bluff where they shared their first kiss high above the old Santa Fe Trail. Beyond the Rock, the hundred-foot-tall gray concrete silos of the grain elevator, where they survived a fight for their lives. To their backs, in the cemetery section outlined by sixty-year-old cedars trimmed shoulder-high of branches, the grave of Cimi's father.

Nick glanced at Cimi's profile as her hair feathered out behind her. He tried to absorb the moment, the emotion he knew was inevitable.

She broke his trance. "Okay, I drove half a mile for this. What's up?"

"I have a memory card"—he held out the card and its plastic case—"that I understand has a spreadsheet showing chemical pollution in the Arkansas from the oil well near Quivira. The hydrologist who created it has gone missing after repeated harassment by Saltwood Exploration."

She peered at the card, then up into Nick's eyes.

"That's the well that was bombed," she said.

"Yes."

"You were . . . of course you were there." She examined him more closely. "You're burned and injured. From the explosion? Tell me you didn't cause that."

"I didn't do it. The guy who did was named Sterrett, and he was following orders from Kevin Perdue, who was recently in the news. They bombed their own crew to work up support for the PETRO Act."

"And you know this because . . ."

"Because . . . I can't tell you. What I'm asking is, will you take a serious risk? Just look at the data or give the card to someone you trust and who is water-science smart, street smart, and mentally tough. Someone who loves the Arkansas as much as you do. Tell no one else. No phone calls, no emails, no texts."

After a moment, she nodded.

"Make a copy," he said, "but don't put it on your hard drive. Drag the file onto another card and hide that card. People have died because of this spreadsheet. Don't go against Saltwood by yourself. This card could kill the PETRO Act, so it'll have to be used soon, and the oil industry goons will go after people who get in their way."

He extended the card on his open palm. She lifted it with her fingertips.

"With your life, Cimi. Be really careful. Let me tell you how careful. The Russians are now brothers with part of the FBI. They told me they'd kill you if I didn't work with them."

She stepped back.

"So, you're a Russian again?"

"No. Never again. You were the only tool they had against me."

"That sounds familiar," she said. "The hero Dog protects women."

A light went on in her eyes.

"That *was* you! Trying to save Kelli Ochs in Wichita. I told Mom it was. Kelli ate once in the diner. She was a sweetheart."

Nick brushed it aside. "Listen, there's no one else I trust with this. This is your chance at age twenty-one to change the world."

"Twenty-two."

The RV rose over the crest of the hill, and Orion signaled that he was going to pull up and park.

"Be well, Cimi. Make it to twenty-three." He turned to his big ride and gripped the door handle.

Cimi said just loudly enough over the wind: "You're a new and better man, my secret agent."

•　•　•

The long road drew Orion and Nick west. To entertain themselves between prairie dog towns, they listened to the radio and put together the week that was.

The Kansas governor that morning had named a new senator to replace Harriet Gayfeather, and it wasn't Luke Meriwether. After spending two days in prayer, Pastor Luke announced quickly, he would run for governor on a pro-military, evangelical ticket.

"But Tuesday, yesterday, the shit hit the fan club in Pastor Luke's church," Orion said. "A bunch of his congregation signed a letter to the paper saying they were leaving, and the TV stations started to look at his personal property, the church's charitable foundation, and rumors of his infidelity."

There also was a rumor, Orion said, that Luke's 15-year-old was pregnant.

"One of my naturists belongs to the church's women's club. She hears things. Ol' Pastor Luke was posing for a photo to go with a newspaper story about the attack, and he roped his family into standing next to him at the pulpit. His wife and kid looked like they wanted to kneecap him. The kid is getting abortion counseling because Jesus Daddy can't have a teenage-mother daughter. And sweet Mrs. Meriwether is planning to write a memoir called *What the Hell.*"

The mysterious gunman from North Dakota, whose fingerprints were found on a rifle near the Quivira explosion site, still hadn't been found. His phone, found in the pickup's camper, was dead, but a forensic investigation found that it had lasted long enough to ping cell towers as far south as Nebraska the day before the explosion.

Crime-scene specialists had matched the North Dakotan's hunting rifle to a slug blown out into the field sixty yards from the crater. They later found a second slug from a different rifle, and the second slug bore minuscule traces of the binary explosive Tannerite used in the bomb.

For lack of a better choice, however, the Dakotan remained the top suspect, in public at least.

Karlton Cooper, Orion said, was determined by the district attorney to have acted in defense of others when he killed Kelli Ochs in church, and a GoFundMe page was started for him in honor of his First Amendment stand for the freedom of religion and his Second Amendment right to pick up a handgun in church and kill someone. Cooper told police that God gave him the revolver. Police and federal agents were unable to determine who had brought it to church; they were saying it must've been bought at a gun show, where no records were kept and no background checks were required.

A team of Wichita police investigators, however, found a print from Cooper's left index finger on a disabled video recorder in the pawnshop where a clerk was killed two days before the church shooting. The print matched several found on a revolver discovered under the front seat of Cooper's Toyota, and a round fired in a ballistics test matched the one that passed through the clerk's chest.

A report on public radio described Cooper as merely a person of interest. In front of TV cameras, the report said, his mother, Ms. Filene Cooper, held her Bible before her heart and described her son as "a trusting but mediocre child who mixed bad luck with bad choices. May Father God bless his soul. I was saved, you know, by Father God and Our Lord and Savior . . ."

Orion turned down the radio and shrugged.

"Poor guy," he said. "He's in a tattered generation, blown ragged at the edge of the hurricane."

"What do you think can be done?"

"Realistically, your generation and the one after it have the hardest path. You all are the lucky people who'll get to determine whether the idea of America is worth saving."

"It's a fascinating time to become an American."

"Take the Constitution. Will it survive as we know it? Or will the things it says be supplanted by almost-the-same ideas, but twisted? Which laws will be enforced? I'm talking about how the government behaves, not silly little things like homicide."

"Well, sure," Nick said. "The tree of liberty, the blood of tyrants; that kind of thing."

"Now, me, I'd like to see the First Amendment put to good use," Orion said. "It'd still protect someone who pokes his head into a crowded theater of armed Second Amendment fanatics and shouts 'Fire!' Although, you know, the Second Amendment isn't even an issue anymore. That's over and done with."

He thumped the steering wheel in fun. "And I have four rifles at home."

Nick said, "I'd have to work a lot harder if it weren't for gun shows. Also, please let Laura know it was the Russian mob who shot up her canoe."

•   •   •

All reporters' questions about Kevin Perdue were referred to Saltwood Exploration's team of civil and criminal lawyers. His biographical page on the company's website was expunged, and his widow deleted every mention of him from her Facebook page.

A couple of twenty-somethings riding dirt bikes discovered Lance Sterrett's Saltwood Exploration pickup along the Arkansas River. They returned with their own pickup that afternoon and relieved the Saltwood truck of its catalytic converter, wheels, tags, jack, and battery. From the cab, they appropriated fishing tackle, a rifle case, and boxes of ammunition as well as a few packaged meals. For good measure they also took the truck's radio, registration, and garage remote before breaking all the windows and mirrors.

Nobody at Saltwood ever again mentioned troubleshooter Lance Sterrett. Joyleen Sterrett didn't either; she was desperately pursuing Pastor Luke's wealth.

Delayed by the late arrival of family members, the funeral for the last of nine oilfield workers was held in southwestern Kansas. No one was allowed to attend except the worker's parents, sisters, girlfriend, and young daughter.

Senator Gayfeather's body, taken to the FBI lab in Virginia for an autopsy, would lie in state under the Capitol dome in Washington. The River Jordan Cathedral in Wichita lobbied to host the funeral, but her office instead chose to return her coffin for a ceremony in the 500-seat Saltwood-donated theater at Wichita State University. Security was expected to be intense: metal-detecting wands, no knives, no outside bottled drinks, no outside signs, small purses of clear plastic only, and a mix of federal, state, and local law enforcement. An offer of assistance from the Cathedral's Almighty Rifles was turned down politely.

Burial would be in Fort Scott National Cemetery, not far from Gayfeather's birthplace in southeast Kansas.

In Washington, the Senate's Republican leader said the PETRO Act was well on its path to passage to protect a vulnerable American industry during these troubled times.

•   •   •

Nick and Orion were motoring west at an RV-appropriate speed, backing up a few cars now and then but easing over to let them pass. In Jetmore, a broad grain elevator redirected the south wind, and two dozen large birds circled on the rising column of air. As they rolled through town and were still three hours' drive from the Colorado state line, Orion pointed out how the pastures were becoming more arid.

"The West begins at the 100th meridian," he said. "Guess where we are."

"For all the things that happen here," Nick said, "Kansas remains a land of subtle beauty."

"You could write a memoir," Orion said. "Except you were allegedly not here when everything happened."

"Man, forget you even thought that."

"The state is screwed up," Orion said. "You're fixing things whether you mean to or not."

A couple of miles down the road, Nick fixed his gaze on a grasshopper that had splatted against the windshield.

"Screwed up? You want screwed? My goal each day is to make sure there's no evidence I was ever here. You don't know me, I don't exist, I'm erasing myself."

"Still," Orion said, "you're a remarkable dude. That's why we're trying to keep you safe."

He pointed his thumb at Nick.

"Laura asked me to sneak you out of Kansas because she likes and trusts you. That's one reason. The second reason is that if you get infected from your injuries this week, I can help."

When Nick started to speak, Orion stared him down. Nick tried again, and Orion held up his palm. "It's important to me to give you good care and to honor Laura's wishes," Orion said. "And I owe you for saving her life."

"But," Nick said, "I don't want to put your life in danger. Once you're associated with me, it'll be like you're back in combat but this time with crazy-ass Americans."

"It's almost that way now," Orion said.

"I won't be able to move freely anywhere without government sponsorship," Nick said. "Anytime I fly or take a train, my face will be recognized by artificial intelligence, and I'll be tracked. If I walk the streets, go to a bank counter, appear anywhere there are cameras, the video spies will have a record of it. It's up to them to have me arrested or not.

"Here's the deal, if you don't mind," Nick continued. "Always remember that I'm grateful for everything you're doing for me and for Laura. I admire you, Sam Orion. I trust you."

Orion nodded. "Sure. Same here."

"In a day or two, pull off outside some county seat where we see a car dealer. Then you go have a vacation, but stay away from Bull Creek for a few days. Let things settle down."

A mile passed. Yuccas bloomed in the ditches next to barbed-wire fences outlining pastures softened by gray-green sagebrush. In a ditch, two turkey vultures raised their featherless red heads as the RV approached but didn't fly away from the roadkill deer they were picking apart.

"I know you're going to be in contact with Laura," Nick said, "but there's a good chance her phone and email are tapped and her house is bugged. She knows that. So don't talk about me or where you left me or what you think I might be doing. You made this trip alone, okay?"

"Secrets within secrets within secrets." Orion checked his mirrors. "I was hoping for a fun vacation, but it's your hide. Laura's and mine too, and it makes me paranoid."

"Sometime the day after tomorrow, okay? Long enough to make sure I'm not sick."

"Excellent. I'm relieved," Orion said. "But today we party. Let's get a pizza and a six-pack in Scott City. That's ninety miles, up on K-96. Then we'll drive north to Monument Rocks, fart around the rest of the afternoon, and catch the sunset glowing on limestone towers. It might be your last view of Kansas at its best."

45

"M y secret agent," Cimi Hernandez had said to Nick. And she had seen him at his worst.

He hoped he wouldn't always need the approval of former girlfriends before he could be happy, but it did feel good.

His mind played out what it might be like to take on Laura Eisenhauer as a partner. She was smart, adaptable, and ruthless, altogether a good choice if he went that way.

Tonight, he'd sleep alone in the cabover bunk. He knew he'd think about Cimi; heaven help him. He'd also consider his short hours with Kelli Ochs, who had turned a crappy life into one of purpose and spirituality. The small metal box with Kelli's mementos was with Laura, who had promised to track down the aunt and mail it to her. Nick would dwell on Laura, the only woman to have drunk his truth serum and lived to complain about the hangover. Laura, the vigilante, who for her own reasons helped push Gayfeather into insanity and waylaid a bit of political corruption.

He was lucky to have gotten off the Eisenhauer ranch alive, to have survived a second trip into the heart of Kansas. Laura was as dangerous as he was, and sly, and fierce. Perhaps it was simply fortunate that she had sent him away, and he had left enthusiastically, before either of them found a fatal flaw in the other.

Nick knew what he had done for the Russians and the FBI, but also for the nation. He was more than glad the FBI adopted the entirely plausible public story of how Gayfeather and Kevin Perdue died. If asked, he'd accept the FBI's equally plausible "secret" cover story that Perdue had killed Gayfeather as part of a conspiracy to sell out both the Chinese and one of the country's largest oil companies.

Nobody brought up in public Harriet Gayfeather's instigation of the bombing that preceded the PETRO Act, but the information was added to Barb Pellen's files. Apparently the present administration wanted that bill to pass, although the bill's future belonged now to Cimarron Hernandez.

Nobody publicly mentioned the secret account Gayfeather had set up in Panama with her Chinese paychecks, or the FBI research that tracked the fund's growth. Nobody mentioned that an FBI faction had delivered Nick Deveraux directly into Russian hands for the ostensible purpose of killing Harriet Gayfeather, and that Gayfeather had arranged the transfer for the purpose of killing Laura Eisenhauer.

In the end, Nick was glad he had done what he did. He had killed, and maybe killing was in his soul as far as he had one. These deaths were justified. In good conscience, he'd use the money from the FBI, Gayfeather, and Orlov to reach the next part of his life.

He had tried to protect others' lives, good lives except maybe for Laura with her anger issues and opportunistic justice. Years ago, he had started down a shadowed path because of vengeance, and he couldn't ignore his own history. He liked the hunt. He liked the idea of killing Gregori Orlov.

Nick glanced at Orion, who had settled into the road's rhythm, fiddling now and then with the radio. Nick said, "Hey," and caught Orion's attention.

"Last week back at the restaurant," Nick said, "you mentioned something about living fully exposed that I didn't think about much at the time. But it's true. None of us is as clean as we think we are."

Orion shrugged. "We are who we are."

Yep, Nick Deveraux thought. I'm still the Dog of the Afterworld.

Acknowledgments

For many years I drove across Quivira National Wildlife Refuge on my way to and from Pawnee Rock, my hometown in Kansas. Finally, in 2010, as I was starting to write *Dog of the Afterworld*, I spent half a day in the refuge. This wonderland of wildlife has lived in my thoughts, and I've been back several times since. Thank you to the good folks who watch over Quivira, from the US Fish and Wildlife Service to conservation groups to the picnicker who cleans up someone else's trash.

For *Saltwood,* I granted myself license to adjust the fictional timeline. The decade that elapsed between when *Dog* was set and the time of *Saltwood* has been compressed to about two and a half years. In addition, the company called Saltwood Exploration, the drilling rig, and the story's leak of chemicals are complete fiction. The acreage of Rice County that Laura Eisenhauer's fictional ranch overlays does exist, but not in the form described in the story. There is nothing wrong with the land, the water, or the people who own the property, and nothing in the story should be inferred to represent the owners in any way. The plot and characters are my own inventions. The mention of any actual corporation or private person in this novel is intended not to disparage their decency or actual practices, but merely to acknowledge their presence in society.

I used many sources while writing *Saltwood.* Among them are books about Kansas and US history and politics, notably Thomas Frank, *What's the Matter with Kansas? How Conservatives Won the Heart of America;* William Frank Zornow, especially the "Quest for Quivira" chapter in *Kansas: A History of the Jayhawk State;* John Rydjord, compiler of the legendary *Kansas Place-Names;* and Anna E. Arnold, *A History of Kansas,* which was published in 1919 by the state of Kansas for its public schools. In that book is a poem by Eugene Fitch Ware, a tiny piece of which appears in this novel.

On the subject of progressive politics a century ago, I attended to the message of William Allen White, the famed editor of the *Emporia Gazette*. I thank Beverly Olson Buller: *From Emporia: The Story of William Allen White;* and the editor himself: *William Allen White: The Autobiography of William Allen White.*

Natural history information was gleaned from Rex Buchanan, ed., *Kansas Geology: An Introduction to Landscapes, Rocks, Minerals, and Fossils;* Michael John Haddock, *Wildflowers & Grasses of Kansas: A Field Guide;* and John L. Zimmerman, *Cheyenne Bottoms: Wetland in Jeopardy.* Websites and particular pages that were helpful included Fish and Wildlife's www.fws.gov/refuge/quivira; iNaturalist's www.inaturalist.org/places/quivira-national-wildlife-refuge#taxon=47126; and Kansas Wildflowers & Grasses, which describes the lovely gayfeather at kswildflower.org.

The Kansas Geological Survey, based at the University of Kansas, helped me understand the state's oil and gas fields and water resources: maps.kgs.ku.edu/oilgas and kgs.ku.edu/water-resources-and-geohydrology. More information about exploration came from the Kansas Independent Oil & Gas Association's website, www.kioga.org.

In addition, practical understanding about Quivira and its nearby towns came from Marci Penner, *The Kansas Guidebook;* Marci Penner and WenDee Rowe, *The Kansas Guidebook 2;* and Pam Grout, *Kansas Curiosities: Quirky Characters, Roadside Oddities & Other Offbeat Stuff.*

Various news and journal articles have been helpful. Among them are the following sources:

Perchloroethylene (perc): Larry Kramer, "Order Bars Classifying Chemical as a Carcinogen, Study: Perc remains in dry-cleaned clothes"; Amudalat Ajasa, "EPA bans two cancer-causing chemicals used in everyday products"; Katherine Burgess, "Kansans drank contaminated water for years. The state didn't tell them"; Jordan Schmidt, "Wichita, Kansas groundwater contamination linked to dry cleaning solvents."

Seismology and fracking: F. Rall Walsh III and Mark D. Zoback, "Oklahoma's recent earthquakes and saltwater disposal"; Steve Thompson and Anna Kuchment, "Seismic Denial? Why Texas won't admit fracking wastewater is causing earthquakes"; Ker Than,

"Oklahoma earthquakes linked to oil and gas wastewater disposal wells, say Stanford researchers."

Water: Allison Kite, "Ogallala Aquifer drops by more than a foot in parts of western Kansas"; Nicole Asbury, "U.S. officials see no need to secure water for Quivira National Wildlife Refuge after ag deal"; Max McCoy, "Hoping for a miracle to save the Ogallala Aquifer? Prepare for the new Dust Bowl."

Church and state: "Forsetti's Justice: Fundamentalism, racism, fear and propaganda: An insider explains why rural, Christian white America will never change"; Miguel De La Torre, "The Death of Christianity in the U.S."; Tim Alberta, "How Politics Poisoned the Evangelical Church"; Stephanie McCrummen, "The Army of God Comes Out of the Shadows."

Drilling in Alaska: Yereth Rosen, "Biden administration plans new limits on oil leasing in Alaska's Arctic National Wildlife Refuge"; Evan Halper, Maxine Joselow, and Chico Harlan, "What Trump's victory could mean for oil companies and climate change policy"; Yereth Rosen, "Oil and gas lease sale in Alaska's Arctic National Wildlife Refuge draws no bids."

A key part of the Saltwood story was formed in my imagination after hearing a public lecture by Dr. Mary Beth Leigh, a microbiologist at the Institute of Arctic Biology at the University of Alaska Fairbanks; she addressed remediation possibilities against a plume of sulfolane spreading underground from an oil refinery in North Pole, Alaska. In 2021, Lois Parshley's article, "The pollution plumes of North Pole" in Environmental Health News, discussed the situation.

Any errors of interpretation of these reports are mine.

Saltwood's epigraph, using material from G.H. Fish's 1891 pamphlet, was found on the Kansas Historical Society website, kansasmemory.org/item/208683.

The hymn "In the Garden" is available in the public domain. The lyrics were written by Charles Austin Miles and published in 1912. The snippet of poetry about "the glory and the dream" is from William Wordsworth's "Ode: Intimations of Immortality," published in 1807, and enhanced, in the political context used by *Saltwood,* by William Manchester's 1974 history, *The Glory and the Dream: A Narrative History of the America, 1932–1972.* The mood of the prayer spoken in Russian by Kevin Perdue in Chapter 32 is found in a Cyrillic gospel tract, Такой была твоя жизнь, *This Was Your Life,* published by Chick Publications. An aphorism about art and happiness was paraphrased from author Chuck Palahniuk's observation that "Art never comes from happiness."

I thank my friends in the Arizona Mystery Writers club in Tucson for being supportive people who understand that writing about the worst impulses of human nature is a necessary part of civilization's attempt to find justice.

After *Dog of the Afterworld* was published, writer Max McCoy of Emporia spent time with me on the phone, offering thoughtful observations about that book and how to approach my next project. His generous advice has been my North Star.

I thank Tracy Million Simmons of Meadowlark Press in Emporia, Kansas, who accepted Saltwood and guided it through production. She and her crew of readers, editors, designers, and publicists have long supported Kansas and Midwestern poets and other authors.

Thanks go to Julie Johnson, who proofread the text and added helpful suggestions. Mystery novelist Mike Graves, who read an advance copy, generously provided good suggestions.

I am fortunate to have had members of my family contribute to the development of *Saltwood.*

My son Nik Unruh was an early reader and frequent provider of pithy and trenchant observations about interesting people and situation. Thanks, Nik.

Dave Leiker, an outstanding landscape and portrait photographer as well as my brother-in-law, patiently guided me on two photography tours of Quivira National Wildlife Refuge and made another trip on his own as he prepared slideshows and videos to accompany *Saltwood.* He also photographed me for the back cover.

My sister, Cheryl Unruh, a top-notch writer and the editor of the journal *105 Meadowlark Reader* at Meadowlark Press, provided insightful guidance on facts, structure, tone, and phrasing in the final drafts of *Saltwood.*

I owe the deepest acknowledgment of all to my beloved partner and enthusiastic beta reader, Julie Scott. Her work in her arts— quilting, piano, and home design, as well as volunteerism and public service during a career of wealth management—has deepened my appreciation for what can be done, and why it should be.

About the Author

Leon Unruh grew up in Pawnee Rock, Kansas, a town midway along the Santa Fe Trail. He wrote for several small newspapers in Kansas and was an editor at dailies in Austin and Dallas, Texas; Wichita, Kansas; and Anchorage, Alaska. He started editing college textbooks and business trade books in 1989, in addition to his newspaper work. He was later the editor at the Alaska Native Language Center at the University of Alaska Fairbanks. He created and operated PawneeRock. org, a website about his hometown's history, work that was honored by the Wet/Dry Routes Chapter of the Santa Fe Trail Association.

Saltwood is the second thriller in Unruh's *Dog of the Afterworld* series.

Unruh also is a co-author of *Final Destinations: A Travel Guide for Remarkable Cemeteries in Texas, New Mexico, Oklahoma, Arkansas, and Louisiana,* written with colleagues at the *Dallas Morning News*. His essays and short stories have appeared in *105 Meadowlark Reader, Ice Box,* and plainchina.org.

Unruh lives in Tucson, Arizona.

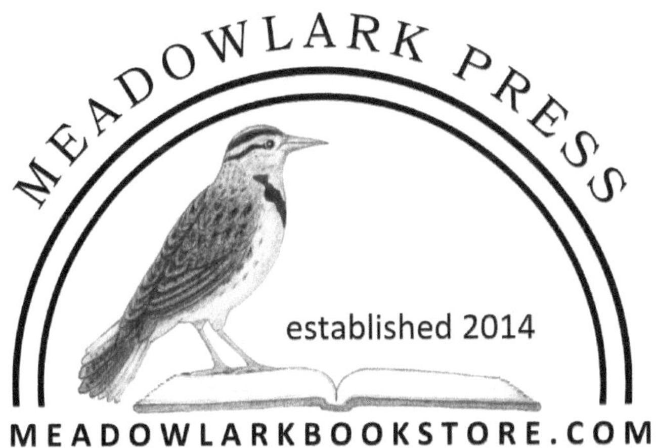

Books are a way to explore, connect, and discover. Reading gives us the gift of living lives and gaining experiences beyond our own. Publishing books is our way of saying—

We love these words,
we want to play a role in preserving them,
and we want to help share them with the world.